TO ⊙
THE SUN

ALSO BY OCTAVIA RANDOLPH

Sidroc the Dane

The Circle of Ceridwen

Ceridwen of Kilton

The Claiming

The Hall of Tyr

Tindr

Silver Hammer, Golden Cross

Wildswept

For Me Fate Wove This

Two Dragons

Water Borne

The Circle of Ceridwen Cookery Book(let)

Light Descending

The Tale of Melkorka: A Novella

Ride: A Novella

BOOK ELEVEN

THE CIRCLE OF CERIDWEN SAGA

TO THE SUN

OCTAVIA RANDOLPH

PYEWACKET PRESS

To the Sun is the eleventh book in
The Circle of Ceridwen Saga by Octavia Randolph
Copyright 2024 Octavia Randolph

ISBN Softcover: 978-1-942044-42-0
ISBN Hardcover: 978-1-942044-43-7

Book cover design by DesignforBooks.com. Cover illustration and maps by
Michael Rohani. Sun image photo credit: Shutterstock/Nazarii_Neshcherenskyi.

Pyewacket Press

The Circle of Ceridwen Saga employs British spellings, alternate spellings,
archaic words, and oftentimes unusual verb to subject placement. This is
intentional. A Glossary of Terms will be found at the end of the novel.

CONTENTS

LIST OF CHARACTERS

Sidroc the Dane, formerly Jarl of Four Stones in South Lindisse, now a wealthy trader on Gotland

Ceridwen, Mistress of the hall Tyrsborg on the island of Gotland, wife to Sidroc

Hrald, son of Ælfwyn and Sidroc, Jarl of the Danish keep of Four Stones in South Lindisse

Yrling, son of Ceridwen and Sidroc, currently living at Four Stones

Gunnvor and **Helga,** cook and serving-woman respectively at Tyrsborg

Eirian, daughter of Ceridwen and Sidroc

Rodiaud, youngest daughter of Ceridwen and Sidroc

Eskil, a Svear warrior and ship-master

Tindr, a bow hunter

Juoksa, a boy of Gotland, son of Tindr and Šeará

Šeará, a Sami woman, wife to Tindr

Jaské, daughter of Tindr and Šeará

Brani, a seaman guide of Eskil

Rannveig, a brewster on Gotland, mother of Tindr

Runulv, a Gotlandic ship-master and trader

Gyda, wife to Runulv

Berse, a weapon-smith, formerly a warrior

Withun, a monk

Bork, an orphan and young warrior under Hrald's care

Sigewif, Abbess of Oundle

Sigferth, King of Jorvik

Ælfred, King of Wessex

Guthrum, late King of the Danes in Angle-land

Thorvi, a Danish star-reader

Aszur, a ship-master and trader of Jorvik

Tofa, a lewd woman of Jorvik

Pega of Mercia, wife to Hrald, and Lady of Four Stones

Jari, a warrior of Four Stones, chief body-guard to Hrald

Kjeld, second in command at Four Stones

Mealla, companion to Pega, a maid of Éireann

Ælfgiva, daughter of Hrald and Pega

Edwin, Lord of Kilton in Wessex

Alwin and **Wystan**, captains of Edwin's body-guard

Wulgan, a Saxon ship-master and trader

Edgyth, Lady of Kilton, mother by adoption to Edwin

Ceric, son of Ceridwen and the late Gyric,
grand-son of the late Lord Godwulf, God-son of
King Ælfred, and older brother to Edwin

Dwynwen, Princess of Ceredigion in Wales, wed to Ceric

Worr, the horse-thegn of Kilton, pledged man of Ceric

Dunnere, priest of Kilton

Tegwedd, a Welsh serving girl to Dwynwen

Garrulf, scop of Kilton

Æthelflaed, Lady of Mercia, daughter
of King Ælfred of Wessex

Wilgyfu, wife to Worr

Ladja, Mistress of Staraya Ladoga

Vermund, King of Novgorod

Davor, a guide thereof

Efim, Prince of Gnezdovo

Karlen, Prince of a river trading post

Demyan, his older brother, also Prince
of the same trading post

Oleg, King of Kyiv, uncle to Karlen and Demyan

Arni and **Farulf**, two Gotlandic adventurers

Emund, brother to Farulf

Sigtrygg, a Svear adventurer

Ælfwyn, formerly Lady of Four Stones,
now wife to Raedwulf of Defenas

Raedwulf, Bailiff of Defenas in Wessex

Burginde, companion and nurse to Ælfwyn

Ealhswith, daughter of Ælfwyn and Sidroc

Blida and **Bettelin,** orphaned siblings of Defenas

Cerd, grandson to Ælfwyn and Ceridwen,
son of Ceric and the late Ashild

Indract and **Lioba**, married couple,
stewards of Raedwulf's hall

Eadward, Prince of Wessex

Ecgwynn, his wife

Eanflad, younger sister to Ælfwyn

Dagmar, daughter of the late Guthrum,
King of the Danes in Angle-land

Asberg, brother-in-law to Ælfwyn, in
command at the fortress of Turcesig

Sister Ælfleda, mother to Ælfwyn
and Eanflad, a nun at Oundle

Congar, a thegn's son of Cantwaraburh

Elfrid, a priest at the cathedral of
Cantwaraburh, uncle to Congar

Sister Bova, brewster at Oundle, formerly
known at Tyrsborg as Sparrow

Brother Balin, a monk at Oundle

Elidon, King of Ceredigion in Wales, uncle to Dwynwen

Anarawd, King of Gwynedd in Wales

Merfyn, King of Powys in Wales

Llywarch, King of Dyfed in Wales

Meurig, King of Morgannwg in Wales

Luned, a woman of Wales

Gwydden, priest to Elidon

Ultan, stable boy in the King's stable at Witanceaster

TO THE SUN MAPS

TO
THE SUN
THE YEAR 896

Land of
the Sámi

Land
of the
Sámi

Norse

Uppsala
Svear

Gotland

Land
of
the
Rus

Viborg   Danes
Åros   Skania
Ribe

Tyrsborg

Öland

Prus

Four
Stones

Frisia
Dorestad

Pomerani

Polanie

Wessex

Kilton

Hunesfleth

Frankland

Paris

TO
THE SUN

MESSAGE BEARERS

Gotland

The Year 896

SIDROC was not certain where he was; all was darkness. Nor did he know how he had found himself here. Had he taken a blow to the head? All he knew was that one of his sons was behind the wall he pressed his hands against – a boy who needed him . . .

He forced himself awake; not a fear-induced jolt, but a summons he gave himself. Despite pulling himself by force of will from the bleakness of the vision, his heart was as tightly clenched as if his fist had replaced it.

When in the past he had startled awake from having ridden the night-mare he knew to reach his arm over his head, and place his palm flat against the sturdy wooden head board of the bed he had built. It was reminder he was in fact not on some field of battle across which men screamed out their death-throes, nor fighting upon the blood-slimed deck of a lurching ship. Often beneath his reaching palm he would feel the grooves of the design he had chiseled there, the great circular interlace from the silver disc bracelet he had placed upon his shield-maiden's wrist. He did this now, extending his arm so that it met that reminder of the here and now. His palm lingered only a moment. The wood under his hand felt too much like the wall he had been pressing against, trying to reach his son. Yet he was here, at Tyrsborg; his wife safe and asleep next him. He drew back his arm and wiped it across the beads of cold sweat which had gathered on his brow.

This was all he was sure of; he was here at his peaceful hall. Was it a night-mare he rode, or a fluttering of his fylgja, that female guardian-spirit of his family, which awakened him? When he had touched his own brow, he sensed the second, his fylgja moving within him, ready with counsel.

It lasted a moment, this freeing sensation, to be replaced by the leaden weight of dread. Yet it seemed confirmation of the trueness of the vision. It was a message, not a night-mare.

One of his sons — or both of them — were in distress. His mouth worked, soundlessly. Hrald. Yrling. Both, he had trusted, were safe and well at Four Stones. Their shared fylgja told him otherwise.

Sidroc must address her, must face her. And he had ever felt her presence most readily under the heavens. He rose, and stood in the dark, pulling on his clothes. Around the margin of the closed shutter high in the gable, the soft blush of dawn was beginning to show.

He opened the door of the treasure room to the gloom of the hall. The sleeping alcoves of Gunnvor, their cook, and Helga, their serving woman, were to the right, both curtains pulled firmly shut. To the left were the alcoves of Eirian, that of her absent brother Yrling, and of their youngest, Rodiaud. He heard a whimper, surely from that child. The heavy wadmal curtain hanging at Rodiaud's alcove had been pushed aside. He moved closer; her box bed was empty. Rodiaud ofttimes would crawl in with her sister, or with one of the older women. He went to Eirian's alcove. The gathering light was enough to see through a gap in the heavy curtain. There was his elder daughter, asleep on her side, her back towards the sleeping Rodiaud, nestled against her older sister, her tiny hands clasped under her chin. At the child's feet, where he was not allowed, he saw the sleeping Flekkr, coiled into a tight ball, his furred tail wrapped around his nose. Here, all was well. But not so with one of his boys.

He stood there, aware of the creeping Sun breaking in from the closed shutters, lightening the hall moment by moment. He returned to the treasure room. His wife was just beginning to stir. He said nothing to her of the vision. So formless it was, he could not yet speak of it. Their day began.

Seated at the broad table Sidroc took two spoons of the boiled oats in his bowl, and no more. Ceridwen noted this, without comment. The hall door was open to the morning and its sounds. The lowing of one of the cows Tindr was milking served as excuse for Sidroc to stand. "I will get a start on the paddock fence," he said. He and Tindr had been repairing the top rail where it had weakened from the stress of the horses leaning against it. He looked to his wife, who gave a quiet smile. He reached for a loaf where they sat piled on the platter, and took it with him. Ceridwen knew it was not for him to eat later.

Never an empty hand, Sidroc thought, when approaching the Gods.

Out in the forecourt between hall and stable, Sidroc left Tindr undisturbed in his milking. Flekkr had followed him out and was frisking at his heels. Sidroc thought almost to drive the dog back, but then gave thought. The animal was a scent-hound. Such were meant to find things. He would keep the dog with him in his appeal. He slipped into the spruce trees beyond the kitchen yard and vanished up the path.

The Dane was headed for the Place of Offering, and its small, fern-bedecked clearing. It was there he spoke to Tyr, and to the Goddess Freyja. Tyr was his fulltrúi, that patron God he had given himself to as a young man. He had come later to the service of Freyja, a dedication foretold by an old woman he had met in Jutland. It had been that white-armed Goddess of love and lust who had helped him secure his shield-maiden, and had kept her under Her protection in the intervening years between first seeing her as a young maid at Four Stones, and making her his wife here on Gotland.

So confused were Sidroc's feelings he would need the aid of both. Tyr and Freyja could guide his hand in casting the bones of augury, but he would need his fylgja's help to discern their meaning. This inner guardian spirit was carried also in the breast of Hrald, and Yrling.

He reached the place, where every year he made Offering in thanks for the bounty Tyrsborg enjoyed. All who lived at the hall stood with him then. But he had come here betweentimes as well, times of doubt and trouble. The low wooden Offering boxes he and Tindr had made their first harvest-tide were sinking into the undergrowth, a few slats of their framework still visible under the furling ferns. A single, tall post crowned with an open platform stood ready to receive what Sidroc had carried with him from the table. He had offered many fowl here over the years. He drew a deep and steadying breath, and entered the space.

"Tyr! Freyja! Every good thing comes from you. And every good thing I share with you." He held the bread loaf aloft, to the heavens, and to the waiting birds, those eyes of Odin, he knew were watching. With a twist of his thumb and forefinger he tore a hunk of the crusted loaf, and placed it in his mouth. Flekkr was nosing in the ferns, and looked, bright-eyed, to him, his folded ear cocked, the second pointing straight up, as always. The dog was here as emblem of finding; he must take part in the Offering as well. Sidroc tore a second piece and tossed it to the hound's quickly snapping jaws. As Flekkr gnawed one-sidedly at it, his master reached up and laid the torn loaf on the Offering platform.

This done, Sidroc drew breath. He needed answers. His right hand rose to his head and his fingers combed through his dark hair, hair now amply streaked with grey. His eyes skimmed the tops of the trees surrounding him. He stilled himself. The fylgja needed quiet, or he needed quiet to hear her. A fluttering again, the slightest movement in his breast. He must ask.

He reached his hand again up to the platform on which he had placed the loaf. His fingers groped, touching, then closing around a cluster of bones there. A knot of feathers, still attached to a piece of gristle was there as well; this he replaced upon the Offering platform. Sidroc opened his calloused palm to the lifting Sun and studied what he had gathered. He had collected nine small bones, some straight, some slightly curved. There was rightness in this. Nine was a sacred number. He could ask three questions, and throw the bones in three equal handfuls. He would cast them here, on the hardened earth at the base of the Offering pole.

He chose three bones, then placed the remaining six on the edge of the Offering platform. His fingers closed about the first three, and he brought his fist to his heart. The words falling from his lips were no more than a hoarse whisper.

"Tyr. Freyja. You will guide my hand, as you ever have. You know before I speak what I will ask. Fylgja, Lady-spirit who runs in the blood of me and mine, answer so I will not mistake you."

Sidroc drew a slow breath, and as he flung the three bones on the ground before him made question.

"Of which son did I dream?"

The delicate bones, the colour of ivory, held an answer. They formed the rune Hagal. ᚾ

"Hrald." His father exhaled the name.

Hagal was the rune his oldest son signed his name with, when he wrote in runes. Hagal stood for hail, water transformed into ice. Hail could destroy tender Spring crops, and also melt to nourish them. Hagal signified a change of direction, a sometimes mystifying one.

Sidroc reached up and pulled the next three bones from the platform. Again he closed his fist around them, and again voiced aloud his question as he held the bones to his breast.

"How grave a danger?"

Sidroc took a step back, and flung the bones so they would fall beneath those first cast.

The three aligned as ᚦ Thorn, one upright, and the two others joining it at an angle to form a point. Thorn indicated a weapon, though it need not be one cast of iron. Thorn could be anger – or lust. Either way it signified a test, as was breeching the defences of a blackthorn tree, or an encircling ring of briar.

Sidroc's lips parted, considering this. He expected a trial, a test. Sidroc had witnessed his son face what he hoped would be the greatest challenge of Hrald's life, facing an older, more experienced warrior in single combat. It was an ordeal Sidroc had wanted to take upon himself, so grave a threat was death at the hands of Thorfast. Was there now another, even more dangerous test awaiting Hrald?

The Dane closed his eyes. This woman-spirit, the fylgja he shared with his son, knew more, and could tell him if he was ready to know.

Sidroc uttered his next words to her. "I will cast again." He bent and retrieved the three bones, blew on them gently to clear them from the shadow of Thorn, and let them drop.

It was a strange cast. One of the fowl bones fell straight out before him. The other two bones fell almost atop each other, at the tip of the first, angled down like a fish hook.

Lagu. ↾

This was the ultimate female rune of power, and one of the most potent of all runic symbols. It carried the sense of water, and all its life-giving and life-destroying qualities. It was the sea carried in our mother's belly in which we swam before our birth, and vital refreshment for all thirsting plants and animals. Water could be unstoppable and beyond control; raging rivers sweeping away all before a surging flood, seas crashing down on a hapless ship, scouring away mast and sail and men. And Lagu held another meaning, that of the madness of sexual desire.

Sidroc stood still, studying this barbed rune. From the self-same bones he had cast first Thorn and then Lagu. Ordeal, trial, pain – and then a waterfall far too easy to be swept off by.

Something moved strongly within Sidroc's breast as these thoughts flashed through his head. He spoke aloud what he felt his fylgja was telling him.

"A woman."

If any knew what lengths a man might countenance to win the woman he wanted, it would be Sidroc. His chest tightened as if his fylgja had grown too large to contain in the presence of this certainty.

He thought now of something Yrling, his uncle, had told him when Sidroc was yet a boy: That all disputes between men were either over women, or silver. It was not far from the truth, Sidroc had learnt. Yet silver was interchangeable. Women were not. Weighed on the scale the finest worked necklace was worth no more than the hack-silver it had been wrought from. But the sole woman a man desired could never be replaced by another.

It took long moments before the Dane reached his hand to the edge of the Offering platform and pulled the last three of the chosen bones. He had learnt much, none of it good.

His final question.

"What can I do?"

Sidroc flung the bones from his hand with a snap of his strong wrist, one which almost instantly revealed the answer awaiting him.

The slender bones fell one straight out, the other two side by side, crossing the first at an angle. He looked down at his cast, then up to the sky. Instead of that rich morning blue which so often roofed their days here, it was a pale and milky shade. He lifted his gaze to its blankness, an echo of what the bones told him.

Nid. ᚾ Nothing. Nid was need, and Nid was hardship. Nid was the two pieces of wood left in times of famine, a stop, an end. Sidroc could not help the boy. Hrald alone must solve this.

It was not a sign without hope. But one must work with Nid to find it. Two sticks could kindle fire, provide light to see the way ahead.

Sidroc had been confronted with this rune before. Again Yrling came to mind, standing with him on a deserted beach in Angle-land, to find both their ships and all their goods stolen. The thief had formed the rune Nid in stone to mock the discoverers. The stunning loss marooned them. Yet that same loss led them at last to capture Four Stones...

Hrald. Sidroc stood, shaking his head, thinking on his son. The greatest hazard to Hrald was not another warrior, but a woman. He let himself exhale, expelling the last bit of air in his lungs, freeing his chest. His fylgja was there, nodding her head at him. When he was a boy his father told him that if their family spirit could be seen, she would appear as a beautiful woman. He imagined her that way for years; Sidroc was interested in women and their beauty. Now that he was older, Sidroc thought of her as not a woman, but almost a child, one as small perhaps as Rodiaud, but infinitely wise, and without guile. He gave silent thanks to her now, though the message had been a hard one.

He bent and picked up the bones of augury, one by one. They should be taken to the beach and released to the waters. It was not an ordinary visit, in which he had come to offer thanks as well as sustenance. Sidroc had come to learn something. He had been granted insight into his dream, and been changed by the knowledge given. He felt impelled to leave by a different route. His head lifted in a final glance up to the Offering platform, the lump of his loaf just visible. Midway up a red pine a jackdaw was scolding impatiently, urging him to leave. He did, whistling to Flekkr where he had lain down in the ferns. Together they began picking their way through the undergrowth and the pines. Beyond their ruddy-barked trunks he could see the Baltic. Man and hound made for the pebbled beach. The water lapped upon the white shingle in a short and restless pulse. Sidroc lowered his hand into the cool and foaming edge, and allowed it to carry off the nine bones of augury.

As they vanished from view Sidroc repeated one thing. Nothing, he told himself. I can do nothing.

He had come out to the coast a short distance from Rannveig's house, not yet in sight around the curve of the promontory. Flekkr trotted at his side, stopping to chase a sea duck paddling in close to shore. Sidroc continued on, walking just behind the mounded pebbles of the tide line. Soon the brewster's garden, and then her house would come in view. From there he would climb the hill to Tyrsborg.

He did not get that far. Sidroc had just rounded a stand of weathered limestone towers when he saw a dragon-ship, sail furled, oaring up to the wooden pier. The careful slowness of its approach was proof those aboard were come to trade, and not raid. Sidroc stood still, taking the craft in. It bore but a few men. Whatever it was carrying warranted little more. He stared at the wind-vane topping the mast, and knew it. Eskil the Svear. This was Eskil's drekar. The tip of its mast had always sported a gilded bronze weather-vane, brilliant in the Sun. It made great show, typical of a rich Svear, Sidroc had always thought.

A graceful slow glide brought the drekar to the pier. The old men who ofttimes clustered at the bench there were not in attendance this early in the day; there was no reaching hand to catch a thrown line. But the steers-man, and the men on the starboard side, were ready to bring her safely alongside the planks of the pier.

All thoughts of Hrald and runic warnings were set aside. Sidroc would meet this ship, and the man he felt must still be its captain. He passed his own ship beached on the shingle, Dauðadagr, and had gained the pier when Eskil lifted his head from where he secured the steering-oar in the stern. Sidroc stood, awaiting him. There was one less than a dozen crew aboard; barely enough to man the drekar and get out of a scrape, if a pursuing ship could not be outrun. But the nature of the men differed from the last time Eskil had landed on these shores. The Svear who commanded men and ship had changed as well. Eskil raised his hand and called out to Sidroc, as if glad to see an old friend. The Dane had already an inkling of what was to come.

Eskil lifted himself over the gunwale, not waiting for a gangplank. The man was as well dressed as always, his tunic fresh, brown boots unscuffed, the long yellow hair carefully parted and plaited in two. He wore but his knife for weapon; behind him were his men and arms. Sidroc had but a working knife belted over his worn work tunic, and as was meet, uttered the first words of greeting to the traveller.

"Eskil. You are more welcome this time, than the last. Though if you come to buy ale for all of us, you will be more welcome still."

The Svear gave a laugh at the memory, and Sidroc grinned.

"How fares your King in Uppsala?" Sidroc said next. It had been in that war-lord's service Eskil had last been here.

Eskil gave a low snort. "Ivar is dead. Me too, nearly. A King's body-guard . . . the plunder is great, but the life is short."

Sidroc was forced to give a single laugh. "I have served as such. To Guthrum, King of the Danes in Angle-land. For reward, he gave me a cuff of red gold. But I was glad when that service was over. Treasure means little if you are not here to enjoy it. And though what we bury will be ours in Asgard, the gleam and heft of it here gives, I think, more pleasure."

The Dane looked again at Eskil's drekar. It was a fine ship, the same he had sailed in on years before as a trader, and then as henchman of Ivar. The Gods had favoured Eskil, to keep him both alive and in command of such a vessel.

"So," Sidroc went on. "We spoke once of you taking up trading, and settling on Gotland. Has that day come?"

Eskil grinned back. "The soundest advice is given by one who has lived it themselves. You have. And so, já, I am ready. And even to settle in Paviken, as you suggest.

"The best news is yet to come," Eskil went on. He craned his neck over his shoulder, as if he could see across the broad expanse of the sea which had carried him here. "I have no interest in the Baltic shore. The trading posts of the Polanie, the Pomeranie – even the Frisians to the west – they cannot entice me."

The Svear was here dismissing quite a source of treasure in this proclamation, and Sidroc awaited the reason.

"I will head east, and east only. And you could partner with me."

Sidroc was just opening his mouth when the Svear went on.

"We will get silk ourselves."

Neither had forgotten the length of red silk that Eskil had procured, and which Sidroc had, over a drunken night of dice, won from him. Before it had come into the Svear's possession such had been passed from hand to hand, along many trade routes, and been sized up and priced by many merchants. The idea of procuring it more directly was enticing.

"Peppercorns," Eskil went on, should his listener require further incentive. "Curls of cinnamon bark. Nutmegs that will sell for their weight in pure silver."

Sidroc had just been addressing his Gods, and must put a stop to such talk. He had a once-broken vow which must be kept.

"I will not leave this island again," he said in answer.

Eskil was not deterred. He seemed in fact to have expected this, and was ready.

"Not you," the Svear assured him. "Not you directly. Your ship, helmed by your man. And your trade goods, to barter for treasures we can now only eye as they pass into the hands of Kings and Princes."

"Or win at dice," Sidroc reminded. It was that costly bolt of red silk he had in mind.

Eskil blinked. "I was drunk," was his even retort. "No matter," Eskil went on. "We will each have a ship, my drekar with me at the oar, yours with your man, well skilled in both sailing and trading. I have a good ship and men, and lack only silver or furs enough to command the goods we seek."

So the Svear needed a stake as well, which he looked to Sidroc to supply. Still, he was willing to risk his drekar and his life, and that was some security. And Sidroc would have his own ship and crew at Eskil's side, to make sure all promises were kept.

Sidroc's expectant silence prompted the Svear to say more.

"We will carry furs from the north; fox and wolf and beaver and ermine. Walrus tusks, and hides. Beeswax is prized in the courts of sultans and caliphs; we will take casks of it. And silver, coin if we can get it, for it is coin they favour; hack if we cannot. With this we can buy silk."

Sidroc's eyes swept the deck of the drekar behind the speaker. Eskil was numbering goods not yet aboard. Indeed, other than the sea chests of the crew and the standard range of casks holding stock fish and water, little cargo could be identified as such. Weaponry there was, easy to spot, spears and shields secured and waiting.

Sidroc shifted his gaze to the men who stood ranged about the deck, watching them. They looked handy enough. But there were not enough of them. Counting its steers-man captain, the dragon-ship held eleven men. Any trader would need twice that number to set out on such a journey. The Dane addressed this lack in his next question.

"With so few men as this?"

The Svear was ready with his answer.

"The folk of Gotland are famed for three things: their sheep, their treasure, and the sailing skills of their men. I thought here I might find some likely takers to round out my crew."

Sidroc had to work to keep a smile from forming. These ten Svear were all Eskil could persuade to join on such a perilous venture. Though he flattered the islanders, he counted on them to step up and take their chances with him. The Dane was not unaware that this might give him added assurance in the venture. Sidroc was known and respected on the island. If he backed his own man and ship, others who had wanted to sail with his captain Runulv and never had the chance would leap to do so. And those throwing in to serve on Eskil's ship could act to ensure the interests of Gotland were given their due.

Eskil began speaking again, content perhaps that the Dane had discerned what he needed about ship and crew.

"When your man is returned he can take the silk north to Birka. Or on to your home land, and Haithabu. Think what it would bring. I have heard of Paris; it could go there. Consider the silver it will bring at Jorvik, which I have also heard tell of. The same with spice. And there are always gems."

Gems, thought Sidroc. Runulv had procured a small sack of them in Paviken, fresh from the Ural Mountains. Runulv had carried them to Paris, on the same voyage on which he had delivered his shield-maiden's son Edwin to Hunefleth.

"Then there is Attar of Rose," Eskil went on. "A single small vial will buy a good horse."

Sidroc's eyes flicked up to the pale sky a moment. If there was one indulgence his shield-maiden desired for herself, it was rose oil. He had not been able to give her any for several years. She still kept the last tiny vial he had won for her, and though it had long been dry, he knew she still opened it at times for the scent that lingered there.

His mind still on his wife, Sidroc saw Eirian appear, basket over her wrist, walking down the hill from Tyrsborg on an errand for her mother. At her side walked Juoksa, the son of Šeará and Tindr. The hound Flekkr stood up from the pier and with a yip of greeting trotted to them. Both the young stopped at the sight of the two men on the wooden planking.

Eirian stood, uncertain whether to approach her father. She knew the yellow-haired man at his side, and knew too his ship. The girl and her mother had been on the trading road last year when that ship drove for shore with frightening speed, and the men aboard jumped down to the beach, shields on their arms, spears in their fists. Despite this, all had ended well from that visit, and she had stood with her mother outside Rannveig's as all drank ale while her father and this stranger spoke. Still, she waited for her father to nod to her. Curious as she was about life beyond the confines of the island she had little fear of approaching the yellow-haired man now. She was glad when her father granted her a slight nod, signaling she could come forward.

Juoksa hung back a few steps, but Eirian walked to the men, a smile on her pretty lips for her father, one which she compressed modestly as she gave a quick curtsey before them.

Sidroc did not let her speak. He knew she might ask of Eskil some question which would allow the man the liberty of speech with her.

"I will be along to the hall soon," he told her. His tone was mild, but his words direct. "Go on your errand now."

She gave a glance at the long dragon-ship behind them. This done, she nodded cheerfully enough and turned toward the trading road. Juoksa did not join her, but lingered, going first to the bench at the end of the pier, and then to his grandmother Rannveig's garden, where he appeared to busy himself amongst a tangle of herbs the brewster used to flavour her ale.

Sidroc was aware the Svear's eyes were fastened on Eirian as she walked off. The Dane made a move to leave, ready with a vague offer to meet later at the brew-house, when Eskil spoke.

"Your daughter."

Sidroc turned to the man.

"What of my daughter?"

"She is a fine maid," Eskil observed.

"Of that I am aware." A moment passed before Sidroc spoke again. "And she is still a child."

"Já." Eskil's quiet admission was followed by a long silence. When he spoke again, the girl was out of sight, having vanished into one of the stalls on the trading road.

"You told me at the Althing that I should find a wife of Gotland. I can wait."

The Dane turned to him fully. He did not mind spinning a yarn from the roving he had been handed. "Gotland born, she is. But she is bound for Wales."

"Wales," repeated Eskil. He was not sure he had heard of it.

"Is it the island to the west of Angle-land?" he asked, squinting across the darkening waters as if he could somehow distinguish it at this distance.

The girl's father shook his head. "It is on the western coast of the great island of Angle-land. But the folk of Wales are their own people, with their own tongue." And fierce they are, he said to himself, from what he had heard from his shield-maiden wife.

"Why there?" A moment later the Svear supplied his own answer. "Your wife — she is of them, perhaps."

"Half," Sidroc conceded. The feisty half, he felt. He was compelled to go on.

"My daughter has been promised. To a Prince. One of a Kingdom in Wales."

"Ah," allowed Eskil. "She has folk there, to help the girl to such a marriage."

"My wife's son is wed to a Princess of that place," Sidroc confirmed.

Sidroc had the pleasure of hearing the Svear draw a deep breath, to which he only nodded. Wherever Eirian set out for, her father suspected she would somehow reach Cymru. It seemed her sole desire. The maid was single minded enough to search for, and find, her grandmother, if she still lived. Kilton was not far from the borders of Cymru, he knew. Ceric, and even Edwin, would help her in that quest. Eirian had told both her parents she had spoken to Edwin about coming to Kilton.

Eskil began to grin.

"Then she is off limits."

"Já. She is off limits."

Eskil gave his head a single shake. "Gotland has maids aplenty," he went on, in attempt to recover. In fact two young women were nearing, baskets of eggs in their hands, and had glanced over long enough to fall quiet at the look of the yellow-haired ship-master, and then, as they moved further off, break into giggling peals of blushing laughter.

Sidroc did not answer; his own words echoed in his head: She is bound for Wales. He had spoken it, and aloud, this truth of what he thought his girl's Fate held for her. His hand rose and he ran his fingers through his hair, as if ordering his thoughts. Both men turned, back to Eskil's ship, and the venture he proposed. Several moments passed, as both considered.

Sidroc's next question gave the Svear real hope. "When?" he posed.

Eskil had given careful thought to this. His eyes shifted to the horizon. A bank of soft grey cloud was now rolling in over the trees from the west, crushing the mild blue sky beneath it. It was a harbinger of cold to come. Winter lay ahead. But Spring meant mud. Those heading to the lands of the Rus then counted themselves lucky if instead they met late ice and snow. And melting snows made for fast and treacherous rapids. Eskil knew that even at the best of times they sometimes would need to roll the ships overland upon birch logs, to avoid rivers too perilous to their hulls. A late Summer departure meant a few of the smaller trading posts they need visit to replenish stores and make minor trades might be closing, but the largest would remain open as the snow flew. Some years that could be right on the heels of the last harvests here. If they left soon they would find fewer opportunities along the banks of the rivers and streams they must travel, but skidding a ship over an ice-bound river was far easier than traversing the miring mud of a warming countryside.

It was either now, or wait for late Spring and its long days.

"Now, before the full Moon." The Moon was not yet at its waxing crescent, so it gave them ten or twelve days.

The Dane considered this response, but gave no sign of assent. The Svear, ever a gaming man, was presenting a challenge to him. It was true; most trading was over, and purses were full. If Sidroc agreed they must begin at once to gather trade goods and supplies, and assemble Gotlandic men for such a daring venture. At least Runulv's ship was still in the water. Harvest was largely over; the grain cut and gleaned, animals as fat as they might grow to carry them over until Spring. If ever it was time for a man to leave his holding in the care of his wife, it was now. And on his own account Sidroc was ready. Osku the Sámi had just been to Gotland, leaving Sidroc the richer in broad pieces of whalebone, marten and beaver pelts, a stack of sealskins, and most valuable of all, walrus hide and tusks. Sidroc had amber as well, worked into shining beads, and unworked in smoky golden lumps. Amongst those bags lay beads fashioned of red amber, which he had been holding back for a rich market. And he had a great deal of silver.

The Svear looked to his ship, and went on. "I have a man with me, who knows the ways. The swiftest routes, the richest trading posts."

Sidroc answered, in measured tones. "I will speak to Runulv. See if he and his knorr are up to it."

"Nej," Eskil answered. "Not his ship. Your own." The Svear tilted his head to the drekar Dauðadagr on the pebbled beach. "She is smaller and lighter than any knorr. Some of the rivers we will use are no more than streams, and need a narrow hull."

Death-Day, thought Sidroc. How Yrling would have leapt at this chance. Both Yrlings, he corrected himself. Well, he would first have to assure Dauðadagr was sea-worthy; she had not been in the water for months.

"What say you," prompted Eskil. He felt he had done his best to sell the scheme to the Dane.

Sidroc answered, though with another question.

"How long will you remain here?"

"Until you say já," Eskil returned, with a nod of his head.

THE VENTURE

SIDROC climbed the hill to Tyrsborg. His wife was sitting in the kitchen yard with Gunnvor, their cook, shelling dried beans to fill waiting pottery jars. He had a moment to study her at work, watching the curl of her fingers as she stripped the beans out. Upon her wrist flashed the silver disc of the bracelet from the night they hand-fasted, as undimmed as she herself.

Ceridwen looked up from the work table, and rose to go to him. She could not fully read the expression on Sidroc's face; he was an expert dice player, good at tæfel too, and could well conceal what was in his mind at the gaming table. But she knew his face too well. Something had happened, that was clear.

He paused by the paddock, where several top rails Tindr had planed in the barn lay ready. The man himself was at work within, smoothing more planks. Tindr looked up when Sidroc's shadow struck the opening, and they nodded. Sidroc stopped at the paddock fence and waited for his wife.

"Eskil the Svear is back," he told her.

Ceridwen's chin lifted in surprise. Without a word she took a few steps to where she might see down the hill, to the pier below. Indeed, a long dragon-ship stood at rest. She went back to Sidroc with her question.

"Did his King send him?" She was not eager to learn of any more veiled threats to the island.

"Nai," Sidroc assured her. "That one is dead. And Eskil glad to have survived him."

He paused a moment before going on, to give such news its due. The Svear was bent on changing his life and deserved that much.

"Nai, he is ready for a life of trading, and came to see me. He proposes that he, with his ship and men, go with Runulv, east, down the river Dnieper. Then south." Sidroc looked from her for a moment down to the Svear's waiting drekar. "Perhaps all the way to Samarkand."

The Svear had not named that fabled golden city in the sand, but Sidroc knew it to be one of the great centres for rare goods; a fountainhead of treasures in the desert. It was, of a sudden, easier for Sidroc to conjure it in his mind, to set a destination for the venture.

"He says he has a man who knows the way. And – Runulv's knorr will not serve. He wants Dauðadagr as the second ship."

"Samarkand," The name fell from Ceridwen's lips with quiet wonder. She knew it as a place trading men spoke of, but none she knew of had ventured there. Amber came from these Baltic shores; furs from the north, silver in great amounts from Angle-land and Frankland. And silver came too from far to the east, coins with flowing writing on them like thread work. The rarest of goods came from the trade routes from the east, silk and spices.

"He would leave now, before the Moon reaches full," Sidroc went on. "Such a journey will take time. Not weeks but months. But if Runulv agreeś, he could return with Death-Day laden with silk."

Ceridwen turned her eyes to those of her husband. A single word passed her lips, and in a whisper. "Cinnamon."

One of the strongest memories of their time together traveling the Baltic coast was the meeting with the rich spice merchant who had given her a precious piece of that rare bark.

Sidroc held her eyes fully. "Já. Sticks of cinnamon."

That had been the night she told him she would travel with him freely, that they might, as man and wife, build a new life together. The memory of cinnamon was intertwined with the winning of her. The spice merchant foretold that his shield-maiden would bear two daughters, and the cinnamon enough to dower the girls. She had sent that stick, along with one found in the Idrisid workbasket he had claimed for her, to Paris. Runulv had traded them there and brought back bars of Frankish iron, sold to Berse the bladesmith here. She had realised enough silver from the weaponsmith to give each girl a handsome start in their married lives to come.

She spoke again. "But – months. And the danger – it is too much to ask Gyda to bear."

Sidroc answered in a low tone, and with respectful gravity in the judgement of Runulv's wife. "That will be Gyda's choice," he countered.

Ceridwen gave a slight nod of her head. After their trade goods had been destroyed in the ware-house fire on the trading road, Gyda had sold her prized silver brooches so Runulv might be able to buy more salt to trade.

The Dane uttered the next in a voice considered, but resolute, as if he stood at a gaming table, ready to push the whole of his silver winnings back into the common pot, come what may.

"If Runulv agrees to go, I will risk all Osku's furs, hides, and walrus tusks. All of it. And all this years' amber from the Polonie trades. Also – one half of our silver."

His eyes, which had been set before him to some unseeable middle distance, now rose and met hers.

"Do you consent?"

Ceridwen could scarcely speak. He had never sent all the furs on a single voyage, but divided them on the two trips Runulv had made in recent Summers. Runulv might set sail for the trading posts of the Pomeranie or Polonie, or head up to Birka, even sail up the raider-infested straits of Dane-mark to Aros. When there were goshawks to sell, or special goods worthy of its noblemen, Paris was the goal. Those were risks they took each trading season. But half their silver – this was years of profits he was willing to wager.

"None of the gold," he assured her. He still had three pieces from the eight she had given him, and he would never lay claim to the twelve he insisted she lay by for her widowhood. But he might risk the thick bracelet of Rus gold he had bought, to replace the one Guthrum had granted him. The thought of this carried his thoughts back to Hrald, who now owned that gold cuff. He gave his head a shake and went on.

"I do not know which God Eskil has dedicated himself to," he told her. "But I know he has found the favour of some God to have lived as long as he has." Sidroc took a moment to consider this. The Svear's fulltrúi was likely Balder, who had certainly bestowed good looks upon him. Another thought arose. Perhaps Loki the Trickster had guided Eskil all this time. That could be believed.

"I challenged him to trade, and now he is back, ready to do so. He helms a good ship, and a man he says knows the route. He has let drop that he needs goods, and one look at his decks tells me he has little or nothing on his own account to trade. I will stake him, provision both ships, make sure able men join him aboard, as he needs another dozen at the oar. And he needs Runulv and Dauðadagr; a single ship has little chance of returning. For all this I will ask two-thirds of what he wins in trade. Should they return with silk and spice Eskil will be a rich man."

If Sidroc adhered to his past practice of giving Runulv a third share of his profits, this could be a gain of significant wealth for both families. And as in every trading venture, captain and crew could trade goods on their own account. These might bring considerable sums, above and beyond the share the men earned from taking part in the voyage. Ceridwen took in the movement of his eyes as he detailed all this, seeing how quickly he had seized upon the idea, and was giving form to the agreement he would seek. Now those eyes, darkly blue and sober, turned upon her face.

She had not answered his question, that of the giving of her consent to such a risk.

"I think back to our first voyage," she offered.

It was like his shield-maiden to conjure the past, holding it up as if to illumine the future. To Sidroc this presaged a hopeful conclusion.

"We had so little," she recalled. "Three of the great millstones you ordered cracked in the fire; you had not yet paid for two of them. Runulv's salt was destroyed by the water you fought it with. We four had to scrimp to come up with goods worthy of the journey. Little as they seem today, it was most of what we owned."

They had overcome that painful loss and made a profitable voyage. There was silence between them, remembering this. The steady stroke of Tindr's plane sounded from within the stable, a rhythm not unlike the lifting and lowering of an oar.

It felt some accord had been reached about the endeavour, some first milestone passed.

"Now I must learn if Runulv will go," Sidroc decided.

"Was that all?" Ceridwen now asked.

A moment passed. He was not going to tell the girl's mother that the Svear had inquired after Eirian, nor share how he had answered Eskil, proclaiming the girl was destined for Wales.

Yet Ceridwen did not take her eyes from his face. There was more; what she did not know, but it prompted her to say the next. Her words were a challenge, though a gentle one.

"Eskil was not the reason you left our bed early."

Sidroc let his eyes flick up to the gable peak of Tyrsborg, before returning to his wife's face. He must tell her.

"Nai. My fylgja was stirring during the night, and granted me a vision."

Ceridwen had taken a step nearer. She was one who believed that a dream, however confused, always held some truth. Her eyes, as green and as questioning as the day they first met, had widened as she waited for him to go on. He did so.

"She told me of trouble, with one close to me, but far away."

Her alertness could hardly be the greater. She looked as if she were about to speak, but he lifted his hand, and went on.

"I went to the Place of Offering and cast bones. It is Hrald."

Sidroc did not want to admit he had at first been uncertain as to which son he had dreamt of, lest she fear for Yrling without cause.

"Our shared fylgja told me. The trouble is a trial, a test; deep distress of some kind. The cause is a woman. And there is nothing I can do to aid him."

"A woman," Ceridwen repeated.

"Já. When he was here he told me he had been wed but briefly, to a daughter of Guthrum. It was clear his attachment to her was strong. Yet he sundered the union when he found her in the presence of another Dane, his arms around her."

Sidroc had not shared this before, but then the tale had been Hrald's to tell. And it had been one with a seeming end.

"So it could be her – his wife," Ceridwen wondered aloud.

Sidroc gave a nod. "It could. Or another," he allowed. Somehow recalling the look on his boy's face as he told of his failed union suggested that it was this first, most wrenching attachment, come back to haunt him.

Another silence fell, one of quite another kind than that concerning trading. It was Ceridwen who broke it.

"When Edwin was here, and I was so troubled about him, you reminded me that no matter how pinioned we are to the lives of our young, they must fly alone. You told me the fluttering of their wings could not knock me from our sky. This truth gave me comfort. Yet – the wind currents buffeting our young are sometimes felt by us, even if we can do nothing . . . "

A smile forced its way to his lips. He let go a deep sigh, and gave a slow shake of his head. "Já," he allowed, and said no more.

He did not wish to remind his shield-maiden of this truth from his own past, crowding in upon his fears for his son: You do not know the depths a man will drop to, for the woman he wants. After they had escaped capture by the Idrisids, Sidroc had been ready to kill his own men, should they have come after and found him. He was spared that unhappy prospect. But all else he had cast off, that he might keep her at his side, and start anew with this woman before him.

✠✠✠✠✠✠✠✠✠✠✠

After Eirian had left him to go to her father on the pier, Juoksa had lingered a while in the herb garden of his grandmother, Rannveig. He watched his friend as she walked from the two men to go about her errand on the trading road. Juoksa did not join her. There amongst the leggy stalks and blown flowers of the brewing herbs, he busied himself, head down, seemingly absorbed. He kept his eyes fixed on the plants he brushed his palm over, and his sensitive nose, attuned to the pungent aromas of farm animals, the cool and verdant fragrance of the forest, and the mineral tang of Sun-bleached limestone, twitched at the rising scents of costmary and thyme. But his ear was cocked to the pier where Eirian's father stood with the yellow-haired stranger. After a while he turned and made his way purposefully back to Tyrsborg, where his mother Šeará and little sister Jaské had been visiting Eirian's mother. Juoksa did not climb the road, but rather went the back way, from the brew-house garden to the

line of trees marking Alrik the joiner's house, just beneath
Tyrsborg. When he arrived his mother and sister had already
left, to make the short walk to their forest house. Juoksa ran
after. He had not far to catch up to them. Ŝeará turned on
the path at the sound of his footfall, her hand in that of Jaské.
Her face, with its angled cheekbones, made her look like a
deer, the name which Juoksa's father had given her. With her
white skin and long pale plaits her son thought she looked
also like Moonlight, even in the dappled shade of the trail.

Ŝeará smiled at her son, but saw the distress he wore.
Juoksa was not sure how to tell her what he had learnt. The
only certainty was that it had made him unhappy. As much
as he loved his father it was hard, using only his hands, to
share such things with him. He spoke to his mother in the
tongue of the Sámi.

"Eirian – she will go. She will leave here." He was slightly
out of breath, which made the message all the more urgent
seeming.

"Eirian will leave?"

Juoksa gave a deep affirmative bob of his chin. "I heard
her father tell a ship captain. He said Eirian will go to Wales,
and wed a Prince."

Eirian had before spoken to him of this place, Wales or
Cymru; she used both words for this distant land. Juoksa
knew only it was so far to the west that the Sun must set
near there. The boy did not know what a Prince was, but
understood all too well the word "wed."

His mother smiled at him. "She must wed one day,
Juoksa."

"Yes. She must wed me. She must wed me!"

This vehemence surprised her. Little Jaské, tired from walking and standing, pulled her hand from that of her mother, and sat down on the moss by the side of the trail. It allowed Ŝeará to more fully address her son. The boy had the near-white hair which crowned her own head, and piercing light blue eyes, almost like those of his father. Those eyes were staring at her now, as if for answers. Juoksa was four Summers younger than Eirian, a great gap at this tender age. Ŝeará saw this mattered not to the boy. Eirian's twin, Yrling, had been patient with her boy, and the two had spent hours in shooting practice with their bows. When Yrling had sailed away with his older brother Hrald, Juoksa felt almost wounded by the loss. But Ŝeará had always thought Juoksa admired Yrling, but did not want to emulate him. She paused as she considered her son, allowing the fierceness of his words to drain away before she answered.

This was not the first time Juoksa had mentioned a future with Eirian; he had built small houses in the woodland, big enough only for her hound Flekkr, but had confided to both his mother and Eirian that one day he would build a larger house for his young neighbour. Eirian had only smiled at this, as the fanciful jest of a little boy. But Ŝeará saw his eyes as he said these things. And never before had Juoksa, young as he was, mentioned a desire to wed anyone.

Ŝeará looked down at her boy. He was shy, and was happiest with his father, out stalking, or at hand-crafts. His very name meant bow, the weapon both father and son hunted with. She imagined that Juoksa looked forward to a life such as Wolf Eyes knew, one spent in forests and meadows. He was dressed as she and little Jaské were, in the soft napped deerskin leggings and tunic she had made for them; Sámi clothing for her Sámi children. But Juoksa had more than once asked that he might dress like his father, in linen and wool. She knew her boy was tending more and more to island ways, just as a young plant will turn to the side where the Sun shines brightest. Juoksa would, she thought, be more than content to remain here on this island, wed a girl from a local farm. If he did he would live in a timber house, as did his bride's family. But Juoksa was half Sámi. Because of his mother he would always know how to build his own round house of straight pine poles and hides. At times Ŝeará regretted that both her young ones were being raised far from the land of her own birth. Yet she could not fault her life here, and its abundance. As did all the Gotlanders, Ŝeará gathered berries, mushrooms, and nuts in great numbers from field and forest. Hens did well here, and gentle cows gave of their milk, far more than did their ren at home. Her husband's bow and snares provided ample game for both his own family and Tyrsborg. The honey from his bees sweetened all their days. They had a generous share of grains and apples from the upland farm. Grain was a luxury to Ŝeará; she and her family could have their fill of barley, oats, and wheat.

Ŝeará took pains to tell both her offspring what she could of her Goddesses, but young Juoksa already marked his hands with the hunting runes as his father did. And Ŝeará was not sorry to be away from the harshness of the Sámi Winters.

Juoksa stood before her with lowered head. His fingers, which he had clenched almost into fists when he had proclaimed that it was he Eirian must wed, had uncurled; his arms now hanging slackly from his narrow shoulders.

Juoksa's eyes were fixed upon the ground, but the smooth white brow was pinched in thought.

Ŝeará must give the boy time. She would not speak rashly, but allow him to find a measure of calmness. This was the Sámi way. Just now she would comfort her son as she could.

"Eirian's folk are not from here, but from other lands," she reminded him, her words low and soft. "She is of their blood. And sometimes blood can call us, far away."

Juoksa's eyes lifted at this, and rested on her face. He had already been planning the big forest house he would build for Eirian, when they were old enough to wed. His mother had told him how a proper village should be arranged, and that the chief's house should front the rest of the houses. His father was like a chief, and so the house Juoksa and Eirian would build would be behind the one his father and mother had made. He would grow to be as great a hunter as his father, and his grand-father would bring many furs from the north to keep Eirian warm.

His mother went on, in the same quiet tone.

"You are like father. Wolf Eyes was raised here, with Grandmother. He has all the forest to wander, and to feed us from. This is what he knows, and loves. He does not wish for more." She smiled down at his questioning face. "Nor any less do I. He is most important to me. Father, and you, and Jaské; Grandmother, and our friends here. When you are older you will know what is most important, what calls you. But you must allow Eirian to follow what calls to her."

Sidroc's work with Tindr at the paddock must wait, and he signed to the man to return to his forest home and the needful tasks awaiting him there. What could not be put off was his determining whether or not he would throw in with Eskil, and the greater part of that decision was not his to make. But he could not approach his captain Runulv without knowing more.

Few good deals were brokered on an empty stomach, and first Sidroc went to his kitchen yard, where Gunnvor ladled up a bowl of boiled oats. Tyrsborg's cows provided milk aplenty for both butter and cheese, and he dropped spoonfuls of tangy kvarg on its steaming surface. A golden dribble of Tindr's honey over this gave him a second chance at the meal he had earlier abandoned.

When Sidroc entered the treasure room of his hall, his wife was within. Upon their bed, from which he had arisen in a state of disquiet, sat two of his fine linen tunics. And in his shield-maiden's hand was the cuff of Rus gold he wore for occasions of note. She smiled wordlessly at him. She knew that a parley of such moment demanded more than the work clothes he was clad in now.

As Sidroc readied himself he spoke.

"I will see Eskil," he told her, "and question his man who has made the journey. If his answers are good, I will be back for horses, so we may head to Runulv's farm."

He went on as if he guessed what she were about to say next. "Gyda will hear all, I promise you. It will not be like the sail to Lindisse."

"It cannot be," she stressed. Gyda had not known the risks Runulv had taken on that voyage; her husband had sheltered her from the truth. Runulv had made that sail to return their sons Ceric and Hrald to Angle-land, obliged by his loyalty to undertake the hazardous crossing. This venture was purely for profit, and neither Runulv nor Gyda should feel beholden to agree to it. "She must know all; the months it may take, and the full danger ahead."

"We will see what Eskil's man says," he answered. He moved to the wall where hung his weapons.

That morning he had worn but a working knife at his side. Now he belted on his seax, that he had won so long ago in Angle-land, copper and silver wires hammered into its grip in a sinuous dance. Eskil had before seen it, but to wear it now was another reminder of the distances its bearer had himself sailed.

She held out the golden cuff for him, and stood before him as he pressed it over his right wrist. With such a weapon and the gold encircling his wrist he was an impressive sight.

"Samarkand or not, you look the part already."

He gave a rueful laugh. "Já. That of a man ready to part with much silver."

Sidroc walked down the hill toward the dragon-ship tied at the pier. It was as tight and as trim as any seafaring band of warriors could ask for, and the object of both care and pride to those who sailed her. The curved prow rose high, ending in an open-mouthed sea serpent, frilled with fin-like sawn ornament behind the jaws. Today the head gaped woodenly at the trading stalls just beyond its reach. The stern was likewise adorned, the carved head facing up to the invisible realms above. A few gashes at the base of both prow and stern told of the spears and swords of men who had been run down by her speed. It was a noble craft, one which Sidroc had admired despite the occasional frictions with the Svear who helmed her. In Sidroc's eyes the ship and the Svear were alike in this.

The gangplank was out, and few men still aboard. A single turn of the Dane's head to the left told him several of Eskil's crew walked the trading road, some at work re-provisioning the ship, others browsing the goods on offer. But Eskil remained aboard, and seated on a cask not far from the steering-oar. Sidroc walked down the wooden pier to him.

The sky over their heads bore the milky, indeterminate quality of the early morning, a curtain dropped from the Heavens to the edge of the Baltic, with little contrast between sea and firmament.

The Dane stopped and addressed the man.

"Still aboard your ship. You are eager to sail," Sidroc jested.

The Svear answered with good-natured directness. "Eager instead for the wealth the sail will bring. To us both."

The Dane tilted his head. "Let us go to Rannveig's," Sidroc now invited. "Your man who knows the route – have him come with you."

Eskil gave a nod. He looked about him; one of the men remaining aboard was gestured forward, and the Svear sent him to the trading road to retrieve a second. Not long after Sidroc was confronted by the guide. Brani was a man nearing forty years, Sidroc guessed, of middle height, and broad of chest, a rough and ready sort. His sandy hair and sun-hardened hands told of long sailing and little shelter. He was missing much of his right ear, an injury not uncommon amongst warriors who had caught a blade there, but wore his hair pulled back by a cord, as if proud of the action this proclaimed. Brani was leather-skinned from salt and sea, and possessed the sharp alertness that told of a man well-versed in both trading and raiding.

The three headed to the brew-house. It would be some hours before it opened, but ale would be forthcoming nonetheless. And it was ever a good place to sit and talk.

Rannveig, with her prime view of both landing stage and trading road, was ready for them. She moved, keys jingling, from her brewing shed to stand at the doorway of her drinking establishment, armed with her own jest for the Svear. The brewster set her hands on her ample hips as she addressed him.

"You are come to inspect the new door jamb you bought me," she ribbed. It had been Sidroc's thrown spear which had cracked the wood nearly its full length, a spear which acted as sudden barrier to the advancing Eskil and his men.

The brewster expected no defence from the Svear, and instead straightened up before Sidroc, opening her hand in welcome to the table nearest the back wall. In short order the men sat grasping pottery cups of her late-Summer ale, flavoured with the tiny but aromatic leaves of the herb thyme. Rannveig, sensing that a discussion of some importance was about to take place, left a jug of the cool stuff upon the table. She rolled up one of the awnings, so they might have view of the ship and sea, and retreated to her brewing-shed.

After the first draught was downed, Sidroc began. He looked first at Eskil, then at the guide Brani.

"Eskil suggests we go after silk. And I have heard of Samarkand."

Brani was the first to react, and did so with widened eyes. His startled tone confirmed his surprise. "Samarkand. Samarkand. That is the trip of a year, just to reach it."

Those eyes shifted from Sidroc to Eskil, then back to the Dane.

"I have not been that far," Brani went on. "I know the Persians rule there, with wealth untold. One must take the Volga to the sea called Caspian to reach it, then overland through sand and high passes strewn with the bones of men who have tried. So lies Samarkand and its treasures. But it is the trip of seven or eight seasons, Summer to Spring twice over, or even more, to go out, and back."

Even so, Sidroc had a question to ask. "Who rules there?"

"Caliphs with more warriors – and wives – than any Dane or Svear could feed, or please. The folk have one God, named Allah, and pray many times a day; and drink no strong drink, not even ale."

Brani shook his head, whether in wonder or in despair it was hard to guess. But he ended with a muttered, "Samarkand . . . "

The man had drawn a line he would not cross, and looked to Eskil with his grievance. "Miklagårdr, on the western shore of the Black Sea. The crown city of the Byzantines. That is what I told you." Brani's eyes moved back to Sidroc. "I have been there twice. From Miklagårdr to Samarkand is seven or eight months, of sand and thirst and heat and cold.

"But from Gotland to Miklagårdr, by river and some hauling, is only four, three if we meet with no trouble. If we are not forced to over-Winter on the way, we could be back by the second planting next Spring. Those of us who return," he added hopefully.

"And if we make Miklagårdr, you will not scorn what we carry back with us. Goods from Cathay are sold there, as commonly as Baltic amber is in Birka."

"And who rules there?" Sidroc was moved to ask. He knew of Miklagårdr, had heard tell of it here on Gotland, but other than its fabled riches knew little.

"Leo is Emperor of all those parts. At least he was when I was last there. A Christian, who prays in a temple larger than any in all of Midgard. He is heir of Basil the Macedonian, but his mother was half Svear. Leo's men will take a fat bag of silver from you to land and trade, but Fate may make that bag puny in your eyes by the time we set our sail for home, decks laden with wrought silver and bronze, gemstones, rare weavings, dyes of blue and red, spice and silk."

Brani grew thoughtful here, remembering. It prompted the Dane to ask another question of the man.

"And you had your share of all this?"

Brani was decently dressed and sported a knife of visible worth, but one might wonder if the rewards of the outing had proved worth the effort and risk. He either had unusual taste for adventure, or had not in fact won enough to retire to a farm with his riches.

Their guide gave a shrug of his brawny shoulders. "I had. But women – and dice . . . "

Eskil laughed.

"What is the surest route?" Sidroc now asked.

Brani lifted his head and squinted out across the Baltic waters. "Sail north, then east through the Gulf of the Finns, up the River Neva to Staraya Ladoga. Then south. There are small rivers from there, but we will run out of water. When we do, then overland, hauling the ships on rollers when we need to, all the way to Kyiv and the River Dnieper. I know the shortest trail to it," he assured them, "and at some posts we might find guides from point to point. From the fortress of

Kyiv, then straight down the Dnieper, in shallow water and deep. The worst is saved for last. Before we reach the Black Sea, we hit the rocky cataracts. We will have to haul the ships out and roll them where there are rapids."

Brani paused long enough that Sidroc cocked his head at him. This prompted an admission from the guide. "The ribs of many ships litter such passages; captains who tried to ride the waters, instead of hauling their ships along the shore."

Eskil had looked sharply away, as if unwilling to contemplate this Fate for his fine ship.

Sidroc said nothing, but the muscle in his cheek rippled, as he clenched his jaw.

Eskil was nodding his head at all this, as if Brani's words had conjured memories of stories he had heard, but had let slip into the recesses of memory.

Brani summed up this portion of the journey. "Leaving now, much will depend on the waters, and the rains."

The guide took breath, and then had something to add. "If the rivers freeze on our way back, we will put the ships on skids, and push them along with tamps, as if oaring on ice."

Sidroc shot a glance at Eskil. This last seemed news to the Svear, but he nodded in agreement to this pronouncement by his guide. Perhaps Eskil, unsure if he would find a partner for the venture, had not delved as deeply into the hardships ahead as he might have.

"And then?" the Dane asked. It was Brani who answered.

"We reach the great inland Black Sea, and skirt the western shores, until we see the towers and domes of Miklagårdr. The Black Sea is sealed off by only the narrowest of openings from greater water. The Emperor controls this.

There lies Miklagårdr. We call it that, "Great City", but those who live there name it Constantinople, for an old King.

"If the weather is against us and we cannot make Miklagårdr, there are other places to trade with profit, goods hard to find here. Novgorod is one, and not far from Lake Ladoga. Rurik was their King, a Svear. His kin control the area. Many of our brothers have joined them there. Kyiv on the River Dnieper is another, also Rus. The slave market there is almost second to none. The Kings of the place are called Rus now, but they are Svear."

Sidroc took a moment, considering all this. Samarkand was but a name, one which for now must remain nothing more. But the chief city of the Byzantines, Miklagårdr, was a most worthy destination, and failing that, this trading post of the Rus, Kyiv, could suffice. He had learnt enough to proceed. He let his eyes fall first on Eskil, then Brani, in turn.

"Eskil's ship is a good one, and mine, Dauðadagr, is another. Both will be richly loaded. I will send seal skins and walrus hides," Sidroc told them, "walrus tusks as well. Pelts of Winter fox, marten, and mink. Amber, almost a hundred weight of it. Casks of Gotland honey. And pure beeswax for the making of tapers, as much of each as we can carry. Ornaments of silver, worked into tiny bells, amulets, and pierced beads."

The Dane might have been detailing the makings of a feast to famished men. Both Eskil and Brani had leant forward at the table, listening to this accounting.

Brani had something to add to the list of goods to trade.

"And we will be rounding up Slavs on route; yellow hair and blue eyes are always prized by the Byzantines."

Sidroc paused. The very name slave came from the Slavs, though untold numbers bought and sold were other captives from other lands.

His shield-maiden had decided feelings about such traffic from her Christian upbringing. Those enslaved passed through Gotland; Eskil himself had sold a young girl to Sidroc's wife. There were slaves aplenty throughout Wessex and Mercia, but they had laws protecting them, and those who possessed them could not without penalty dispense with their lives. It was common that when Lords and Ladies died, they would free a number of their slaves as an Offering to the Christian God. More to the point, and to his own experience, he and his shield-maiden had been captured by Idrisids and were destined for slavery; he as a bonded body-guard to some potentate, she as a pleasure-woman kept behind walls. He must speak here.

"There will be no slaves brought upon Death-Day," he decided. "It is against the desire of Freyja, whose good will we need."

It was Eskil who questioned this.

"Freyja?"

"Já. My wife – Freyja has ever watched her. On your own ship you may deal as you like, Eskil. But know that Freyja has two eyes, and as Dauðadagr sails with you, she will be watching you both.

"Besides," the Dane added, turning to a practical aspect, "slaves need to be captured, and are not easily given up by their families. We make this journey to trade, not to raid. Slaves must be fed, and when you arrive, cleaned up enough to be appealing to a buyer. Why add all this to your efforts when you have such goods to trade as you will carry, lashed upon your very decks?"

Eskil made protest. "We will need slaves to help with the hauling."

Sidroc lifted his eyes out across the water, and kept them there. His next words were cool, but decided.

"You are saying the good men of Gotland, and your Svear, are not up to the task? That the backs of your men will not bear such a test of strength?"

Now it was become a point of pride.

Eskil and Brani looked at each other. They knew the entire venture depended upon this Dane to fund it. Neither had failed to notice the broad bracelet of red gold encircling his right wrist, proof of past success. The older man shrugged his shoulders, and awaited his captain's answer.

The Svear let the potential insult pass.

"Well . . . if you bring the Gods into it," Eskil pondered aloud.

Sidroc's retort closed the topic. "The Gods are always part of it."

That afternoon three men rode up to Runulv's farm. It had grown to considerable size over the years Runulv had sailed for Sidroc, and was now home to his family of six, as well as three serving women, one who was wed to a man who helped Runulv with ploughing and the care of the many cattle and sheep they had accrued. The outbuildings had grown in proportion, and all was kept as trim as was the knorr in which Runulv had made his fortune.

The mistress of the farm, Gyda, was out in the work yard with one of the serving women, gathering in clothes hung to dry. The day had featured no bright Sun, but the general aridness of the island air had crisped them nonetheless. She recognized Sidroc on his black stallion, and at the barking of the dogs, her two oldest boys, both of whom had been in the barn, went to greet him. The other two horsemen were strangers, and she called out to Runulv, at work repairing one of their iron cauldrons at the small forge behind the house.

Runulv appeared, still clad in his leathern apron, and raised his hand to his friend. As the horsemen neared he recalled the yellow-haired man at Sidroc's side. Runulv had been here at his farm when Eskil's drekar had landed last time, bearing a demand from the King in Uppsala. But he had seen the Svear when he, with all the men of Gotland, gathered at the hastily called Althing to hear the terms. The smile on Runulv's face would have faded, but for the look on Sidroc's own, which bore no sign of ill tidings.

Gyda approached with Runulv, her serving woman behind her. As the men swung down from their horses Gyda turned, a signal to the woman to ready ale. Sidroc noted that today Runulv's wife wore a fine pair of gold-chased Gotlandic brooches on the straps of her over-gown, shaped like the elongated heads of cats. She owned three sets of brooches of high workmanship, a source of pride to both her and her ship-master husband. Sidroc was about to present her with the chance to have some of pure gold.

After Runulv's first words of welcome, Sidroc gestured to the men with him.

"Two men of the Svear, who would have us join the trading trip of a lifetime," he said as introduction. "Eskil you will recall, late of the service of the Uppsala King. Brani" – and the man bobbed his head in answer – "is his guide."

Sidroc paused a moment, one freighted with import. "To the treasures of Miklagårdr."

Gyda's hand rose in surprise, and Runulv stood, open-mouthed. It was much to take in, and Sidroc knew this. He was asking Runulv to throw in with these men, and travel to lands utterly unknown to the Gotlander. The Dane had the advantage in that he had prior dealings with Eskil, good and ill, and had many times gamed with him, which, Sidroc held, was ever a swift way to learn of a man's character. Now Runulv must be able to form his own conclusion about with whom he would risk his life. And Sidroc wanted Eskil to see the enviable life Runulv had built on his trading wealth, so he understood what was at stake in joining the adventure.

"Would you hear more?" Sidroc posed. He turned his eyes as well on Gyda; she must endorse the venture and its hazards as surely as Runulv.

Gyda paused but a moment. "I will fetch ale," she answered.

The four sat down at a kitchen work table, and when ale and cups had been placed upon it, Sidroc gestured to Gyda to sit as well. She had not often been privy to the planning stages of Runulv's trading ventures, but of this she must know all. Their two oldest boys were there as well, seated upon a random bench some distance away. They were too young to join the adventure, but not too young to hear for what, and to where, their father would sail.

The plan was repeated. Runulv asked a question of the route. "Lake Ladoga – why sail so far north, only to sail south again?"

Brani gave answer. "The tribes we will meet. The River Neva will be friendlier to us than the River Dvina. We will join the waters of the Dnieper just the same. And we must stop at Novgorod, a trading post of the Rus. If we need more men, we will find them there."

All were aware that by that point they may have lost a man or two through sickness or misfortune. A source of eager and trustworthy replacements was nothing to be scorned.

After the couple had heard all that could be told, and the ale jug had been refilled over several rounds, Runulv turned to Gyda. He asked of her no question, only held her in his gaze. She had said nothing throughout, and for her answer only placed her hand on top of his and gave it a squeeze. But she nodded her head, and a slight smile came to her lips.

"My sister's oldest boys – one of them will be able to come and live here to help with the heavy work, until you return."

Thus it was decided.

Runulv looked to his guests, and asked the same question Sidroc had of Eskil.

"When?"

"Now," Eskil answered. "To set sail before the full Moon."

Runulv gave his brown hair a shake of surprise.

"I will need to do some work on the knorr," he countered.

"Nai," Sidroc told him. "Not your ship. You will sail Dauðadagr. She is lighter and faster."

Runulv blew out a breath. "Death-Day," he considered. "You should change her name." But he grinned.

※※※※※※※※※※

Four men rode back to the pebbled shore upon which Dauðadagr lay beached. Tied to his saddle Runulv had two stout lengths of walrus hide line, and would waste no time getting the drekar into the foaming shallows.

"We will put her in, see what water she takes on," Runulv noted. The straked boards of her hull, well-tarred as they had been, would have dried and shrunk during the months out of water.

Even lying there, canted to one side high and dry, Death-Day had to his steady eyes a kind of rare attraction. The ship-captain's knorr, as sturdy and faithful a friend as she had been, was clumsy in comparison; a dray-horse next to a King's long-legged mount. Runulv had sailed Dauðadagr a few times, pleasure outings up or down the coastline prompted by the pleadings of Sidroc's son Yrling, who fancied himself the trim little dragon-ship's rightful owner. The boy was avid enough, hands on the oaken steering-oar at all times, standing next to Runulv as the Gotland captain talked to him about reading the roll of the waves, the catch of the sharp and hazardous currents, and the pale treachery of the limestone sea-shelf projecting under the clear water beneath their keel. Now Runulv would sail her across the Baltic, up the narrow Gulf of the Finns, and down rivers far distant from these shores. As he prepared to guide her out into the cool and waiting Baltic he could not help but think ahead, of the long sailing in river waters awaiting them.

With help from a few of Eskil's crew, the four righted her and pushed her into the foaming shallows. They tied her alongside the Svear's own ship, that her crew might keep watch on her. Now again in the water, Dauðadagr's pine planks would swell to a tight fit, closing any gaps. Those remaining after two days would be stuffed with a sticky mass of tar and wool fleece, and tar daubed as well on any places on the hull wanting its preserving coat.

Once she was secured, Runulv rode off into the countryside, ready to alert all his usual crew that sailing season was not in fact over, and the chance for the fattest purses they had ever hoisted lay before those willing to take on the challenge.

Only one thing more remained to be fixed. The terms of the partnership between Dane and Svear had not been formally agreed upon, and after seeing Runulv off, Sidroc boarded the drekar to accomplish just that. The Svear awaited him. The two took up seats on chests stored in the stern, not far behind the steering-oar Eskil would soon man.

The crew were mostly ashore; Rannveig had opened her brew-house to all comers, and from the activity and aromas issuing from her kitchen yard it was clear that Gudfrid was griddling up oat cakes and tending to a pot of fish stew.

"We will be true partners, and go half," Eskil began.

"Half?" the Dane asked, with lifted eyebrows. He glanced around the empty deck. "You bring one man who knows the way, and your ship," he reminded, in a tone that indicated the paucity of Eskil's contribution. And the daring to go, Sidroc added silently.

Still, he must make his bargain; it was only just, given his backing the entire venture. He would start high, and ease the Svear into the deal he wanted.

"You will sail on my silver, with able Gotland men to round out your crew, men who will join because of Runulv, who is my captain. My goods will be your stake, unless this decking we sit upon hides more than a stowaway rat. A three-quarters share of all goods you return with is mine, or you can sail alone, with your eleven men."

The Svear looked as though he might let go a howl of protest, but mastered himself. He looked from left to right, as if for answers, then pulled a three-legged stool nearer them. Eskil took a small handful of coins from his belt and laid them on its top.

"Here are ten parts; the whole of our profit," he said, straightening ten silver discs into a row. "Equal parts," he added, for in fact a few of the coins were but half pieces. "These are our winnings; the gain of both ships." He then pulled a few away from the rest. "Four parts of the whole will be mine, and six yours."

Given what Sidroc would stake – his fine drekar, all the goods, and the life of Runulv – it was not enough. Still, it forced Sidroc to consider. Eskil too was risking his ship, and his life. And the Svear had brought him a chance to procure the kind of goods, and realise the kind of gain, that might never come again.

Sidroc's right hand went to the coins, moving them, whole and half pieces, into two new groupings. He looked on them, then gave a nod of his head.

"A two-thirds share for me, and a third for you," he responded. "True partners," Sidroc ended, offering his hand.

The Svear took that hand. Adorned with gold as it was, it seemed both emblem of this pact, and promise of reward.

This concluded, it gave Sidroc time to bid Eskil walk down the trading road with him, to turn up to the rise where stood the forge of Berse the weapon-smith. The man was Sidroc's age, give or take a Summer or two, but possessed two abilities the Dane felt vital to help ensure the success of the venture to Miklagårdr. Berse was a trained warrior who in his youth had been an active raider, ranging through the Baltic, testing the spear points, knives, and swords his father had forged. And he was a skilled blade smith, able if needed to repair or even forge new weapons for the combined crews. Berse was as well widely known in these parts of Gotland, and just as widely respected. It had been Sidroc and Berse Eskil had called for, on the Svear's last visit to this bay. If Berse would sail, it would help attract good men to join him.

The ringing of iron beating upon iron met their ears as they approached the low-slung but open-walled forge. There was the weapon-smith at work, hammering away at a spear-point, its tip still smoking red from the fire. One of Berse's sons was tending the hearth, the second stood ready by the quenching pot to take the spear-head. Berse glanced up at his visitors, his massive right arm in motion, and sweat from the fire beaded on his brow. He gave a nod and continued on, gesturing with his head that the son by the quenching pot take over. The boy did so, with a transfer of the hammer and point from father to son so deft that scarce a moment more passed before the finishing blows were struck. Berse watched the boy's work with care, and when his son looked up at him, holding the finished spear-head aloft, was met with a nod of approval from his father.

As Berse joined his guests they heard the hiss of the quenching pot behind them. The weapon-smith gave a satisfied smile, and looked to the two who had sought him out.

The smith possessed an additional attraction beyond his skill making and wielding weapons. Of all those men of Gotland Sidroc knew, Berse was the most eager for gain. It was not just lust for silver, but the adventure which brought it. It was only fair that Sidroc tell him of this chance, should the man decide to leave his forge. With two sons also at work at hammer and tongs he was not abandoning his trade, just absenting himself for a chance at significant profit.

The Dane made the proposition as direct as time was short.

"Eskil will sail for Miklagårdr in his drekar at the next full Moon. And Runulv will sail for me, in Dauðadagr. They will not return until Spring. But when they do, it will be laden with treasure from Byzantium. I know you have ventured to the east. Will you go now, and have your part in the winnings?"

Berse looked as though long-awaited news had at last reached him. His weathered face lit from the grin now creasing it.

"Miklagårdr. I have never been so far. Even if we make Kyiv we will return rich. I have been told you can buy in Kyiv at half the price of Birka. And in Miklagårdr at half the price of Kyiv."

The weapon-smith went on, in even greater gladness. "Long have I wished to see the forges of the Byzantines. I have ten, twelve good blades to take, to show them Weland's art as practised here on Gotland."

"Good. Your arm will prove doubly handy then, ready to repair any iron needed, and to impress the warriors of Miklagårdr with your craft."

"A triple benefit if I am aboard," said Berse, with a note of protest. "My own arm to fight if we are attacked."

So Berse acknowledged the danger, and without Sidroc mentioning it, offered himself. Sidroc gave a slow nod of grateful acceptance. He had already decided on the next declaration, if the blade-smith agreed to go.

"And you will sail on Eskil's drekar," he said, with a glance at both men. Berse's presence would be an added level of surety to Sidroc's ends. The men of Gotland who wished to sail with the Svear would be thus under the direct leadership of one they knew and trusted.

Sidroc turned now to Eskil, without giving him time to weigh in. "Thor smiles on you to have gained such a crewman," he summed.

Berse was grinning from ear to ear. Eskil's drekar was one of the finest ever to grace their shores, and now he would be aboard, a valued crewman of a Svear who once threatened them.

Sidroc must further add to the smith's accomplishments, so Eskil truly understood his value. "And a good story teller," he added, with a grin of his own. "He will fill your ears with tales to while away the long hours." Eskil opened his mouth, then closed it. Indeed, the Svear had already been subject to what he wagered was the entire story of Gotland.

The day had been long, one full of the promise of triumph. Sidroc returned to Tyrsborg with growing confidence in the outing, with Runulv and Berse both eager to take part. Ceridwen greeted him outside at their well; she was drawing up water for her grape vine, twining over the bench by the front door in the hall's gable end. Its purple grapes grew plumper every day. He took the line from her and finished the final pull, then carried the wooden bucket to the base of the vine.

He had said nothing yet, but it was clear he was pleased; his look and manner spoke this.

"All is in order," he told her, as he canted the bucket over to drench the knotty roots of the vine. "Runulv and Gyda were eager for the chance. And Berse will join; with him aboard Eskil's ship, fronting ten or more islanders, it will be almost as much a Gotland ship as will be Dauðadagr, helmed by Runulv."

The mistress of Tyrsborg was about to speak her joy at this, when he went on.

"But they cannot reach Samarkand; it is too far. Their goal lies at the great city of Byzantium, Miklagårdr, on the Black Sea. It has a second name, Constantinople." Sidroc thought a moment, recalling what he had heard of it. "It is, I think, the largest of all cities, and at the crossroad of east and west. And it must be the richest, perhaps richer than Samarkand."

She took this in. She had heard of Constantinople at Kilton, from the stories of the priest Dunnere. It was a vast fortress of the eastern Christians, named for an Emperor in a long line of Caesars, Constantine. It must be grand indeed, beyond her compassing if it be the largest of all cities. Yet there remained in his voice a wistful note as he named the desert city beyond their reach.

"Samarkand – it is an ancient place," she suggested. "It will wait for you."

"Já. Samarkand will wait," he agreed. He leant near and kissed her brow line. She was not surprised at what he said next.

"That map the priest gave you at the trading post– can you find it?"

"It is safe in the corner of my clothes chest. I will bring it here, where the light is best."

She entered the hall, and then the treasure room, wherein they slept. For all the thousands of times she had opened her clothes chest in the years since she laid the vellum within, she had never before lifted it out. The last time they had looked at it was the third day after their arrival here, when she had asked Sidroc to show her just where they had landed. Once her new clothes chest had been built she had flattened the vellum and consigned it there; it had been subject to much stress, crushing, and wet on their way to Gotland. Now she parted the folded lengths of yet unsewn linen and wool and took it out.

Sidroc had taken a seat on her favourite bench, that beneath the grape. The vellum was not much broader than the length of his two hands, palm to fingertips, but it had been the longest of the scraps she had to choose from. She remembered with what diligence she had copied out the forms of land, and the spidery veins of rivers, from the far larger map the Mercian priest had shown her. Gotland was not even upon the chart; the priest had wished to show her routes to trading towns along the eastern Baltic border where they might settle.

Ceridwen watched Sidroc's eyes trace the coastline, beginning with the first of two marks she had made, indicating two trading posts they had visited on their travels following their escape from the Idrisids.

She saw his brow furrow, as her lines petered out. He even turned the vellum over, as if hopeful more was drawn upon the back.

"He did not show you the best of maps," he decided.

She was forced to laugh. "Eardwulf was trying to help us to a safe port, where we might live unmolested," she reminded. "Not to Miklagårdr to buy sticks of cinnamon."

"We did find a safe port, no thanks to map or priest," he returned. Still, he could not resist a smile. Gotland had been their first sighting, and their lasting home.

He looked again at the vellum. "This," he thought aloud, as he pointed to a waving line heading south, "must be the Vistula." His eyes rose to another line, extending at the furthest right of the map. "And this, the mouth of the Dvina."

He gave his head a shake. "Eskil's man Brani has been all the way to Miklagårdr, twice. But Berse and Runulv, and all the men of Gotland, will return with the same knowledge."

He handed back the vellum, which for never being looked at, had not lost its power as emblem of their new life together. She held it to her breast as she carried it to the treasure room and laid it again beneath its deep shroud of fabric.

All evening Sidroc felt a thrill of latent energy flowing through him. His commitment to the venture was vast, but that of the men going, greater still. He was risking half of all the silver he had won through trade and gaming over these past dozen years, that and every trade good he could place his hands upon. He could lose all. But good men of Gotland could die. The two drekars, fast as they were and captained by shrewd and able men, could meet shipwreck before they landed at the mouth of the Neva. Once river borne, the ships could be wracked by rocky cataracts, the men set upon by raiders, and massacred. Fever could fell them all, as surely as a reaper's scythe. Yet he knew if he were not bound by the vow he had made to Freyja and Tyr never to again set sail, he would himself go.

Or would he, he asked himself. He was standing in the dim light of the treasure room, unbuckling the belt of his seax, thinking these things. His shield-maiden was already abed, and he had just locked the doors, knowing daughters and serving women were safely asleep. The steep roof of Tyrsborg sheltered so much precious to him.

He finished undressing and moved to the bed. He drew back the covers and laid down. He was not sure if she drowsed, but he would not let her sleep, not now, feeling as he did. He had left the cresset burning; he wished to see her body and her movements. His lips upon her face made her stir, and she murmured as he pulled her atop him. His hands upon her hips and breasts made demand, one only she could answer. Her response, yielding, yet with rising passion of her own, was fired by the desire he stoked in her.

But after she had fallen into sleep, warmed by his embrace, he was again visited by thoughts of his son Hrald. Nothing gave pleasure like the right woman, and nothing else could give such pain.

SHE FORGETS NOTHING

"WE NEED A MEAD CASK, full of sheep's fat."
This was Brani, the guide for the journey
from Tyrsborg to Miklagårdr. He stood with his captain
Eskil, and with Sidroc and Runulv on the shingle beach, not
far from the end of the wooden pier where Eskil's ship and
Death-Day were moored.

The faces of those Brani addressed told him he need say
more. "To grease the rollers we will use, to push the ship out
of water for portage overland."

All knew the ships would run out of river water on the
way south to the Black Sea. And Brani had promised he knew
the shortest water routes, but it meant abandoning dwindled
streams and setting out through grasslands and over hills to
reach the next navigable river. The ships would need to be
hauled overland.

"Also a stout axle, with two iron-rimmed wheels
attached," Brani went on. "To move her." Here the guide
tilted his head towards Death-Day, lying cocked on her keel
in shallow water.

The eyes of all lifted to that trim drekar, the pride of
Sidroc's son Yrling, and the ship upon which a young Sidroc

and the first Yrling had sailed the North Sea to plunder Angle-land.

"And for Sharp Tooth as well," Eskil offered, with a nod at his own drekar. "She will need such an axle."

Sidroc cast a quick look at the Svear; it was the first time he had ever named his ship in his presence, and a sign of growing confidence in the partnership to share it.

But Brani shook his head. "Nej. She is too big for the narrow waterways we will meet. Sharp Tooth gets left at Gnezdovo, or even Novgorod. We will buy small boats there to take us onward." The guide paused a moment. "You will buy," he corrected himself, and grinned.

Eskil's lips parted. Brani had not mentioned this, that he could not make the full voyage in his own ship. It was as good as his home; at this point he had no other, and he would be parted from it.

Brani shifted his eyes from the drekar back to Eskil. "There are tribes along the way, with dugouts. We can leave your ship on their banks, and venture on from there." The guide looked again at Dauðadagr. "She ought to serve. But portage will be rough. We can haul her past the most treacherous rapids, carrying her in parts if we need to."

It was Sidroc's turn to take a deep breath. Ribs could be knocked out of a ship, rivets pulled, and the keel left with just half its inner structure clinging to it. Mast and spars were not much more than peeled and smoothed tree trunks, and lashed together compactly could be carried or dropped by lines to be reassembled later. With his limited sailing past Sidroc knew these things, but had done none of them.

His hand rose to his hair, and he pushed it back away from his face as he took this in. Well, if Dauðadagr need be taken apart and hauled in pieces, Runulv would be there to put her to rights again. He looked over to his captain. There was a thoughtful furrow on Runulv's brow, but he was nodding his head at Brani as if up to the task.

Brani, thinking ahead, mentioned another necessity for ship-faring men. "Tar we will find on the banks near the fort of Gnezdovo, a ready supply to dress our planks and water proof our lines."

All nodded; there was neither ship building nor repair without pine tar. It sealed and kept from rot wooden hulls, hempen rigging lines and much else as well. Birch tar had special qualities beyond these, and could waterproof boots and still allow moisture to escape the leather, ensuring dry feet.

"And we will need," the guide went on, "ready at hand – not packed away – items of slight worth, but great show, to offer to those we meet along the waterways. Iron work such as strap hinges, small locks with paired keys, harness fittings, and buckles. Also, a few things of real value. Shears that cut sharply and meet true will be greatly prized; these will be gifts to chiefs. For the women, beads and silver trinkets of all kinds. Coins especially they favour, drilled so they may be hung from a necklace. We must have enough of all this, ready at hand so we are not delayed."

Sidroc took careful note of this list. Berse and his sons had time to knock out any number of small pieces of useful ironwork, and blade-smith as he was, Berse was expert at the fashioning of shears. From his own stores Sidroc had bags of brightly coloured glass beads, many brought back by Runulv on his trading runs. Here on the trading road there were silver smiths to work the unblemished coins he could provide into ornaments, either by drilling and attaching a small silver ring, or soldering a tiny channel of silver so the piece would always hang flat.

"What will they offer in return for these things?" Runulv wished to know.

"That we will not end with arrows in our backs, as we row away," Brani answered.

<hr/>

That afternoon Sidroc returned to the beach. As he approached the brew-house, he spotted Eirian seated within. Rannveig had not yet opened, but with the canvas awnings rolled half-way up it was a good place from which to watch the wooden pier and any ships tied there. The girl was perched on the edge of a bench, elbows on knees, her chin resting on her interlaced hands. Her gaze was trained on Eskil's drekar, rising gently on the incoming swells of the tide. To Sidroc, this did not bode well.

His shadow fell across her, and she turned her head and saw him. She jumped up, and then came out to stand before him.

Eirian had a smile for her father, as was usual for the girl. Her question surprised him, as it had not to do with the Svear, but with Eirian's twinned brother.

"When do you think Yrling will return?"

Sidroc paused, his eyes shifting to the heavens before returning to his daughter's questioning face.

"Before he arrives fronting five ships, I hope." It was a blithe response, a feeling not shared by Eirian, who only blinked her blue eyes at him. He went on, by way of explanation. "That would be a great feat, but we would like him back before then."

"He and Hrald sailed together," the girl reminded. "Edwin said I would be welcome at Kilton. Could not Runulv take me to Hunefleth, as he did with Edwin?"

The breadth of the girl's pondering forced him to take thought. A simple question about her brother leapt to Edwin, Kilton, and then Runulv, to take her to the mouth of the Seine in Frankland.

If Sidroc were to entrust Eirian on that journey, he would have to ask Runulv to take her all the way around that vast island, and deliver her to Kilton. There would be no consigning her to a strange captain to carry her to the Saxon shore, to then find some envoy of the King of Wessex to carry her on, overland. And Runulv was now destined for Miklagårdr. Sidroc could address none of this, and so asked a question of his own.

"And once at Kilton, what would you do there?"

She rocked forward a little on her toes, as if in anticipation of that day. "See Ceric again, and Edwin. And see where mother was a girl. And take mother's messages to them both. She might have letters for them," she guessed. "And meet the wife of Ceric, the princess. I want to know Dwynwen. She is of Wales. As I am, in part. She might help me find Grandmother."

Sidroc gave his lowered head a shake. Clearly she had been thinking of such a journey. It was almost as if he was hearing his own words to Eskil come back to him. All she lacked was telling him she would then wed a Prince.

Eirian's next words were a further surprise. "Perhaps from there, I could see Hrald at Four Stones. And check up on Yrling," she added, with a sly smile.

The girl's persistence was as great as her twin's. Sidroc must admire her single-mindedness. He must also curb her imaginings.

"For now, Runulv sets sail east for me. When you are older we will see about your journeying to Kilton, or Four Stones."

Her face lit. To Eirian, this was as good as a promise.

Rannveig appeared, coming round from the corner of the brew-house. She was teaching Eirian the craft of brewing ale and making mead, and today would be another lesson. Eirian almost ran to her, such was her gladness at her father's words.

⊱⊰⊱⊰⊱⊰⊱⊰⊱⊰

"She likes to hear of Sparrow," Rannveig told the girl's mother. The brewing lesson was over, and Ceridwen had walked down the hill to visit with her friend. They sat at a work table before the brewing shed. Rodiaud was with them, seated on the ground, stacking crockery cups and pots of various sizes, and singing as she did so. Eirian was now wandering the confines of the brewster's garden with Juoksa. She and Rannveig had worked on two different fla-voured ales, for the first rolling dried rose hips to a crumble between their palms to let them steep in the brew, and for the second, thyme and sage leaves. From where the brewster and Ceridwen sat, it was clear Eirian was telling Juoksa of this as she brushed her hand over the plants. Though her herb garden was mostly blown, with seedheads foremost, it was still a time of great interest to the brewster. Herb flow-ers gave delight, but seeds and dried leaves imparted flavour. Like an old woman, Rannveig thought, and smiled to herself.

"Eirian would like to meet Sparrow," her mother agreed.

Rannveig recalled what Hrald had told her of Sparrow since she had left Gotland. "Eirian says she wants to brew as well as she does, called to provide ale and mead for a hall of a hundred folk. Folk of importance," the brewster added, for Hrald had pointed out that Sister Bova's ale was dipped out to men and women of great learning and standing.

Rannveig took a breath, looking at the two youngsters. Juoksa was hanging on every word Eirian spoke, nodding his head in near frantic agreement at something she had just told him.

"She asked me today if you would give her a piece of gold, as you gave Sparrow, when she leaves."

Ceridwen turned to her. "She forgets nothing," she murmured of her daughter.

"They are two of a kind, Yrling and Eirian; having shared a womb they cannot help it. Both know what they want. But Eirian is no mischief-maker."

Their eyes travelled again to the youngsters amongst the herbs. They had now lifted their heads and were looking at the two ships afloat at the wooden pier; the large war-ship of the Svear, and the far smaller drekar owned by Sidroc.

They two were talking of the ships, that was clear, especially that of Eskil's. Eirian had pointed at it, and Juoksa, with waving hands, was indicating that Eskil came perhaps from the west, where the Sun set.

Ceridwen watched in silence. "I think she is telling Juoksa of how much she wants to sail away."

Indeed, Juoksa's shy smile and shake of his head suggested he did not agree with what Eirian had just said about the big ship.

"We do not have our children," Ceridwen said aloud. It rose, brimming in her heart, and she must share it with her good friend. "They are wholly of us, but apart. They are given us, only to make lives of their own, follow desires which may take them far from our lives, if never from our hearts. I came to this island, and my children will leave it. All that we have built here, amongst the community of folk, dear friends, the children and grand-children of others, generations out of mind of Gotlanders. Even Sidroc's father is here."

Rannveig listened. "True. They are not born for us to keep."

A smile formed upon her lips, then passed. "At times I thought Tindr would be mine forever; a blessing to me but a sorrow for him. If Ŝeará did not come . . . " She did not finish this thought. "Now, with her, and Juoksa and Jaské, it is all I could have hoped for Tindr."

Mention of Tindr reminded Ceridwen of his older sisters, snatched away by the fever which spared Tindr's life but took his hearing. Rannveig had endured much; both women had.

"You lost your girls. And Dagr. I lost my first girl. And her father.

"Yrling is off. He promised to return . . . "

Rannveig gave a considered nod of her head. "With his five ships, if I recall."

Ceridwen had to smile. "Já. Fronting five ships. How long will that take him, I wonder. I would rejoice to find him rowing ashore in a boat like that Sidroc and I arrived in."

The brewster again nodded her head.

"Though our girls were taken by fever, Frigg blessed me with Tindr, who wants nothing more than to stay here."

They looked back at the two. The brewster was the next to speak. "If Eirian leaves, Juoksa will grieve." Rannveig gave a sigh. "She is years older. But he is fixed on her. Ŝeará told me. And anyone can see it."

Ceridwen murmured agreement. An attachment formed at an early age was nothing the girl's mother would scorn. She had seen it with her oldest son, and Ashild.

A great clatter of pottery interrupted them. The tower Rodiaud had built of cups had toppled over, luckily breaking none of them. The child looked up to see if she were to be scolded, and was met by nothing more than the lightest of reprimands. She nodded her head gravely, then laughed.

"This little one," Rannveig predicted. "She is yours, to keep."

RUNAWAY

Lindisse

Y RLING had left Four Stones with careful planning, riding out shortly before the evening meal. The hall was thus fully occupied, kitchen yard bustling with fire-stokers, cooks chaffing and a few at times cuffing their many helpers, serving folk appearing amongst the work tables with waiting salvers of wood and bronze to be piled high, and others with jugs and ewers to be filled. Those who would partake of this under the roof of Four Stones gathered within. Yrling had witnessed this for months, and tonight would miss it. He had ridden round to the Place of Offering, where his traps lay stockpiled. He had secreted them in a stand of bushes not far from the large mound which Hrald had told him covered Toki, their father's cousin, whom their father had been forced to kill.

Yrling lashed his packs on as carefully as he could, though his horse skittered and whinnied at the effort of pulling the ties through the saddle rings. What with cooking kit and a slight shelter there would be hardly room for him in the saddle. He had not packed tidily enough, and he knew it. Besides provender and clothing he had as well his shield and spear to account for. Both were sized for his height, the shield only slightly smaller than the disc a grown man would carry, and his spear was that length used for throwing. He slipped the shield on his back by its leathern thong, and set the spear upright against a tree to take it up last. He worked in haste, knowing that near to the hall as he was, he could be discovered. Yet few ever ventured here, and he muttered this reminder as assurance to himself as he lashed on the second bag. That stable boy Bork was one who did; his father lay under a small mound off to one side of Toki's. The mound was grass-covered, and Yrling had seen Bork here, pulling weedy growth from it. Today no one visited; it was late in the day. Yrling was alone.

At last ready, he hoisted himself up into the seat, finding it awkward to clear the saddle with his leg over the lumpy packs. The gelding Hrald had presented him with upon his arrival at Four Stones was a beautiful animal, a deep burnished red chestnut, and larger than any horse Yrling had ridden at home. The fine saddle and brass-trimmed bridle of ruddy brown leather almost perfectly matched the beast's hide. He knew the horse to be a valuable one, just as the long knife Hrald had given him held value. Still, both were gifts, and now his. His throwing spear was another gift, and he was taking them all.

Yrling turned his horse's head south to the stream beyond the big beech. The spring that fed the wells within the hall yards cascaded out beyond the kitchen yard door, and joined the water flowing there. He guided his horse to its pebbled bottom, where he trusted their scent could not be picked up. In the glancing afternoon Sun the flow was clear as well water, and sticklebacks and minnows darted in it. He had walked out here with the great hound Frost, and recalled the dog splashing and playing with the fingerlings, streaking and silverly, as he thought of them, in the refracted light. A pang struck him then. The hound's mate Myrkri was about to whelp, and he would not be there for that.

He rode south, keeping to the stream bed. Quarrelling jackdaws along the bank cocked their heads at him, one more thing for them to complain of. Dusk began to fall about him, the ripening grassland shading from gold to russet to brown, and then to leaden grey. The boy had ridden this way before, and found what he knew was here, the stream broadening out to water meadow, and then as it thickened with sedge, a mere. A wood, dim now, loomed beyond. He turned then, and moved his horse across it, the suck of the beast's hoofs and the wailing cry of a few late flying curlews the only sound. A water vole swam ahead of him, a dark but tiny point splitting the water, before vanishing within a clump of sedge. The nests of moorhens were abandoned this late, untidy clusters of dead reeds floating on rafts of tangled sticks and rotten logs. Some nests still held the remains of a clutch of the moorhens' spotted eggs. Yrling looked down on all this, mindful all the while of his horse's footing. It was north he was heading, and he hoped the stratagem of moving through the water, and then keeping fast to the sodden mere-lands, would thwart any, man or hound, in tracking him. Frost, a coursing animal, was a sight hound, not a scent hound; Yrling could thank Thor for that. He saw a tall cairn of piled stone, and turned towards the trees beyond it.

Yrling reached the wood and could do no more than just
enter; dark had fully fallen. He could not risk losing his horse
to a stumble over an unseen root. The boy made his camp.
He freed his mount from packs and saddle, sat on a downed
tree trunk, and pulled bread and a slab of cold pig from his
food bag. He would not hazard lighting any fire; it was not
cold, and he had both blankets from his bed to wrap himself
in. There was no water at hand, but his horse had drunk
freely along their sodden route. On the morrow he would
find the road he sought.

He did not sleep well. The ground was hard beneath
him, and in the little light he had not been able to clear it of
stones, nor select a better site. The squared calf hide he had
as ground cloth kept rising damp away, but nothing more.
And there were neither pines nor spruces at hand, offering
needled boughs to cut and serve as cushioning, upon which
he could unroll it. Every crack and creak of the trees gave
rise to minor startle, as if they foretold those who might be
following him. His thoughts could not help but drift to Four
Stones. Each night Yrling sat at the crowded table of those
youths beginning their training. When he did not appear in
the hall, it might be some time before he was missed. But
at some point his brother or his brother's wife, the Lady
Pega, would have looked over and wondered at his not being
there. Still, boys were often late, though they risked a cold or
meagre meal if they were. The men on the palisade had seen
him ride out; they would have been questioned by now, he
thought. Dressed as he was for a late afternoon jaunt, they
could not have known where he truly rode.

Yrling fell into a fitful sleep, jerking awake in the broad
light of day. He had wanted to be up at dawn, and swore an

oath at himself, heard only by his gelding, browsing nearby. He scrambled to ready both horse and himself, shoving more bread into his mouth, making the animal shy from him as he heaved the packs again up and tying them to the saddle rings.

The boy had taken pains to question the warriors of Four Stones about the Caesar's roads crossing Lindisse. It was part of his plan. He asked of these byways heading in all directions, so that none, if they recalled his asking, could pin his interest to any certain spot. But Yrling had marked well in his mind where the roads of stone leading north would be found. He wished to travel as quickly as his horse's strength allowed, and riding alongside, or upon the Caesar's roads, was key to his escape.

Now he emerged from the wood, scanning across the marsh lest he see any riders at a distance. Ducks rose from the reeds, nothing more. He moved out, and back towards the stone cairn he had spotted. This too he had scouted before. It marked a boundary between Hrald's lands and those of the man Haward, but more than that, marked a trail head. It led to a Caeser's road. Yrling had gone this far in the past, down the narrow track until it opened up, allowing him to see the remains of a laid road. Parts of it had been lost in the mere behind him, but as the soil dried, more and more of the gravel and stone it had been built with could be seen. He urged his horse forward, walking alongside the tumbled and uneven surface to save the animal's hooves. He could not help but feel a ripple of exhilaration in gaining it.

Yet he knew he must be cautious. The roads of the Caesars were the most heavily travelled, and so would leave him the most exposed. There were many dangers here. It was not like Gotland. Here he could meet with brigands and other evil-doers, who might try to rob him of his horse, his goods, and if he resisted, perhaps his life. If he was beset, he could not even use the protection of being the brother of Jarl Hrald, as he might be held for ransom. No thought shamed him more than that of being led back to the gates of Four Stones and bargained for. He would not let that happen.

Now he took sight along this road, north and heading to the great trading centre of Jorvik.

He touched his heels to his gelding and moved on. The morning as it unfolded was proving to be a fine one. He had no leathern cape to fend off rain, and thought that he should get one for his future use. Everything could be had in Jorvik; any number of men had told him that. Now he was away from Four Stones and headed there, and with no sign of men or dogs at his heels. This thought furrowed his brow for a moment, thinking of grey-coated Frost, and his mate, Myrkri. The arrival of the pups would be the first of what he would miss, and he had been all but promised one. There would be more he would miss, he knew, but the surety of freedom lured him on.

The Sun was at the highest point in its arc when Yrling noticed something ahead, two figures which had been partially obscured by the overhanging boughs of a tree. He slowed his horse to get a better look, then nudged him forward with his heels. In the road stood a small and dark donkey, wearing only a halter to which a trailing lead was affixed. A man clad in a similarly dark gown was bent over a pack saddle lying on the side of the road. Yrling saw it was a monk, a holy man of the Christians; he had seen plenty at Oundle, and stayed overnight in their hall there as well. This one was above middle age, with the top of his head free from the grey hairs that fringed above his ears. He was slight of form, but Yrling's father had always told him that such men could be full of sinewy strength.

The monk straightened up as Yrling approached. His gelding tossed his head and gave a whinny of greeting, which the donkey returned, stretching its furred neck and blasting an unexpectedly loud bray for such a small creature. The monk had lifted his hand in a hopeful gesture.

The boy reined up. He saw at a glance what had happened; one of the leathern straps securing the donkey's wooden pack harness had snapped. Everything must have dislodged, which explained the scattered packs, none of them large, now upon the grass.

Yrling got off his horse. He was in a hurry, but one could not ignore a traveller in need.

He muttered a greeting in the tongue of Angle-land, which the monk returned.

"I am Withun. Of the monastery of Streaneshalch, before it was laid waste," the man went on. He paused. The boy before him was not even born when Danes plundered and burnt it. "Blessed Hild was its founding Abbess, long before my time, may she rest in peace."

Yrling only nodded; he was squatting now and looking at the broken pack strap. Both of them reaching across the breast were worn, and the one on the right had finally given way. He rose and reached for his saddle. There behind his cantle was rolled his hide ground cloth. It was big enough. He could cut two strips from the long end of it, to replace those worn. Each was fastened to the wooden pack frame by doubled rings of iron, and tethered to a larger central ring at the donkey's breast. All he need do was cut the strips and thread them through to adjust them. He glanced up at Withun. The monk's gown was belted with a mere length of twisted hempen rope; nothing he could have used to serve as a strap.

Yrling knelt down and scored through the end of his ground cloth, having the monk hold it taut against the ground as he did. He had no shears, but two firm slices for each new strap served. Then he pulled out the worn and broken straps, and threaded the new through the rings.

The unencumbered donkey had gone to stand in the shade cast by Yrling's horse. Both animals rested there, head to rump, swishing their respective tails as they waited.

Yrling held the small beast's lead while Withun lifted pad and pack saddle onto the donkey's back, and adjusted the new breast straps into the doubled rings.

When he was done the monk pressed his hands together. "You were Heaven-sent my boy, as sure as any angel who descends to answer prayers."

Yrling cocked his head. He knew that angels had wings, which sounded like it would be useful, and that some of them also had swords, so he could not complain.

"Do you have a letter?" Yrling asked, as he did not know what else to say. He knew that monks often bore such messages on behalf of those who could not themselves travel.

The man blinked, and bobbed his head. "That I do, for the Holy Mother Abbess Sigewif, at Oundle." All about the monk's countenance spoke of his eagerness to be in the company of such an august personage as was the Abbess of Oundle.

Yrling felt his face change; he could not stop the grin of recognition from spreading across it. It was all he could do to keep from crying out that he knew the stern old woman, had sat at her work table, and been made to write out, under her steely gaze, what she had dictated. He assumed a look of what he hoped was tedium, an attempt which was not successful, as the man's next words proved.

"You have heard of her," he said. "Been perhaps in her presence. I will stand before her myself, if the Prioress favours me with that attendance. The Abbess is a Princess by birth, but shunned all that. Her King-brother is now St Edmund, and may we be perpetually in his regard." The man fell silent a long moment, before naming one even closer to Four Stones. "There is now in Oundle Church the grave of one Ashild, who died in its protection. You would know of her?"

Yrling ducked his head so quickly he may have been afraid of being hit. Ashild of Four Stones was no kin to him, but was half-sister to Hrald. And Yrling knew Hrald grieved her loss; he had once shadowed his brother when he went, seemingly alone, into the stone church of Oundle, and watched Hrald approach the white expanse of the ledger stone covering his lost sister. Hrald had knelt, and bowed his head at the letters carved there.

Yrling shook his head.

The monk lifted his face, squinting against the Sun in the sky.

"If you know of Oundle, tell me how much journeying lies ahead. My little grey friend can go on and on, but these old bones of mine weary."

Yrling took a breath. He did not want this old man to think he was of the very hall that had been such a support to the folk at Oundle. Yet to dissemble, to lie to the man, even send him off on the wrong track . . . something within him made his belly churn at this.

"You will reach there tomorrow, or the day after if you linger on the way. Follow the Caesar's road; it becomes a track, but keep on. You will see a stone cairn. Head south from there. You will see another cairn; it marks an ox-cart track. Follow that, with the woodland on your left. The ox track will open to a road, leading to Oundle."

The monk was nodding his head to all this, as if knocking it into memory.

"Blessings upon you, my boy. When I have safely arrived, let me say a prayer for you, and name you at the altar."

Yrling almost sputtered. He must think of a likely name, one which, should the old man share it at the abbey, would not be connected with himself.

"Ulf," he offered. It was the most common name he could think of, and would have to serve.

The monk looked surprised. "Ulf. Ulf from . . . "

"Jutland," Yrling said. Though it was a vast place, and the home of his father, it was only a name to him, one faraway.

"Your speech is strange," the cleric went on. "Now I know why. You are not of these parts."

Yrling feared the man was about to ask where he was heading, or why he was upon the road, and alone. He reached for his saddle and pulled himself up into it, signaling he was about to ride off. The monk was unperturbed.

"Nay, not of these parts," he repeated. "But then, neither am I. I am Kentish born."

Yrling knew this lay south, but nothing more. He turned his horse's head.

The monk bobbed his stubbled chin. "Ulf from Jutland. I shall pray for you at Oundle's altar."

The ride from Four Stones to Jorvik was six days, five in the long light of Summer, if roads were dry. His second day out, after boiling up his dinner, Yrling realised his food stores would not last through the next. It had not been easy gathering food for the trip. Though he was welcome there at any time to eat, he had felt himself almost pilfering from the kitchen yard as he snuck small amounts of oats and barley away, dropping handfuls from casks in the store-houses into small linen bags. He had helped himself to fresh picked apples and pears, asked for boiled eggs as if he would take them away and soon eat them, begged for a hunk of smoked pig haunch, and most daring of all for a lad raised to be truthful, had not only lifted a few items of cooking gear, but reached in and grabbed a whole cheese when one of the spring houses was open. Yet such filching had not been enough. He was hungry at night and again when he awoke in the morning. He was used to having his fill, and now faced sudden want. The men he had spoken to who had made the trip had pack horses with them, laden with provender. The slackness in his leathern food bag told him he would need to stop and seek provisions.

Yrling had a small sum of silver, the same which his mother had given him when he and Hrald had taken ship. It was significant only to her that she had placed five and thirty silver pieces into the small purse at his belt, the same she had once ridden off with. But then, her boy was in the care of Hrald, and heading to a hall of riches. This, and what he now carried with him in horse and weaponry, was all Yrling had to make his way with.

The boy had passed a few tracks that looked worn enough to lead to farmsteads. He resolved to follow the next and see if it carried him to food. He turned down such a track, one well rutted by the wheels of carts. The trees about him thinned, then opened to pasturage, dotted with white-bodied sheep. The croft was just beyond, an assemblage of timber buildings large and small. A dog came running out, barking and snapping, but a boy about his own age appeared from a work shed and whistled the dog quiet. A woman, and then a man appeared, both from behind a small barn, and as he neared the wattle fence surrounding their thatched house, a string of children came tumbling out over the threshold. The man moved haltingly; he had once suffered some hurt to one of his legs, that was clear.

The woman wore paired bronze brooches at the shoulder straps of her gown, telling Yrling she was a Dane. She was not to his eyes young, but had as yet no grey in her brown hair, which was tied back in a kerchief of dark blue. She stood and narrowed her eyes as she looked up at him.

Yrling bobbed his head and greeted her in Norse. She nodded her head in return. The dog, a smooth coated hound, was circling his horse, making the animal toss its head, and the boy collared him. Yrling gave a nod of thanks to the boy; he did indeed look the same age. But Yrling was astride a fine horse, with a big knife at his side, almost a sword, and bore also the shield and spear of a warrior. The farm boy, still holding the hound, walked a little behind Yrling that he might see the shield, with its dark field and red zigzag.

"I need food," Yrling began, looking at the woman. "To buy," he added hastily, lest they think he begged. "I have silver."

The woman looked at her husband, his face as hard as flint. He made no sound of assent, only gave his wife a slight nod, as if this was women's business, and she in charge of stores.

It gave Yrling a chance to look over the holding, which was tidy enough. To one side of the house lay two fields, one in which reaped grains lay drying, the second lined with rows of partly-harvested vegetables, and yellowing pot herbs. He could hear a couple of unseen cows mooing; they would need milkers to make butter and cheese, with so many young ones to feed. The fowl houses had hens aplenty roosting along its low roof, and strutting behind their enclosure.

"How many days?" the woman asked.

"Three or four."

"Heading to Jorvik," she answered, with a bob of her head. "Rob you blind they will, so watch the scales when you pay up. The lead weight they show you first, and balance before your eyes – some will change that in a flash for one heavier or lighter, making you pay more, or get less."

This warning delivered, she returned to her questioning.

"Eggs? How many? I can spare four loaves, no more; they will go hard, but spread with butter they will serve. We have smoked pig – I can spare some of the shoulder – and I have a cured cheese or two you can have. Skirrets. And pears.

"Barley? Oats?"

"All of it. If you please," he added, trying to be polite at the offered bounty.

She gave a nod of her chin, and then gave him a hard and long look. "You are young to be warring. About my Rig's age," she guessed, glancing at her son. "Like him, you are growing."

Yrling glanced over at the snub-nosed boy, holding the panting hound back by the collar. He was pretty sure Rig was the name the God Heimdall took once when travelling in disguise. If this Rig was in fact of Godly origin it was well hidden. The boy's mouth had opened when Yrling rode in and had yet to close.

The man finally spoke. Yrling had been uncomfortably aware how he had been eyeing his horse, and his weaponry. The knife at Yrling's side was no ordinary weapon; it had been that Hrald had worn when he arrived on Gotland. The tooled leathern scabbard alone was eye-catching, the hilt with its beaten copper and silver wire ornamentation something to covet. Dusty as he was, with such a mount, and wearing such steel, Yrling spoke of wealth. Alone as he was, it made him a target. On Gotland he would have been welcomed at any strange farm, and made to sit with the family and partake of their meal before heading on. Here he had been warned never to get off his horse when he sought food.

"One of Sigferth's men, eh?" the man asked. The horse was unusually fine for such a young rider.

This was gratifying to hear, and made Yrling sit up a bit straighter in the saddle. The way his questioner tilted his chin northward made him wonder if this was not the name of the Dane who ruled Jorvik.

"His kin," Yrling answered. That should put an end to any thought of mischief in the man's head.

The woman had left and was gathering new eggs in her apron that she might set them to boil in her kitchen yard. That started, she took Yrling's empty food bag and vanished with it, first into a storehouse, then opened a small structure which must be their smoke-house. The boy and man remained, staring up at Yrling, and several of the small children were also standing, gape-mouthed, looking at him. He was glad when the woman appeared, his bag lumpy with food. She gestured him nearer a work table and he nudged his horse to it. She pulled everything from the bag, naming it as she did so, in a kind of righteous triumph.

"And salt," she added, holding up a tiny, stoppered tube of hollowed-out birch. He had not asked for this, and knew how vital it was in giving flavour to the whole.

After he had seen it all, she repacked it. Yrling took the bag and twisted round in the saddle to tie it in the ring on his off side.

Now he must pay. He had no idea what the food was worth, and looked uncertainly to the woman.

"Coins or hack?" she asked. Every word from her seemed its own wary demand.

"Coins. I have coins." Indeed, those which his mother had given him were all silver coins of Ælfred of Wessex, collected by Rannveig at the brew-house and given to her. Their purity was well known, he had since learnt.

Yrling reached for his belt and the pouch there. He pulled out two coins; they were small, but might be enough.

He held them out to her. She picked up one and held it before her eye. "Is this of Guthrum?" she wanted to know.

Yrling shook his head. "They are made by Ælfred, King of Wessex."

"Not of Guthrum," she muttered.

"They are pure, nip one if you like," he answered.

She shook her head. "Silver is silver. Here at least. In Jorvik, beware."

With the newly bought abundance Yrling feasted that night. He boiled up some barley with the skirrets, and thickened this with half a loaf of oat bread. He pared slices of the smoked pig, and cut a hunk from the salty cheese as well, both of which gave savour to the bland simplicity of the browis. After a long day in the saddle he was hungry and eager to partake of the contents of his small soapstone pot. When he had camped with his father on Gotland, or the family made the trip to the Althing and passed a few nights there, he had helped at the cook-fire. But he must keep himself from thinking overlong of those gladsome outings on that distant island, or the time he had ridden out overnight in great anticipation with Kjeld and a few other men to check on the western boundary of Four Stones. Camping alone was far different than with family or companions, and to break the silence he found himself speaking aloud to his horse as he kindled his fire and tended it.

A ferry awaited at the banks of the Humber, a flat barge on which folk, goods, and animals could be carried over the vastness of the broad river, to continue their journey on the northly road. It was a vessel Yrling had resolved not to board. It would take him well out of his way to ride west to where his horse could safely ford the smaller tributaries, but he would not risk being seen and remembered by the ferrymen in charge of the craft. The way the men of Four Stones had spoken of it, the crossing was a small adventure in itself, and it pained him to forego it. But when he neared the banks of the great estuary he began skirting the edge, over high ground and through marsh, until the swift current narrowed enough to offer passage for his horse. He had never forded any stream deeper than the hock of a horse, and before he started across he got off his animal and retied his saddle bags to fix them as high as he could. As he did so, Yrling remembered his mother telling him that she had once need to ford a broad river; he did not recall which, nor even if she had named it. She feared the girth loosening or breaking under the stress of the crossing, and she could not swim. Yrling could swim; his father had made certain of that, but the thought of mishap with girth or packs made him tighten the first and doubly secure the second.

The river here was many horse-lengths wide, and Yrling was glad it was late Summer and the current not at its full. Still, he held his breath a moment as he pressed his horse forward, hoping that the beast could make it across at a walk. The gelding pricked his ears forward and stepped out, but then with a little plunge lost the footing beneath its hooves, and was in up to its broad breast. Yrling's low boots filled with water, and he nearly lost one of them when his left foot slipped from his stirrup. But his horse, big as he was, swam strongly forward, and soon enough was in contact with the mud leading to the northern bank. Ears back, the chestnut scrambled up upon the bank. Once on the grass of the other side, Yrling jumped off, both to empty his wet boots and to lavish praise on his gelding. This diversion took a full day, for then he must ride east to pick up the Caesar's road again, but when he made his camp that night he was across, and no one had noted his passage.

The next morning Yrling passed a marker the men of Four Stones had told him of, for the broadness of the road of pounded dirt crossing it spoke of much traffic. That road led due east, to the sea, and a small landing place with a wooden pier for the loading and unloading of goods such as horses, sheep, and cattle bound for points up or down the coast, or even to Dane-mark, where good examples of all were prized. He knew now he was only two days from Jorvik.

At midday he turned off into a grassy clearing to eat something and rest his horse; a serpentine stream lacing through it made it ideal, and both he and his horse were athirst. Whenever Yrling paused on the road, he always did so out of sight, moving into the trees or into any clearing at hand which offered a copse to screen him from view. Today after eating a couple of pears and boiled eggs he allowed himself to linger. He had already refilled his water flask, but his horse would welcome the chance to fully drink. He let himself lie back, knees up, and close his eyes against the strong Sun over his head. The low hum of bees hovering above the clover blossoms around him filled his ears, that and the gentle plashing of the water hitting larger rocks in the stream. On the other side of the meandering rill, osiers grew, their slender branches sighing against each other in the breeze.

A deep breath escaped Yrling's lips. No longer had he any fear of being found. He had planned it well, he thought, starting out south, any trail lost in the stream bed and then marshland, only to double back and head north to his true destination. He retraced those first few hours in his memory, vaguely aware they no longer mattered, and his plans for what came next did.

Quiet as it was, it made him aware of a distant jingling, like that of harness rings and bridle bits, and the steady clank of iron-rimmed wheels against the stones of the road. A waggon, surely, and perhaps one flanked by riders. He jumped up. The road was almost arrow straight at this point, a common feature of many of those built by the Caesars, and he would surely be seen if he attempted to ride away now. Yrling did not relish discovery, even though he had just decided he had little to fear. Nothing had been unpacked, he had only pulled the eggs and pears from his food bag. He made quick decision, and reached for the rein of his browsing animal, and pulled him into the trees. He did not want the gelding to call out a whinnied greeting, as it had to the monk's donkey. Yrling secreted himself by his horse's side, choosing the furthest side of the clearing, to give himself the longest view of the approaching waggon. He hoped it was a crofter and his son, driving goods home from Jorvik; nothing more.

Before it came into sight the growing clatter told Yrling that it was more than a waggon and a single horseman. He looked behind him. The trees were far too thick to lead his horse through quietly. He must hope the waggon would pass on, and when it was out of hearing, he could then be on his way.

Though he kept his hand fast on the rein, Yrling turned his horse's head away from the road, in the faint hope that the nearing waggon would warrant no interest from the beast. The clank of the iron rims grew louder, until Yrling could hear men's voices as well. Through the foliage he now saw two horsemen, holding spears upright in their fists, leading a waggon.

Yrling's own spear was tied in two places alongside his saddle. He fought the desire to pull it.

Next came an open-sided wooden waggon, one with a double railing around it. Pulling it were two heavy draught horses in full harness. In the waggon bed stood ten or twelve men and women, their hands bound before them, and tied to the upper railing. They ringed three sides of the waggon, the back gate only being left clear. A few knelt, perhaps unable to stand longer, though it meant their bound wrists were kept awkwardly high. All the folk were young, Yrling saw. Behind this freighted waggon rode two more men.

Slavers, Yrling told himself. These are slavers. His breath had caught in his throat as if it were trapped, and he was of a sudden aware of the hammering of his heart, sounding like a beaten drum inside his chest.

The men guarding the enslaved were Danes; their weapons told Yrling that, and the captives were of Angle-land. At least the women dressed as did his own, and Hrald's mother, in long-sleeved gowns without shoulder brooches. The smudged faces and unkempt hair of both men and women suggested they had been on the road a few days. Yrling thought back. The landing pier he was told of, the turning for which was marked by the cairn – were these folk of Angle-land themselves headed for transport from that place? But he himself was also a Dane; if he were found, would they leave him alone, let him pass? He did not wish to find out.

One of the horsemen in the lead turned his head to look into the clearing. The stream was in clear view. He called out, raising his hand to halt the progress of the waggon.

Yrling fought against a rising tide of fear as the waggon rolled up and then into the clearing. They too needed water, and here was a ready source. Yrling watched, cursing under his breath, as the horsemen dismounted. The driver stepped down from the waggon board and joined the men as they dropped to their knees at the stream bank and dipped up water in handled wooden cups. Their freed horses, slack-reined, lowered their necks and joined them. Yrling had lately drunk of it, and knew it was cool and sweet. His horse moved behind him, and he placed a hand on the beast's muzzle, willing it to silence.

When the five men had drunk their fill, and dipped in their leathern flasks as well, they turned to the waggon, in which their human freight waited. It was hard for Yrling to scan those faces, and see the wretchedness there, made the sharper by the obvious thirst evinced as a few tried to swallow with tight throats. How long had it been since they had been allowed food or drink, he wondered. They would have some now, as two of the Danes approached the waggon gate at the rear, unhooked it, and climbed aboard. The other three had taken up their spears and now held them at the ready against any escape. As the folk were freed, one by one, some rubbed their chafed wrists, while others scrambled down as quickly as they could to the stream bank, there to fling themselves face down to the water. Two of the captives may have been man and wife, and a second woman her kin, for the man helped both of them down, and laid a protective arm around one. A growled order from one of the guards made him drop his half embrace. They made their way to the bank with the rest. As they knelt or lay at its edge, with only their mouths or cupped hands to slake their thirst, two of the slavers let their spear shafts slide through their fists and the butt end rest upon the grass. The horses were still drinking, and those in harness now also led forward to join them.

Many moments passed, in which Yrling could not imagine what thoughts ran through the captives' minds as they drank their fill in a rare respite from bondage.

One of the guards began to get restive, and moved towards the bank as if to hurry the folk back up to their feet.

It was enough to trigger the actions of a young man who lay closest to the pair of draught horses, the great animals still standing with necks lowered to the water. The man leapt up, and screened by the team of horses, made a run for it, dashing through the trees on the opposite side of the clearing from where Yrling and his horse stood in hiding.

The act spurred all the captives, men and women. Men yelled and women screamed, in encouragement or fear. One followed in the wake of the first to break for the trees; two others fled across the road, others in ones and twos made for different points, the depths of the greenwood their goal. The draught horses snorted and backed from the water, turning the waggon to partially block the view of that portion of the stream where most of the captives had been drinking, and where a few still stood, uncertain. All the guards were on foot, and for the thickness of the undergrowth beyond the osiers, could not have followed their charges into the trees otherwise. They bellowed out orders to halt, and one flung his spear, which found home in the back of one of the men who crossed the road, aiming for the trees there. One of the captives made almost straight for where a wide-eyed boy stood concealed with his horse. Yrling would be discovered. His thumping heart stilled enough to hear an inner voice command him Go, an order as urgent as the voice issuing it was soft.

As the fleeing captive neared him, Yrling stepped forward enough from the overhanding boughs that he might mount. Despite the threat of a thrown spear, he must make his own break for it. The Danes were now all chasing after their escaping human cargo. They had killed one, but it had proven little deterrent. They could not afford further loss if they could help it.

Yrling scrambled up upon his horse, a fistful of the animal's mane in his right hand for leverage. The driverless waggon was now blocking part of his access to the road, and the other four of the Danes' horses, also loose, wheeled about, shying from the yells of their owners and the folk dodging and running amongst them. The captive nearing him gave a wild look at Yrling, then crashed onward into the shrubby growth. The man had no way of knowing if Yrling was another Dane attempting to deprive him of his freedom, or his life.

Now clear of the tree line, Yrling kicked his gelding. The animal gave a snorting whinny and with a half rear, took off. With a yank of the rein Yrling drove the animal around the waggon and into the road towards Jorvik. One of the slavers near the team turned and saw the unexpected pair. Here was an obvious prize, a healthy lad on a strong horse. Both held true value. The Dane grabbed the reins of the nearest horse and swung himself up, and after. Yrling could hear the man's pursuit, and hear too the yells and shouted oaths from the Danes in the clearing, calling out that they needed him there. A boy on a fast horse is hard to catch, and the slaves they already had were at risk of escaping.

Yrling was pursued only a short distance, yet lashed his horse with his rein ends until he dare look back to an empty road. His heart was pounding; more so, Yrling thought, than that great organ which beat inside his animal's broad breast. They slowed, both heaving for breath. Some voice within Yrling had told him Go, and he had. If this was his fylgja, it was the first time she had ever spoken, or the first he had paid attention. A face rose to his mind, that of his father, followed by that of his brother Hrald. How much he wanted either by his side.

Yrling slackened his horse even further, giving the strong neck a series of pats. A jolt of energy had shot from the pit of his belly as he had shown himself and fled, and he nearly trembled from the force of it, still coursing through his body. He took a gulping intake of air, trying to free himself from the fright. The next breaths he drew were quiet and deep. He shook his head in quick dismissal at the image of his father, and of Hrald. They were not here, and as it turned out he did not need them. He made a run for it and won out. The voice he had heard – if it was in fact his guiding-spirit, his fylgja – well, he had listened. His father often talked about how certain Gods could watch men, and this felt almost like that, to Yrling. He was worthy of attention, no matter that it was a spirit shared by his kin; she had been there, watching.

When he made camp that night Yrling fell into the deepest sleep to have visited him upon the road. It was when he took a draught of water from his flask at dawn that he thought of the captives. For one, that water from the stream was the last thing he tasted. But at least some of them must have escaped.

Moving on under a grey morning sky he began to see folk ahead. The Caesar's road of stone was met at an angle by a broad road of pounded earth, from which folk joined it. Some, staff in hand, drove cattle with the help of a dog. Others were pushing vegetables in hand wains, or walking by the head of ox drawn carts loaded with hard and sooty charcoal, woven cages of living spotted fowl, grunting red-bristled swine, bags of newly threshed grains, or the lead-lined wooden casks that told Yrling they were filled with salt. All headed, like him, to Jorvik. He fell in with them, a sole horseman amongst so many walking or driving small waggons. Others of their kind passed them, heading from the great trading town to their crofts or other, smaller trading towns.

As they neared Jorvik the road branched off, leading to the different gates giving access within. Yrling did not know which to choose; only that once inside he sought the riverside on which ships docked. The timber palisade surrounding the town was not high, and the extent of roof peaks beyond told of a myriad of structures. The southern gate was before him, and he chose that. The gates themselves were broad, the doors swung wide at this hour of the day. Tolls-men stood waiting, ready to assess a tax on any entering to sell. There were two of them, and two more serving as guards, with a strong box of iron on a tree stump between them.

All fell in line, waiting their turn at admission. Restless and thirsting horses, lowing cows, bleating sheep and all who led them filed through. Yrling swung down from his horse, as he saw others who had mounts do. Before him was a small waggon crammed with fowl, from which several cocks, unmindful that it was midday, crowed lustily from their wicker cages.

His turn came. The tolls-man to his right gestured him forward. The man was as heavily armed as any good warrior, sword and knife at hip, and at his feet behind him resting against the timber wall, shield and spear.

"What are you trading?" the tolls-man asked.

"Nothing. Only my service. Aboard a ship."

The tolls-man cast his eyes over the kit tied to the saddle rings. It looked meagre enough. "If you sell the horse, you will be taxed then," the tolls-man announced. With a slight jerk of his chin, the man dismissed him to pass through.

Once inside Yrling's eyes swam with the sheer size of the place. Countless timber buildings, crowned with steep gable roofs of thatch, rose before him. Lane after lane extended out in a grid from the toll-gate, each passage seemingly thronged with folk and beasts. It was not pounded earth they trod; each street was planked with wood, an aid to damping down mud and dust. In nearly every lane he spotted guards, patrolling in pairs, shields on their backs, spears in their hands. These moved slowly, looking on, clearly in no need of buying or selling.

From a woman standing at one corner, basket over her wrist and holding up a small loaf, Yrling learnt that the quickest way to the riverfront was skirting the palisade until it opened up. He was glad to mount his horse and move it and himself out of the crowded thoroughfare. As he made his way he looked down on streets of leather-workers and comb-carvers, weavers and sellers of cloth. Bead-makers in glass and others who needed fire were clustered together, as were the forges of the smiths, closest to the river and the water needed should fire escape their hearths.

Near the smiths he saw another woman upon a corner, one standing quite alone. Unlike the loaf seller on the crowded corner, she held nothing in her hands. This woman was brightly clad in blue and red, with waves of yellow hair escaping from her head wrap. She smiled at the young man approaching her, upon his good horse.

Yrling nearly craned his head behind him in his confusion. But the woman's eyes were fastened on him; she meant no other. He returned her smile, with all the uncertainty he felt.

As he neared her lips parted, and from them emerged her pink tongue, protruding slowly and meaningfully at him.

Yrling stared at her. He felt abashed, and felt also colour flame his cheek. He ducked his head, but not before he saw her laugh softly, aware now of how young he was. The sound of her laughter released them both from her spell, and he moved on.

He was glad to reach the riverside. This was the broad River Ouse, upon which the men of Caesar had built their settlement long ago. He got off his horse and led the animal along the planked boardwalk on the water's bank. Other than the open landscape on the opposite shore, the river margin was as teeming as were many of the other precincts, but all who had shop here were shipwrights, stitchers of sailcloth, winders of line, knotters of netting, and such like trades. From the banks projected stout wooden piers, at which were tied fishing boats, trading knorrs, and several lean dragon-ships. Yrling had to slow to take in the sight of these drekars, some twice the length of Dauðadagr back at home.

Nearly all of the ships had men aboard them, either active in lading or hauling off the goods they carried. Other craft lay quiet with just a man or two left as watch. Yrling approached a drekar with one such seaman standing near the curved prow.

"I am looking for the ship-master Aszur," he told him, after a respectful bob of his head in greeting. "He owns three drekars."

The man gave a returning nod. "The dwarf. He sailed, yestermorn. He was tied up here; I saw him set sail."

Yrling rocked back on his heels, nearly bumping his horse's nose. He could not explain why, but he had fully expected Aszur would be here.

"Do you know where he headed?" It was a foolish question, Yrling knew it. He could not swim after him, even if the man knew where he was headed.

He questioned shook his head.

All Yrling could do was nod in silent acceptance, and move on. He was hungry and thirsty and his horse was too. He needed a place where his gelding could browse, and the riverbank was nearly all wooden planking and refuse piles. He must care for his animal, then find a strange captain to offer his services to. Who knew when Aszur would be back at Jorvik again.

The lad walked along, glancing up at the ships tied and waiting. He passed half a score or more of such vessels, trying to assess which was a likely one to take him on. One was a sturdy knorr, fairly heavily laden, on which two men worked. It was tied stern closest to the planking Yrling and his horse trod. In that stern stood a short but broad figure, his back to Yrling. At midship by the upright mast was a wiry man, his hair fixed in a long silvery plait. He was facing Yrling, and the boy gave a start at seeing him. It was Thorvi, Aszur's cousin whom they had picked up in Aros.

Thorvi knew the night sky more fully than the lines of his palm, and Yrling remembered him, and the man's skill. The lad raised his hand in greeting, taking a few steps onto the pier, and Thorvi grinned back.

JORVIK

A SZUR the Dwarf turned in the stern of his tethered ship. Someone had called his name, a high-pitched, almost wavering call, one of a youth whose voice had lately broken. He looked up from where he had been coiling hempen line, and out to the wooden pier holding fast his knorr. There stood a boy he recalled.

"Aszur," Yrling called again. The boy tried to grin, but the shipmaster could read the uncertainty on the lad's face.

"Yrling, brother of Hrald," the boy called, placing his hand on his chest to remind the dwarf of the connection. Though Yrling had grown, Aszur knew the boy at once; one did not forget so keen a youth. The boy spoke again. "I thought you had sailed." There was no hiding the relief on the lad's face.

"So we did, but a fraying line on our rigging stopped us. It has been replaced."

Aszur took in the lad's travel-grimed clothes. The horse behind him was nearly as dusty. Of escort there was none. Yrling was alone all right, and glad to see a friendly face from his past. The lad's next words were a question, one posed with furrowed brow.

"Where is your drekar?"

"Two I have sold; the best I have moored not far. But it is my knorr I need, for the trip I now take." His upper lip curled up just enough that the gold-wrapped tooth glinted in the sunlight.

Having said this much, it was the turn of the diminutive ship-master to make inquiry. He did not fail to note how the boy's face had fallen at this news.

"Why are you here," demanded Aszur. The voice was deep, almost booming, and issuing from so short a form might surprise the hearer.

Aszur well remembered this boy's brother, a rich young Jarl, one baptised a Christian and heeding that faith of mercy and forgiveness. He remembered too the care Hrald had taken of the boy. Something was amiss, to find the youth here and alone. The dwarf's next words suggested what it might be.

"I cannot be guilty of harbouring a fugitive. Or a felon."

Yrling straightened up. He answered with no little defiance in his tone. "I am neither. I left of my own free will, and did no wrong." Here Yrling looked also to Thorvi, as if for support. Thorvi gave a noncommittal nod.

"Your brother is Jarl," Aszur went on. "Did he know of your leaving?"

"Nej."

"Did any at his hall?"

Again, Yrling must give his head a quick shake.

"Nej."

"Then you have stolen away." Aszur looked meaningfully at the horse.

Yrling was quick to defend himself. "The animal is mine. Given me by Hrald." He could not keep a trace of petulance from his tone.

"You said if I seek passage again, to seek Aszur," the boy protested.

"I told that to your brother. Not you."

The lad seemed to have answer for everything.

"But I do not seek passage – only to work for you, to serve on your ship."

The ship-master had no time to render his opinion of this.

"I want to sail with you," Yrling spouted, and took a step nearer. "I will work hard. And you will teach me all I must know to handle a ship." He looked now to Thorvi, whose silver hair made his face look younger than his years. "And teach me to be a star-reader, like you, Thorvi, so I can sail through the night."

This forced a grin from Thorvi, one which he tried to suppress.

"I know a lot already," Yrling went on, looking again to Aszur. "You saw that back in Gotland, when we sailed around the whole island. On Death-Day. She is my ship," he reminded.

It was true that the shipmaster and the boy had made that sail.

Yrling lifted his hand to Aszur's ship. He said the next with all the conviction that he felt, remembering that a few words of praise might go a long way in convincing a man to do that which you wished. "I want to be able to sail Death-Day as well as you helm your own ship."

Perhaps the man considered, for it took him a moment to answer.

"And the horse?"

This caught the boy up short. Though he considered the animal to be a gift, and thus his, Yrling did not feel right about selling it. He sputtered out his response.

"Can you keep him for me, while we are gone . . . ?"

Aszur cocked his large head. Another moment passed, as he looked from horse to boy. "I have carried such beasts before," he allowed. He almost smiled now; at least Yrling caught a glimpse of gold. "And he may be useful to you."

"Then it is settled," Yrling answered. He had often heard his father use these words to close any agreement, and felt no little triumph in his dealing.

Aszur still held the line he had been coiling, and now glanced down at it as he continued his winding.

"We cast off on the morning tide. A crew of eight, not counting Thorvi and me. Nine now, with you. We sail south, for Hunefleth in Frankland, at the mouth of the Seine."

"Frankland! I want to see that place – I want to see much more."

The dwarf nodded.

"Right now you will see about fodder for your horse. He cannot eat seaweed. We will coast as we can, but some beaches are nothing but sand. And – there is the matter of your fee. I do not carry unseasoned hands without silver. You will learn at my expense, and eat as well, unless your food bag is enchanted by Frigg and she ever refills it when it empties."

Yrling listened, slack-jawed. He had not thought that he would have to pay to serve aboard Aszur's ship. And his horse would need a roll of hay, perhaps two; there was no doubt of that. He dug in his purse, almost fearful to ask what the dwarf demanded, lest he not have enough.

But Aszur waved him off. "My fee I will tell you when we land, and have judged of what use you were." The man looked at the gelding, now nosing Yrling in the back. "But your beast cannot wait. Go down to the eastern gate; there you will find many horses for sale, and the hay to feed them." He pointed down the narrow walkway, hemmed in with stalls supplying goods for ships. "Do not pay more than one-eighth eyrir, one eighth of an ounce of silver, a roll. Buy two, and do not let them cheat you; have them roll it before your eyes so you see it is free from mould. One-eighth eyrir per roll. Walk away if they insist on more. You will not get far. They will call you back, soon enough."

Yrling recalled what the woman on the road had told him. "Will they rob you blind here?"

Aszur tossed back his head and gave a laugh. "Nej. But with fodder, you need to be mindful not to make your beast sick."

Yrling gave a nod. "A woman I bought food from on the way here said they would switch the scale weights when you were not looking."

The dwarf gave a snort. "Likely the kind who would do that herself," he countered. "Best not be trying that, with the agents of Sigferth all about."

"Sigferth?"

"He is King of Jorvik, since last year. At least he calls himself King. He wants this port to rival the best trading towns known. Any cheat will be treated sharply."

"Sigferth," Yrling said again. "The woman's husband looked at me, and my horse, and mentioned him – asked if I was one of his men, even. I told him I was kin to Sigferth."

Aszur let out a low laugh, while shaking his head in wonder. "You are quick, my boy. Thinking like that will stand you in good stead."

The ship-master looked about him. He gave a nod to Thorvi and then spoke to Yrling.

"Come. I will go with you to buy hay."

Aszur heaved a gangplank over the gunwale, and using a sea chest to reach the side, stepped over and came smartly down the incline to the planking of the pier where Yrling and his horse stood. The dwarf's legs were badly bowed, and he swayed from side to side like a water-logged boat as he walked, but there was no mistaking the confidence, even hint of swagger as he did so. Despite his lack of stature, Aszur was one who most folk would watch with interest, and no disdain. The great head, crowned with waving dark brown hair which rested on his shoulders, was made the more striking by eyes nearly the colour of amber. The gold-wrapped upper front tooth was more than eye-catching; it proclaimed wealth, and a man who was not afraid to flaunt it, as well as one who cared for his appearance. The legs, short and deeply bandied, seemed near to fully clad in the knee-high boots of deep brown leather he wore. His tunic of fine weave reached nearly to those knees, and was twice-belted. The first was a broad tooled strap from which hung three leathern pouches, for purse, steel striker and flint, and those other items necessary to the man. The breadth of this belt, and the care with which its brown leather had been stamped and embellished made it a signal part of his appearance. The second, narrower belt, wrapped over the first, held a knife encased in a darkly tanned scabbard, and long enough to serve nearly as a sword. In all, Aszur was of estimable appearance. His upper body, with its powerful, almost barrel chest and thick arms, seemed destined for a man of considerable size. Yet Yrling noticed as the man gained the pier that he was now far taller than Aszur, by at least the span of a palm, he guessed. Aszur noticed it too.

"You are thinking that this year you are taller than me," he suggested, as they walked side by side towards the roadway.

Yrling was indeed noticing just that, and gave a little start. The dwarf was looking straight ahead.

"Many over the age of twelve Summers are taller than me," Aszur observed. "I am used to it. But few – few are more canny than me, and fewer, better sailors."

Yrling felt moved to add an observation of his own. "And you are strong, too," he offered. "I remember how you often handled the dropped sail, heavy as it was, and how you swung yourself from ship to ship when we anchored along the way."

The ship-master gave a nod at this, one Yrling noted from the tail of his eye. They looked an odd pairing as they walked along the crowded byways. Yrling was but a lad, yet with his shield on his back and spear in his hand looked every bit a warrior in training. As if I were kin of the King here, he told himself. And why should he not be seen as such – his real kin, his own brother, was Jarl of Four Stones in Lindisse. At his side Aszur looked one who had seen and done much, and made the most of what Fate had handed him. And no one would forget that dwarfs knew gems, and metals, and the magic thereof. The gold-wrapped tooth Aszur sported seemed proof of that. The Sagas were filled with such tales.

As they walked they passed a dark-haired woman, alone as was the yellow-haired one who had smiled at Yrling. Like the yellow-haired one, this one had no basket of eggs or bread over her wrist, and held nothing in her hand to show to hungry passers-by. She smiled at Aszur, and then looked as well to Yrling. Aszur gave the woman a nod, and smiled back before they passed on.

"That woman – do you know her?" Yrling wanted to know. "On my way past the forges another woman smiled at me. One with wavy hair of yellow."

Aszur turned his head to look at the lad. "Only a smile?"

"Then she . . . she stuck out her tongue at me. But slowly."

The dwarf gave a low laugh, and then took a deep breath, a sound which to Yrling was akin to a great bellows filling.

"Tofa. She is a good girl. A little eager at times. You were wise to move on."

As they neared the eastern gate, the stalls and workshops gave way to larger plots, including those of folk who lived here in Jorvik. These kept their own cow or two, and a few even had horses. Then came the paddocks of the horse traders, and on the other side of the toll gate, those paddocks at which horses and oxen could be kept under watch while their owners traded. Just before they reached these, the two saw a single stall where some trader had set out his wares. It was in fact less than a stall, merely the back of an old ox cart used to display his goods. A few casks also held items clustered upon them, oil cressets and leathern bags of different sorts, as well as a few things of cast bronze. It was a hotch-potch of goods, but then, many traders arrived with such. The man who offered these things was still in the act of setting them out, and as he was well away from the main trading lanes, looked up with hopeful air at the party who approached.

The trader's eye skipped first to the horse; it was a worthy beast, a chestnut with a single white stocking, and blazed nose. He looked then at the figure leading the animal, not much more than a boy, but one dressed in the way of a warrior, shield on back, and throwing spear in his free hand. By his side swayed a bandy-legged dwarf; not the smallest the trader had ever seen, but still shorter than the growing boy. Despite his stunted size the dwarf had an air of self-assurance about him, and when he opened his mouth to speak to the boy, a flash of gold glinted beneath his upper lip.

The trader straightened up when they neared his wares. Aszur sized up most of the goods in little more than a glance; the leathern bags creased and worn, the bronze work, pins and buckles, not much above hack.

A bolt of striped cloth lay atop a cask. The fabric was richly figured twill, in deep shades of green, and worked up would make a handsome tunic. The trader saw Aszur's eyes go to it.

"Quality work," the man promised. Though he was surely no man of Angle-land from how he dressed, his accent told both Aszur and Yrling that he was no Dane.

"Svear?" guessed the ship-master. He was asking of the cloth, but the man answered for himself.

"From no one place. I trade along the coasts of Frisia, mostly."

Aszur took up the cloth and unfolded the top length of it. It had a puncture by one corner, not fatal to its use. But as he held it up even the short distance his arms allowed, he saw three more. Surely it had been hit by arrows as it had sat bundled upon some ship's deck.

Still holding the green cloth up, Aszur canted his head to the trader.

"A few small slices," the man assured him. "Nothing a good seamstress will not make short work of."

Aszur let the fabric drop. The trader reached over and at once refolded it to hide the punctures.

"What is in the jugs?" Aszur wanted to know, looking over at what rested on the cart bed. These were three small but squat jugs of glazed crockery, with wooden stoppers, heavily waxed. The seal had been broken on all of them, so someone had checked the contents. They sat amongst slumping sacks of some other unknown goods, grain perhaps.

The trader gave a slight shrug. "Some kind of red. Paint or madder-dye. Smells bad."

The dwarf made gesture that he wished to see within. The trader pulled a short knife from his belt and used it to pry open the wooden stopper. Aszur reached with both hands to tip the crock nearer him.

A dark red mass lay within, so dark it looked nearly like dried blood. But it was wet; Aszur let a fingertip touch the stuff, and withdrew it to the light. Some substance scarlet-red sat there. He drew the finger to his nose, took a sniff. It was indeed not a pleasant fragrance. But it was neither the mineral smell of copper-based paint, nor the vegetal aroma of madder. He let the crock tip back, and set the wooden stopper into its wide mouth.

"I am in need of madder, to dye my sails. This is going rancid, but will still serve. Let me see the other two crocks."

The man dutifully opened the others for Aszur to inspect. After he had finished, Aszur spent a long while in thought, as if he deliberated on such risky material as was this madder.

Few others had passed down the lane during this, but now two of the King's guards went strolling by, hands on their sword pommels, moving slowly, looking from right to left. It seemed to prompt speech from the trader.

"If you buy two crocks, the third is yours."

Aszur cocked his mighty head. "Three pots of near-rancid madder for the price of two. I will see if the dye cauldrons can be heated soon enough, while it will still throw its colour on my sails."

"It will serve, it will serve," the man muttered.

"I will be back tomorrow if it does not," came Aszur's answer. He laid out a few pieces of hack silver on the man's scale, and with Yrling's help stacked the crocks in the boy's now-depleted food bag.

They turned away, moving towards the horse paddocks and their supply of hay.

Aszur kept his eyes straight ahead as they did so, but now had something to share with Yrling. The voice, pitched low, thrilled with discovery, one he seemed eager to share.

"You spoke of being robbed blind here. Stolen goods in the hands of fools never repay. That rascal let a small fortune drop from his grasp. And to me."

"The madder for your sails?"

"It is not madder. It is kermes, from the oak forests behind such cities as Pisa."

Yrling had never heard of either kermes or Pisa.

"Pisa lies north of Rome. Kermes is a costly dye, made from a beetle. No red is more precious nor more rare. Such finds its way to places like Samarkand."

"Samarkand." The name alone carried with it the sound of high adventure. "Where is that?"

"Sail east to Gotland. Keep sailing, across the Baltic and then down rivers to inland seas. Then cross mountains and deserts. There lies the golden city of Samarkand."

"You have been?"

"Never."

"Then we should go," Yrling answered. The excitement in his words made the dwarf look over to him. The boy was not too tall for Aszur to reach up and ruffle his brown hair, and he did so now.

⌘⌘⌘⌘⌘⌘⌘⌘⌘⌘

The hay now secured to the saddle rings of Yrling's horse, the party turned back to the riverfront. They progressed past stalls from which goods of wrought sheet copper stood, then those from which objects shaped of treen were displayed. Wooden spoons, ladles and scoops stood upright in wooden pails, almost beckoning to be taken up and handled. Many of these men and women were cup-makers, turning out wooden cups of all sizes, some with handles, some without. The ground about their workshops was thick with wood shavings. From their overhead awnings the handled cups, dangling on string, thumped merrily against each other in the breeze.

Yrling saw the yellow-haired woman who earlier had been standing alone by the forges of the smiths, she who had stuck out her tongue at him. The woman was again on a corner, a different one. She noticed them both. The woman gave a slight smile to Yrling, but then focused her gaze on Aszur. She gave Aszur a wink.

The dwarf lifted his hand and smiled in return. The two moved on.

"She likes you," Yrling offered, and turned his head back over his shoulder at the woman. She waved in return.

Aszur laughed. "Tofa likes most men. It is her job."

Yrling was ready with his next question.

"Is she a lewd woman?"

He knew about such, from the young men of Four Stones. He had never met a lewd woman, nor even knowingly seen one amongst the women of the village or hall, and was quite interested to learn more.

Aszur laughed his merriest now. "She is. Lewd – and shrewd, both. But one who gives honest value in exchange for the silver you bring her."

The boy was not sure what to say to this, or even what question to ask. He was grown aware of women, and of the urgings of his body. There had been girls, especially in the past few months since he arrived Four Stones, who he had found himself looking at, and even thinking of. Yrling could not help but turn back his head in hope of again viewing this object of their discourse. But Tofa was nowhere to be seen.

Aszur wished to check up on the rest of his crew, and so they stopped at several brew-houses to look for them. Three were together, throwing dice at one establishment, and the remaining five were sitting and drinking with a group of other sea-faring men at a second. Final lading would be that dusk, and now the men should expect a horse amongst the cargo. They looked at the beast, and the boy who led him. This would entail the lashing of casks and chests to make space for the animal behind the mast, and this was briefly discussed.

"My young friend Yrling will be joining us as crew," Aszur told them, which made the boy's heart swell with sudden pride.

Then Aszur and Yrling turned their faces towards the Ouse. Not far from the brew-houses they approached a small clearing, in which a wooden platform stood. No one was about, and Yrling wondered aloud what it was.

"The slave market. When there are folk to sell, they are brought here, with Sigferth's men to watch and exact their tax."

Yrling said nothing, only studied the empty staging. It was worn; many men and women must have climbed the three steps up, and stood there to be exhibited before buyers.

When it was behind them Yrling spoke. He wanted to forget what had happened, but seeing the platform made it all real again.

"I was chased by slavers on my way here to Jorvik."

Aszur looked at him. "And –?"

"I had my horse, and outran them. They were chasing all their slaves, who had run off. They had untied them so they could drink at the stream I had stopped at. I was there, hidden in the trees when they rolled in."

Aszur considered the possible outcome of the boy having been taken; the lengths his older brother would have gone to in redeeming him, if the boy could convince the slavers to even try, before he was transported to Dane-mark, and mayhap points far to the east. There was no need to scold the lad now; it was clear he had been shaken by the episode. And Aszur had something to add, from his own experience.

"I was once wary of slavers myself," the dwarf admitted. "For folk such as me, the smaller you are, the more you are worth as a play-thing to Kings and nobles." Aszur looked to Yrling, who had cocked his head in interest at this. "When I was young boys used to taunt me with this, as my Fate." Aszur paused a moment, as his eyes flicked to the heavens. "I no longer fear it.

"I am grown too old to be amusing, now. My skill lies at the steering-oar. My legs, bent as they are, are strong enough to hold me upright, but it is the force of my arms and shoulders directing the oar through the waves that the Gods have granted me. That and the skill to read the sea. I am most valuable there, and have made my way as steers-man a long time. Even when set upon, crews have defended me from capture. No man can ask more."

The lad was silent a while, in simple agreement. Knowing your companions valued you enough to defend your life and freedom was the highest honour.

"So you have given yourself to Njord?" Yrling offered.

"Já. The God of the Sea has been my patron. And he wed a woman of the tribe of giants, so he knows what it is like to be small."

Aszur had ended with a short laugh, but this gave Yrling much to think about. The question he next asked was direct.

"Is your father short?"

Aszur set his jaw, as if in thought. "From what I have heard, he was of normal height." A longer pause followed. "When I was little, and they could see I was not quite right, he left."

"Oh." Yrling did not know what more to say about this.

"How did you become a ship-master?"

"Most of my strength is in my upper body. Farming is hard with short legs. I can drive a waggon, and walk behind a plough. But I always wanted more. I liked ships. To me, they have beauty. As certain women do."

Here the dark-haired woman they had seen earlier walked by, and winked at them. Aszur winked back, before he went on.

"And at my height I am not so easily hit by a swinging spar," he jested.

"Tell me about your tooth," Yrling next prompted.

Aszur smiled so broadly that the lad saw the glimmer of gold more fully than he ever had.

"It was broken, when I was young." The dwarf looked at Yrling as if gauging his own age. "Two or three Summers less than you, I think."

"In a fight?" It was hard to keep the note of excitement out of his voice, but the lad tried.

"Já. A fight. Being the size I was, I had to scrap my way up." Aszur paused long enough for Yrling to see his face cloud at the memory of what must have been a hard boyhood.

"Another boy tried to punch me. I ducked, and his fist hit only air. I laughed. Next thing I knew, his boot was in my mouth. He kicked me, and broke my tooth off short."

"Ah."

"He fell, knocked off balance by his kick, and I jumped on him. I tried to break his leg by twisting it, but he screamed. For his mother. The others laughed so hard at him I rolled off."

"Then you got gold and made a new tooth," Yrling suggested.

Aszur laughed, and answered with a shake of his big head. "Then I looked even uglier, for many years, with a broken tooth. It was later I won gold, and had the stump wrapped in it."

Yrling studied the man. "You are not ugly," he decided.

Aszur was quiet at this. The boy went on. "My father has a scar. He got it when he was young. It goes from under his left eye down to his chin. And it is wide. He thinks he is ugly; I heard him once say so. But he is not. And you are not, either."

HARD LANDING

THORVI bent low over the sleeping Yrling. It was the first night upon the knorr, and the ship was gliding over the dark water of the River Ouse. The trees lining the banks were dusky clumps, tall but formless. The star-reader shook the boy's shoulder, and hissed out an order.

"Wake now. The sky is clear and shows every Summer star and wanderer."

Yrling groaned in protest, but began to stir. Groggy as he was, he had no idea how long he had slept. An oil lamp sat not far from where he lay, half sheltered from the breeze by an open box on end. By its light Yrling could see a tall man at the steering-oar, one of the crew who had relieved Aszur for this watch. The dwarf's solid form could just be seen in the stern, lying on his bedroll, back to the steering-oar. Yrling rolled to his knees, ready to stand.

"Nej," answered Thorvi. "Stay on your back, just shift your feet towards the mast. You will see all the heavens this way."

The star-reader was in fact lying down next Yrling, and was soon shoulder to shoulder with him. Looking straight up, the sail, gently luffing in the light wind, no longer obscured their view of the heavens. That sky was blue-black, streaked with stars, the brightest of which Yrling knew. He settled back down and blinked his eyes to fully open them. The rhythmic creak of wood upon wood rose from the deck, that sound which had lulled him to sleep. The soft soughing of wind in the sail, and the chime and clang of random metal served as chorus to Thorvi's voice as he pointed out the twinkling frameworks above their heads.

"Which is the star, always hanging in the north?" he wanted to know.

Yrling blinked again. There were almost too many stars for him to discern that one which served as pointer to the lands of the Sámi.

"Look for the patterns," Thorvi advised. "Shapes that you know."

Everything looked a sparkling jumble to Yrling's eyes. A dense river of stars, clotted together like curds of cream, bisected the dark dome above them, making it even more difficult to resolve any one star. Then the boy gave a twitch.

He pushed himself upon his elbows, and looked behind them. There was the northly star, bright and bold, at the end of the pattern called the woman's chariot. His hand lifted up in the air. "The leading star is there, where Freyja's great cats are hitched to her waggon. We head due south; it is behind us," the lad declared.

It made Thorvi give a grunt of approval. "Knowing where to begin looking is always a good start."

Yrling's eyes adjusted to the star light, allowing him to pick out more from the milky band spanning from north to south right over their heads. Thorvi asked him about that thick cluster.

"Look up where Heimdall lives, guarding the passage of Bifrost to the realm of the Gods. Three bright stars shine foremost, in a wedge like the point of an arrow."

One shining point was indeed so bright that it helped Yrling link it in an arrowhead shape to the others.

"There is another shape partly in the arrowhead," Yrling decided. "One like the body of a long-winged bird, flying overhead."

Thorvi's voice showed his satisfaction that the boy had picked this out. "It is a swan, oaring across the sky. The bright star at its head points north-east at this time of year. We could sail to Norway by it."

This one star by night could take us there, thought Yrling. The star-reading skill was one he must master.

Yrling's horse was near, drowsing on its feet, and now gave a low nicker. The animal was nought but a dark form, the burnished chestnut of its true coat muted in this owl-light. Only the single white stocking was clear.

Yrling turned back to the star-reader. "Do you know every star?"

Thorvi's low laugh did not disguise his pride in being asked this question.

"Give me a clear night and I could guide us right to Asgard," Thorvi answered. He took sight again, and pointed out a luminous body just over the horizon. "Sleep again," he ordered Yrling. "That blue wanderer calls out that dawn is nigh. Soon the Sun, and not me, will wake you again."

The boy blinked his eyes open again to a grey dawn. It would be a fair day; Thorvi had told him so. During his chores upon deck he found himself lifting his head, up over where the mast and sail curtained his view. Up there lay the stars, and the larger wanderers too. Yrling's thought came as a discovery: the stars he had studied last night in the depths of the night were still above him, hidden in the bright blue dome roofing Midgard. Those brilliant points of light he had gazed upon and puzzled over were always there. They would have shifted in the sky, but they were there, above him. As a thought it gave a strange sense of comfort. He was reminded of his father telling him that even if he could not see the Gods, they were still there.

Later Yrling told Thorvi about this. "The stars," he began," casting his eyes up into a cloudless sky of blue. "They are still there."

"They are," Thorvi agreed. The boy was more thoughtful than he looked. "And at dusk and dawn, when you see them appear, and then fade, you are sure of that. But none can see them in the day, except the Gods that walk amongst them."

So Yrling's time upon the knorr began. Food was dear at Jorvik, and Aszur sailed with the bare minimum of stores from there. When they stopped at the few hamlets dotting the banks to refresh their water, buy bread and fresh provisions, the lad was, as the newest member of the crew, ordered to carry the bulk of these goods, and did so without comment or complaint. At each stop he took his chestnut ashore so the animal might stretch its legs and crop green grass. Yrling managed the sail with the other crew, scrubbed down the deck with a bucket of sea water and a knotted mass of old hempen line balled in his fist, helped parcel out the provender so that each man received an equal share, and was allowed to handle the iron anchor with oversight from Thorvi. In the light winds of the Ouse he sat at the oar block and got a taste of rowing a far heavier ship than was Death-Day. Yrling's palms were reddened with coming blisters and his shoulders burned from effort, but he learnt the needful skill of keeping in time with his brethren as they pushed, and then pulled the long oars through the green water. He was chided for not affixing the lid to the water cask firmly enough, and praised with a single nod when Aszur glanced at how well he had coiled a spar line to keep it free from tangling and out of the way.

As interesting as the long sail down the River Ouse and the broad Humber had been, there was something fine about being in open waters again. The sea water had a distinct smell to river water; the air felt different. Fresh water ducks gave way to seabirds, both paddling near their hull, and flying purposefully overhead. The knorr skirted the shore, the green coast to starboard, and endless rippling waves of blue to port. They would do so, Yrling had been told, until they reached the broad channel, across which lay Frankland. From there Hunefleth at the mouth of the Seine would be their goal.

With the open sea to port, the knorr rode swiftly with a smart wind billowing her square sail. In late morning Thorvi gestured Yrling over to his side. The newest mate had just finished his twice-daily task of mucking out the straw-covered area occupied by his gelding, which was tethered by two halter lines to keep the beast secure. Yrling was glad to straighten up and join the star-reader, who greeted him with a question.

"What do you see that helps you steer this ship?"

Yrling looked about him, and settled on the view to starboard. He could not help but give a short laugh. "The coast. It is right here, and I can follow it."

"And what of the coast?"

The boy had to think a while before answering. "What of it?"

"How can you tell the depth of the water, or if fresh river water runs into it? What do you see when you look down into it? What do you hear? What if fog or dark hid the shore from you? On the sea at night, you will hear waves crashing on shore, even from a distance.

"Within sight of land like this, take a deep breath through your nose. Let it out, and take a sniff. Can you smell that land? When you sail to the far north you can smell the resin of pines and firs. But here – do you smell smoke from a distant farm? You can smell many things coming from the land, especially if there is mist."

This was much to answer, but Thorvi did not seem to expect a response. He posed these questions to test the boy's senses. And in fact the star-reader went on.

"You see the coast. What more do you see to help you steer?"

Yrling looked about at sea and sky, then looked up.

"Ah – there is the Sun," he supplied.

"Which every morning of your life has risen in the east," Thorvi agreed. "Thus you know east, west, north and south, from it. Tell me how more you can use it."

"It is low in Winter, but high in Summer, over my head at midday." He thought a moment. "The Sun is never so high here in Summer in Angle-land as it is on Gotland."

"Nor so low in Winter," nodded Thorvi. "Good. And you can sight with it, given any land ahead. Where did the Sun rise today, against that land? Where will it rise tomorrow?

"What else do you see?" Thorvi posed.

Yrling looked over the gunwale. "Over there, only water."

"Nej. Not only water. You see the horizon. If we were not coasting that is all you would see, that edge where water meets sky. Stars and wanderers too will arise from over that horizon as the Sun sets. And what is that," he asked of a sudden, pointing at a bird on the wing.

"A bird."

"What kind?"

"I cannot ken at this distance. One I do not know. Long legs."

"Já. It is a crane. It cannot rest in water. It flies to land to fish in shallow water."

"In the open sea, a land bird will lead you to shore. Whales will follow shoals of fish which near the coast as well. You must use all you can see to help you steer your course."

Yrling thought of something the star-reader had yet to mention.

"My father has a Sun-stone. Or did have; he gave it to Runulv, who sails for him."

Thorvi gave a nod of his head. "Such crystals will find the Sun for you, in a clouded sky," he agreed.

So the lessons from Thorvi went on, stargazing at night, and by day learning to read waves and water currents and noting the flight of birds.

Yrling had imagined that perhaps now they would take advantage of the open water and drive a bit further away from shore, the better to catch the wind. But Aszur held a steady course, merely skirting the coast, and, the boy saw, scanning the shoreline as he did. Yrling had no idea what he looked for; they had made a stop when leaving the Humber to take on fresh water and food, and more fodder for his horse, who was even now tossing the hay into the air as he ate.

It was mid-morning when something came into view. Yrling stood, as was usual when he was not at his chores, with Aszur at the steering-oar. The dwarf was telling him about the hazards of shoaling waters, a threat Yrling well knew from the limestone shelf surrounding parts of his home island. Now the steers-man fell quiet, save for a slight puff of breath, a sound of discovery. Yrling turned his head to starboard, to what Aszur had seen. A wooden pier jutted out into the water. Yrling stared at it, then scanned the trees of the shoreline behind that pier. It was, he knew of a sudden, a pier he had seen before, straight on, when he and Hrald approached Saltfleet, Aszur at the steering-oar as he was now.

Sure enough, the dwarf was readying to tack and make that pier; his ordered command to his crew confirmed it. They would land, and here at Saltfleet.

Yrling began to sputter out a protest. Eyes wide in disbelief, he turned his head to Aszur. "But – we – we are going to Hunefleth!"

"We are going to Hunefleth," Aszur agreed, eyes still steady on the pier. "But you are heading back to Four Stones."

No one need lay hands on Yrling to convince him of this. The note of decision in the ship-captain's voice was itself an iron manacle.

The boy felt as deflated as was the sail, now being dropped in preparation to land. Thorvi had moved up to the prow, and was whistling out a sharp greeting. Sure enough the single man who had been stationed as look-out at the mouth of the pier was now joined by several more, coming from the two buildings on shore.

As they neared, it was Aszur who bellowed out their request to land. Hands still upon the oar, the strength of his deep voice lent a certain gravity to his message.

"I return something strayed from your Jarl. A horse. Also a boy."

Indeed, between the downed sail and the nearness of the approaching knorr, those gathering on the pier could see this for themselves. A chorus of whistles and cheers rose from their throats.

The dwarf's next words were uttered for Yrling alone. "Their cries of welcome will be as nothing to your brother's relief at having you back. That is, once the birching you deserve is over."

Yrling could not speak; his chagrin was too great. Heat rose to his head, and he felt sure his face flamed. At last he stammered out a question.

"Did you always plan to bring me here?"

Aszur would not dissemble.

"I did. I set my own course, and take care of myself. None but a fool would make an enemy of the Jarl of South Lindisse. It would be but a matter of time before he heard that you had taken ship with me.

"Besides," the dwarf went on. "Why should I break trust with your brother? Harbouring you would be no less than that. From what I saw of him, he would not deal thusly with me."

The end of the pier grew closer, but Aszur went on. "Why did you break trust with your own brother?"

Yrling had never considered his leaving like this. He had been ready to accuse Aszur of betraying him, and now saw he himself had betrayed his own brother. And Hrald had given him his own knife, and one of the better horses at Four Stones.

His shame was such he could scarce answer. Still, he must defend his action. "I wanted . . . more. To see more. Do more. I want to sail."

"You want to sail," Aszur repeated. "So did I, at your age. But you must hold faith with your Jarl. You owe him service. Instead you have stolen his horse and caused him endless worry."

A thrill of alarm shot through Yrling's belly at this. He had meant none of this.

Thorvi had thrown a line to the men standing on the pier; the knorr was pulled close. It hit the side of the pier with a dull thud, one echoed within the lad aboard.

***

Thorvi stayed with the knorr and the rest of the crew. There was a supply waggon offered to Aszur, as his stature made it difficult to ride. He was good at driving horses, though, and could stand on a waggon board and do so. Today however he was content to sit upon it, a wooden box under his feet, while a crestfallen Yrling paced his horse alongside, with an escort, the boy thought, to make sure he did not bolt. He had already been subjected to good natured chaffing from the men at Saltfleet, and was to hear more of it from the four who escorted the waggon to Four Stones. He had no heart for any of it, so downcast was he, both at the forfeit of a new life at sea, and at his growing realisation that his act had likely caused his brother real distress.

As nearly always happened with approaching parties, one of the escort was sent ahead to tell of their near arrival. Yrling wanted to beg that this not happen, but then considered that his sudden appearance might cause even more upset. As it was he feared Hrald himself might ride out to meet them.

This did not happen. In fact, when they gained the road leading through the village, he was almost surprised to see nothing out of the ordinary. None of the cottars paid them any mind as they passed, and there was no group clustered at the open gates of the palisade to greet him.

It was when they passed through those broad gates that Yrling saw his brother. Hrald stood in the stable yard, his wife Pega next him. Her great hound Frost was next her, sitting obediently at her feet, his noble head cocked at the party's approach. The dog stood, with a thump of his tail, as he recognised Yrling. But the lightest touch of Pega's hand at the hound's head made the animal fold his haunches again, and sit. Jari stood off to Hrald's left, and Kjeld was off to the other side. Jari looked like the giant he was, and had his arms crossed over his massive chest. Kjeld's face was less stern, but Yrling did not know if he could call it a look of actual relief at his return. He had no time to do more than glance at these two as he pressed his horse closer to his brother.

Yrling could not tell from Hrald's face how angry he was; he looked, the boy realised, a bit like their father when something untoward had happened. A glimpse at the young Lady of Four Stones told Yrling that she had lately been crying. The woman who helped her, Mealla, held Pega's babe, and Mealla was scowling over the child's shoulder at Yrling as he neared.

Yrling got off his horse. He had been taught by his father to do so, as a sign of respect for those of greater power who stood before him. Just now he needed every reserve of good conduct to ease his way.

Aszur pulled up the waggon. He stood upon the waggon board and addressed the Jarl of Four Stones.

"I return to you what is yours," he said. "One horse. One boy. The horse was fed using silver belonging to the boy. The boy – the boy is a good sailor, and was of use to me."

Yrling hung his head, unable to withstand praise at a time like this. Still, he heard it.

His brother spoke, his words low and grave. "I will give you silver for them, both."

"Aszur will not accept silver from Jarl Hrald. You are one with whom I have shared a good passage, out to Gotland, and back. And the drekar you awarded me – that was recompense enough."

The dwarf glanced over at Yrling, and dropped the tone of his voice even lower.

"He should be birched."

Yrling cast a furtive glance at Hrald, and saw to his relief that a slight smile had formed upon his brother's lips, one quickly repressed. Aszur's next words were more welcome.

"But he is a good sailor."

This final pronouncement hung in the air a moment, a kind of tribute to the runaway he never expected. Then Hrald, with the slightest gesture of his hand, beckoned him forward, and Yrling found himself in his brother's strong embrace. The Lady Pega hugged him as well, tears flowing down her cheeks as she did so. Being cried over like this was worse than Yrling expected. It made him feel a small boy again.

It did not last long, for after Hrald released his brother he spoke to the ship-master who had delivered him.

"I did not expect to see you again, Aszur Gold-Tooth. Having returned something of value to me, you must sit at my table."

The dwarf flashed a broad smile at the name Hrald had bestowed on him, one which made the precious metal in his mouth glint brightly as he did. He was more commonly known as Aszur the Dwarf, but this new moniker more than suited him.

He gave a nod, and began to scramble down from the waggon. It was impossible not to watch him as he did; the waggon board was a high one, the kind most women would need ample help in ascending or descending. Yet bowed as his legs were, they were sure-footed, and in two simple moves he stood, boots on the hard-packed ground of the yard.

The Lady of Four Stones, eyes still reddened from her tears, moved to the open door of her hall, and with a slight gesture of her small hands welcomed their guest. Hrald inclined his head to his young brother, that he might go before them. It made Yrling feel glaringly exposed, and again that he was almost under watch. But he went, following Pega in, as Hrald and Aszur fell in behind him.

Two serving women were already stationed near the high table, one holding a basin of water for the rinsing of hands, the second with a towel of linen. Yrling hung back, allowing the use of both to Aszur first. It was clear from the dwarf's pleased expression that such an offer of ablution before taking ale was a novel act. He made full use of both, and when he finished with the towel returned it to she who had offered it with a wink of his eye. She was both young and comely, and found herself dropping a curtsy as she dropped her own eyes.

Yrling dipped his finger-tips into the basin and shook them in the air. His brother's wife, standing at the side of the woman holding the basin, widened her eyes at him, and he took a breath and plunged both hands in. He truly needed the towel now, and as the maid offered it he paused and looked at her. She was one always about the hall and the high table, but now having seen Aszur admiring her, Yrling took note of her himself. She only blushed in response to his gaze.

Jari was standing just next to Hrald, and as they moved to the table Yrling felt it was almost more difficult to be in his presence than that of his brother. He now understood he had worried Hrald. But something about Jari told Yrling he had disappointed the body-guard. Hrald was kin; he had to forgive him. But Jari was so important that Yrling did not know how he could overcome his fall of esteem in the Tyr-hand's eyes. And he was so big. If he was to be birched, he hoped it would be Kjeld and not Jari with the branch in his hand.

They took their places at the high table. The chair reserved for esteemed guests had been brought out for Aszur, and a footstool placed before it. Hrald and Pega sat in their carved chairs, with Aszur at Hrald's right. Jari took his usual place on the bench to the right of the Jarl, just past their guest, and Kjeld sat at the left of the Lady of Four Stones. Mealla, that Lady's companion, carried the babe out, with a piercing look at Yrling as she did. With a gesture of his hand Hrald placed Yrling not on the other side of Jari, but motioned him to the end of the table. Yrling felt himself to be as cut off from the family and head warriors of Four Stones as he had been on the road.

"There is a story to tell," Hrald began, after the first swallow of ale had been taken. He looked first to his young brother, then to Aszur. Hrald's tone, while low and calm, carried more of command than invitation about it.

Yrling knew he must speak. He opened his mouth and a squeak came forth. Cheeks flaming, he took another sip of ale. The cup he clenched in his hand was of bronze, and felt as heavy as lead.

"I wanted to go to Jorvik," he began. "The town you are always talking about," he went on, with a beseeching look at first Jari and then Kjeld. The faces of both men were so near to wearing a scowl that Yrling hurried on. The boy had rarely seen Kjeld without a smile, and Jari looked one false word away from pulling his knife.

"I wanted to find Aszur," Yrling went on, with a significant look to the ship-captain, as if he had some share in his own actions.

Hrald sat listening, saying nothing. To Yrling it was almost as if their father sat there, one long to listen and slow to act. But when act he did, it was decisive.

"I wanted to sail, to see more of Angle-land. And Frankland too," Yrling ended.

At last his brother spoke. To Yrling's ears he did so not as his older brother, but as the Jarl of Four Stones.

"You wanted," Hrald repeated. He let that hang in the air before he went on.

"Did you not think of what your disappearance would cost us? Did you think of the distress to my wife, in whose care you have been entrusted?" Hrald glanced now at the Lady Pega, whose tears of relief were scarcely dried. "Did you think of the worry to me, knowing you had set out in an unknown land, one whose ways are so different from that of your Gotland home? Did you guess that we searched for you, sending men in every direction after you? I need those men, here, and at the ready should my hall and lands need defending. You took them from that, and from their needful work about the hall and valley of horses. You disrupted all. Is that what you wanted?"

Yrling's face felt so hot that he thought it truly aflame. Dropping his head availed not; he must face his brother under these just words.

"Then there is the horse, as good a gelding as my stock can yield. I did not bestow him on you so you would steal away like a thief."

Yrling's mouth began to open, as if in protest. He had thought the horse truly his, and no theft was greater than horse-theft.

Hrald read that expression and answered it. "Yes. The horse is yours, as is that knife at your belt. But is this the way you repay gifts, and repay my trust in you, that you are worthy of such things?"

Yrling could take no more. The tears he had been fighting welled in his eyes and escaped. He did not snivel; he pressed his lips tightly together to keep from making a sound. But his shame was there upon his face for all to see.

"I did not think of any of this," he rasped out. "I am sorry for the trouble I caused. Forgive me, Hrald."

Yrling made it through this without bawling, but feeling estranged as he was from his brother, must quickly append this plea. "Forgive me, my Jarl."

He forced his eyes to meet those, dark blue and seemingly angry, with which Hrald stared back at him.

The Jarl of Four Stones let a long and low breath escape, one which gave his little brother time to compose himself. Still, his answer was stern enough.

"I accept you back into my hall," was what he said.

Yrling swallowed, hard. He nodded his head with lowered eyes.

Hrald turned his head to the woman standing there with the ale jug. A new lightness was in his next words. "Now we will have mead," he instructed, "so we might drink to my brother's return to the hall."

Yrling was made to tell the whole story of his adventure. It was with some little relief that he watched Jari unfold his meaty arms and lean forward over the table as the tale was told. There were exclamations from Kjeld on the cunning with which Yrling had planned his route; Hrald's second in command had headed the search party heading south, and as good a tracker as Kjeld was, had lost the hoof prints of Yrling's chestnut in the mere just as the boy had hoped. Lady Pega murmured a few kind words to the report of the assistance Yrling had rendered to the monk, which he hoped would go some way in restoring him to her good graces. And all listened intently to the episode of the slavers. Yrling, watching his brother's face, could tell how grave a danger he had escaped. But it was Jari who spoke.

"You could be shackled to the oar, pulling towards Jutland now," he gruffed. Jari's face, still sprinkled with freckles despite the weathering of the years, rose in thoughtful contemplation. "From there, sold on to work the salt mines in Frankland, where in a few years you would look an old man. You could be sent off to Fes, and the caliphs there. Or just left a thrall in Jutland, doing the work you watch oxen do here."

There were worse things as well, abuses which the Tyr-hand did not enumerate. Boys could be used in the same shameful way girls suffered.

These grim possibilities seemed the more real for Jari's quiet tone, and Yrling was forced to gulp away the rising lump in his throat.

After this those seated at the high table dispersed. Yrling fled the hall in relief, and went to the paddock to check on his horse. The animal had not been short of feed on their adventure, but he had not the tools to care for coat and hooves on the road as he did here. And now returned to his fellows, the boy saw how the gelding had missed certain of them, falling into standing by the same two mares whose company he seemed to favour. He chirruped to the beast as he neared, and the glossy head rose in welcome. Yrling thought he might get a comb from the stable, the long fair mane could use smartening up.

He turned to do so, and saw the stable-boy Bork almost behind him. Yrling had not noticed him at this arrival, though like Mul and his sons, Bork was generally ready whenever riders entered through the palisade. He quickly reminded himself that there was no reason he should take notice of such a one.

Bork spoke, without any other greeting. "We went to look for you."

"We?"

"Já. Many of us. I went with the Jarl, and ten men, and me."

Hearing that Bork had been selected for the search party led by Hrald did not sweeten Yrling's mood.

"Well. You did not find me."

"The Jarl sent men all over. He – he was worried about you."

This went unanswered. Yrling remembered the way Hrald had looked at him when he arrived with Aszur, and did not want to think about it.

Bork stood before him, uneasily shifting from foot to foot. He had always been taller than Yrling and seemed to have shot up even more. Then Yrling caught a glimpse of a silver chain about the stableboy's neck, one of fine workmanship. Yrling's hand went slowly to it. Though Bork twitched in response, Yrling pulled from beneath Bork's tunic a small, well-wrought cross of silver. It bore an uncanny resemblance to that Yrling had Offered as a sacrifice in the beech tree down by the Place of Offering.

Yrling let the cross drop from his grasp, falling on the outside of Bork's brown tunic. He let his eyes lock on Bork's.

"That looks like my cross."

"You threw it away."

"I did not. I Offered it to the Gods."

"It was not wanted. It fell to the ground."

Yrling was not sure what to say to this. It gave Bork a chance to further defend his act.

"It is holy, and was a gift of Lady Ælfwyn. When you were baptised."

Bork had been baptised late as well, but had received no such sacramental gift. To treat anything given from the hand of the Jarl's mother like that, let alone a sacred object, was unthinkable to him.

Still, Yrling had swift answer. "Well. She is not here any more. But do you think she would be happy that you stole it?"

"I saved it, not stole it."

Yrling's eyes flared, and he said the next with all the recklessness he felt.

"You are a thief, just like your father, who was killed for it."

Water was come into Bork's eyes, and he worked to control his voice as he answered this charge.

"My father did not throw the spear – the man called Are did. Not my father . . . "

"But it was your father who tried to steal a horse, and was killed for it."

"We were hungry . . . " Bork's voice had trailed off, then found root in a new truth. "You took a horse, too."

Yrling was about to fire back that he needed that horse, when he realised that this was the same answer Bork's father would have given. It stopped him, and he gave his head a small jerk. He no longer knew what to say. He did not care about the little cross Lady Ælfwyn gave him, and did not know why he was provoking Bork over it. It was the grievance of a sullen child; one he no longer wanted to take up. He had been to Jorvik on his own, and seen a lot, and almost gone to Frankland too. Yrling let his eyes rest a moment on the animal before them and said the first thing he thought of.

"Horses are good," he put forth. "On a horse you can do lots."

Bork was so surprised that he just nodded. Then he made bold to speak.

"Myrkri had her pups," he offered. "They are penned in the old grain house by the side of the kitchen yard. There are four of them. Their eyes just opened. Jari said first litters are sometimes small. But he is happy with them. There is no runt amongst them."

As one they moved towards the paddock gate so they might visit them. Yrling was aware he had never willingly done anything, even an act so slight as this, with Bork before. He gave his head a small nod, in acknowledgment. Bork was here at Four Stones and would stay here. And Bork worked hard and gave Hrald no cause for concern, as he himself just had. As they neared the shed they saw Myrkri standing behind the wattle fence, the tumbling mass of her dark young at her paws. Yrling turned his attention to the mewling pups. I only hope Hrald will still give me one, he thought.

⫷⫸⫷⫸⫷⫸⫷⫸⫷⫸

Aszur Gold-Tooth must stay the night; there was no heading back to Saltfleet that day. Having returned the miscreant in good order and refused any silver, he was treated by all with the deference awarded an honoured guest. Jari himself took him about the keep, pointing out the many changes and additions which had been affected since he, as a young hot-head, had stormed through the kitchen yard door at the side of Hrald's father. The Tyr-hand took Aszur round both halls, the barns and paddocks, to end at a lingering appraisal of the kitchen yard, where, by one of the brew-sheds, they sat pulling at deep cups of foaming ale. Any, seeing the two together, might have grinned; the ruddy-haired giant and the dwarf made a unique but fitting pair, for despite the difference in size, both men sported barrel-chests, large heads, and brawny arms.

Aszur again sat at Hrald's side that night, and when the salvers had been cleared away, and Wilgot the dark-clad priest had ended a rambling story about toiling in vineyards, the dwarf of a sudden stood, opened his gold-adorned mouth, and sang. It was a song of the sea, one of his own making, and in praise of the beauty and dangers of the salty, watery way on which he earned his living. Aszur's voice in song was as deep and resonant as that with which he spoke, and all fell silent at his skill.

Not long after this the hall began to break up for the night. Aszur Gold-Tooth would sleep in an alcove near the treasure room, and Yrling, who lived with Jari and his wife Inga, began to make his way with them out the door to the small timber house which was theirs. Inga had already greeted the boy, clutching him so firmly to her bosom the breath was pressed out of him, and now, with a reproachful cluck, she went ahead. But nearing the door of the house Jari stopped. His silence around Yrling had been notable, though the boy had noticed with what apparent pleasure the Tyr-hand had spent the afternoon with Aszur. Yrling feared what might come next. There was no birch whip at hand, but was a cuff about to fall from that mighty, maimed hand?

Instead Jari turned to Yrling, and in the thrown torch light, lifted his good, left hand to the boy's head. Thumb and forefinger closed around Yrling's right earlobe. There was a little glitter in the Tyr-hand's eyes; Yrling could see that. Jari pinched that earlobe, just enough to make Yrling flinch, and gave a sharp but quick twist. Then he let the boy go.

"You make me glad Inga gave me girls," he said. Then Jari let out a laugh.

The waggon to take the dwarf back to Saltfleet stood ready in the morning, awaiting only the paired horses to draw it. He would ride back with the same escort, and after the hall had broken its fast, and most had quitted their benches for the first tasks of the day, Yrling moved from his accustomed table forward, to where Hrald now sat alone with Aszur. The two glanced his way as he neared, and he heard the mission now awaiting the ship-captain.

"I have kermes to sell at Hunefleth," Aszur told Hrald.

Yrling had to bite his lip; he had been at Aszur's side when he had made that lucky buy. And he had thought he would see the mouth of the Seine, and Hunefleth too, with the savvy trader. He watched as his brother and Aszur exchanged banter about such a valued win as was that dye-stuff. Now they gave him a nod, and rose; it was time for Aszur to leave.

Yrling felt almost as down as he had when the wooden pier of Saltfleet had come into view, and realised his short-lived adventure to be over. He felt a kind of betrayal, even though he knew the dwarf had not lied, nor even really misled him. Aszur must live by his own lights, as did all men. Yet the pang Yrling felt was deep, and real. The dwarf could not leave him like this.

Aszur seemed to feel this as well. Hrald had gone ahead, leaving the two of them alone within the hall. Yrling had said nothing, just walked slowly at the side of the dwarf toward the heavy door, now fully open to the waiting day.

"When you are older, if you still aim to sail with me, seek me out at Jorvik," Aszur finally said.

There was no response, yet the ship-captain felt the boy was not sulking, just stung.

A long moment followed. "We spoke of Samarkand," Aszur recalled.

Yrling turned his head sharply to face the man. The ship-master went on.

"Such a trip is not to be undertaken lightly. But I have a taste for sights and smells and tastes unlike those I know. Also – a taste for gold." He smiled now, and said the next. "How can I not, when it is always in my mouth?

"One day you and I might head there."

Yrling's intake of breath was so deep that it took him a moment to respond.

"Do you mean it? You and me, to Samarkand – the golden city?"

Aszur just nodded.

"We cannot sail there; only part way," he cautioned. "There are shaggy beasts, far larger than horses, and with huge hooves, which men ride long distances across the sand. Beasts which need little water, and carry not only men but silk and spices to and from Samarkand."

"We will ride them?"

Again, Aszur nodded. "I have met men who have done so." The dwarf thought a moment, recalling what he had been told of these beasts. "Their gait is an odd one, they sway and pitch like a ship." He gave a short laugh at this. "Ideal for we seamen."

It only remained for Yrling to exact a pledge of good faith.

"Do you swear on Odin's eye?"

"I can swear that if, and when, you are ready – as long as you are grown – we will speak of it. Perhaps your brother will stake us, who knows. If not, I know many in Jorvik, where my repute is such that rich traders will supply us with what we need to risk our lives."

This would have to suffice, and to Yrling it was more than enough.

The dwarf's thick hand had gone to his neck, and he was pulling something out from under the collar of his tunic.

"Here is a pledge to you," he said, passing the warm piece of metal to the boy. "I have worn it many a year. It will remind you of our voyage to come."

It was a bronze hammer of Thor, one suggestive of an anchor, with upturned arms.

Yrling took it, and dropped it over his own neck. It felt more than an amulet, and a true bond of friendship. He had to clear his throat to utter his thanks.

"I will find you, Aszur Gold-Tooth, and we will sail together, and win gold in that golden city."

CAUSE TO LIVE

Wessex

EDWIN landed at Hunefleth ten days after leaving the hall Tyrsborg, on the eastern coast of Gotland. There were paired goshawks aboard Runulv's knorr, and the ship-captain offered to take the young Lord of Kilton with him, down the Seine, and to the stone city of Paris. There the raptors and all else aboard – fine bronze work in the way of decorative strap hinges and box locks from the eastern reaches of the Baltic, six pure white miniver pelts, and fully three score of long beeswax tapers dipped by Tindr – would find buyers. Edwin had been tempted by Runulv's tales of the riches there, but he could not in good conscience allow further delay. He had not returned to Wessex when expected with the King's merchant Wulgan, and at this point there must be concerns for his safety. Still, he must ask Runulv of the wonders of Paris.

Runulv had a good eye for detail and described the island of Paris, its stone streets, and the striking way in which the folk therein dressed, which to the Gotlander seemed to be the donning of festival clothing each and every day. Edwin listened to all and then wondered something aloud.

"You must have seen some fine women there."

At this Runulv had laughed. "The King surrounds himself with such. He has readily supplied them with goods he has bought from me."

It gave the Lord of Kilton pause. Men of power commanded much more than mere land and treasure.

"Are they his kept women?"

Runulv cocked his head and gave a slight shrug. "His women, or relations; I do not know. But he is not alone in his wealth. There are wine merchants there as rich as warlords." Runulv at this point knew of Edwin's failed mission to Dorestad, and so said the next.

"You might wed one of their daughters."

Edwin grinned, but shook his lowered head. If truth be told, he had no stomach just then for further adventure. His right fore-arm, sliced from wrist to elbow by the razor edge of Sidroc's sword, was still healing. And he had been away too long.

It would be one thing to return to Kilton with a bride, but he was not. He was mightily concerned with telling his mother and brother about his foray to Gotland, as he knew he must. There would, he trusted, be another chance to journey to Paris.

Runulv had been to Hunefleth five times. On each visit the port grew in size and importance, moving from a needed supply point for fresh water and provender to a small trading centre in its own right. Runulv did not deposit Edwin there, after refreshing his own stores, but scouted for a reputable captain to take his charge across the channel to the Saxon shore. Edwin was not ready to reveal himself fully to the chosen ship-master; he told the man only that he was on his way to Witanceaster, and needed passage to Swanawic. There he knew he would find the King's men answering for the collection of tolls, and could arrange a small escort to take him to Ælfred.

His assumption proved right, and after a rough but mercifully safe crossing Edwin and his body-guards Alwin and Wystan were given not only the loan of horses at Swanawic, but two of the King's men to ride with them to Witanceaster.

As they neared the doubled walls of the great burh Edwin could not help but recall with what expectation he had approached these same gates for St Mary's Day. He had been summoned directly by the King, but the end had been nought but disappointment. Here at Witanceaster Ælfred had made an unthinkable proposal, that Edwin wed Ealhswith, the daughter of Four Stones. The following, and fruitless journey to Frisia had only compounded his frustration. Here he was returning to the King, empty handed. He could scarcely think that Ælfred would be pleased at the ill-Fortune seeming to follow the monarch's choices for Edwin.

The Lord of Kilton and his two body-guards were given lodging in one of the small timber guest buildings near the great hall. They had been offered hot food, the convenience of the bathing shed, and the assurance the King would see Edwin later that day. Edwin took advantage of the time, setting off alone through the great burh, trying to lose himself and his thoughts. At one point he turned the corner of a narrow street lined with work sheds to see a square, fronted by the stone cathedral in which he had attended Mass on St Mary's Day. It was there he had sighted a striking young woman, dark of hair and sombre of expression, and learnt she was Dagmar, daughter of dead King Guthrum of the Danes. He turned from the building so sharply that he nearly ran into a man crossing behind him. It was Wulgan, the merchant ship master who had carried Edwin from Swanawic to Frisia.

After this initial surprise the older man greeted Edwin warmly. "I am but recently returned myself to Witanceaster, and have stopped here but a few days," he explained. The relief, even satisfaction, of the merchant captain's countenance seemed sincere. He took a moment to study the young man before him.

"It relieves me, Sir, to see your face," he went on. "To return without you, and with no report of when you might return – well, it was no gladsome admission to make."

Edwin had cause to wonder if Ælfred had been greatly displeased in him for not returning with his envoy. Wulgan seemed to read this on the young Lord's face, and countered it.

"But the King had just report of your action upon my ship," Wulgan assured Edwin. "I detailed your efforts, and those of your two men. The King listened with interest, and appreciation."

This was heartening. Yet of a sudden Edwin saw he might be in the King's presence by himself.

"Is the Bailiff of Defenas here?" he asked. There were few councillors closer to the ear of the King than Raedwulf, and despite his new connection to Four Stones, Edwin wished the man could be at his side.

Wulgan shook his head. "Back at his own hall," he admitted. Wulgan went on.

"I also had the unhappy task of telling the King of the death of Count Gerolf. He understood why no union with the daughters could be achieved. And I related how upon hearing this, you bid me fare-well at Dorestad and took ship for the Baltic."

The merchant sensed Edwin's discomfiture, and made offer. "If you will allow me, I will join you in your interview."

Thus it was that shortly before all gathered to sup in the great hall, Edwin and Wulgan were admitted to the small timber building which Ælfred used as study.

As with Edwin's first meeting with the King, a serving man poured mead from a silver ewer into three cups, gold for the King, and silver for his two guests. To Edwin the King did not seem as hale as he had at their last meeting. Dark circles hollowed the area underneath the blue eyes, and his skin seemed almost sallow under the weathering of the Sun. Yet both were greeted most cordially, Wulgan as an old and trusted confidant, Edwin as the hope for Kilton's future he had ever been.

"Wulgan has made high remark of your prowess and courage upon his ship," the King noted after they had taken their first swallows of the golden liquid.

This was gratifying, falling from the lips of the King, and Edwin allowed himself a modest nod of acknowledgment. What the King next said warmed the Lord of Kilton far more than any mead could have.

"I think, if my recollection is correct, your brother Ceric never fought at sea." Ælfred paused in thought, then went on. "But Godwin had. And on a ship built with his mother's silver."

The King shifted subject and tone in his next words.

"You did not return with Wulgan," he pointed out.

"No, my Lord. A Friesian trader offered to take me on to Gotland, where he was heading." A moment passed before Edwin went on. "I wished to see my Lady Mother."

"Ah," said the King, with a nod of his head. "The Lady Ceridwen. And was this accomplished?

"It was. She is well. And asks that for the sake of both Gyric and Godwin of Kilton, she be remembered to you."

"You mother is a woman who would be recalled warmly on her own account," the King returned.

"I have gifts for you to carry, on your return to Kilton," Ælfred went on. "One for Elidon, King of Ceredigion. I am greatly pleased that his niece has entered into the hall of Kilton. Raedwulf has told me of Ceric, and his wedding the maid," he added. The King left it at that.

Ælfred did not seem to be aware of the circumstances of the Welsh princess's arrival at Kilton, or if he did, considered the matter of Ceric wedding the bride intended for Edwin of little account. What mattered was the connection with Kilton.

"The Friesian daughters – there will be more choices for you, here and abroad," he counselled. "Now, with Winter on its way, concern for kith and kine will best serve you."

All Edwin could do was nod his head in acceptance. "I thank you, my Lord."

Despite the praise of his fighting skills, and the fact that Wulgan had supported him by his presence, the interview felt less than successful. It felt a weak directive to go home and take care of his burh, and almost a dismissal. It was not; Edwin understood that. Even the King was taxed with caring for the daily wants of his folk, and these spanned the entire Kingdom.

Ælfred granted two of his men to ride to Kilton with Edwin, Alwin, and Wystan. Edwin was grateful for the additional cover; he had gifts from the King he was responsible for, and five well-armed men on fast horses would give any random brigands pause. Nearing home, Edwin reviewed in his mind all that he must relate upon arrival. Once on his own lands he felt a flush of relief to be back. The possibility which had summoned him away seemed far distant in memory and experience. Frisia was a wasteland of water, confused and confusing. Here his meadows were still green, and his orchards, having yielded up most of their fruit, ready to receive their Winter's rest.

Yet as he rode in through the gates his face could not help but reveal that his errand fell short. Wystan had ridden ahead, and the hall entire was there to greet him. His mother Edgyth stood at the centre of the group, Ceric at one side, Worr at the other. The priest Dunnere was there as well. Edwin got off his dusty horse and Edgyth came to him for a quick embrace. The moment she stepped back he saw she knew the trip had not been fruitful. He had no time to respond in word, for from the tail of his eye Edwin saw a red-gowned Dwynwen approach. She was nearly running, then stopped short before him, to give a grave and deep curtsey, with her child's smile lighting her face. At the neck of her gown she wore the pin she favoured, a silver circle of a coiling dragon with garnet eyes. Then his brother embraced him in welcome.

Ceric, Worr, Dunnere and Edgyth all went with Edwin to the treasure room. Edwin would have liked to have spoken with his mother privately, but he realised these were the only advisors he possessed. His grandmother Modwynn, and the monk Cadmar were gone. He must be more open with those councillors left to him.

Before they sat down at the small table within, Edwin's hand went to his tunic neck. He had all three small parcels of gold, sewn into sleeves of tawed leather, laying against his chest. Edwin pulled them forth now. He placed them upon the table, the fine interlacing of their stitching untouched. He had made no offer of bride-price.

All were silent. The gesture said much, and they would learn more. His mother poured out the welcome ale. During the lift of his gold-rimmed cup Edwin's sleeve fell back a short amount. Worr was seated at Edwin's right, and saw the tip of a scar at his wrist, terminating just by the golden bracelet he wore. The scar was new, and from a fresh wound. The horse-thegn's eyes shifted to meet those of Edwin. The moment that passed was silent but full of import.

Edwin began by telling of his return to Witanceaster.

"I have just come from the King. When I landed at Swanawic his men gave me escort to Witanceaster. I hoped Ælfred would be there. He was, and I could tell him myself that the plan to wed one of Count Gerolf's daughters had been dashed. Gerolf had died just the night prior. His hall was in mourning, and Ælfred's envoy Fremund warned me that the girls would now be dependent on an older half-brother for their dowers."

Edgyth made a soft murmur. "There will be another, my boy," she said.

Such words of consolation had reached Edwin's ears too many times, and he gave his head a short nod, almost a jerk, at hearing them once again. His mother saw this, and felt her boy's frustration. It was confounding, this difficulty in obtaining a suitable bride for her son. When she, and before her Modwynn, had wed, these were well-considered matches between wealthy and landed families. Strategic, of course, in the combining of properties and assets, but not freighted with the need to continually build and shore the defences of Wessex. Just as she must make allowances for Ælfred's desire to wed Edwin to the daughter of Four Stones, she understood the King's attempt to pair her son with a wealthy Friesian, and one whose father, Count Gerolf, had been useful in fighting the Danes. Of worthy women there were many, but at the level the Lord of Kilton was expected to wed, very few.

Her boy's losses ran deeper than she guessed. Edgyth knew of one young woman who had caught Edwin's eye, the Lady Pega, when he appealed to Æthelred in Gleaweceaster to buy cattle. She had, Edwin had told her, been set aside for some unnamed suitor. The second Edgyth had no knowledge of, one he had glimpsed while called to Witanceaster for the disastrous meeting with Ealhswith of Four Stones. Now Edwin knew much more of both. Each were out of Edwin's reach, the first having been promised to the Jarl of Four Stones, the second having been discarded by him.

To turn his thoughts from this sad litany he described the rest of his travels.

"I sailed with a merchant captain who has journeyed many times for Ælfred, Wulgan by name. While we were out by the Isle of Wiht a war ship of Danes attacked us. We were larger and had more men, but they would not relent. Wulgan prepared war-fire, there on the deck, and his archers shot arrows aflame with it into their sail and lines. At last they tried to ram us; their ship was lost to them. We were in danger of catching fire too, and must leap down upon their deck and fight hand to hand. We killed them all, save six. Wulgan brought them aboard, and set them to the oar. Their ship burnt to the water line behind us."

Edgyth had her hands clasped to her breast as her son related this. Ceric and Worr asked more of this adventure; Worr had heard of war-fire but never seen it kindled. Edwin related all in the same straightforward manner he had heard both of them tell of their exploits, with no embellishment nor attempt to draw special attention to their own actions. Alwin and Wystan had been at Edwin's side, and the entire hall would soon hear from them about the action.

"And then I – I went on to Gotland."

"Gotland?" This was Worr, in a tone bordering on wonder.

"I met a Friesian trader who was heading there. He took us." Edwin paused, thinking of how best to frame his reason for the voyage. He repeated what he had told the King. It was the best part of his journey; he understood that now. "I wanted to see Lady Ceridwen."

Edgyth at once responded with the warmth she had always held for the boys' mother.

"Is she still well? Does she thrive?" The Lady was leaning forward towards her son in hope of affirmation to these queries.

"They are all well," Edwin said. "Her daughter Eirian, a maid of twelve or thirteen years, was free in telling me of her desire to voyage here, and from hence to Wales."

It took a moment for those listening to connect this desire to the young maid.

"Ah," said Edgyth. "Ceridwen is half-Welsh."

Edwin nodded. "She wishes to come here to Kilton, to see where her mother lived. And she seeks her grandmother, a Welshwoman. But she told me no one knows her name."

"She will be most welcome here," Edgyth answered. She looked to Dunnere, and went on. "You, and Dwynwen, may be able to guide her in her search." She turned back to her son. "Tell us of Gotland, Edwin," she urged. "Ceric has warm memory of the folk there." She smiled at he named.

It prodded Edwin to turn to one of his packs. Ceridwen had sent Edgyth a gift. They were five cut gems, four opals and a large rounded turquoise, which could be set into the binding of a book. No gift could prove better for the devout Edgyth.

After Edwin had told all he wished to tell, Lady Edgyth and Dunnere left them. There would, both knew, be details that Edwin might wish to share only with Ceric and Worr. But the three, alone, sat in near-silence a while. Worr rose to go. Edwin looked up at him, but could not bring himself to speak. With a nod the horse-thegn left the brothers alone.

Edwin did not wait for Ceric to rise as well.

"Our mother – she wishes to see you." In fact, the Mistress of Tyrsborg had told Edwin she yearned to see Ceric. But if she had now been privy to Edwin's words, she would readily forgive his reticence.

Ceric drew breath. His head dropped forward, chin lowered. The day he had parted with her on the wooden pier before Rannveig's brew-house lived on in memory. Once again he was revisited by the shame he felt at his callous treatment of her at that parting.

"She has a pottery imprint of Cerd's hand," Edwin went on. "Hrald brought it to her. It is to her like a holy relic."

Ceric exhaled a long breath and looked away. "I was not kind to her when I left with Hrald. I have regretted it over long years." He looked back at his brother. "She deserves only good."

This made Edwin catch his own breath. "I never knew her, not as you did," he reminded him. He looked at Ceric and felt again the sting of envy: You are from the man she loved. And I, from the man she feared.

But he found himself telling Ceric a truth, "I was glad to see her."

His brother nodded. In the silence that followed Ceric's eyes rested upon the top of the table, darkened with years and use. Edwin's hand moved again to his cup. Ceric saw the tip of a red scar on his brother's arm, at the right wrist, and just above the bracelet of red gold he wore. The tunic sleeve was loose. As Edwin watched, Ceric took the hem of the sleeve in his fingers and pulled it up. The scar went on, broadening as it went, to terminate in a doubled cross-work of thread, the fibre now showing almost black. Someone had sewn this wound.

His brother had mentioned nothing about taking an injury during the sea battle. Ceric looked his question to Edwin. It would have been easy for Edwin to lie about its source, but he could not.

"It happened on Gotland," he said. "I wanted to spar with the Dane."

"To spar with him?"

"Yes. He bested me."

Ceric found it hard to believe that Sidroc would have taken up a weapon against his brother. He answered the only way he could, a remembrance of his own past, in a voice just above a murmur. "I too got hurt, sparring," he reminded.

"You should show it to Lady Edgyth," Ceric went on, wishing nothing of this nature to be withheld from that good woman. "She has seen many wounds in her life. Including those caused by friendly sparring."

Edwin did not answer at once. When he did his voice had dropped a note.

"I was trying to kill him."

"Kill him?"

"Yes. I was angry."

"Over Godwin, our uncle?" Ceric asked.

Edwin swallowed.

"Yes. Over Godwin. Or so I thought. I was angry at our mother. Angry that she still loved me."

All Ceric could do was nod. He could understand this. He asked another question.

"Did you go to our uncle's grave?"

"Yes. Mother took me. The cross you carried is still there. Still upright."

Ceric nodded wordlessly. Edwin moved on.

"The deaf hunter, Tindr. He took us out into the forest, and to a great burial mound."

Looking back at it, this overnight adventure had been the best hours of the entire voyage, and some glimmer of that shown now on Edwin's face.

"Tindr," Ceric repeated. "He taught Hrald and me so much. Showed us so much."

"Yes," Edwin admitted. Like how to be content with whatever lot you are given. "His life – he has everything he wants. And he is deaf."

They sat in silence. The journey, despite the adventure of the sea battle, had proved fruitless as far as Edwin's finding a wife. Ceric wished to address this, but could hardly do so in any direct manner, when he was now wed to Dwynwen of Ceredigion, who Edwin had carried from Wales to be his own bride. Still, he felt he must say something.

"That Frisian Count, Gerolf – you were never able to see the daughters."

Edwin shook his head, and sighed. "I heard them wailing. My timing could not have been worse. And," he added, "I heard from others the girls had likely been left but little as their portion. Their dowry would have been rich enough, but with their father dead . . . "

"They are of good blood, though," Ceric hazarded. "And Ælfred approved of the match."

Edwin gave a small sputter. "Fremund, my guide there – when I asked his opinion of the girls' comeliness, could say nothing more encouraging than they possessed a comfortable aspect." Edwin's lips cracked into a smile, one at his own expense. "As if they were cushioned chairs.

"It was," he summed, "not enough to tempt me to return."

Later, Edwin walked past the stable. He saw Worr standing within at one of the work tables there, and stepped inside the dimness. Worr turned from the saddle before him.

Edwin met the horse-thegn's gaze and spoke. "About the Dane. You were right."

His eyes dropped to his right arm. Worr took the sleeve and pulled it up to the elbow. Again, Edwin did not resist. As a sword cut it was evidence of unusual control, to leave that stinging cut without grievously damaging the arm.

If the young Lord of Kilton had drawn blood from the Dane, he would have said so. His silence confirmed that he had not.

"Was she there?" was Worr's only question.

"Yes. She saw it all. My insult to her was the cause of the strike."

Worr gave a shake of his head. "The fact that he left you alive is proof of how he values her."

Edwin could do no more than nod agreement.

That night alone in the treasure room he recalled Worr's words. Ceric would not fight back when Edwin had punched him. Sidroc would not take his hand, or his life, despite being sorely provoked. It was but another lesson in restraint.

When Ceric left the treasure room he found Dwynwen sitting at the small table in their bower. An ink-dipped feather tip was in her hand, and a piece of white birch bark before her. Despite the slight chill of the day the door was open for better light. She was at her drawing, painting the odd glyphs and swirls that held meaning for her. She looked up at Ceric, and spoke.

"Edwin did not like Frisia," she guessed.

Ceric could only agree. "He found no wife, so the long trip did not reward him." His brother had now twice travelled far to win a bride.

Dwynwen closed her eyes a long moment, and then opened them. "I think she will come to him," she decided.

A few days later Lady Edgyth was in the pleasure garden with the serving woman Mindred. The latter held a basket

and knife, while the Lady, on her hands and knees, dug at
the roots of a patch of bonewort. Edgyth had been taught at
Glastunburh that now, at the end of its growing season, the
roots would be richest in that healing efficacy she sought.

It was a cool, even chilly day, with a brisk breeze ruffling
the waters below into white caps. Edgyth thought they
worked alone in the garden, until Tegwedd stood up from
where she had been sitting, on a low bench at the base of a
tangle of climbing rose. The girl was near the top of the stone
steps leading down the cliff face. Edgyth arose and went to
her. Tegwedd could now speak the tongue of Wessex, and
gave a quick and jolting curtsey to the Lady of Kilton.

"Where is your mistress, the Princess, Lady Dwynwen?"

Tegwedd turned her head. "She is below, with her waves,"
she answered. "She told me to stay up here," she added, lest
she be accused of neglecting her duty.

Edgyth knew the ward-men on the cliff to the right were
at work, watching the beach from the blind secreted there.
She did not fear for Dwynwen's safety, though she heard
report that more than once the men had need to climb down
the steps in haste when the Princess vanished from view,
having grown too near the base of the cliff face for them to
see her. Edgyth moved closer to the first stone step. From this
angle she too could only see a portion of the shingle beach
below. But she continued along the edge of the precipice,
taking care to keep well away from the drop of the sheer cliff.
Then Dwynwen came into view, standing still on the piled
shingle. Her arms were outstretched in front of her, palms
down, over the incoming foam at her feet. The small head
was lifted, chin up, gazing over the sea. The girl was either
at prayer, or some other communion with the water lapping

at her feet and stretching far away. All the way to Cymru, thought Edgyth.

Perhaps Dwynwen, knowing the great distances Edwin had travelled by sea, was put more in mind of her own water-washed shores. She had lost her home, in the way that all brides lost their homes, for all travelled to the homes of their husbands.

Edgyth finished with her task, and took the basket of bonewort with her to her bower. But washing her hands in her basin again put her in mind of Dwynwen, conjuring at the sea edge. On a shelf near the Lady of Kilton's clothes chest sat the hardened case which Lady Luned had sent her as gift. Within lay an heirloom, an old harp of Cymru. Edgyth went to it. It was, she felt, something sent in trust for the girl they now shared. The leathern case had been stained dark red. She laid it on the top of the chest and considered it.

Small cracks had found their way into its surface as it was being moulded into the oval shape of the harp it would protect. But the case itself was as firm as if it had been formed out of metal. Edgyth opened it, and lifted out the harp. It was also red, its finish crackled with time. Such lap harps could have any number of strings, from six to thirty. This, from Dwynwen's home, carried eight, a span which could easily be set to sing, or be stilled, by hands as small as hers. When it was plucked or strummed it sat upright, as all harps did, against the left shoulder. Edgyth wondered how Dwynwen, who favoured her left hand, would hold it.

It did not matter if Dwynwen took it up. The Lady of Kilton merely wished to place the harp, gift of her step-mother and reminder of her Welsh home, where the girl would see it. Perhaps she would derive comfort from it. There was a sense of wistfulness in the girl's pose; that and a kind of summoning in the expression of her arms, held straight out as if beckoning something, or someone, near.

Edgyth replaced the instrument in its case and carried it to the pavilion of the pleasure garden. One climbing the steps from the beach would see it clearly. The harp had a little wooden stand so it would sit upright on the table, and the Lady prepared to set it thus. The breeze was such that as soon as she lifted it from its leathern case, the harp began to play. Struck by the wind, the strings hummed, as if unseen hands had been laid against them. Edgyth placed the frame upright in its cradle, awaiting her young daughter-in-law. Another puff of breeze and the strings thrummed. Edgyth recalled taking the harp to Garrulf, their scop, and his considering the old instrument. "Many songs are within," he had told her. Here, unbidden by human hands, they seemed eager to be heard.

Tegwedd was there at the top of the steps, but did not see Lady Edgyth come and go. When Dwynwen ascended, her eyes met the red harp. She saw, and almost at the same moment, heard it. It was calling to her. It was not only from Ceredigion, but of her father's hall, one of the many things Luned had packed up and brought with them when they moved to Elidon's fortress by the sea. Sudden joy moved in her small breast. Luned had sent this as gift to Lady Edgyth. And Lady Edgyth must have placed it here for her.

Dwynwen came to the harp, thrilling to the sound the strings made as they trembled under the touch of the breeze. Sounding unaided by human touch as it was, it was almost a living thing. She took a moment to regard it. Dwynwen knew the horses from whose long tails these hairs had been plucked, to form these strings. The tuning pegs around which they were anchored were carved of bone from the ankles of their goats. Still standing, she placed her fingers on the strings. Now she sat, and pulled the harp into her lap, nestling it into her right shoulder. Her arms encircled it. She held it thus, contrary as it were, to common usage. But as in so much else, it was natural to her.

Dwynwen could sing, but her voice was not the piping pitch of many young girls. Her voice in song took on a huskier note, more womanly, and more affecting. Her fingers plucked at the strings. And she began to sing.

The burh of Kilton kept a special meadow, removed from its paddocks within its palisade, where mares in foal were pastured. It was enough removed from the bustle of the keep that its denizens could peacefully graze and stretch their legs as their girths thickened with coming young. Worr was riding out with a couple of the stablemen to bring a few of the mares closer to term back to the confines of the foaling paddock. Ceric always took interest in the horses of the burh, and had accompanied the horse-thegn. He rode, as was usual, the bay stallion Hrald had presented him years ago as a parting gift from Four Stones. The animal was reminder of the long ride Worr had made with him, on which Ceric had presented Hrald, then only of five-and-ten Summers, with a ring tunic Ceric had ordered for his friend. And it was the trip on which he had pushed a linen bag holding a golden silk gown across a table to Ashild. The stallion Ceric rode had ever been his favourite since the day Hrald had given it, and in fact, three of the mares they now watched in the pasture were his offspring.

When Worr had inspected the mares, he chose five of the twelve to be led back to Kilton. The mares lacked even halters, and Worr slipped neck ropes over the heads of two of them. The other three would follow, such was the herd instinct even amongst the mares. The two stablemen with their charges fell in behind them as they readied to leave.

As they turned their horses back for home, they passed the mouth of a road leading east from the burh.

"Begu," Ceric said, looking down the road.

The horse-thegn understood the suddenness of this mention. The road leading to her hamlet was there.

"Yes, Begu," Worr agreed. He gave a smile at the thought of her.

"It was just you and I, riding together, when you took me to meet her," Ceric remembered.

"Just so," Worr answered.

"She gave her house to a woman who was kind to her," Ceric went on.

"Yes," the horse-thegn said. "She noticed every act of kindness. Though she expected none."

Begu was off in her new life now, wed to a man she had known as a child, and was now mother to his own children.

Worr held the woman in thought for a long moment, as other faces arose.

"You have known some women of high remark, Ceric. Ashild. Begu. And now the Princess of Ceredigion."

There was a lesson there, Worr felt. Each woman had a message to bear for Ceric. And Ashild of course had given him a son. Dwynwen held unlimited promise, but like the

Lady Edgyth, Worr harboured no further expectations for her, having seen what good she had already wrought in returning Ceric to one who could take pleasure in his life. Anything beyond this was benison.

"The Bailiff of Defenas is much taken with her," Ceric said.

Worr nodded. "It would be a hard heart indeed who is not taken by the winsomeness of your Lady-wife."

Ceric gave a short laugh, recalling the surety of her address to the Bailiff. But he went on in all seriousness, just as Dwynwen had. "She made clear to your father-in-law her connection, not only to the King of Ceredigion, but of every Kingdom and Princely holding of the Cymry. She is kin to all, through Rhodri Mawr. I had not thought of that before."

Ceric held a moment on this reflection, one of great meaning. Then he went on.

"So often the Welsh have been a scourge to us. Mercia and Wessex have been at war with them for many years, and some of their Kings and Princes have joined with the Danes against us. But Elidon was rare in abstaining, and sought connection with Wessex. He has achieved it through Dwynwen."

Ceric paused here, recalling what his wife had said to Raedwulf on this matter. "Though when Raedwulf spoke of this, Dwynwen was quick to correct him, claiming that Elidon had nothing to do with it. It was rather the Lady Luned who was responsible for her coming here."

A woman, thought Ceric, to whom I owe more than I can say.

"I think Raedwulf sees the Peace-weaver she could be," Ceric continued. "He may, I think, ask Dwynwen and me to go to Cymru, visit its Kingdoms, bring gifts and expressions of friendship to its war-chiefs.'

Worr answered in a long exhalation. "Ah. The time could scarcely be bettered. With Haesten dead, and no other Danish war-mongerer nipping at our heels to take his place, yes. There have been only scattered incursions since his death."

And Worr understood his father-in-law's desire to place Ceric in a position of importance, and bring him to the forefront in stabilizing relations with Wales. With Ælfred ailing this was never more important. The King with his bouts of bleeding sickness might live a year or two longer. The knowledge of the King's increasing weakness was kept from most, but Raedwulf with his close relation to Ælfred was privy to the growing concerns. Upon Ælfred's death his son Eadward would be crowned King of Wessex, and likely without contest from his same-aged kin. His sister Æthelflaed had too firm a grasp on Mercia for any connection to her late mother to arise and attempt to claim the throne of Wessex.

"It is perhaps not a question of if I will be asked, but when I will be asked," Ceric went on. "If I were to go and undertake such a journey, I would want you by my side, Worr. It would mean an absence from Kilton, Wilgyfu, and your boys."

The horse-thegn's answer came as readily and firmly as could be hoped. "There is no asking, Ceric. I am your man. I will be with you."

Worr gave thought, and spoke again. "Kilton is well protected. Edwin has his captains, Alwin and Wystan. In fighting skill they are two of the best young warriors to have come through this hall."

Ceric could not but speak the next truth. "Yet there is no councillor. None like Cadmar, or Lady Modwynn."

"He must find his way without one," Worr countered. "He has, I think, made great strides this last year. That will continue."

Raedwulf had also spoken to Ceric about serving Eadward directly, when he was made King. He would not broach this to Worr, not yet. Now he must ready himself for what immediate use he could be put to, for his God-father and King, Ælfred of Wessex.

On his return from this ride, Ceric had gone to the bower house he shared with Dwynwen. She was not there. He retraced his steps and entered the hall of Kilton, near-empty now in mid-day. A few women worked at the large looms set against the side door, passing their charged shuttles through the warp strings. Other women, their young at their feet, stood nearby, wooden spindles whirring as they dropped from their fingers, spinning the mass of roving at their shoulders into fine and thin yarn.

There were however two more figures, seated at the end of the high table. At the tall stool at which he ever sat was Garrulf, the scop. Perched before him on the end of the broad face of the table sat Dwynwen. Faint music surrounded them, the plucking of strings. Dwynwen was gowned in red, as she often was, and it took Ceric a moment to make out that upon her lap she cradled the red Welsh harp sent by her step-mother, Lady Luned.

Ceric did not near them. He would not disturb the two, but just allowed his eyes to rest on Garrulf's absorbed expression as he leant near the young Lady Dwynwen to hear all. After a moment Ceric soundlessly withdrew.

Garrulf knew of this song, the lay of Trystan and Esyllt, which begins when Esyllt heals Trystan, the nephew of King Marc, of a grievous wound. Garrulf had never recited it, and now the small Princess taught him it. She knew it in the tongue of the Cymry, and must take time to render the words so he could understand, and sing them so all could hear. Master scop as Garrulf was, his ready ear and quick mind bent readily to the task.

But Dwynwen changed the ending of the lay. After they had drunk from the same cup, the love of the King's nephew and the Princess of Éireann did not lead to madness and disgrace. King Marc tracked them to the forest whence they had fled. But when the King found his wife in the arms of his nephew Trystan, he did not leave his sword between the sleeping pair, to remind them of their wrong-doing, and warn them he had found them. In Dwynwen's telling, the King was moved by their beauty and devotion, and left instead his gold ring at their feet, as a sign of blessing in their life ahead. As Dwynwen taught Garrulf, the two lovers remained in the forest. Trystan no longer fought the wars of any man, and Esyllt used her healing powers only for themselves and the woodland creatures who approached her for help. In their leafy bower they built a life of quiet and peace. The Welsh Princess had wrought the ending as she wished it.

Every dusk when the hall of Kilton gathered, Dwynwen wore the golden fillet around her brow at table. Ceric had placed it there the first night they had supped in the hall as man and wife. Like the cup she lifted to her lips, it had been owned by Ceridwen, the mother of Ceric. Ceric placed his own golden fillet on his head, that worn by his father, Gyric. The silver cups they lifted to drink their ale or mead were those once held by Ceridwen and Gyric, and all four names were engravened on the golden rims. Dwynwen never sipped from hers without touching her own name, and that of Ceridwen.

Garrulf had a new song to play, a new tale to tell, for all within the hall that night. The air Dwynwen plucked out he had spun into a melody that rose and dropped, carrying listeners off as if they rode a wave. Only three had heard it before this night. Edwin, Lord of Kilton, had sat in King Elidon's hall while it was played in the tongue of Cymru. The scop of Kilton had taken tune and tale into his ears and hands as the small Princess sat before him, singing and playing for him.

Dwynwen knew this story by heart; she had lived by it, and had made bold to change the Fate of those sung of. Now, rendered into the tongue all spoke, the hall entire could enjoy it. And a few, carefully listening and considering, understood the tale on its deepest level. Three sat at the high table who played the parts Garrulf sang of. Ceric was the wounded Trystan, scarcely clinging to life. Dwynwen was the healer, Princess Esyllt. And Edwin was akin to King Marc, who must surrender his young wife to a greater love.

All listened with interest. Some were enraptured. At the end of the lay, as all hearing called out acclaim for Garrulf's skill, he stood, and holding his harp before him, bowed to Dwynwen in acknowledgment.

The next morning Ceric went to Lady Edgyth. She was still in her bower house, but all night the story Garrulf had sung resounded in his ears. He had not heard it before, but he felt he had lived it.

"That song last night – it is true," he told his aunt. "Dwynwen saved my life. I could not have lived without her."

Edgyth was much moved by this, just as in the hushed dimness of the hall she had been moved by the tale sung by the scop. These were the same words the girl had used privately to her, and in her letter to Lady Luned. Dwynwen had vowed to save the life of Ceric. And she had in fact done so.

"She gave me cause to live," Ceric ended.

The Lady Edgyth, who knew much of love and more of hope, leant forward to kiss him on his brow.

TO STARAYA LADOGA

Gotland, and Points East

THE winds did not always favour the small convoy setting out. Both ships were fast and sailing in tandem was a pleasure with the wind at their sterns. Death-Day had been re-sailed since Sidroc had brought her to Gotland, and sported the narrow interwoven strips of linsey-woolsey common to that island's sailing vessels. The strips crossed each other at an angle, and half of them had been dyed ochre yellow. Interwoven with the undyed strips, the sail once unfurled made handsome show, a billowing and golden-hued wind catcher which by its very colouring presaged riches to come.

Sharp Tooth's larger sail was all of apiece, for it was made of long vertical lengths of linsey-woolsey sewn together. But every other panel had been dyed woad blue, so that its stripes were just as eye-catching as was Death-Day's intricate interlace. And Eskil's ship was crowned by its gilded wind-vane, from which a handful of dark ribbands fluttered, giving its steers-man clear indication of the breeze. Yet there was no one of real account to admire their passage, as their crews saw nothing more than a few late-trawling fishing boats on their way.

When the winds turned contrary, Eskil's larger drekar took the lead, with Dauðadagr sailing or rowing in her wake. Still, it took fully three days to approach the Gulf of the Finns, sailing steadily north and eastward.

Once in the gulf to Staraya Ladoga they felt the first glimmering of their destination, facing the rising Sun, and feeling their eastward draw to it. One morning around their cook-fire, as they squinted against the first rays breaking over the dark sea, Runulv said, "They say the Gods arose in the east."

As the lifting orb pierced the horizon with ever-growing brilliance, it was easy to accept such a notion, and that the Sun brought renewal not just to Midgard where dwelt man, but at Asgard too.

Brani answered. "One thing I have seen, much treasure lives in the east. And we will get our share."

Now they were deeply in the Gulf of the Finns. When crossing the Baltic, Berse the blade-smith had kept the men on Sharp Tooth amused by singing at the top of his lungs. But now, in narrowing waters with strange tribes perhaps behind the trees and out of sight, he kept his silence. Here and there from the banks rose burial mounds, most grassed over, but two or three of naked rock. Men had died here, and lately, on this very route. Still, the mounds, so like those of home, told that the same customs were observed after death.

As Brani the guide had promised, a small trading post at the mouth of the River Neva welcomed them upon arrival.

The folk at this post spoke Norse, and their own tongue as well, one which Eskil remarked had no backbone to it. They traded for ale and fresh bread, handing over silver fragments from a deep purse of hack kept by Runulv.

This first segment of the journey was the shortest, yet was observed with due ceremony by both captains, each Offering a rooster to the river ahead. They had left the waters of the Baltic, and their homes, and now began the long inland journey to bring them to the Black Sea, and from thence, the splendours of Miklagårdr.

Gotland knew late Summer, but it was fully Autumn here, the trees a rusty gold, long grasses yellowing along the banks, and in pale blue skies above, masses of heavy-bodied ducks flying on their southern route. These flew low overhead, as if having just alighted from some near marshland opening from the Neva. Their cries and squawks made the men lift their heads to them. This early in the adventure none could be wistful at their southerly path, yet more than one noted the plaintive eagerness to be on their way to warmer Winter quarters. The crews glanced skyward, and then back to the tasks at hand. They were sailing, and when the wind faltered, rowing, against the current on their way to Lake Ladoga, but the Neva was plenty wide, broad enough so they might drop anchor for a few hours' rest at night.

Three days saw them entering the waters of Lake Ladoga, rimmed in places with brown rock cliffs crowned with tall and slender pines. They skirted the shore, Sharp Tooth in the lead, finding beaches of fine sand as well as sheer and rocky crags, until at Brani's order they turned south down a broad waterway. It was there they sighted the settlement of Staraya Ladoga.

As an encampment it was impressive enough, a palisade of heavy pine trunks spiked to ward off the unwanted, encircling a good assortment of pitched timber roofs. There was but one wooden pier, bereft now of any vessel, but of length and breadth enough to accommodate several ships. A number of smaller boats were hauled up upon a grassy shore. A broad gate facing the water fronted the settlement, its doubled doors solidly shut. They had only just begun to take this in when a horn rang out. It had not issued from the town itself, but from some hidden ward-man on the shore.

Both Eskil and Runulv had been waiting for this. Eskil slowed the motion of his drekar, dropping sail and allowing Dauðadagr to come alongside and pass. They had agreed that for safety's sake the smaller Death-Day would approach first; she was more maneuverable in case they need beat a hasty retreat. They had no reason to expect anything but the welcome afforded all traders, yet caution was ever the road trod by the wise.

This switch complete, both captains looked to the small boxes they had at the ready, laden with gifts to ease their entry. Where possible, Eskil would present on behalf of both ships. They sailed as one, on a shared voyage, and both the Svear and Runulv knew conserving these trinkets now might spare them trouble later. But such a place of importance as was Staraya Ladoga demanded a gift from each ship.

Before the palisade gates were swung open, they heard the clamour of what sounded a host of hounds, barking excitedly. This pack was foremost crossing into the open, held tightly by leads in the hands of no fewer than three men. There was perhaps a dozen of hounds, some of which now, sighting the ships, raised their muzzles to the air and gave full voice, baying at them.

Berse, who was at this point standing near Eskil at the steering oar, joined his own low voice to the din. "A welcome party. Of dogs," he muttered.

The Svear gave a short laugh. "Let us not be fed to them, like bones," he agreed. Eskil nodded his head to his second in command, who took the steering oar. His men had already shipped their oars, as had Runulv's, on Dauðadagr. Eskil stooped to retrieve the small chest of gifts, and then moved forward to the prow, Berse at one shoulder, Brani at the other.

"Make a gesture of offering with the box, but let them speak first," Brani hissed. They had grown close enough to scan the faces of those awaiting them. "They can see we are Svear."

Behind the hounds and their handlers was now a mixed group of men and women, eyes alert but visages hard to gauge. A few well-armed warriors bearing spears and shields flanked them, but the delegation conveyed more expectant curiosity than anything. The men were dressed alike, in gathered, loose leggings which ended at the calf to meet their leg wrappings. The women dressed much like those of the Svear or Gotland, with a long-sleeved under-gown over which was placed a sleeveless gown fastened with paired brooches at the shoulders. What differed was the amount of silver draped from brooch to brooch, and hung about their necks; chains and ropes of silver, beads of silver interspersed with those of glass, and most striking of all, ornaments of silver wrapped about, or dangling from their head wraps.

Runulv, taking this in, was glad Sidroc had provided so much in the way of this favoured metal. And the presence of so many women was reassuring. He glanced back to Eskil, who nodding in return, signed that Dauðadagr should give way for the larger ship to land first.

As soon as they grew near enough, the Svear called out from his prow. He knew they cut a fine figure; Sharp Tooth was wholly praiseworthy, and the smaller drekar with her was nothing to dismiss. Indeed, the eyes of the delegation on the shore were shifting from prow to prow, from one curling sea dragon's head to the other. The men holding the hounds had stilled them enough so the arriving captain might be heard.

"I am Eskil, come to trade in Miklagårdr," he began. There was seemingly no one leader to address, so he spoke generally to the crowd. "I sail with my friend Runulv, a Gotlander. My man Brani has passed this way before –" Eskil paused a moment, judging the best way to proceed, and decided on flattery – "and has known your generous welcome."

There was no response, so he went on. "We need water, ale, and bread, and to pass in peace through your waters on our way."

He was still holding the wooden box, and now lifted it toward the assembled. A few of them looked at each other, then at the guards. These responded by allowing their spears to rest back on their shoulders. It was a woman in the middle of life who made gesture to enter. She was as heavily adorned with silver as were her sisters, but made decision for all.

Four only from the paired ships went ashore, the two captains, Brani, and Berse. The gates were swung shut behind them, an unwelcome sound. Those remaining aboard were deprived of their captains and charged with the safety of the ships; those within the fortress cut off from all assistance should it be needed. Yet once behind the palisade the four found themselves surrounded by the everyday life of thriving folk, amongst workshops and barns and fowl houses and romping children and women hanging out wrung woollens in the tepid warmth of the Sun.

The main hall was set back amidst all this, but by its greater size proclaimed that here lived the chieftain. It was built of rough timber, with a timber plank roof upon which a thick layer of moss had taken hold, giving it the air of a forest retreat. The brilliant green of the moss made fine contrast with the roughly planed and deep brown timbers of the structure, and all the eye fell upon had the look of a natural prosperity. The door was open, and they were led to it by a smaller segment of the welcoming party, which followed them in. The header of the opening was low, forcing those entering to bow their heads as they crossed over, the best defence to attack. Eskil never crossed such a threshold without his fingers on the hilt of his sword, both to keep it from striking the jamb, and to feel its steel ready at hand.

The dimness of any timber hall demands time for the eyes to adjust, and it was near midday, making the contrast the greater. But as the three paused after crossing the threshold, they were caught unawares by a near dazzling display of metal work hung upon the wall they faced. This was festooned with weaponry of every description, knives and swords of shapes known and unknown to the visitors, hung upon the upright planks with spear points and shield bosses of prodigious size, all glinting under the flames of iron torches thrusting from the same wall. It was a use of burning oil only the wealthiest or most prideful would entertain, and here at midday, with no feasting crowd to marvel at it. In fact, the hall seemed utterly empty. Then they saw it was not.

A woman stood at one end of the long table before that festooned wall, spinning. Her hair, long to her waist and grey as a wood dove's wing, proclaimed her age. As they watched her, a handful of dogs tumbled over the threshold behind them, to swirl around the table with thumping tails and settle beneath it. These must be the favoured of the pack.

The spinster turned to the men who advanced, and set down her spindle on a basket heaped with dark roving. A movement of her shoulder shifted her shawl enough for the visitors to glimpse the immense amount of gold hanging from her brooches. Eskil and Runulv, side to side, looked to each other. This then was Mistress of the hall.

Two of the guards now escorted the four to where she stood awaiting them. As they neared she moved to the mid-point of the long table, one dark and well-scarred with years of use. She sat upon a short bench set there, of crude make but laid with a cushion covered in a highly-figured cloth. She lifted her hand and spoke to two serving women, young and of a comeliness which Eskil could not fail to notice, who came forward to attend her. She then was alone; it was clear to the visitors they need not await her husband or son.

A kind of sour ale was poured into pottery cups. When all were filled the old woman stood a moment, lifting her own cup, and saluted her visitors with it, indicating with her head they should do the same. Her eyes were a warm, but light brown, and still bright.

She took in her visitors with those bright eyes. She saw they had taken pains to smarten themselves up before landing, and presented themselves in clean tunics and leggings. Two were formidably armed with knives and swords she gauged at once as blades of worth. The tallest was yellow-haired and a man of considerable good looks, with high cheekbones and cool blue eyes which lent a steely air to his countenance. He moved with an assurance close to a strutting cock; a walk which drew the eyes of women.

At his side was a brown-haired man of sturdy build, a wide brow, and firm chin. The openness of expression on his face gave it an attractiveness it did not naturally possess; it was a face to be trusted. He wore no sword at waist, but from its grip she guessed his knife was Frankish, thus no trifling weapon. He must be far-travelled to be wearing that, or lucky to have won it.

Both these men bore small wooden boxes, handsel she knew with which they hoped to buy their passage down the river. By the side of the brown-haired one was a man older than both, sword-girt, with curly, greying brown hair, close clipped grey beard, and the body of a wrestler. The fourth was a weathered seaman who had lost an ear.

Her first words surprised them. "So late," she mused.

The puzzled look on her guests' faces drove her to say more.

"Late in the season. You have craft, or you are fools. Perhaps both." She turned her eyes first on Eskil, then Runulv. A smile cracked her lips. "Yet I welcome you. A woman likes a man with daring."

This last seemed to be addressed to Eskil, one young enough to be son, if not her grandson. Few men knew better how to return such a remark to a woman than Eskil.

"Not too late, honoured Lady, to win your favour upon our passing," he began.

She grinned now, revealing the loss of few side teeth.

Both Eskil and Runulv had set down their boxes to take up the proffered ale. The Svear judged that it was not too soon to present their host with some token from within. His eyes met the Gotlander's for a moment, and the Svear lifted the lid on his first. Both Eskil and Runulv were practiced in presenting gifts, keeping the box closed, revealing the offering with ceremony, and if more than one gift was expected, then slowly, one by one, as if each were the final.

Eskil cast his eyes into the box. Bedecked as she was with gold, he could not offer her trinkets of silver. But he had something golden to present, and did so. He pulled a small linen pouch from the box, loosened the drawstring, and laid it before her.

Her hands, blue-veined, but with fingers still straight, went to it. She uncovered a small cup, one carved of amber. It was no larger than a hen's egg, but as a piece of worked amber was of exceptional worth. As she held it up, the torch light, flaming behind her, struck it, making it almost glow with a deep yellow lustre. She did not try to hide her delight, which made the three before her value her pleasure in it.

It was Runulv's turn. He took his own look within the box before him, vexed with the same quandary which Eskil had faced. Brani had told them to have at the ready iron shears which met sharply and cut truly, as gifts for the leaders of tribes they met along the riverways. Berse had made up four pair, for the four largest trading posts they would pass on their way. Staraya Ladoga was one. Runulv had placed two pair in this box prior to landing. As Fate had willed it, he chose one larger, and one smaller pair. The smaller was the perfect size for a woman's hand. He ignored the silver ornaments, as Eskil had done, and lifted out a pair of newly forged shears, gleaming darkly in its oiled finish. Runulv's wife Gyda, thinking ahead, had given him a scrap piece of woollen goods to travel with these shears, for as she pointed out, "No sale without a slice," when it came to such tools; one must see how well they performed.

The old woman was more than happy to do so, slipping thumb and first two fingers into the looped handles, and then closing the iron jaws upon the wool. The blades cut as cleanly as a razor.

The recipient of this gift placed the shears on the table top, next to her new amber cup. She seemed ready now to talk. She straightened up, and gestured to the serving women to pour out more of the sour ale. A soft chiming came from the old woman whenever she moved, the sound of many ingots' worth of gold ornaments striking each other.

"I am Ladja, and Mistress here. My husband is dead, and my son, our chieftain, is off to the eastern hills just now.

"What men are you, and from where?"

Again, she looked first to Eskil.

"I am Eskil, a Svear. Late of the body-guard of Ivar, dead King of Uppsala, but now turned to trade."

She nodded. "A dead King is no King," she reflected.

The Svear was forced to give a small laugh at this truth.

A moment passed, one in which it was difficult for the four arrivals to keep their eyes upon the face of the woman before them, so distracted they were by the wealth she bore upon her person. Around her neck were strands of metallic beads, each carrying as many as a rich woman of Gotland would wear. But most women of Gotland would be wearing silver. These were gilt, and some of them mayhap solid gold. Other strands were festooned with golden coins and tiny golden ornaments. In a single twisted coil about her neck lay a torc of gold. Runulv, so practiced in gauging the weight of metal, knew it for what it was, a ring equally a full ingot of that rare metal. In the light thrown by the oil lamps she glimmered as if dressed in starlight, and there was no silver upon her.

"You are eyeing my gold," Ladja said. The words could have been barbed, but she wore a smile on her weathered face. "I am glad you take pleasure in it. When a woman grows old, it is good to present something of beauty for others to look at. And," she went on, placing a hand upon her bosom for a moment, "I am proud of my wealth. No one, I think, is as rich as Ladja."

She pondered this a moment in silence, and the men could only nod their heads in agreement. Certainly none had ever seen such a display as she wore before them now.

From then on, the words 'rich as Ladja' became a kind of byword between her four guests, signifying wealth of such a standard that would be hard to compass.

The lady looked now to the brown-haired man next Eskil, one who met her gaze with a small bow of his head. His words, though, rang with simple and unaffected pride.

"I am a Gotlander, Runulv by name. A free trader of a free folk. I sail my own ship, a broad knorr, and trade on behalf of a Dane well known on the island." He remembered the war-ship Dauðadagr just outside the gates. "The drekar I sail now – it is his. I sail on his behalf."

"Gotland," Ladja repeated.

Runulv nodded, and looked to he who sat at his left. "Berse is a weapon-smith, also of Gotland."

The old woman's eyes turned to Berse. She had noted the man and his sword before, but now her brown eyes rested upon him. Seated, he seemed to be only slightly above middle height, but the use of hammer and tongs had given him the shoulders and arms to be the envy of any son of Thor.

"Gotland," she said again, still looking at the smith. "I knew a boy from Gotland. You – you may be of an age to know him, as well."

She fell into thought, the gaze of her eyes dropping into the cup she held. Berse, one always ready to hear more, asked of her a question.

"Did you then come to Gotland?"

It roused her. She lifted her head and gave it a shake. "I could have. The boy – for he was not much more than that – he offered to take me there."

This was enough for Berse. He had indeed the burliness of his trade, and now leant forward, propping his meaty arms on the table, and spoke again. "Men's lives are built on stories, Mistress Ladja. Those of travel and adventure are the best," he ended in encouragement.

She went on, her face in turns shadowed and then lightening with memory. "I lived on Öland then, a long worm of an island, but I am wholly Rus. I was captured, as a maid, in the very yard you crossed to reach this door. It was before our great palisade was built," she offered, with a feeble laugh.

"Amongst the attackers was a rich farmer from Öland, who claimed me as part of his booty. I was left untouched; he meant me for the second wife of his eldest son. He sailed off with me and much other booty. But that first wife, a clumsy, ugly woman, shrieked when she saw me, and would have none of it.

"The old man hardly knew what to do with me. His wife took my gold." Her fingers rose to touch a large ring of that rare metal, suspended from the very centre of one of her necklaces. "This piece; given me by the man I loved here. I was pledged to him before my capture." The pause she took gave her breath, and the near-whisper of her next words did not hide her umbrage. "I had for years to watch her wear it."

Again she stopped, as if in bitter memory. Yet she gave a sigh, and went on, signalling the serving women for more ale.

The sourness of the brew began to make Berse fear he might suffer from belly-ache; yet the potency of it led him to continue quaffing. The women behind them holding the ewers proved no sluggards in keeping all the cups filled, and he could not be bested in his drinking by the woman before him. Ladja took another draught and went on.

"I became a woman of the household, not yet a thrall nor a freewoman, but something betwixt. The farm was large and prosperous, and I worked hard, as much as any other. I had a son there, with a man of my choosing."

Berse could not trace the thread from Öland to a man of Gotland, and must ask of it. "But the boy you met – he of Gotland?"

Ladja nodded, and the smile returned to her thin lips. "He had been treated harshly by some Rus. He was a fisherman; his ship was stolen at sea, and he was forced to leap overboard to his death. His featherbed saved him. He washed ashore in Öland. He was brought to the farm where I lived. But he had lost all; had no ship, and it was late to sail with others; he must wait until Spring and better weather.

"His name was Dagr."

Berse sputtered, nearly choking on his ale.

"Dagr?"

"Did you know him? He found his ship, beached in Spring, and set sail. Did he reach his island?"

"He did," Berse assured her. "Dagr hailed from the south of the island. But he wed a maid from our parts, on the eastern shore, from a good farm known for its apples. They moved to the coast so Dagr could keep fishing. That is where I met him. His wife, Rannveig, is a brewster, and all gather at her brew-house. Dagr told me the story of his boat being run down by Rus raiders, and being cast overboard, and how he lived to spend the Winter on Öland."

Berse took pause here, half in wonder, and half in need to slow his tumbling words.

"He and Rannveig had children. A boy survived, Tindr, who grew to be the best hunter on Gotland."

"He was not a fisher, as was his father?"

"Nai. Tindr was called to the woodland."

"Does he live, still?"

"Dagr? Nai, he died years ago, on his fishing boat. But his boat was found, and Rannveig had a great stone carved and painted for him, down in the south, where Dagr came from."

He studied the woman. Even the weapon-smith could detect the note of wistfulness in the old women's eyes. He asked about it.

"So – you knew him there, on Öland."

"I did. For all of that Winter. He was a sweet boy."

Mazed with lines as her face was, there was no hiding the warmth which flickered a moment in her eyes.

"You did not go with him back to Gotland, though he asked you to. Tell us why."

She gave a laugh. "I am Rus, of Staraya Ladoga, and would let nothing stop me until I could return. My boy was old enough when I found my chance to slip away. I gave him the choice to stay, or go with me. He joined me. Before we left I reclaimed my gold and took all I felt I was owed."

Ladja did not say how she recovered her gold, but the grim satisfaction on her face suggested it may not have been easily parted from the old man's wife. Still, the gold was hers, and the Gods will help the just even a score.

"It took us many weeks to reach here," Ladja went on, "and I had been gone eight years. The man I was pledged to, thinking me dead, had wed, and had children of his own, two daughters. But when I landed and walked through that gate he turned to his wife, and nodded in dismissal.

"Oh, she was sent away with gold; shed no tears for her. The marriage was not of their choosing, and she was, I think, glad to palm her gold, and go. From that day on I became his rightful wife, as I had always been.

"We had a score of Winters together. I wept and tore my hair when he died. He was a good warrior, and a good chieftain. He claimed my son for his own, and we had two more, now dead; and daughters aplenty, some of whom met you when you landed.

"Yet over the years I did not forget Dagr's name, nor his face. When one grows old, these things rise from our youth and give us comfort, those we have touched, and who touched us."

It was a striking tale, and perhaps helped along by the potency of the ale, no one was more struck by it than Berse, who despite his brawn had the soul of a skald. By the time

Ladja had finished, he found himself blinking a film of mist from his eyes. That water served to prompt him to action.

Berse, like many metal-smiths, carried a large pouch at his waist while travelling, filled with small tools: files, punches, a pincher, and the like. It was something ready-made he reached for now. He unwrapped the cord to the toggle, opened the flap, and drew something out. It was a square-sided bell, one not wrought, but cast of green brass, carefully patinated. When he moved it to her by its stem it gave off a single mellow clang. He cleared his throat and spoke.

"Your tale has charmed my ears. I would like to give you this, Mistress Ladja, as reminder of your telling, and our hearing."

This was accepted as readily as were amber cup and iron shears, but she looked upon the giver with real warmth.

The sunlight was creeping past the open door, reminding the two captains of the need to rouse themselves. The weather remained fair; they hoped now to secure fresh provisions and take their leave. But Ladja would have none of it.

"You will stay the night," she told them, an offer with more than a note of order in it. "I would speak more to this one," she ended, with a glance to Berse. She could further sweeten the offer, and did so.

"Also the food you will be given will far outstrip the salt fish and hard loaves in your casks. You will sup with me and my folk in this hall. I will send smoked pig, grain, and vegetables to the ships; your men may cook on the shore and liven their appetites."

She had a final word before they stood up. The Mistress of the hall scanned their faces, then ended by fixing on that handsome one belonging to Eskil.

"Do not touch my women while you are here," she warned them. "At Novgorod, at Kyiv, you will be offered women. These are my own."

Runulv must bite back his smile, and Berse shifted his eyes to the door lest he grin. Only the Svear responded, a slight gesture of his hands to deflect a baseless suspicion. It made Ladja laugh.

That night was held a feast of welcome; none could gainsay that. Ladja's daughters and their husbands and all her men, some two score, gathered within to partake of it. There was a roasted goat, which had been splayed to cook the faster, then forked into savoury shreds; a potage of fresh water fish with the roundest grains of wheat the men had ever seen; and plums which had been roasted in the fire with honey, then spread, oozing with sweetness, on fresh seeded bread.

They were allowed to return to their ships for the night, to find the men in good spirits, having been brought a cask of the sour beer, and the promised provender.

On the morrow, having procured the needed supplies from Ladja's stores with silver coins, they bid her fare-well.

"You will have a gift for me, from Miklagårdr, on your return," she said as dismissal. It was not so much hint as command, and both Eskil and Runulv nodded their heads with proper gravity. She extended a hand towards them in a kind of benediction. "And may every merchant meet your price, and your profit far exceed your outlay."

Then she drew Berse's bell from her sleeve, and rang it. "You need bring me nothing," she told him, "save the tales of what Miklagårdr teaches you."

WHAT HAVE
YOU BROUGHT ME?

THEIR next goal was due south, the trading post of Novgorod, a newly made seat of Rus power. It was through these waterways that Svear had travelled a few generations ago, and settled, to be given the name Rus by the local tribes. They now controlled much of the water route south. The founding Rus had arrived by river ways; it was a name akin to the word row, and row the two crews did.

The forests of long needled pines and firs which had lined the Gulf of the Finns and the shores of Lake Ladoga fell off. The prows of the two drekars now rose over plains, creased with flowing water. Late Summer as it was, the river they followed lacked water, and was in parts shallow enough to give cause for concern lest they stove in or get snagged on the larger boulders now visible above the surface. There was no wind to catch sail, nor if there had been would it have been safe to raise it. They oared and punted their way south along the water channel, snaking through marshland and quaking bogs. They heard and saw almost no birds, not even water fowl, and were at times plagued by swarms of tiny, biting flies. It was forsaken country, after the snug prosperity of Mistress Ladja's hall.

Dauðadagr had a draught shallow enough to keep her and her men afloat, though heavily laden as she was, Runulv had never a more trying time scanning the water ahead for half-hidden hazards. Being the smaller vessel, she led the way, with Runulv at times having one or more of his men walk upon the muddy shore to scan the placid waters and call out the location of rock ledges or sunken boulders.

Sharp Tooth with her greater weight was at risk enough that her crew spent four days walking alongside her, some upon the bank, some trudging through the water, hands along her hull, to help see her way. Only Eskil and a few men were left aboard, armed with oars to help steer her safely through such passages.

Their guide Brani had warned of shallow waters, and of portages to come, but neither captain had bargained for this so soon after leaving the depths of Lake Ladoga. Eskil did not relish the possibility of abandoning Sharp Tooth on the banks of this unnamed waterway, unwatched and uncared for, doubling up men and goods on Death-Day until they reached Novgorod and the chance to buy smaller boats. This concern, one shared by Runulv, went unvoiced by both men. Speaking of unprofitable ends could draw them near.

Despite the bog mud they saw signs of trade along the banks. In a few dryer places stood crude open structures, yet roofed, much like stalls, which spoke of the display of goods earlier in the Summer. On the fourth morning, as they rowed and punted themselves through a broader part of the river, the men in the prow of Dauðadagr were startled by an arrow whizzing past to land on the other bank. One gave up a yell of alarm, and all aboard dove for cover. There is no enemy so unnerving as one who cannot be seen. Runulv at the steering-oar dropped to his knees, but held the rudder below the water line. Eskil's men scrambled for bows of their own, and Berse clapped his helmet, ever at the ready, upon his head. But beyond this random shot, no aggression followed.

When Novgorod came into sight, all heaved a sigh of relief. It was, like Staraya Ladoga, set behind a palisade of fairly recent make. The difference was Novgorod ranged far along the bank, encased in a rectangle of palings. The land here was higher, grassy, but still mostly treeless. The sharply pointed pines which formed the palisade, and the planks from which the buildings within had been pounded together must have been floated from up or down stream.

It was folk they sighted first, working along the banks, a group of women and boys at a task upon the ground not easy to discern at a distance. These looked up at the drekars, and with sharp whistles and shrill cries left what they were doing, and made haste for the rear of the palisade.

Runulv's own experience meeting unknown tribes in his trading told him how to proceed. "Oars up, and stand the ship," he ordered. He turned back to face Sharp Tooth and gave out a shrill whistle himself. "Their chief will come to meet us."

Both ships dropped anchor. Looking at their retreating forms Runulv had just enough time to guess the folk at work were Slav. Their broad faces, high cheekbones, and light yellow hair suggested as much.

Aboard Sharp Tooth Brani was saying much the same, and more. "The Rus chief will summon us closer. All of us must have our hands free of weapons." Here Brani shot a glance at Berse. The wearing of a helmet would be read as a foretoken of violence. Berse heaved a half-sigh, half-oath, but pulled it from his head.

Brani went on. "He will ask our business, and our route. He will ask for a silver ingot that we might pass; perhaps two, for we are two ships. You must not bargain, not now, but supply what he asks. He will invite us to land, and offer many things to buy. It is then you can bargain, after he has given us food and drink."

No cry of alarm or other clamour arose from behind the palisade, and the two drekars waited in some suspense for the main gates to open. When they did, about a score of men walked out, armed as if the body-guard to the single man they fronted. He was belted with a sword and knife, but had no shield upon his back; the weapons were mere signs of estate. His body-guard carried long knives, but more importantly, bows in their hands and quivers of fletched arrows at their hips. As they came to a halt, each man drew an arrow from the leathern quiver he sported and nocked it to the bow string. To those men aboard their ships, it was a welcome sight that the bow itself was kept low, at knee height. The archers were nonetheless entirely ready to let fly if needed.

Their war-chief was a man in the middle of life, tall, fair-haired, and dressed in a grey woollen tunic embellished with broad bands of tablet weaving in the brightest of yarns. Upon his head he wore a cap of black fur, pine marten, perhaps. He looked a Svear, but with a broadness across the cheekbones that told of a Slav mother. His beard was of prodigious length, a wavy yellow grizzled with grey. After he joined the row in which his men stood, he planted his feet and placed his hands on his hips.

"I am Vermund, King of Novgorod," he began. His expression was as fixed and stern to be nearly a scowl.

Upon the drekars an oath escaped the lips of Brani, who muttered under his breath, "King?"

Runulv stood in plain sight to the self-named monarch, alone and undefended. But back on Sharp Tooth Brani hissed to Eskil. "He has amassed much silver since I was here, to claim that title; or by using it shows he thinks himself the equal to the King of Kyiv, further down river."

Eskil did not care if the man before him claimed to be King of all Serkland and Cathay, as long as he was permitted to buy provisions and pass down river. He pulled himself up and called out.

"We salute you, King Vermund, and greet you with gifts. I am Eskil, a Svear like your forefathers. Runulv" – and here Eskil lifted his hand to the smaller drekar – "is a Gotlander. Our goal is Miklagårdr."

Vermund's immoveable mouth had softened into a grin, and Eskil pressed his advantage. "We know of your open-handedness to your Baltic brothers; my man who has stopped here before has sung of his reception. Now we would land and resupply our ships."

The King was ready, and receptive. "Hah! I thought as much."

He spoke in Norse, but with a kind of halting cadence which required a moment for his listeners to understand. But his lifted arm gestured them to land. "Come in. We will talk of what you will need, and what help I am willing to give."

Neither Eskil nor Runulv need be parted from their crews, for all were waved in through the gates. Yet this gave concern to both captains; no ship was ever left unwatched by a few trusted crew, and their drekars were laden with goods.

Vermund read the furrow which had formed on the Svear's brow correctly, and spoke.

"Your ships are safe. You are Vermund's guest, and none would pilfer from such a King."

The suggestion that the ships and their contents were now, for the duration, Vermund's property was not reassuring, but it must suffice.

Both captains had their gift box in hand, and led the way through the gates behind Vermund and his body-guard. The fortress was divided into two distinct precincts. To the left lay animal paddocks in which herds of milk cows, goats, and horses stood and browsed. Runulv noted these last were not much larger, and no more long-legged, than the native Gotland horses. Yet the breadth across the chest and a broader barrel told of animals with strong wind, which could canter long distances without fear of foundering.

Arrayed directly before them were barns and granaries and such like structures, with the kitchen yard and its outbuildings and storehouses running towards the rear wall of the palisade. Two wells were there; with the river at their gate the soil would readily yield well-water.

To the right lay the dwellings and workshops. All were built of upright timber, and all roofed with wooden planks, upon which were set slabs of sod, covered in now yellowing grasses.

A great many of Vermund's folk were about, drawn by the arrival of the newcomers and curious to see them. Runulv noted again the many who reminded him of the Slavs he had seen and had dealings with at the trading posts of the Polanie on the Baltic shore.

Two such yellow-haired women stood by the open door of the largest hall, each dressed in gowns, one of red and one of blue, nearly covered with bright thread work, with the hems of their skirts bordered with three broad bands of woven tablet-weaving. Vermund was at this point walking just before the visitors, and the women's faces were wreathed in smiles as he approached. Both of these women were comely, and were enough bedecked with silver as to make the captains assume these were two of his wives. If this was their everyday attire, Runulv wondered what their festival dress might be.

Vermund turned, and with a few words in an unknown tongue ordered his men to escort the main body of the crews to the kitchen yard. Eskil wanted Brani and Berse with them, so made request to the King, who, granting it with an air of benevolence, led the four inside the hall.

Within there was nothing to arrest the eye, no glittering display of won weaponry as they had seen at Staraya Ladoga. Still, the upright timbers and beams holding the roof had been carved in handsome fashion, in designs neither Norse nor in the style of any carving either Eskil or Runulv had seen. These featured no sinuous interlacing, but instead a kind of blocky energy of paired opposing shapes and slanted lines. Some of the shapes might have been birds; others antlered deer.

Serving folk were at work at one of the tables, lighting oil cressets with fire they caught with straws from that banked up at one end of the fire-pit. The cressets were of a make unknown to the captains, with a deep pottery vessel holding the oil, and not a shallow dish.

All of the score of Vermund's body-guard followed them in, and dividing themselves neatly into two groups, stood by at the tables to the right and left of the head table, where they would have clear view of their King and his visitors.

Vermund went to the high-backed chair awaiting him, one of rude make but with hundreds of small iron disks, no larger than nail heads, hammered into its frame. They lent a dull gleam to the piece, suitable to the man who now sat upon it. The rest took their places on benches.

Vermund's supposed wives had vanished into some recess or hallway when the greater party entered, but now reappeared with three younger females, mayhap their daughters. These set not cups of pottery or bronze or even silver before the men, but tall beakers of pale greenish glass. They were Rhenish; both Runulv and Eskil knew them at a glance. They were flared from bottom to top, with rings of darker coloured glass spun around them, making the grasping of the beaker the easier. And they were perfectly matched, with only that placed before Vermund of different make, for it was a stemmed goblet, but also of green glass. Runulv shifted his eyes to see if anything had been placed before the body-guard. As he had guessed it had not, the better to stay alert to danger to their King.

The wives now began filling those glass vessels, beginning with that of Vermund. They carried each a long-necked pottery jug, holding it from the looped handle as they poured. It was wine; each man knew it at once by colour and aroma. It swirled, as red as blood into their glasses.

King Vermund took up his glass goblet. "From the Greeks, and their stronghold of Miklagårdr," he told them.

They each took a potent sip, save for Berse, who was unstinting in his mouthful. After the first taste, the women now returned with pitchers of water, meant for adding to the wine. Eskil and Runulv were quick to water theirs, less their thinking and dealing become addled.

This over, the King's eyes shifted to the wooden boxes sitting before the two captains.

"What have you brought me," asked Vermund, a demand not unexpected by his guests.

The two had discussed this last night, when Runulv had come aboard Eskil's ship, and were ready. Sidroc had added a few weapons to their store of potential gifts, knives and well-tooled leathern scabbards. The blades he had Berse's sons hammer up, and for the scabbards, he asked one of the leather-workers on the road to make up in haste. As they approached Novgorod Eskil and Runulv had decided that this might be occasion to present such.

Both captains opened their boxes in tandem, and both pulled from it a sheathed knife.

"Gotland-made," said Runulv with a note of pride.

Vermund's eyes widened, and he reached for one and held it in his hands. It was too much for Berse, who must speak.

"Forged by my own flesh and blood. Not these hands of mine," he added, with a laugh, "but those of my sons."

They were fine examples of the blade-makers' craft, pattern-welded, with all the rippling movement which could be conjured by the twisting and hammering together of many thin pieces of steel.

Vermund left the first knife unsheathed, and pulled the second, holding it closer to the flame of the cresset to admire the work.

He lifted his eyes to those of the weapon-smith. "You make such blades yourself?"

"I do," Berse confirmed. "Knives, spear points, and swords. Helmets also."

Vermund leant back in his chair, as if considering the smith.

Runulv and Eskil were hit with a sobering realization, one which took the other two a moment longer to grasp. Weapon-smiths were the most prized of all workers in metal. Such were subject to kidnap, ransom, and even forced service. In the Sagas of old, Weland the Smith had been crippled to keep him from fleeing his captors, so skillful was he.

Berse's eyes rolled up to the rafters, and his hand closed around his beaker so he might drink again. His mouth was of a sudden dry.

Eskil must speak, and did so as he opened the lid of his box. He was ready with a diversion.

"We have also these," he said, placing a handful of silver ornaments before the King.

His women, hovering behind the table, let out little gasps of pleasure at seeing them.

"Beads," Eskil described, poking some of graceful pierced design, "small silver bells" – and here he picked one up and rattled it, so that all might hear its merry tinkle – "and coins, ready to wear. Purest silver. From Angle-land," he remembered to add, for Sidroc had reminded him that the further distant anything hailed from, the more it was prized.

The females were now leaning over the table, chattering amongst themselves. One of the youngest reached forward as if to choose from the offerings, to have her hand slapped by another. It was enough of a distraction that Vermund ordered them all from his presence. Their squabbling could be heard all the way out.

The King returned to business.

"Give me an ingot each of silver," he commanded. "There are tribes between here and Gnezdovo who will not receive you as I have. They are savages and eat the flesh of those they capture. I will send a man with you as escort past their villages, without whom you might end up in a cauldron."

As the four were taking this in, Vermund spoke again.

"Why do you sail so late? You are fools to be only at my door, with Winter at your heels."

Eskil gave answer. "My man Brani has visited you in the past, and made the full journey to Miklagårdr. He knows we can do so again, even by ice."

The King had given the guide scant notice, but now studied him.

"How many wives did I have then," he demanded.

Brani took a breath. "It was five Harvests past," he recalled. "Your wife with the waving hair; I recall her. I sailed with a Svear captain named Hedin; he was thrown from a boat by rapids in the Dnieper cataracts. We did not find his body."

"So you have made the Winter journey," Vermund summed.

"Once," Brani allowed. "And a second trip to Miklagårdr, earlier, setting out in Spring."

Vermund folded his arms. He rested his gaze on Eskil, and then Runulv.

"Give me an ingot of silver each. Because I like you I will sell you wolf skin tunics and leggings. Without them you will die, or lose arms and legs to frostbite."

The two captains looked at each other. All aboard had brought the warmest Winter clothing they owned, heavy woollen wadmal tunics, fur-lined hoods, and water-proof capes of tanned leather. Eskil knew the Winters in Uppsala were more severe than those on Gotland, but thought them all adequately kitted out.

But Brani caught his captain's eye, and nodded that Eskil accept the offer. Eskil felt he had little choice. Such outfits would be costly, but if they needed them it would be silver well spent, and they could be sold back home to those heading north to the lands of the Sámi.

"For the onward journey we need food and water as well," Eskil added.

"And the use of my horses to haul your ships overland," was Vermund's answer.

Brani had warned them of this, that to make the best time they could not search out water routes, but would need to transport the ships to the next navigable water.

"I thought we could make it to Gnezdovo," Brani offered.

"Not now; there is not water enough."

So it went on, with Vermund badgering and cajoling the adventurers in regards to their kit. Runulv and Eskil were silently adding up what all this might cost. They would be leaving a fortune at this threshold.

At last the King gave a whistle, drawing serving women to the table. The wine was poured afresh, and Eskil did not water his, nor did Vermund. He was now in good humour, and of a mind to inquire of his neighbours, and tell of himself.

"I have not asked you of Queen Ladja," he posed. "Her health is good?"

It took a moment for Eskil to answer, so surprised was he with the honourific.

"Ladja, Mistress of Staraya Ladoga? We found her well."

"All her gold," Vermund muttered with a shake of his head.

Eskil uttered a sound of agreement, and made bold to add the next. "And we found her welcoming. But protective of her women."

"Ah," Vermund answered. "She promised that I might offer you some. So I will, on your return." The King gave a snort of laughter, then went on. "Ladja is a modest woman. She is as much Queen of Staraya Ladoga as I am King of Novgorod."

The four listening did their best to look impressed. There was the King of Kyiv, but away from his ears any of these chiefs could name themselves as they wished, and Vermund did so. He leant closer to his visitors and spoke again.

"She is pure Rus, born there at the lake, but her son is half Svear. That is why she liked you."

And, thought Berse, liked those of us from Gotland, for she carries memories of Dagr . . .

Vermund had more to tell. "My folk are Svear, mixed with Slav," he went on. He paused a moment before giving a laugh. "As I am! I am kin to Oleg, King of Kyiv. We are both kin to Rurik, first chief here. My folk grew rich slaving amongst the Slavs, driving them long distances to send them down river to Miklagårdr. But my father kept many of the best Slav men and women to be his own. Those who spotted you first are all my half-brothers and sisters, the younger ones my own sons and daughters. They are kin, but there are many in thrall to me. But slaves are a small part of my riches and my power. Horses, silver, glass, and spice – I deal with all traders, and all raiders; the Khazars, the Bulgars, even the Pechenegs."

This final tribe named made Brani jerk his head in alarm; they must be fierce indeed.

King Vermund did not notice. Fully warmed to the task of impressing his visitors, his claims rose as he lifted his cup again.

"Fortune smiles on all who I let pass. Down river, those who you meet know you have my approval. They will hasten to speed your way. Speak my name in Miklagårdr and merchants will bow to you!"

This boast nearly prompted Runulv to inquire why they then needed one of his men as escort to the next trading post, but he refrained. If they must head over land, Vermund's word perhaps carried less weight than it did on the river banks. Instead, Runulv asked a question which had been on his mind since they had entered the treeless steppe. He wondered how the hall was kept warm in such harsh Winters. At home, and in Svear-land too, vast stacks of firewood would be piled under the eaves, or under separate cover, awaiting the cold. And everyday cooking and washing took wood as well. In this treeless clime, how did Vermund keep his folk fed and warm?

The Gotlander voiced his question in the form of a statement, aware that to some tribes a question was considered too direct, and could be read as an insult.

"I see no trees, King Vermund, no firewood. Yet your folk look well fed, and thriving."

Vermund gave another cry of triumph. "Hah! Trees are for timber, not the cooking pit. Our Summers are long, the grasses grow tall. The dung of all my animals is gathered to dry. Cattle, horse, sheep – all their dung is dried, then wrapped in long grass which my folk cut. The women are very good at it; they were at this work when they spotted your ships. They form logs of dung and grass, narrow to the eye but easy to take fire, and long to burn."

The day wore on. Vermund was as eager to share the customs and ways of his own folk as he was to extract news of the lands rimming the Baltic. Of this his visitors had little, other than the fact that the King of the Svear was again a new man. Eskil was careful not to name himself as one of the dead King's body-guard, lest Vermund fault him in his duty, or worse, consider him as a candidate for his own. And the goods the King of Novgorod wished to sell them were displayed, chief amongst them the tunics and leggings of wolf skin. These were to be worn fur side in, over woollen tunics and leggings, and were well cut, and solidly stitched together with leathern thongs.

"East of us – nothing but wolves," Vermund muttered, in answer to where so many pelts could be obtained.

That night the crews of both ships joined them to sup in the hall. River fish again made up the main part of the meal, boiled up in a milky broth in which great quantities of green and tangy water herbs swam. Amongst Vermund's herds were many milking goats, and his guests were treated to a variety of cheeses, both soft, and salted and cured, from those thrifty beasts. These were smeared on slabs of unleavened bread, torn from flat discs as wide as the large griddles on which they had been baked. Sprinkled with salt, the blistered and crackling bread was used as well to sop up the fish stew. It was a meal as satisfying as it was simple.

Late in the evening the King's guests retreated to their ships for the night. Eskil and Runulv had full bellies, but lighter purses.

"At Miklagårdr it will all come back to us," Eskil claimed to Runulv as they parted. "And we will be rich as Ladja."

THE WHEELED SHIPS

ESKIL and Runulv and their crews left King Vermund with not one, but three of his men. The first was he who would escort them as far as the river trading post of Gnezdovo. Only the first part of the journey could be made by water, and for this Vermund supplied three horses as well. These animals, and their two drivers, would drag the drekars over grassland when the waters ran too shallowly or too randomly to follow. The goal was the River Dnieper, and the shortest route to it demanded portage.

This would be slow and tedious work. But the party began well enough, on the water, and with the escort, Davor by name, upon Dauðadagr in the lead. Sharp Tooth could follow at close distance, as rowing in such shallow water as they were, either ship could be smartly halted and thus avoid collision. The horses were ridden, with the third led, on the bank. Their harnesses were aboard Sharp Tooth, along with the wheeled axle and cradle she would need. This could have been knocked up cheaply by the wheelwright on the trading road who had made the same for Death-Day, and Eskil did not spare Brani when reminding him of this. He was not overly harsh, however, for he was in secret glad that he need not surrender his ship so soon. Vermund had warned them that at last the cataracts of the Dnieper would force them to leave both ships behind. Of Runulv's insistence that he would not do so with Dauðadagr, Vermund clicked his teeth, and with a gimlet eye studied the small drekar. "She is a fine ship," the King conceded. He gave a shrug. "And it is your burial mound."

On the fourth day out from Novgorod Sharp Tooth, whose draught was only slightly deeper than Dauðadagr, struck mud. The crew jumped down into the water to lighten the load, but she was held fast. They began the labourious task of unloading, hoping to refloat her enough so they might tow her downstream another day or so. Meanwhile Davor was walking ahead, wading to gauge the coming depth. He returned muddied from hip to foot, and with a face which spoke of defeat.

There was nothing for it but haul both drekars out. It was here the notched log rollers Brani had demanded were first put to use. They were laid in a row upon the bank, the distance of a man's wrist to elbow apart, and the notch, the width of the keel, slathered with the sheep's fat they had laid by for this use. Once the keel of the ship was pushed into the first notch, it could be guided with surety into or out of the water. Both ships were hauled out in this way, and then pushed into the wheeled cradles. Sharp Tooth could then be reloaded, and the horses hitched up.

The wheeled axles featured a pair of large iron-rimmed wooden wheels, bridged by a short axle fitted with a cradle into which the keel would rest. A horse, or oxen, or men themselves could then be roped to the prow, and pull her forward. A ship so loaded needed to be steadied along the way, for she was liable to topple over rough ground. The horse and its driver could do only so much; the men with their hands along the hull must guide her, and act as brake too, when they met any downward slope.

It took a full day to unload Sharp Tooth of almost all cargo, and haul her up over the bank. They had worked under a hot Sun, so that the sweat poured freely from the labourers; but as soon as the golden orb lowered in the sky the warmth fled, falling as cool as any late Harvest-tide night. It was the first chill they had felt, foretokening cold days and nights to follow. Eskil's men camped on the bank amidst all their kit and goods, and at dawn began the task of reloading her.

On the morrow Dauðadagr was far easier to work with. She was still free-floating and so her prow could be angled to the bank where it was lowest. Fully loaded as she was, she was too heavy to haul from the water, and her crew passed bales and casks of smaller wares hand to hand over her side to those waiting on the bank to lighten her. When she was rid of half her goods, the log rollers were made ready on the muddy margin, and a single horse pulling and her crew pushing got her up and onto the grass. Runulv was not happy to see her emerge, hull and keel dripping and glistening, from out her natural element. In this heat her straked planking would quickly dry out. He had a small quantity of tar aboard, as did Eskil, but Brani had promised that further down river they would find natural tar in pits, for the taking.

This began a week of slow going through the parched grasses. One horse was hitched to Dauðadagr, and two to Sharp Tooth, their drivers walking beside the animals. The prow was only lifted after the animals had made a start; then the entire ship, as ungainly as it looked out of water, could move ahead. Davor their escort stood aboard Death-Day, as it gave him a vantage point from which to scan the landscape before them. Eskil's ship as well had two ever-changing men upon it, beginning with Brani in the prow and Berse in the stern, so that they might watch the flanks and rear as they progressed. Eskil's men aboard would whistle out their warning if needed.

Davor was a wiry and scrappy sort, of middle age, but nimble enough for the rigours of his task. He had a brass horn hung from his waist, so that he could signal ahead and identify the party as one under Vermund's protection. At times when they crossed rivulets of water he blew it; these must be borders of some sort. The water yielded up by such streams was welcome; it was thirsty work, walking alongside the ships, and they need at times to push them ahead with steadying hands as the horses pulled them over hillocks. Neither Eskil nor Runulv stinted in this, and took their places amongst their men. They worked under a pitiless Sun, with no tree cover to take their noon day rest under. The best they could do was throw themselves down in the scant shade cast by the hulls of their wheeled ships.

One morning as they were breaking their camp one of their number stood up, bowl still in hand, and growled out an oath. All heads rose to the horizon. Necks turned, eyes scanning the amber-hued grasses waving about them. Horsemen surrounded them, no fewer than a score, pacing their beasts steadily forward. Each horseman held an upright spear in his right fist, and from several spears long coloured ribbands jittered in the breeze. Each man was followed by a second horse, one unencumbered by pack; a fresh mount.

Davor, seated by the cook-fire, was quick to rise and hold his horn to his lips. He sounded it, the same low and sonorous tune the men had heard him play to an empty landscape. The horsemen did not slow, nor did they hasten. All the crew of both ships were now on their feet. Each had their most needful war-kit near them at all times, and now were in the act of taking up spears and shields. Those who owned swords belted them on. Berse was never far from his helmet, one he was proud of, with a great flowing moustache in hammered steel matching his own. He dropped it upon his head. Eskil had a helmet of worth but let it lie in his arms pack at his feet.

"Who are they," the Svear asked Brani. Davor was steadily sounding his horn, so he must ask his own man.

"Some Turkic folk," Brani muttered. "I think Khazars, from the number of horses."

Davor now began walking forward, alone, to meet the horsemen. Eskil, seeing this, made move to join the man, but Brani pulled him back. Runulv had come up to Eskil's shoulder, and added his own counsel.

"Vermund gave us this man for just this reason," he reminded.

If Runulv had his way the men would have their weapons near, but not to hand. The Gotlander was a trader foremost, one who knew any move to weaponry could prompt violence when none was intended. He was ready to defend his goods and his life to the last, but would await evidence requiring that. It was true they were encircled, yet these plainsmen came forward not with war-whoops but with studied attention. The way they eyed the ships told that they had seen such before. Let Davor, and the gifts they carried, speak for them.

Their escort was now doing just that. Davor had walked boldly toward the men, and was engaged in a guttural and hurtling discourse with two of them. All the horseman were dressed alike, in dark-hued open tunics which crossed over their chests and fastened with toggles of bone or antler. Their leggings were close upon their legs, and dark-tanned leathern boots rose almost to their knees. Their saddles seemed scarcely more than woven pads strapped over with bands of leather, but their stirrups, shiny and open-worked, were wrought with skill. Upon their heads sat peaked caps of sheepskin, with round brims of curly fleece shading their creased faces.

As he spoke to these plainsmen Davor kept his horn firmly in hand, and used it almost as extension of his arm to drive home his message. The two he conferred with had dropped the rein from their left hands, and were gesticulating with them just as freely. They pointed to the three horses Vermund had lent them, and much discussion ensued, with Davor speaking ever more rapidly in answer. Then the leaders' gaze was turned upon the crews themselves. It was hard to read what was transpiring; no anger showed upon the faces of the horsemen, so perhaps the party was not guilty of trespass. And the attitude of the other plainsmen surrounding them had changed. They let their reins go slack, and let the butts of their spears hit the ground to rest their arms.

After an anxious while Davor turned back to the ship crews. His face, which had been full of serious intent when approaching and dealing with the horsemen, now bore a wide grin. He allowed them to see it a moment, then resumed his neutral mien.

"You will give them gifts now," he instructed the captains when he reached them. "These are Khazars, horse traders, and they recognised our animals as theirs. I had to remind them my King had bought the beasts at good price."

Davor took thought before he went on.

"They are slavers, almost without equal. Their King has three score slave women to warm his bed, and five and twenty wives. Each of these women have a gelded man to guard them."

This made his listeners pause, if not at the number of females, then at the sheer quantity of men who had suffered the gelding knife under this King.

"They will let us pass unhindered?" Eskil asked, with a glance at the Khazars.

"They will only lighten your load of gifts," Davor returned. "As you will guess, they are proud of their women, who they keep well hidden. If you have more women's things as you offered to Vermund's wives and daughters, give them those. A bead or two to each man, and for the chiefs I spoke with, one of the silver coins each for necklaces. For as in all places, a man shows his prestige by decking his wife in beads and trinkets."

It took no more than this for Eskil and Runulv to retrieve their wooden boxes. The Khazars urged their mounts forward, and came one by one to receive the tiny bells, pierced silver beads, and finger rings of twisted silver the captains dropped, one from each, into their open palms. The two who led the tribe were each presented with two silver coins, ready to be added to a necklace by a hanging ring or sleeve. The older of these chief men flashed a smile as he accepted his, then lifted his hand to gesture to the three horses hobbled by the ships. He spoke something, which Davor told them of.

"Your horses. He says they are better than he remembered, and that he sold them too cheaply. But he wishes you good journeying."

The adventurers had known hot days and chill nights crossing the steppes. Now the rains began. The grasses they had trodden were flattened by it, and the ground oozed with mud. The horses, sturdy as they were, strained in their harnesses, ears flattened against the rain, and every man was needed to push. Brani had made this portage before, if not in such trying weather, and with Runulv hammered up a push-bar each for the stern of the ships. They were made of a spare oar, and had room for one man on either side of the keel. It was crushing work, and no one man could be at it long, but it spared the horses the greater strain. At times the rain pelted down heavily enough that the ships needed bailing, and so those slogging through the mud, guiding the ships with their hands, were also spelled by taking up buckets and scoops and tossing what water they could over the gunwale.

This went on for ten days. Vermund had provided them with the dung filled grass logs with which to boil their grain and soften the dried meat he sold them. In the driving rain no fire could be struck from tinder and flint, not even in the shelter of the hulls; the wet wind extinguished every attempt. The men were left to soak the leathery strips of meat they carried in cold water, making them barely soft enough to chew.

Their food stores were at the point of exhaustion, as were the sodden men themselves, when the skies cleared. Davor assured them they were not far from the trading post of Gnezdovo, and deep waters for their ships. And Fate favoured them. A small caravan of oxcarts appeared, flanked by men on horses. With them was a flock of some score of sheep, kept in check by two dogs. These were not Khazars; when Davor returned from his parley with them he told them they were Bulgars, heading back to their Winter quarters on the Volga River to the east. They had grain and sheep's cheese to offer in exchange for silver, but Davor could not persuade them to part with a single animal. Indeed, the sheep were fine beasts, with long waving fleece of white.

"In Gnezdovo you will have your fill of meat, and bread too," he promised, as they loaded the bags of grain aboard. The sheep's cheese was packed in skins of leather shaped like round boxes, for Davor said the Bulgars, often on the move, shunned anything so heavy as crocks.

Brani was near Eskil as Davor said this, and added his own promise in the ear of his captain. "If the Prince be the same as I saw on my last journey, you will be offered more than meat and bread." Eskil was eager to learn more, but Brani only grinned. The words of Mistress Ladja came to mind, but Eskil could not dwell on them. First they must reach the fortress.

The Sun had returned, and with it a wind that forced all to pull on their warmest woollens. It turned sharply cold, but that same wind dried all their belongings, their leathern packs paling as they returned to their original hue. Troublesome as they had been, the rains had served good purpose, for the straked planking of the ships' hulls was now as tight as if they had never left the waterways. On the overmorrow from their meeting with the Bulgars they came to a stream, broad and deep enough to lay the rollers and heave Death-Day in, and on the next Sharp Tooth was able to join her. Again afloat and rowing the men felt a kind of jubilation. They were no longer beasts of burden, like the horses walking alongside the banks. It was thus they saw the palisade of Gnezdovo rise before them.

Gnezdovo was ruled by a Prince, one Efim, whose expectations of Eskil and Runulv were greater than those of King Vermund. Davor had warned the nearer one came to Kyiv the steeper the tariff they would pay, for they grew near to Oleg, the Kyiivan King. Like that King, the Prince of Gnezdovo was Rus, and of Svear blood. The two captains were surprised at his youth, and Brani leant near both to tell them this must be the kin of the old man he had met on his last journey. Efim was of mid height, stockily built, green-eyed, and with a countenance that turned as rapidly from a scowl to a smile as did skittering clouds on a Spring day. His folk around and within the palisade were a mix of people, some amber-skinned and chestnut-haired, others with angled eyes and black hair. Slavs were there as well, in abundance, many with blue eyes and flaxen yellow hair, most of them seeming slaves by the plainness of their dress.

Prince Efim greeted all with an indulgent remark, asked of Vermund at Novgorod, and hearing he was well, demanded two full ingots of silver from each captain. He let it be known that half an ingot from each ship was collected as his own due to Oleg, the King of Kyiv. In return Efim was open-handed in refilling their supplies of wheat, and gave them sacks of millet and barley as well. He offered also additional casks of the meat of cattle, the flesh of which had been smoked, dried, and cut into long hardened strips.

The Prince bade them welcome with a reminder of his fore-sires, and a promise for their stay. "My father and his father before him were known for their unstinting hospitality. No man shall say the less of me."

First the party must wash, and don a greatly needed change of clothing. When afloat the men had ample water in which to wash. But weeks of hauling under a hot Sun with scant water supplies, followed by the mud of cold and soaking rains had done nothing to aid the men in basic cleanliness. The wash house at Gnezdovo was put to task with men and clothes being scrubbed. It offered a luxury few of the adventurers had encountered, a man whose sole task it was to cut hair, trim and shape beards and moustaches, and expertly clean, cut, and file fingernails. He was also skilled in lifting embedded splinters from calloused palms, extracting them with steel needles and pointed tip tweezers. Eskil, proud of his good looks as he was, availed himself at length of the steaming facility, and had the man employ his sharp shears to trim both his yellow hair and beard. Runulv too, aware of the roughness of his visage after these past weeks, had his hair cut, as did Berse. Gotlanders had a certain pride in how they presented themselves to the larger world, and it was only meet that they should sit at this Prince's table as the respectable and prosperous men they were.

Efim's hall was a large one, well filled with men and women when the travellers were summoned by the striking of a gong to join them. His men and women sat apart, men on the right side of the longhouse, and women on the left. The serving folk were of both sexes, and moved with deftness and speed amongst the tables lining the walls. The Prince sat in the centre of the high table, as expected, flanked by two of his body-guard. Eskil, Runulv, Berse, and Brani all sat to his left, the benches to his right being filled by his picked warriors, along with two men of considerable age who might have been aged kin or advisors. Davor and the two horse drovers sat with the rest of the party, scattered amongst the men of the hall.

Loaves of flat bread were carried out, with tubs of salted butter and crumbly dry cheese. Bowls of fresh fish stew were placed before them, and then another of pungent goat, boiled up with nutty millet. Into their cups of bronze was poured a grassy yet tangy ale, fresh enough to foam freely as it fell from the jugs the women held. Every man of them had lost flesh, and they ate their fill, and more.

When this was cleared away, small dishes were set before them, of dried fruit which had been boiled in honey and spice. Tiny spoons of white metal were furnished with which to scoop up this sweetness. Each bowl contained a single dark red clove, softened by cooking. None of Efim's guests failed to recognize it for what it was, and after the fruit had been swallowed, placed the clove into their mouths to savour as the delicacy it was. Some of those with wives at home almost had thought to set aside the clove to offer as a rare gift; Runulv was one, but warmed by food and drink, shook his head and with a smile to himself promised he would carry back at least ten cloves to Gyda on his return to Gotland.

It had grown dark during the meal, and oil cressets were lit by men who came with long metal holders, like those which hold rush lights. These cressets were fixed to the upright timbers supporting the roof, and cast their flickering glow over the heads of those who supped, almost as if they dined under moonlight.

At the end of the meal a troupe of musicians entered, playing as they did so, a raucous piping of shrill flutes, beating of skin drums, and clashing of brass cymbals. The last to enter was an old man singing in a reedy quaver. It was an assault to the ears of most of the crew, but those more widely travelled amongst them took it in for the entertainment it was. As they grew used to the din even those who had first grimaced at the racket were, after another cup of ale, nodding their heads in time to the frantic beat of the drums.

This went on for some time, until Efim of a sudden stood up, and clapped his hands. At this signal the music ceased, and every woman in the place rose, turned towards their Prince with a smile, and left. They were replaced almost at once by a different group of females, five in number, who tripped in, brightly clad in many layered skirts and shawls, with small head kerchiefs tied at the nape of the neck. Upon these kerchiefs was sewn a line of fringe, so that it fell upon the brows of the women, almost like their own hair. Their fairness told the guests that every one was a Slav, and all must admit they were an uncommonly fine group of women.

They wore wristlets of black fabric to which were attached countless little strips of silvery metal, which jingled and tinkled as they moved their supple wrists. They shook their hands in the air over their heads as they rushed in, filling the space with a chiming which seemed to shoot from their very fingers. They needed no such herald, for the eyes of every man in the hall were already fixed upon them. The musicians struck up at once at their entrance.

The women took their places in two rows before the high table, staggered in their placement so that each could be seen and appreciated by those seated before them. And they began to dance.

The women held their arms up in the air, while whirling so that their skirts flew up past their stockinged knees, to their bare thighs. Certain of their viewers found it difficult to resist the urge to duck their own heads low in attempt to glimpse more as the flurry of skirts and flesh whirled before them. The dancers dipped and straightened, took small jumps with pointed feet encased in shoes of coloured leather, and switched from front row to back and place to place so that it was hard to fasten the eye on any one of them. They wore smiles as fixed as their hands and bodies were fluid. At times they made sharp yawping cries, almost like that of birds.

None of Efim's guests had seen such dancing before, save Brani in Miklagårdr, whose grin was nearly as broad as the coast of the Black Sea it sat upon.

Despite the drink they had consumed the visitors refrained from calling out whooping cries of approval at the display; Brani had sternly warned them when in the halls of their hosts, they must observe the actions of their hosts and his own men. These sat watching, but with an air of cool detachment, which Eskil, at work trying to contain the widening of his eyes, could only ascribe to the regularity with which Efim's men were treated to such entertainments.

When it ended, the women dipped low to the table, then straightened up, panting in a way to further beguile their watchers, for their cheeks were now rosy from exertion.

Prince Efim rose, and addressed his guests. "My dancers will extend their talents to you, my guests," he told them, with a gesture to the four. "They will be yours for this night. But they must make the choice of which man they will pair with."

Indeed, the women were now standing in a single line, looking boldly at the men and unabashedly smiling at those who caught their eye. It was almost too much for the adventurers to believe, something out of the tales of Asgard, and the halls of Freyja and Odin.

Eskil, a great appreciator of female beauty, was nonetheless capable of being charmed by any of the women before him. Yet it was they, not him, who would choose.

Runulv stood up. He had enjoyed the display as much as any man. But the image of Gyda, and the boys she had given him, rose in his mind. With a bow to Efim he excused himself, and to his ship, grateful that the Prince had only smiled at his choice to withdraw.

Berse had been widowed for several years, but as his sons were grown, and he was of independent nature, had not found need to wed again. He was more than happy to remain, and winked at the women in hope of drawing one of them over. One on the end, slightly shorter and plumper than her sisters, smiled back.

Brani had not sat at the high table the last time he was here, under the protection of Prince Efim's late father. Nor had he been invited to share in any pleasures to follow. He was now more than eager to partake of this boon granted by their host.

There remained three guests, and five dancers. The women hesitated, a few of them whispering to each other and even blushing as they considered the adventurers who were all but beckoning to them at the table. At last one of the women tossed her head and walked, chin held high, to stand before Eskil. Her act prompted her sisters to do the same, and it was no little gratification to Berse that one in the middle came, nearly running, to choose him. Two more wavered before Brani, who awaited with a hopeful grin, and at the last moment one made decision and stepped towards the guide. It mattered not to Brani; the women were enough alike they may have been twinned.

It left one girl unpartnered. Berse turned his eyes to she who had first smiled at him, but then hesitated. He looked to Efim. "It would be a sad thing, and a discredit to us, to leave one of these beautiful women un-warmed tonight. I ask that she might join with her sister, and me."

Berse's companions turned to him. He was the eldest man at that table, and with his grizzled beard looked it. Those he had sailed with appeared to doubt the truth behind this seeming boast. Berse said nothing, but in response merely lifted an elbow off the table and flexed his mighty right arm.

Efim, who took seeming delight in much of what his guests said, again laughed, and slapped his hand upon the table. "If they are willing to share your favour," he returned, with a look at the two in question.

They were, and nodded their assent.

The dancers lodged in a women's hall set aside for such performers, and that is where they would escort their guests. They filed out, three of them, each with a dancer on their arm, and in the case of the blade-smith, one with an arm linked through each of his.

On the morrow Davor and the two drovers took their leave, heading back to Novgorod. The three horses still bore their slight harnesses, now augmented with a saddle pad and stirrups. Davor was heartily thanked by those he had escorted.

Efim joined in their leave-taking of Vermund's men, and ordered their food bags amply filled for their return. As they rode off the Prince, standing in the open gates with his guests, turned to Eskil. The Svear had spent a most satisfactory night, and Runulv had since joined them to break their fast and prepare their own departure. Even now both crews were at work on Sharp Tooth and Dauðadagr, carrying aboard food stores, and rolling casks of water up the gangplanks.

"Your man knows the way from here," the Prince suggested, in a voice that conveyed some little doubt.

Brani nodded. He had not been sorry to have Davor as escort, and he had tried to mark the ways in which they had travelled in his own memory. This was the third time he had made the journey from Staraya Ladoga to Gnezdovo, and each had traced a slightly different path. There was nothing upon the steppes to build marking cairns from, no stones to pile nor trees to fell and form into tripods. And with a change of seasons such could avail nothing. The snows would be mantling the plains upon their return, but snow and ice could give them faster hauling than ever the dried grass had given. Brani carried a smooth stick, and it was rather the act of notching into it that he logged the number of days' travel from post to post, and recording it thereupon. This, the Sun, and the stars at night he would depend upon. He cleared his throat and answered the Prince.

"The ways of the Dnieper I well recall," he offered.

This made Efim laugh. "Indeed. And if you have been twice through and lived, the river and its falls have taught you something worth the knowing."

The guide nodded, and soberly.

"I have enjoyed your company, and hope to see you on your return," Efim went on. "May the river Gods keep you." He turned his head to the men at their final lading, then back to the captains. "But – I think you fools for having no slaves, when you can buy so cheaply from me. The Pechenegs and other tribes strike when you are most vulnerable, at the unloading and loading of your ships along the way. If slaves are at this labour, you are free to defend both them and cargo."

Eskil listened, but then raised his hand to the statue in the stern of Death-Day. Prince Efim had before noted this carving, and its single eye of glinting quartz. "Odin, All-Father, watches us," Eskil asserted. "Also, in the matter of slaves, we have the favour of white-armed Freyja. Her watchful eyes will make up for the lack of them."

No one was more surprised to hear this than his companions. The Svear was not devout; he had offered a perfunctory fowl at their departure from Gotland, but his muttered prayer was no more than the words, To Odin. Other than the hard hauling of their wheeled ships the Gods had so far favoured this effort; perhaps it was this that gave the Svear a new confidence in their providence.

Both Vermund and Efim had offered them more than one night's shelter in their halls. The captains had demurred. Racing against cold weather as they were, they felt an urgent need to forge ahead. They were not half-way yet; at the next stop they could perhaps rest a few days.

Set off they must. Berse had parted with two of his green brass bells, a gift for each of the dancers who had graced him with their favour, and the women stood amongst the other well-wishers on the shore, chiming the tiny tongues of the clappers in farewell. The crews rowed but slowly downstream as they scanned for the tar pits both Brani and then Efim had told them of. The banks had been treeless for time out of mind, but a forest of pines must have grown here, to have sunk into the earth and by its natural forces rendered into tar. The place was easy to find, for a small open shed was there. Dauðadagr nosed to the bank, and half her men leapt off with buckets and wooden spades. Six buckets, three for each ship, were filled with the sticky substance, and wooden covers pounded over to keep the tar from oozing should the bucket be upset. Each ship had the shorn fleece of an entire Gotland sheep to mix with the tar, the best caulking any hull could want. Runulv, concerned with the abuse the ships might be subjected to, even to the dismantling of Death-Day, demanded no less than this.

TWO PRINCES

W HEN there was water enough, they hoisted sail, or on still days rowed. As they entered shallows half the men stood on deck, punting with their oars against the pebbled bottom. The second half leapt ashore to lighten the load. There, roped to the prow, they towed the drekars onward from the banks. Slogging through the water would have helped those aboard in their efforts not to ram the prow into the banks and lodge there, but the streams now ran cold, and boots and shoes rot and fall apart under such usage. The choice was to unload, heave the ships out, and haul them overland on their wheeled axles, or stick to punting and towing. Either was heavy work, but following dwindling water without running aground was the more exacting.

As the two captains considered their choices an answer appeared. The smell of a cook-fire one morning alerted them to a settlement ahead. Pushing on, they sighted peaked tents along the bank, and a number of horses browsing. Several were mares with this year's foals at their sides. Men arose from near the cook-fire, and came from the tents, led by an old man with a deeply creased face, and a white beard lying upon his robed chest. They were archers, with the swathed fabric upon their heads which marked certain eastern traders to be found in Birka or Ribe. Their turbans hid hair to their knees, Eskil had heard, and the curved swords at their sides held a razor's edge. Those aboard the ships called out to them, and were waved ashore.

Brani had no knowledge of their tongue, but the two captains, used to trading without words, gestured their need to buy horses. But the animals were not for sale, at any price. There was no silver Eskil could show their owners to part with a single one of them.

Besides their horses the men had trained falcons, hooded and tethered to uprights outside one of their several tents. Runulv had carried any number of goshawks raised and trained by his brother Ring to Paris, and his eyes were drawn to the spotted birds. One of the turbaned men stood near the falcons, and Runulv approached where the birds waited, talons hooked over their perches. The Gotlander had no desire to buy such a bird with much arduous journeying still ahead, and the take of a single raptor, no matter how skilled a hunter, would add nothing to the food stores required by so many. But his interest alone was enough for the man to launch into what seemed a detailed declamation of the falcon's abilities.

Runulv's admiration for the bird was such that their leader, noticing his regard, came and joined. The old man was nearly toothless, but despite his wheezing lisp, spoke with energy and apparent pride to Runulv. He then gave order to he guarding the birds, who vanished into a tent to return with a gauntlet of leather.

It was handed to Runulv, who, well familiar with raptors, pulled it on and extended his arm. The old man gently nudged the falcon onto the Gotlander's wrist so he might fully admire so fine a hunter. Runulv said just what he would have of any good goshawk, uttering words of praise.

All this was enough to soften the resolve of the old fellow, and he would at least use his horses to haul the drekars out, and on to their axles. Again the ships must be partially unloaded, the log rollers spaced and greased. Harnesses the turbaned men possessed, and made it clear through their gestures that when they struck their tents, the posts and fabric were pulled along in a kind of drag sledge over the grassland. It took all day for the crews to unload, haul out, settle the hulls into the axles, and then reload. By then the Sun was rapidly lowering in the sky, and they were invited to sup there on the banks. From Sharp Tooth and Dauðadagr came their tripods and cauldrons, grain and dried meat. Their hosts produced meal and salt, which mixed with water was deftly slapped into flatbreads and baked on slabs of smooth stone used as griddles. A golden oil poured from a small jug was dribbled over these, and then more salt. The crews had rarely tasted better bread. The same could not be said of the drink passed, fermented mare's milk which almost bubbled and crackled in the mouth. Yet drink they must, the grinning faces of their hosts demanded it.

The crews slept that night on the banks, wrapped in woollen blankets. In the morning both groups broke camp, but not before a long oration by their host's chief. None of the party knew what benediction or cautionary tale he was bestowing, between his gasps and wheezes. Then from a pouch at his waist, he pulled forth an even smaller folded piece of leather. From it he produced a gift each for Eskil and Runulv, placing it in their right palms. They looked down on a small circle of glass, like unto a finger ring.

Such rings were fragile and could only be worn at table, or likewise festivities. Runulv wondered if it might be a kind of pass, or safe conduct, which the old chief had bestowed on them.

"Kyiv," he told the captains, the first word he had spoken which they kenned. By pointing to his eye and then southeastward, he gestured his meaning.

Brani spoke for the old man. "You are to show them at Kyiv," he suggested.

Both captains nodded their heads in thanks. To keep the rings safe Runulv and Eskil tucked them in the inner slit of their belts, where nothing could strike against and shatter them. They must hold value, or the old chieftain would not have bestowed them as he did.

The captains countered with gifts of their own, a whole silver coin, pierced for hanging, from each.

But the old chieftain was not done. As he watched the men take up the pull ropes, and others prepare to push from the sterns, his eyes misted. He gestured to a younger man, who gave him a large leathern flask, which the old man then presented, head nodding, to the captains.

"Mare's milk," acknowledged Eskil, through gritted teeth.

"Well fermented," Runulv had to add.

They parted, the turbaned men on horseback, some with falcons on their wrists, the Svear and Gotlanders pulling and pushing their ships. The mounted group readied to turn their horses' heads east, the prows of the ships relentlessly south. Even with sails furled and masts lowered the wheeled ships were a striking sight, and the horsemen stood some time to see them off.

Berse, by dint of his age and general esteem, was relieved from the actual hauling, acting as goad and rhythm-keeper to the efforts, so that the men drove forward in time, just as they did at the oar block. He sang as well, the kind of working chant that men have ever laboured under.

Seamen all, they had become beasts of burden. The men pulling wrapped the hempen line, each to each across their waists and up across their chests, to lie against a thick pad folded from cowhide which reached from breast to shoulder. Those taking a turn at the push bars at the stern plodded forward, heads down, with arms fully outstretched. Their captains made sure that all men had equal time serving as lookouts aboard; save for a noon time break it was their only daily respite.

Every fourth day they had to stop and take a full day of rest, lest their aching backs and strained legs give out. Each dawn the Sun rose later to their right, and dropped quicker into the western sky. It grew cold enough at arising that the men donned heavy woollen tunics. With the hauling they were dripping with sweat an hour later, but harnessed as they were, could not strip down to their linen. At mid-day they freed themselves, and some even went shirtless to cool their skin. Then, when shivering, they pulled their woollen tunics back over their heads.

They still followed the waterway as they could. It split into many rivulets, and grew to marsh, driving them to firmer ground. As they moved forward the landscape began to change. From the endless plain of grass, clumps of bushes arose. Deer emerged, with spotted coats though they were grown animals. Burdened as the crew was, there was no going after them, and the beasts sprang away with all the speed and nimbleness of their kind.

"We are nearing two fortresses," Brani told them. Sure enough, by leading them slightly to the east, they discovered a larger watercourse, and began to follow it south. Within a day it widened into a breadth to support the hulls of their ships. They scouted onward, and finding a place where the bank was least steep, unloaded enough so they might haul the ships over and in. They were cautious in this, setting many lookouts, recalling the warning of Prince Efim that they were at their most vulnerable to attack while shifting cargo from land to ship.

"Our late start has served us well, so far," Eskil said to Runulv, as they prepared to again take up their positions in the stern by their steering oars. They had been able to obtain enough provender from the large settlements, and except for the errant arrow which had crossed Death-Day's prow early on, had met no resistance nor threat to their progress.

The water was deep enough to row, but without wind enough to sail. Still, time at the oar was welcome to men who had been bodily pulling and pushing the ships over uneven ground, and even more so as the current they now rode favoured them.

A burial ground came into view, along the eastern bank. A line of grassy mounds rose there, nearly touching each other, as if the folk they covered had been linked in life as they were in death. They saw why; there was further to the east, up a tributary, a palisade positioned well back.

"There will be ward-men here, guards to bring us to shore," Brani remembered. But in fact as they rowed along they saw no one, even at the mouth of the stream leading to the walls. The place was strangely silent, with none moving outside the palisade. The water was there so scant that they determined not to follow, but instead kept on for the second trading post Brani said they would find. They found they had made the right choice, as a smudge of smoke rose, telling of cook-fires ahead.

This second fortress stood on a rise above the plain, one more striking for the weeks they had spent traversing flat ground. The banks of the waterway grew sandy, and brown sand was seen along the trails leading up to the palisade. A stream cut through the bank, leading behind the fortress, a waterway too slight for any craft as large as theirs. The fortress ahead was a considerable one, and fenced all round with a spiked palisade. When the two ships were spotted from a tower fronting it, horns and whistles rang out, and these echoes had not died on the air before the gates were thrown open and a troop of horsemen, spears in hand, raced towards them. Both captains gave orders to ship oars, and both crews made haste in arming themselves.

Eskil had a war-kit befitting one who had served in the King of the Svear's body-guard, and his second in command upon Sharp Tooth now approached him, dragging the pack from the stern which held Eskil's ring shirt and helmet. The Svear had his eyes trained on the men now urging their horses towards the ships, and glanced down but a moment. He gave a single shake of his head, and strode forward to the prow, to be nearer Death-Day's stern. Every man of his had either spear or bow in hand, and those who owned helmets or war-caps had them upon their heads. Eskil had only his sword at his side, just as he had been wearing before the uproar. Shields were there for the taking; he walked past his.

Upon Dauðadagr its captain was even more lightly armed. Runulv wore no sword now, and had never possessed one. He had his knife at his waist, and was as handy with a spear as any Gotlander who earned his silver by trading and not raiding could hope to be. Berse was at this point once again upon the Gotlandic ship, and moved alongside his brother islander. The blade-smith was bristling with arms and armour of his own fashioning, making the contrast between him and the all but unarmed Runulv all the greater.

Runulv surrendered the steering oar to one of his crew, and both captains grew as close to the other as they could.

"Baying hounds or charging horses?" was the choice Runulv offered to the Svear, for it seemed these were how they had been greeted. But both men had time to exchange a grin before they turned to face the welcoming party.

Indeed, the leader of the troop of horsemen had reined in his horse, and now cantered up and down along the bank, taking in both ships. Forty-odd crew men, all armed, looked back at him. The leader turned his horse, an animal with a quantity of jingling silver ornaments attached to his traps, and rode back to the two men who held neither spear nor bow. He leant back in his saddle and considered the two.

The man who studied them was little more than a youth, but his mount, horse-trappings, and dress distinguished him as a chieftain. His hair was light brown, worn long under a peaked cap of some glossy black fur. Over his tunic was one of tooled leather, stained nearly black, and his weapon belts, holding knife and sword, sported silver buckles which gleamed in the weak sunlight. The spear in his fist was adorned with ribbands of red and yellow tied to the shaft, which streamed out in the breeze.

The young man had fastened his eyes upon Eskil and Runulv, but other than shifting his gaze from one to the next, made no move to speak or otherwise acknowledge them. The two captains for their part kept an easy attitude before those horsemen massed before them, Eskil going so far as to hook his thumbs into his belt as if bored.

"Hah!" the young rider exclaimed. His eyes were the blue-green of a turquoise stone, and they narrowed and then opened wide as he studied them. "Your men are armed and ready to fight. You two hold nothing, and only await me. You are their captains, and ready to trade."

He who announced this concluded with a smile of satisfaction at his findings. He now lifted his spear in the air, in a kind of salute. The fluttering ribbands touched the long and blowing mane of his horse, a dark bay, making the animal shake his head and sound the line of tiny bells affixed to his breast strap.

"I am Karlen, Prince," the young man told them. "My brother Demyan is also Prince. Follow me."

Karlen turned his horse and joined the rest of his men. On Sharp Tooth Brani had come up to Eskil. "He was a boy when I was here," he whispered. "But his brother, I remember. A hot-head, quick to take offense. Hedin had two slave girls, and was forced to part with them here."

Eskil took a slow breath. At least they carried nothing in that way these brothers could covet. The captain Brani had last sailed with lost first two women, and then his life, on his way to Miklagårdr.

The Svear and the Gotlander left the body of the crew onboard, again taking only Brani and Berse with them. They hoped to pay their due to continue their passage, re-provision the ships, and be on their way. As the four passed through the palisade gates they all shared a similar foreboding. The place had more the air of a garrison than any hall they had yet visited on this eastward route. There were few women and children to be seen, and those they glimpsed made haste to disappear into any near doorway, or slink behind some work shed. The life of the work yard was different as well; no coopers were at work, steaming and bending slatted wood into casks and barrels, no leather worker bent over a straddled bench cutting and stitching endless shoes or packs; even the noise from the kitchen yard, ever the hub of any settlement, was muted. Workers were there, slaves all by the look of them, trundling goods or prodding animals on their way.

The palisade they passed through was timber, as was the largest of the structures within, but most of the smaller buildings were cut of sod, thick blocks of it. These, like the timber hall, were roofed with a few precious planks of wood, then laid over with slabs of sod from which grasses, now yellowing, sprang.

The four walked in, escorted by Prince Karlen and his horsemen, who all but surrounded them. Nor did Karlen dismount when another man approached on foot. This was sure to be his brother, for he was dressed in the same fineness as was Karlen. The sword at his waist was one of exceptional worth; all could gauge that merely from the tooled sheath and silver-chased hilt. The man himself wore the same style of cap as his younger brother, one of dark and glistening fur. But his own hair was nearly as dark as the pelts his cap had been sewn from, and he was swarthy of skin. Only his eyes told of their kinship, for he had the same turquoise eyes, now turned upon those standing before him.

"I am Demyan, Prince," he said. "I want three ingots of pure silver from each of your ships for your passage, and one healthy slave each. Then I will permit you to buy the supplies you need, and tomorrow or the next day, continue down river."

The man had not even waited to be told their names and mission. The baldness of his demands was hard to hear; Runulv, known on Gotland for his even temper and coolness of head, found his hands instinctively clenching into fists. For Eskil, who had worked long years to control his own quickness to anger, it was even worse.

Yet the Svear mastered himself and spoke first. "I am Eskil, a Svear, and once a body-guard for Ivar, King at Uppsala. We have no thralls aboard." He tilted his head to he who stood at his shoulder. "Runulv is a free Gotlander, as are all his crew, and most of mine."

Runulv must speak. It would be a fine line between standing up to such a chief, and direct and dangerous insult, but he would try to draw it. "The silver we will pay, but not one of our men will we surrender." He let this rest a moment in the air before going on. "Know that Oleg, the King of Kyiv expects us, and will hear if we are delayed, or have complaint with how we were treated. For he will hear that Prince Karlen greeted us worthily, but Prince Demyan did not live up to his reputation."

At this last the other three from the ships looked quickly to Runulv, nearly jolted by his claim that the Kyiivan King was awaiting them. Karlen, still upon his horse, gave a laugh of approval as he looked down at Runulv.

Demyan squinted at the Gotlander. "Bosh! I no more believe you than I do the gibbering old sooth-sayers who read the entrails of birds. I demand a man each."

Eskil remained silent. Runulv had boldly spoken and deserved the chance to follow the path he had cleared. Berse squared up his sizable bulk. Armed as he was he did not think this mad Prince would try to claim him. But he was aware that with his special skills at the forge he might be such a forfeit.

The older brother's words gave Runulv pause, and put him in mind of one they had lately met. Runulv's hand went to his belt. Inside the slit secreted there lay the glass ring the toothless old chief had given him. Eskil, seeing what Runulv sought, drew forth his own ring from his belt.

Both men extended their palms to the Prince, so that he might see what they held. Those on horseback moved in a bit closer. Runulv let his eyes meet those of Eskil. Silence would be best, a silence that allowed whatever meaning was held in the glass rings to speak.

"Huh!" grunted Demyan. He shook his head as if to free himself of some unpleasant thought. When he spoke it was an entirely new question.

"What reputation," Demyan wanted to know. He was eager to learn more, and lifted his hand to the open door of the hall. It gave Runulv time to mutter to Eskil.

"Mare's milk," he said, in thankful memory.

※※※※※※※※※※

Their trials were not entirely over. At the Princes' table, over ale of remarkable bitterness, Demyan had another demand. Eskil and Runulv had already presented the three ingots of silver each, an eye-watering amount to hand over. Each was as long and as thick as a strong man's forefinger.

Demyan had closed his hand over them as soon as the scale had shown him full value. The brass armature and dishes still hung from a rafter above the table, and the place was smoky with burning tallow. Karlen was sitting with them as well, and had possession of the box in which the scale weights were kept. Demyan looked to his brother, who plucked out a good-sized cube of lead from the flat wooden box and placed it in one of the scale dishes, making the opposing arm swing high.

Prince Demyan took another swallow of his ale. The drink was bitter enough to seem poisoned to Berse and the two captains, and though Brani, tasting it, winced along with them, a nod of his head told the others this was in fact the local draught. Runulv was not alone in yearning for a deep cup of Rannveig's soft and herbal brew.

Demyan lowered his cup and looked first at his guests, and then at the scale. "You will take one of our men, with his horn, with you. He will blow it, alerting the Pechenegs that you are friendly to me. If you want his service, balance this scale in silver. If you do not, you are free to go, but you will likely die."

Eskil had heard enough. With some little effort, he kept his voice down. "We have just paid you six ingots of silver. Your man with the horn is part of that. There is no more we will pay, to reach the King of Kyiv."

This was decided enough that all eyes had shifted to the older Prince to see how he would react. Perhaps recalling the rings of glass he had been shown, Demyan offered another idea. "Then you will throw dice with me," he decided.

Eskil had to smile. As long as he kept his head clear he was a better than average dice player. He was of a sudden glad the ale had been so bitter. "I will game with you," he agreed. "But only for what we each stake."

The Svear was in good practice, for he had in fact been playing at nearly every day's end with certain of his crew, casting the dice upon a rare cleared area of the deck. Eskil won more than he lost, and did not mind now trying to take some silver from this arrogant Rus.

Svear and Rus reached for their belts at the same time. From his purse Eskil drew forth a small pile of coinage, whole and half pieces. Demyan produced a handful of finger rings, all of silver. From another pouch the Rus pulled out his dice, as did Eskil. There would be no confusing them, as those Demyan owned were nearly black, of jet or some other dusky stone. Eskil's were carved from walrus tusk, and were white, with the drilled holes designating numbers coloured red. The Rus Prince pushed his dice onto the table in front of Eskil.

It was common in every place the Svear had gamed that one check the dice proffered. A simple holding of the dice in the hand and rotating each one to make certain it carried the correct number of marks was the first test. As a young man Eskil had nearly throttled a dice player in Uppsala who was using a set with no sides carrying either one or two holes, and two which had been drilled with four and five. Another test was tossing a single die several times to see if its fall favoured a certain side. This was almost certain evidence that the die had been weighted with lead powder poured through the drill mark.

Eskil placed his dice before Demyan, and reached for those of the Rus. The man bared his teeth at this, with a grimace fierce enough that Eskil assumed this custom was entirely unknown here. That, or the dice of the Rus were fixed. He had no choice but to take up the dark cubes and play.

After a few throws, Eskil lost, then lost again. The grimace of the Rus was become a grin. After the third game the Svear pushed the black dice away.

"As your skill is so great, you will not mind playing with my own dice these next three games," he told the man.

Karlen honked out a laugh, and his older brother shot a glance his way, but was forced to rise to the challenge. Eskil won two of the next three games, enough to suggest to some at the table that either the black dice were faulty, or Demyan was favoured this night by an unusually strong hamingja, guiding his hand.

It took resolve for the Svear to call an end to play. He had begun to see a rhythm in the numbers and sequence the Rus called out, and felt a few more games might reveal enough that he could best the man at his own ruse. And end up with a slit throat, Eskil reminded himself.

As it happened, serving men were now come into the hall, dragging trestles in front of alcoves, hoisting table tops and benches and setting them in place. The afternoon had slipped away and the time to sup was upon them. Prince Demyan scooped up the silver he had won, and stood. Karlen stood as well.

"You four will stay here," Demyan told them, more order than invitation. Karlen softened this with his own words. "I will have food and drink sent to your ships, and eat with them myself. I have not been north of Novgorod, and they can tell me much." The young Prince flashed a smile. "I might even throw dice with them."

With this both Princes left them, amid the growing bustle of the coming meal.

"Will there be dancing women," Berse wondered aloud. They had heard the titters of females, coming from the hallways, which were screened from their view by thick curtains hung from brass rings and rods. He did not keep the note of hope from his voice as he said the next. "There might be entertainment ahead, such as that Prince Efim provided."

Eskil was quick to respond. "If there is, it would come with a hefty tariff," he reminded. "Better we sleep tonight, and push off as we can tomorrow."

Indeed, none of the four wished to spend another day in Demyan's company. His men filed in, and afterwards a quantity of women as well, who sat upon the opposite side of the fire-pit from the men. If either Prince was wed, no woman sat at his side, but the females seated together were in no manner worthy of scorn. The adventurers were guarded in how they looked at them, less they give offence, but all could discern they were women from many tribes and peoples, some fair-haired and blue-eyed, some with dusky skin and brilliant dark eyes, and still others with straight black hair and slanted eyes. The meal was of unusual savour, a thick stew made from the haunch of a deer, well hung, and with that pungent richness that aged meat imparts. For drink there was more of the bitter ale, made more palatable with such a highly-flavoured dish.

No entertainment was offered, and when Eskil deemed it appropriate he yawned mightily, signaling his need for sleep. The four expected they would be permitted to return to their ships and their men for the night, but this was not to be. They were escorted to a small timber building, no larger than a storehouse, given an oil lamp, and shut in for the night. The place was well outfitted with alcoves, bedding, and all needful for a night's sleep, but it was no consolation to hear a key turn in the box lock in the stout door, locking them in. There was but one small window, mercifully unlocked, but other than that they were veritable prisoners.

Berse spoke. "At least, as close to the barn as we are, they will not fire the house and roast us alive," he offered. At this Brani nearly upset the lamp, but caught it up in time to prevent it spilling and possibly igniting the planked floor. He had complaint of his own to make.

"And Karlen is out with the ships, gaming with our brothers, hearing and telling stories . . . " He needn't go on. All felt the youth was enjoying a far better time than the older contingent sequestered first with Demyan, and now locked in for the night.

In the morning, after all had broken their fast over bowls of boiled grain, Demyan spoke.

"Now you unload your ships."

Eskil and Runulv blinked in surprise. Before they could protest, Demyan stood up from the table and with a wave of his hand had them follow. The palisade gates, closed when the four had entered the main hall, were now opened, and they passed out onto the sandy roadway fronting the banks.

There in the water by the two drekars sat four small boats, and Demyan's men were even now ferrying more from the upstream tributary they had seen on their approach. Those vessels before them were nothing more than dugouts, fashioned from the trunks of mighty trees, which had been hollowed out. The two larger being brought were a kind of almost flat-bottomed river boat, which took well to shallow and often swift waters. Young Prince Karlen was one of the men within the lead boat making its way toward them.

The two captains took all this in, looking first at each other and then at Prince Demyan.

Demyan gave answer before they could speak. "These are your boats," he told them, pointing to the dugouts, and the larger boats now landing. "Those with flat bottoms we call karvs. You are thinking you can buy boats further down river. This late in the season you will find none to sell them. And if you could, they would not be as good as ours."

Eskil and Runulv turned to each other. Both feared this imperious Prince was about to exact even more silver for the use of these craft. Yet as Demyan went on, it became clear the dugouts and karvs were included in the three ingots of silver each captain had paid.

The older Prince had moved on, and was already gesturing to the crews of Sharp Tooth and Dauðadagr to begin their unlading.

"We will haul them up here," Demyan said, turning back to the two captains and then pointing to a wide swathe of sand running almost like a beach along the river bank. "If you return your ships will be waiting for you."

Eskil's mouth opened, ready to take issue with the speculative nature of this statement. Demyan gave a shake of his dark head and laughed. "Those of you who return," he amended.

This exchange was lost on Runulv. He was sorely aware that he must make decision now – forge ahead with

Death-Day, or leave her here on the shores to collect later. He stood on the bank, eyes shifting between the assembled dugouts and the two karvs. The dugouts were primitive craft, but all knew of their toughness and buoyancy. The karvs looked little more than barges with higher hulls, but came with masts and a sail, both now lying flat on their decks. The Gotlander's eyes shifted to Dauðadagr. She was small for a drekar, but none seeing her could question her sleek beauty, nor the quality of her workmanship. And he had at this point spent long weeks sailing her, and even hauling her, to reach this river bank. His trading knorr at home felt a trusted friend, but this small drekar had become akin to a lover. His eyes lifted to the carved wooden form of Odin, stalwart in the stern, his one quartz eye glinting.

Runulv shook his head. He looked for, and saw Brani, and waved him over. He had but one question for the guide.

"You have done this journey before; can Dauðadagr endure it?"

Brani drew a breath, and let it out in a great and audible sigh. His own eyes went back and forth, gauging the size of the larger of the river boats to that of Death-Day. At last he spoke.

"She cannot; not all the way. There are rapids and cascades ahead, and much portage. We will have to carry and drag the boats down steep paths, and in other places lower them with ropes from cliffs. There is one waterfall, called Aeifur, so high, we will have to break her apart to lower her."

Runulv, and Sidroc too, had been warned of this. But they had rivets and tar aplenty aboard, and Berse and his kit to forge any fasteners they lost in the process.

To one side of them Sharp Tooth was alive with her crew moving chests, casks and crates forward, ready to be lowered to the waiting banks, and then loaded to the smaller vessels. Runulv's men had begun the same, but now had slowed, watching the uncertain look on their captain's face as he stood with Brani.

"I want to take her as far as I can," Runulv answered. He looked again at the dugouts and karvs, then back to Death-Day. He could not leave her here, not this soon.

"We will take all the offered boats. Even if we must leave Dauðadagr behind at some point, those of us aboard her could continue on in the karvs and dugouts."

He drew closer to his ship. "We will take Dauðadagr," he told his waiting crew. Runulv was not a little gratified that a cheer rose from the throats of a few of his men, and one of them, standing in the stern, placed his hand on the carved beard of All-Father and made as if giving it a celebratory tug.

"We must lighten her as much as we can, to give us a shallower draught," he ordered next.

Eskil, busy directing the unlading of Sharp Tooth, heard this, and absented himself to join Runulv. Prince Demyan was himself fully engaged in the task of emptying the ship, directing its crew to line up the goods to be transferred on the bank.

"We are taking Dauðadagr," Runulv told Eskil. "And every boat offered to us."

The Svear was not surprised. Runulv had warned that he would not be easily parted from the ship he had been entrusted with. For Eskil and the much larger Sharp Tooth there was no choice.

Now young Prince Karlen jumped down from the river boat he had been guiding, and neared. He was grinning, the wind blowing his long hair in a line of soft brown from under the rim of his dark furred cap.

Karlen came to stand before the two captains. "You would not pay for a guide of my brother's choosing. So I will go."

These words from the younger Prince startled them as much as the order to unload their ships from the elder brother. Karlen went on, still grinning.

"I will take you to Kyiv, if the river Gods will it, but I can go no further. It will take us forty days if we meet with no trouble. At Kyiv I will leave you. You must face the Dnieper and her rapids alone. I will live there in Kyiv with Oleg the King until you return. If you do not," he added thoughtfully, "Oleg will send me back when he can."

The young Prince went on, in further explanation. "Some traders we never see again. They are swallowed by the rapids, or killed by Pechenegs, or thrown into viper pits for false dealing in Miklagårdr." He smiled again, the careless smile of a youth who still believed none of these things could happen to him.

"Why?" was all Eskil could ask.

"Winter is coming. I have nothing to do here," came the answer. "And I passed last night amongst your men, and heard much from them of Gotland, and of the Svear.

"My mother is full Svear," Karlen went on. "She traded at Birka, forming beads from glass rod. Before my father became Prince he went there to trade furs, met her and brought her back."

Karlen pulled at a cord about his neck, which once revealed, held three cylinders of swirled and coloured glass.

"This is her work, what she was making when he walked into her stall and saw her." He glanced over to his older brother, haranguing the men of Sharp Tooth as they passed goods and supplies over the gunwale and to the bank. "He was Demyan's father too. You passed his grave when you floated past those mounds up river. But my mother lives, and is in the women's hall, with my sisters."

Neither captain was sorry to hear this young Prince would be their guide. As he was to go with them, once again Runulv must speak of Death-Day. "I am taking my ship," he told Karlen.

The Prince paused but a moment, before he grinned again. "If she were mine, I would take her too," he affirmed. A moment later he was deep in thought.

"You are two and forty men," Karlen told them. "Four in each dugout; eight on each karv. Ten on your war-ship."

Demyan had now joined, and was told that only Sharp Tooth would be left behind in his care, while Death-Day would sail onward. To Runulv's surprise, he only shrugged his shoulders at this boldness. "If she makes it to Miklagårdr you will be a fine sight, sailing before those great walls of stone," he said. He looked to his younger brother.

"If I do not let him go he will only make mischief here," he told the captains. He looked to his brother. "You had better bring me something rare from Kyiv," he urged, which only made Karlen laugh. A moment later Demyan had turned back to the task of ordering the ships.

Of the two karvs, one would serve as vanguard and lead. The four dugouts would follow, then the second of the karvs. Death-Day would bring up the rear.

Once again the notched rollers were brought forth, so that Sharp Tooth could be pushed and pulled out of the water and onto the sandy beach awaiting her.

Then began the labour of sorting and lading. Sharp Tooth's oars would be left behind, but each dugout came equipped with paddles, and plenty of hempen line with which to securely lash cargo. The two karvs, with their nearly flat hulls, had their own masts and sails, the mast lying flat by the keelson, the sail furled upon its spar next to the mast. These must be inspected, the mastlock checked for cracks, the sails unrolled upon the grass to make certain they were sound.

Eskil and Runulv took pains to divide what they carried. Most of the more valuable of the trading goods would be placed on Death-Day and the two larger boats, with smaller quantities of food and other supplies. Each of the crew would have his own sea chest on the boat he would man, and each of the seven vessels receive provisions appropriate to the number of crew they carried.

"Unless we are well-favoured, and no river God envies us, we will lose one boat at least," Brani cautioned. This occasioned more re-packing, scrambling through the packs, placing smaller amounts of their rarest and best trade goods in the dugouts as well. It was both taxing mental work and demanding manual labour to do this, and by the end Eskil and Runulv barely had memory of which goods were on which boat, so alike were the many wooden casks and chests and leathern packs now divided between them.

Karlen and Demyan, familiar with the vessels, directed the lashing of the goods into the dugouts, forming a near-netting of hempen line around them, for as Karlen pointed out, "When you meet fast water it is too easy to lose cargo."

It prompted a question from Eskil. "Should the men be lashed, each to each?"

Karlen shook his head. "They will just be dragged into rocks, and killed the quicker. Better for them to be thrown free. They might surface near enough to shore to pull themselves out."

Runulv could not help wishing Karlen could make the entire passage to Miklagårdr with them. The young Prince spoke so easily of the hazards ahead, as if immune to such handling. If his youthful confidence served as protection, let it extend to all, thought Runulv.

They set off, later in the day than any had hoped, but with an eye to making use of every daylight hour. Eskil helmed the lead river boat, and gave a long look back at Sharp Tooth, keel over and alone on the sandy shore. Forsaking her was harder than he had thought. Then he must turn his eyes down river, and to the convoy he led. Instead of two vessels, they were now seven, and Runulv on Death-Day, bringing up the rear, was scarce within hailing distance. Karlen went with Eskil in the van, ready with his brass horn to sound their approach. In fact, the Prince had two horns, one looped over his shoulder and secured to his belt by a tether, and a second he produced from his pack. Brani, it was decided, should sail with Runulv. They had but two guides; should they lose Karlen in the first boat, Brani would be tasked with getting them to Kyiv.

After weeks of plodding progress, the swiftness with which the small boats moved came as a freeing sensation. Runulv must keep Death-Day in the very centre of the waterway, its deepest channel, while the dugouts and almost flat-bottomed karvs nearly sprinted ahead. The current bore them southward, eager, it seemed, to speed them on their way.

None of the craft save Death-Day was large enough to sleep aboard, and after Karlen had blown signal with his horn, they landed at dusk each night to set camp on the banks. There they kindled fire so they might eat and warm themselves, and sleep ashore. On the fourth day out they awoke to snow.

THE KING OF KYIV

SNOW kept falling, first in wet and clumping clots, then as it grew colder, in flakes like bushels of down tipped from the sky. Yet it did not impede their progress. If anything, it made the route clearer, the white-mantled banks standing in sharp contrast to the dark water. It allowed them to sail longer into the dusk. In boats so small, the flotilla moved with more swift assurance than it had since crossing the Baltic and entering the gulf leading to Staraya Ladoga. With the current in their favour, the men in the dugouts need do only light paddling. Those in the karvs could use the sail, which grew half-frozen in the wet, but still caught the wind blowing from the west. Only Runulv, standing steadfastly at Death-Day's steering oar, had a hard time of it. He used the ochre and white sail but sparingly. So narrow were certain parts of the passage he dare not risk any loss of control. Eight of his nine crew manned the oars at their rowing blocks. The last stood, oar in hands, at the prow, ready to push Death-Day's hull from any shallow which might snag her. In this they had the advantage of following in the wake of the boats before them, but they must remain mindful of the drekar's deeper draught.

The stillness surrounding them was broken only by their own voices, and the sounding of the brass horn Prince Karlen held to his lips. To some eyes it might have seemed he blew it at random, but when Eskil questioned him he laughed.

"The Pechenegs are active now, even in snow. Late in the year as it is, other hostile tribes have left the river banks to return to their Winter quarters. But the Pechenegs – they are everywhere."

"Why do they not show themselves," the Svear asked. Eskil even turned his head at this, looking port and then starboard at banks holding little but snow.

"They will," Karlen assured him. "They have spotted us, and heard my horn. They are massing down river, or deciding amongst themselves who will have the pleasure of meeting us."

"Will they be in boats?"

Karlen gave a shake of his head. The furred brim of his cap was laden with snowflakes, and some of them took flight at his action.

"They will emerge in narrow places, where we must slow, or places screened by rock."

"Have you fought them?"

Karlen's eyes widened. "The Pechenegs? Even King Oleg does not fight them. There is no fighting them; they are too many, and too fierce. Their Gods are their own, and demand that they eat the flesh of the men they take in battle. There is no ransom, or slaving for them, only that one end. And there is no trade without them, so all pay to pass down their waterways."

Better friends than enemies, thought Eskil, though it seemed none but their own could be truly called a friend to such a folk.

Though snow now blanketed the ground, it was not so sharply cold that the crews had recourse to the wolf-skin suits they had procured from Vermund. Northmen all, they were supplied with tunics and leggings of heavy wadmal, woollens densely woven and warm even when wet. There was not a Gotlander amongst them who did not carry sheep-skins of their curly-fleeced lamm for added warmth, fashioned into sleeveless tunics or merely fastened whole around the shoulders with a broad bronze circular pin. And all the men sported what furs they owned, those they had taken in the hunt themselves, or had traded for. Caps of squirrel or beaver, necklets of foxtail, cow and deer-hide leather mittens fashioned by wives and mothers, lined with furred hare-skin. Some men had prized seal-skin capes to shield them from the rain, and all had hide ground cloths, thick blankets, and sheep-skins to warm them in their sleep. They slept four to a tent, save the men aboard Dauðadagr, who bunked down on the deck between bales and casks, and under the slight shelter of oiled tarpaulins. Their cook-fire was kindled under an open lean-to. Under its shelter a large iron cauldron could be filled with grain, dried and smoked meat or salted fish, and for the first weeks, chunks of cabbage, beetroot, turnip, and onion from the stores of Gnezdovo. There was now shrubby growth and saplings along the banks, and every dusk more was gathered and cut and laid to dry by the fire, ready to be fuel itself next night.

The snow stopped, but the wind from the west continued. As they paddled and oared down river, weak sunlight returned, enough to melt the fallen mantle of white.

"There will be more," Karlen cautioned, one night as they sat around their fire. The ground was sodden, but only the smallest ridges of snow could be seen, well away from the river bank. "But once you make it down the Dnieper, the weather will warm again. In Miklagårdr it snows but rarely, and on the other side of it, it is Summer all year round."

This could scarcely be believed, but Karlen went on before he could be questioned. "You will only be allowed a month to trade in Miklagårdr; then you must leave. When you return you will be in the depths of our Rus Winter. If the Dnieper is frozen enough, you will speed along on ice. On the rim of the Black Sea you will find tribes from whom to buy long skis. Fitted to axles such as you have, you can push the boats along with tamps attached to your paddles, almost as quickly as if you yourself wore skates of bone.

"But if the ice is not thick, or if it is rotten in places, you run the risk of the hull falling through. Your men will be thrown from the boats into the ice water, and quickly die."

There were no grim tidings the young Prince could not smile at, and he did so now. It was a habit of youth that the older men had become accustomed to, especially those with sons of their own.

The Moon had gone from crescent to full and waned to half when the Pechenegs appeared. The flotilla was nearing Kyiv, and all save the Prince had almost taken hold of the belief that their progress had in fact been undetected.

The tribe came upon them near dusk, as they slowed, looking for suitable ground to make their camp. Karlen had warned the Pechenegs would surprise them at an awkward moment, and they were in the act of navigating around a small island, up thrusting in the waterway at a bend in the course. The island itself was no more than an atoll of four horse-lengths long, and no more than two wide, but it was set with boulders, carried there from a time of greater river flow, and crowned with a copse of now-barren birch trees. Karlen directed Eskil to stay to port, naming it as the deeper of the channels, but gestured that the smaller dugouts could pass on the starboard side of the islet.

Through the gathering gloom, Runulv could still see that Eskil's river boat had taken the port channel, and he guided Death-Day slowly forward, her men all standing at the gunwales and punting. Ahead they heard Karlen's horn ring out, signal at this time of day to both the flotilla and any who might be watching and awaiting them. The time to land was nigh.

By the time Runulv emerged round the islet, he saw the boats before him beginning to land on the western bank. A clearing was there, free of reedy growth at the water's marge, and the worn bank itself having shown much evidence of having been used to haul the prows of small craft upon. There was more to see than this. A line of figures now stepped forward from the scant growth at the edge of the clearing. They may have been sitting or lying in wait, but now they arose, two score or more of men. A moment later they had drawn their bows from their backs and nocked an arrow into every bow string. They took aim, an arrow for every man upon the landing boats.

Karlen had ceased blowing his horn, and now let out a sharp cry of recognition. He was in the bow of the karv Eskil captained, and the Svear in the stern at the steering oar. Without looking back to Eskil the young Prince leapt down from the bow and onto the bank.

Karlen took a few steps forward. He had let drop his horn, which hung from its tether from his shoulder, and though he wore a sword, left his hands empty as he approached.

In answer the archers moved forward as a single man. It allowed all those still aboard to see them more fully. The men were dressed nearly alike, in long robes which crossed over at an angle in the front. The opening of the robe left their tightly clad legs free for rapid movement. Angular caps of some stiff material crowned their heads, with an upturned brim and peaked top. These caps were dark, as were their robes, but the belts circling the archers' waists were of brightly dyed leather, in red, blue, or rich brown. Under their caps dark hair streamed over their shoulders, and their beards, though wispy, reached nearly to their belts on some of the elders.

As the archers moved nearer Karlen, their encampment was revealed, a series of conical tents pitched in staggered order. It was clear the boating party would have been stopped here regardless of their own need to eat and take shelter for the night.

One of the archers had now broken from the line, and went to meet Karlen. The man still held his bow before him, arrow at the ready, until he was within a man's length of the Prince. Karlen did not speak as he awaited him, and those afloat behind him had cause to mutter an admiring word at the young man's pluck.

When the leader had spent a moment looking into the face of the Prince, he spoke. It was a tongue unknown to all upon the boats, but Karlen answered, and with certainty of tone.

The Pecheneg chief answered, and this made Karlen turn back to those awaiting him. He pointed to Eskil in the lead boat, and Runulv on Dauðadagr. He gestured both join him. Eskil jumped down upon the bank. Runulv had Death-Day brought ahull one of the dugouts, and lowered himself into it, and from thence to the bank. Though Prince Karlen had motioned only the two captains ashore, two more men followed, not to be denied. Berse was close on the heels of Runulv, as was Brani in following Eskil. They moved forward, to stand slightly behind the captains, a supporting presence in the face of the fierce Pecheneg glaring at them.

They stood there, five, fronted by Karlen; and the Pecheneg chief, backed by perhaps five and forty. Daylight was fading, each moment growing dimmer, which to those waiting to hear what the demand might be only seemed to increase the sense of threat.

Karlen and the chief spoke more, then the Prince turned back to the two captains.

"He says you have gold."

"I do not have gold," Runulv responded, with some little edge in his voice.

He could have almost laughed at this. The single goal of this trip was to return with goods that would earn them gold. But despite the worth of everything that Sidroc had loaded upon Dauðadagr for Runulv to trade, there was no gold amongst it.

They watched Karlen turn back to the chief and speak, gesturing to him. The Pecheneg responded, going on at some length, until his pause allowed Karlen to answer. The chief replied, never lowering his nocked arrow, pointed at Karlen's heart.

The Prince listened, nodding, then turned again to the four behind him.

"Without gold you will forfeit a tenth-part of all you carry. You will be stopped down river by their brethren and asked again. If you produce no gold, you will lose another tenth of your goods. This will go on until you are left with nothing, only your lives. If you still have gold amongst you hidden, then you will all die."

This demand was left to settle in their ears a long moment. Runulv cast his eyes about, as if for answers. It led him to speak.

"Why gold?"

It was not a foolish question; they could give a fourteen-weight in silver to equal a weight of gold. Both captains had sharp memory of the weighty ingots they had already parted with.

"Gold comes from the Sun," Karlen answered. "Also it is the most precious of metals to all men. The Pechenegs extract that which you most value, which is why the last price would be your lives."

"I have no gold."

It was all Runulv could say, for it was the truth. There was no use in turning to Eskil. He knew the stake the Svear had put up was his ship and his ten men. The Dane had supplied all else.

Karlen was relating this to the Pecheneg chief when Berse spoke. He had well noted the ragged condition of the Pechenegs' hair and beards, and took thought.

"Your box," he instructed Runulv. "No man who owns clean-cutting shears would have so ragged a beard. They are cutting their hair and beards with their knives. Offer him those."

The blade-smith said only this, then strode back to the bank, there to order that Runulv's treasure box be handed down. He returned to find all eyes turned to him.

He stopped before Runulv, who made a small nod to the Pecheneg chief, and lifted the lid.

Runulv drew out a large pair of iron shears. He turned them in his hand, so that the looped handles were foremost, and respectfully offered the gift to the chief.

There was no disputing that he was well pleased with the iron cutters. The chief snapped the blades together a few times, listening to the click of the handles as the blades met. He held them out to a few of his men who had drawn nearer. The chief even pulled up the tip of his beard, and tested the sharpness of the blade upon it. A finger's length of scraggly beard fell to the damp ground. He smiled at the result.

As momentary distraction the shears served their part. But such a gift was not enough. After the initial show of pleased acceptance with the shears, the chief fastened them to his belt by the tail of the leather strip spanning his waist. He then returned to the requirement that gold must be forthcoming.

"He says he will number all your packs and chests and casks, and seize one tenth part of them at random." Karlen thought about this, and added on his own, "You might lose some of your stock fish, of no real value save that you count on it against hunger. Or he might carry off the chest filled with blades forged by our friend here," he suggested, with a look at Berse. "Not a treasure you wish to part with, this far from Miklagárdr."

The four men looked at each other, and then glanced over to where their brothers waited, watching from the boats. Each captain felt assured that none of his crew possessed even a grain of gold. Yet they might be forced to ask, thus revealing they were taken by surprise at this demand. The Pecheneg chief, tired of waiting, turned towards the boats as if ready to begin his selection.

Eskil made a move. His hand went to his belt, not to the purse which held his silver, but to the second pouch, in which he kept fire-striker and flint, his dice, and a few talismans he valued. He fished about, and pulled out a tiny leathern drawstring bag. Heaving a sigh, he pulled it open and showed his fellows what lay in his palm.

It was a tiny golden figurine, an idol of some kind, with a bald head, round belly, and arms outstretched. It was smaller than his thumb, but being of gold, was the greater part of his personal stake.

The Svear now held it out between thumb and forefinger. They heard his sigh as he extended his hand to the Pecheneg chief as an offering. The effect was immediate.

The chief took it and held it up before him, occasioning those men nearest to him to gather closer that they might see. A stream of excited words fell from the chief, the tone alone indicating his excitement.

While the Pechenegs gathered about their chief, acclaiming at the tribute just handed over, the Svear spoke in a low tone to his fellows.

"I took it from the body of Ivar, when he was killed," Eskil admitted. "I do not know what it is. Some small God."

"No lesser God," Runulv corrected, "to be wrought of pure gold."

The Svear must nod agreement to this.

Runulv had another thought. "Ivar, your King?"

"Já. Ivar, King of the Svear." Eskil's eyes shifted to the Pecheneg chief, holding the idol aloft in admiration. "But he died like any other man."

"Well," the Gotlander summed. "It – and Ivar – served you well now. All of us."

After this the Pechenegs seemed almost to ignore them. Despite the growing darkness, neither of the captains wanted to remain at the clearing, yet Karlen cautioned that the Pechenegs must be the first to depart. All Runulv and Eskil could do was begin to set their own camp for the night, hewing to the bank and close to their boats.

Deeper in the clearing, the Pechenegs moved about, striking fire and filling their own cauldron. The rising aroma was savoury of smell, but the adventurers were too distant to see with what they filled it. When it was quite dark and their own browis almost ready, a Pecheneg approached, and summoned Karlen and the two captains to follow him. They rose, with both captains casting a look back at the men they left.

Once around the Pecheneg fire, they were seated opposite the chief. The rising steam from the bubbling cauldron helped to disguise their unease, or so they hoped. Only Karlen seemed unconcerned, his face as open and expectant as ever. A bronze ladle was dipped into the steaming mixture, and wooden bowls and spoons handed first to the chief, Prince Karlen, and the two captains. All the other Pecheneg warriors then were handed bowls. The Pecheneg chief said something, a sharp and high cry, perhaps a benediction of some kind. Then he lifted the bowl close to his mouth and began spooning the contents.

Within was a gruel studded with thick chunks of meat.

"What is this," Eskil wondered aloud.

Runulv was thinking the same. When amongst strange tribes, they must accept food and drink to avoid offending their hosts. Even the pungent mare's milk, fermented as it was, could be tolerated, if drunk between spoonfuls of stew. In Paris Runulv had spoken to traders who watched men roast snakes and eat their flesh as a delicacy, and were forced to feign pleasure when offered a taste. But then he thought, this was not too far from the relishing of fingerling eels, which all enjoyed. And most men on long hunting trips, when warring, or in hard times at home would catch and eat anything which would not poison them. Extreme hunger would drive any man to eat the flesh of animals even repugnant to them. But this from the Pecheneg's cooking pot which they all chewed . . . it was not horse-meat, he felt sure, though it had a certain sweetness to it. Then Runulv decided it was indeed the flesh of a horse. Recalling what he had been warned by Efim, he would rather think that.

Eskil's thoughts ran in a similar track. They had glimpsed the ruddy spotted deer, unlike the animals hunted at their homes; perhaps it was this. As Eskil took another spoonful he glanced over at Karlen. The Prince had his eyes lowered, and was chewing thoughtfully. Perhaps, it struck Eskil, even reverently.

A second bowl was happily not pressed upon them, and they rose when the Pecheneg chief nodded dismissal. They made their slight bows to their hosts, and returned to their own cook-fire. There had perhaps never been a night when either Eskil or Runulv had wished so much for a cup of ale, or better, strong wine, to wash away the flavour in their mouths. They did not speak of this, or wonder together about the nature of what they had just partaken. Speaking of things only made them more real.

They awakened to an icy dawn. The Pechenegs were all afoot, had struck their tents, and looked ready to depart. There was no sign of a cook-fire having been kindled by them, no smell of a browis or porridge or anything else warming upon which to begin the day. Eskil and Karlen shared a tent, and as they rose from it the Svear spoke. "No breaking of the fast, for them?"

Karlen shook his head. "They take but one meal a day, at dusk. The one we shared with them. King Oleg told me that the Pechenegs find eating more often a waste of their time. They travel vast distances in a day." Those before them looked ready to vanish behind the skeletal saplings by which they had made their camp.

All Eskil could do was lower his head, and give it a shake.

"I know we could not make a start on an empty belly," he said. His men were already poking up the fire from the night before, to heat their porridge. They had started it last night, filling their largest cauldron with river water, and dropping in barley. When it had been brought to the simmer, a griddle was laid on top, to keep rain or snow out. Now it needed only re-warming.

The Pecheneg chief called out to them, and Karlen rose to meet him. He was gone only a few moments, and as soon as he had turned back to the bank, the Pechenegs moved into the trees.

"He gave me this, to show, if we are stopped by their brethren," Karlen explained, holding up a small, flat, woven pouch. It looked formed from something akin to tablet woven bands, and had a thin plaited loop so that it could be worn around the neck. From the bottom of the small pouch was suspended a dark tassel of some kind, the length of a man's hand. It looked almost like the tips of a horse's tail. Eskil touched it. It was not. Each strand was much too fine to be horse tail. It was the hair of a man, or woman.

Karlen's fingers had gone to the top of the pouch. It was to his surprise, sewn shut, and not a real pouch at all. It felt nothing was within.

"Only evil spirits," the young Prince suggested. "We will not cut it open, to see."

Those listening had nothing to say to this. Yet Karlen slipped the suspect pouch over his head without comment. Now the Pechenegs were well out of sight he gestured to Eskil and Runulv. Karlen pulled his furred cap from his head, and stuck his hand inside the woollen lining around the brim. He held a single large coin of gold in his fingers.

"You would not have ended up in that pot," he assured them. And he grinned.

⚬⚬⚬⚬⚬⚬⚬⚬⚬⚬⚬⚬

The days had grown short. With a waning Moon and unknown territory, camp must be set early and struck late. The waterway opened by stages into a broad river. There was more wet, in the way of sleet, at times driven nearly sideways by a wind blowing from the west. Any day cold enough for light snow to fall was counted as a relief. Snow could be shaken off or brushed away. By the time the fortress of Kyiv came into sight the band was exhausted, hungry, and travel worn. Some of them were on their second and thus last pair of boots, the first having disintegrated after hauling the ships through waterways and soaking steppe land, and now enduring near-continual wet due to the slight shelter of the open dugouts and karvs. Crowded as all the craft were with crew, goods, and supplies, it was nigh impossible to afford any protection to the men within. Cowhides and oiled tarpaulins lashed over their trade goods were re-tied to give the men's feet some coverage, but the need for each crewman to paddle unfettered limited the protection any such covering could give.

Prince Karlen had known the same hardship as all of them, and though no hope of fabled reward awaited him in Miklagårdr, he relished the outing as the adventure it was: a group of men, of which he was assuredly the youngest, undertaking travel through lands rife with watchful enemies, in an unforgiving near-Winter landscape. He could join them for this one leg only, but circumscribed as the Prince's life was, he avidly partook of their shared fortunes.

Karlen sounded his horn as they approached, and in response the flotilla was led into a tributary off the main waterway, where every man of them was waved ashore and through the palisade gates. Kyiv gave them a welcome like no other.

The settlement sat on a considerable rise, affording it a far-reaching view of the vastness of the river and the land around it. It added as well to its seeming importance. A fresh fall of snow mantled both banks, and had settled upon the edges of the palisade walls. Arriving within they found it to be not much larger than the fortresses in which Karlen and Demyan, Efim, Vermund, and Lady Ladja held sway. But Kyiv was conspicuously richer, both in folk and goods. Behind the palisade was a veritable marketplace, a host of stalls and workshops, all crowned in white from the snow still blowing through the air. Most were quiet now, but in Summer the place would have thrummed with traders. For some Kyiv was the terminus of a merchant mission, the goal for many heading from the north or south, also for the plainsmen travelling from the east or west. And it would be here the band of Svear and Gotlanders would pick up the river Dnieper.

Its King, Oleg, was a man in his fourth decade. He looked Svear, with fair hair and a beard just showing grey at the chin. He strode towards the arrivals, dressed in a heavy tunic of quilted leather, a cap of white fox fur upon his head. He greeted Karlen with the joy of an uncle, holding the young man by the shoulders, and kissing him on both cheeks, something only Runulv had ever observed on his travels.

"I am Oleg," he told the newcomers, his hand still on Karlen's shoulder. "We are the Kyiivan Rus, and I their King. I have been so since Karlen was a small boy. My people are Svear, Slav, Severians, Dregoviches, and Magyar – every sort."

And of every sort they were. Despite the cold, many had followed their King out to greet the visitors. As far as dress and features, it seemed representatives of each tribe the crew had encountered were here, living at Kyiv. The notable wealth of the place was seen at once in the costume of the many women about, brightly garbed and with heavy rings of silver about their necks. Each one looked a full ingot's worth, by Runulv's reckoning, and some women sported several. Karlen gave answer to Runulv's questioning look. "Their husbands know success in trading, and compete to show this in how much silver their wives bear."

Runulv and Berse were further surprised to see the single round box brooches that Gotland women sported to fix their shawls. These were silver-gilt, and some looked to be wrought of pure gold, just as the wealthiest of island women wore upon their breasts. Some merchant must have brought them back from his trading on the island, to a fortress rich enough for men to bedeck their wives as were the women of Gotland.

Oleg led them to his hall, one no larger than that of Karlen and Demyan, but with every upright timber column and rafter adorned with carvings of leaping beasts and swimming fish. The stone-lined fire-pit was long, alit, and glowing with warmth. As they entered, several big grey-furred wolf hounds rose from under the high table and came, plumed tails wagging, to greet the King. The animals were not the small sturdy scent hounds used to chase wolves in the far north. These dogs seemed to have been crossed with long-legged coursing hounds, to give them the powerful muzzles of the first, and the speed of the second. Prince Efim, who had sold them the wolf-pelt clothing, had complained that to the east was nothing but wolves, and with such dogs Oleg was prepared for the chase.

Wine was brought, of a strength that even the scent of it rising from the cup made the head swim. Hardship was forgotten. Here they could replenish depleted stores, secure new boots and other items, and most needed of all, spend a few days in warmth and rest.

Such was the comfort all felt that Eskil and Runulv nearly forgot they bore something to show the King. Eskil recalled this, with a jerk, and his hand went to his belt. It nudged the memory of Runulv as well, and he did the same. Each pulled out the small ring of green glass they had been given by the tribe with the mares and falcons. They held them in their palms before the King, and Eskil said the rings bore some kind of message for him.

Oleg laughed. "They are Avars, and love their animals more than their women. The rings are Rus, a sign of favour. They thought much of you." He reached his hand out and picked up the one Eskil held forth, then dropped it back into his palm. "Keep them, for luck." The King allowed a moment to pass before he smiled again and said the next. "They also mean you have a taste for fermented mare's milk."

⬧⬧⬧⬧⬧⬧⬧⬧⬧⬧

They spent fully four days at Kyiv, housed both in the main hall and a secondary one for the King's unwed warriors. Oleg had made no demand of silver, and sold them the supplies they needed at fair prices. At the end of the second day Runulv and Eskil began to worry what might be demanded of them to be allowed passage on the Dnieper. They spoke to Karlen about this. The young Prince had fallen easily into the life of his kinsman, and seemed even more content at Kyiv than he had been at his own hall.

"My friends wonder how they can please you, King Oleg, to repay your hospitality, and assure your blessing on their way to Miklagårdr," Karlen offered that night.

This was a pretty speech from the Prince, and a gratifying one for the two captains to hear.

Oleg steepled his fingers, lowered his head to his fingertips, and gave thought. "They have carried you here in good time, for I had want of you, Karlen. There is a woman here I would have you wed. You will meet her presently, and if she is to your liking, she will travel back to you at Gnezdovo in fair weather." The King lifted his hand towards the roof, which all knew was at that moment being shrouded in fresh snow.

The news that Oleg had a bride in mind for the young man brought a smile to his handsome face. Indeed, the women of Kyiv were second to none as far as comeliness. Many were slaves, but even the women of the household were of exceptional looks. Oleg guarded them with care, and did not allow them to be subject to casual use.

The King raised his face, looked to the two captains, and answered. "If you make Miklagårdr, I seek one thing. A crystal as clear as rippled water, and shaped as a sphere. One as large as my fist."

Runulv drew breath. Rock crystal came from distant Basra, and several smaller spheres had been carried to Gotland, there to be mounted in silver and worn by rich women. Ceridwen wore such about her neck at times, and Runulv knew Sidroc had won the undressed sphere at dice from Eskil. And he had just last year taken two small silver-mounted balls of crystal to Paris, and sold them to good account.

"As large as your fist," Runulv repeated. "If Miklagårdr holds such crystals, we will bring you one."

Oleg smiled. "Then may you reach Miklagårdr, and back," he told them.

The mention of a woman Oleg had selected for Karlen made Eskil think of his own lack of a wife. Here at Kyiv were beautiful women, be they yellow-haired, raven-locked, blest with tousled ruddy curls, or with tresses that soft brown of the female blackbird's breast. He might take his pick, exchange some silver for her, and spend a night with her before he left. He would not think of subjecting his choice to the onward journey, but he felt he could trust Karlen and Oleg to take good care of her until his return. He would even buy a second woman, to act as her serving maid, so she might have what comfort she could in his absence, and on the way back to Gotland.

In the morning he shared his scheme with Runulv after they had broken their fast. Brani was with them as well, and both listened with widening eyes to the Svear's plan.

Brani spoke first. "You will regret your haste. There are thousands of women in Miklagårdr who await you. Wait, and buy there."

Runulv too urged against it, but for different reasons. "You will have to bring any woman back alive, through ways we have just passed," he pointed out. After what they had gone through to reach this far, this was no small consideration.

Runulv had more to add. "Sidroc told me you seek to settle on Gotland. If that is true, you need a Gotland woman as your partner and wife. My wife Gyda – she has cousins, good and honest girls, hard working. And as pretty as those here," he added, thinking of Gyda when they wed. "You will want such a woman. The day you take one to wife, it will give you needed standing on the island, to wed into such a family."

Eskil had to agree this was a point, yet was torn. The women moving about them were more than alluring, and who knew what choice women Oleg was keeping in reserve, one of which he might part with to become his wife? Eskil argued this, and more.

"Take your pleasure here if you must," Runulv summed. None had forgotten that in the morning they must bid farewell to Karlen and Kyiv, and take on the Dnieper alone. "But if you would settle on Gotland, wed a girl of good Gotlandic stock."

The Svear took this in, knowing the rightness of it. But he could not help but shoot back his retort. "Sidroc did not."

Runulv paused. "Ceridwen and Sidroc – they are different."

Eskil's light blue eyes shifted to one side. He said no more, but must admit to the truth of this statement.

SWIFT AND
ROCKY WATERS

LEAVING Kyiv, the Dnieper pulled them sharply east, almost as if it flowed toward the rising Sun. The first four days were much like those which had preceded them north of Kyiv, with cautious travel along a fairly broad channel, one with sanded islets demanding care from Runulv lest he snag his keel. A man was always ready in the bow, testing the depths with his oar.

On the fifth day out this changed. Here they found the best journeying they had known since making land at the end of the Gulf of the Finns. These upper reaches of the Dnieper deepened so that their boats could sail abreast. Eskil and Brani took the lead in the first karv, and just behind came two dugouts, paddling almost in tandem, then the second karv, flanked by two more dugouts. Dauðadagr brought up the rear, though with her larger sail she might have been the flagship of the flotilla. Both karvs raised their masts and unfurled their small sails to catch a wind that blew steadily from the west, speeding their eastward progress. Those crew paddling in the dugouts need not exert themselves overmuch; the buoyancy of their small craft combined with the swiftness of the water made for light work.

The adventurers had found rare favour in having escort much of the way provided by their various hosts. Karlen had entrusted the small tasseled pouch to Brani, and Brani had his own horn to blow in warning. And the Prince taught him, and the two captains, a few words in the Pecheneg tongue. These perhaps equated to proclamations of friendship, or of having already met the tariff set for passage; none of the three were truly certain. What was certain was they had now only Brani as pilot.

The Dnieper was in fact their true guide, as they were pulled inexorably east. They were twelve days on an ever-widening river, with banks which changed from grassland to patchy woodland. Each dusk they drove for shore, secured their craft by dragging the dugouts wholly out, with the larger karvs staked to the shore by lines. Dauðadagr stayed in, Runulv just driving the prow into the sand, and securing her there with iron anchor from her stern, and bowline staked to the shore.

They made their camp each afternoon, hammering their tent poles with wooden mallets into unforgiving ground, setting up the lean-to sheltering their cook-fire, and pitching their tents. The gathering of more fuel was of prime importance, searching for dead wood on the ground, and knocking broken branches out of low-boughed trees. It had grown too cold for Runulv and his crew to sleep aboard Death-Day, and they joined the rest of their companions in warming themselves as best they could around the fire before retreating to their tents. The fire was kept glowing all night, for warmth, and against wolves, whose eerie yowls they heard more often than they wished. A few of the men conjectured a pack followed them, sensing that aboard their boats were the skins of many of their fellow beasts. For this and other reasons the fire was stoked all night. They set watches to feed it, and tend to the cauldron of porridge, which once cooked was swung to a bed of rock to keep warm.

Snow fell, just as it had at Kyiv, and the Sun, low on the horizon and often lost in cloud-girt skies, afforded no warmth. Despite this, there was not sustained cold to ice the river, and it flowed freely and unfettered. Yet each day grew shorter as they neared that turning of the Sun back to its climb in the heavens. Some men donned their wolf-pelt tunics and leggings, but others, at Brani's urging, kept to their woollens and sheepskins alone. "When we reach the Black Sea we will sail into warmth. And Miklagårdr, when we land there, will be as mild as a cool Spring day. But when we return here and approach Kyiv and beyond, Winter will be at its coldest. Then we will go wolf-clad."

Looking back later at the first days of their passage through the cataracts, Runulv's memory became as murky as the churning waters they risked their lives upon. They had suffered hardship to reach this far, to the brink of this greatest challenge of the Dnieper cataracts. Perhaps expected dangers were always thus; once met, they must be placed at a distance so that one could undertake to repeat the same action. Runulv had known fierce squalls at sea, and his knorr had even suffered being dismasted in a storm. He had not sworn off sailing, no more than Brani, having made this transit twice before, was deterred from again attempting to cross the rapids to reach Miklagårdr. The greatest gain was nearly almost always preceded by great risk. They had been warned the cataracts and cascades of the Dnieper would prove treacherous.

The rapid runs were nine in number, seven of which were impassable by water, and of these several memorable enough to have earned a name, which Brani well recalled. Besides these there were innumerable stretches of fast water where decision must be made to haul the boats out and push and pull them overland upon the shore, or attempt to ride the rapids out downstream to quieter water.

When they were twelve days out from Kyiv the water quickened with a new urgency. "We near the first rapid," Brani told them. "Tomorrow or the next day the banks will change from sand and soil, to stone. The river will narrow between banks of solid rock, and cliffs of rock will stand like islands in the middle of the flow."

They found he was right. Next day they sailed around a bend, watching the landscape transform from shallow bank to gently mounded hills. It was at junctures like this Brani would sound his horn, blowing out the few notes the Prince had used to announce their coming, should Pechenegs await. No notice was needed. These banks were washed and barren. It had rained the day before, and any snow which may have lain upon them was now dissolved into the waters rushing under their hulls.

Brani again lifted the horn to his lips and rang out the three blasts that signalled a halt. It was just mid-day, the Sun at its highest point, barely glimpsed in the overcast above them. All boats drove near to shore, finding any anchorage they could.

They did not unload here. Brani had stopped them a distance from the actual rapids, warning that here began the drop in elevation they must traverse in following the Dnieper down on its way to meet the Black Sea. From here the current could catch any vessel and drag it relentlessly onward, crashing into huge boulders strewn across the riverway, fracturing a planked boat like the karvs into splinters, and wedging the dugouts between rocks, oftentimes upside down. They must all secure the boats and walk them down and through this first cataract. Half the crew quit the boats, and would take up lines from bow and stern to guide the craft as close to shore as might keep them afloat. The other half would remain aboard, using paddles and oars to steer their vessels forward. Only when they grew closer could they gauge if there was enough water at the bank's edge to permit the passage of Dauðadagr.

So they set off. Eskil stayed aboard the lead karv, while Brani held the bow line and walked nearly equal to his captain on the rock of the bank. Three others walked with Brani, holding hempen lines and acting both guide and brake to the karv's progress. Eskil had raised the steering oar, as the best passage was at starboard. He took up a paddle with the three crew remaining with him on board, punting the craft along, and away from the boulder-strewn course. At times the men on shore must slacken their hold so that the karv could deviate around a rock too close to the bank, and then be drawn back.

As they began this approach, and with the rest of the flotilla near behind so they might profit from the course taken by the first craft, a rumbling sound began to fill their ears. It was the deep roaring of torrents of water, water forced through narrow channels and tumbling angrily through the impediment blocking its swiftest course. Yet the men could scarcely raise their eyes to what was ahead, paying full attention to the hindrances threatening their hulls. Another slight bend in the riverway brought the noise to a tumultuous crescendo. There in the middle of the river bed rose two upright slabs of solid rock, each the height of three men. The water sluicing between these columns of stone and the huge boulders flanking them made a din no sounding of horns or drums could be heard above.

As soon as they could see this, the pull upon their boats became extreme, as if the compression of the river from these columns had been increased five-fold. The men on shore fought from being pulled into the water, just as those aboard pushed with all their might and main upon their paddles to spare the hull being dashed up against the boulders they were being sucked towards.

There was no way that Brani, nor any of the men, could run back to Dauðadagr to apprise her crew of what lay ahead. Aboard the drekar, they saw the straining of the men upon the banks, along with the mighty dipping and heaving of the hulls of the dugouts and karvs.

Berse was amongst Runulv's crew, and with his avowed strength had offered that he take up the stern line to guide the drekar on her way. His brawn was put to the test, as he had both hands wrapped about the line to serve as brake against the suck of the current.

Like Eskil, Runulv must abandon his steering oar, pulling it up to safety from the water lest it be crushed in an unlucky lunge toward the rock bank. As he heaved it out he turned to see the carving of Odin, always standing to attention behind him in the stern. The lone quartz eye looked dull under grey skies, but Runulv knew All-Father never slept. He muttered a single word, that of Odin's name, and meant it as prayer.

That prayer was answered, in the form of Brani and several other men running back to Death-Day from the boats which had already cleared the danger. Some carried hempen line in their hands, ready to fling it aboard the drekar, others held paddles to use as tamps, pressing her hull away from shore. Even shouted commands could not be heard above the roar of the cataract, but none were needed. These were seasoned crew, used to working as a unit, and skilled enough to see and answer any need to keep their craft from disaster.

Dauðadagr made it through, though not without so much bumping and scraping of her keel and hull that Runulv feared that any moment she might stove in. She did not. Sidroc had long ago told him of her building, and Runulv at this point had intimate knowledge of the ship's ways and ability. But when he finally leapt ashore in the calm water where the others awaited him, one word was on his lips: Odin.

They made camp, then and there; they could go no further. They were all splashed with icy water, and must rub themselves dry and warm. Those who had walked to steady the boats had soaked leggings, and those who had remained aboard had wet arms and tunics.

"This first is called 'Do not sleep,'" Brani told them. They could still hear the rumbling of the water behind them, and picture its flows between the rock cliff islands.

That morning was the last the crew were ever all aboard their boats. Until they reached the end of the rapids, whenever the boats touched water at least half the men would trudge alongside, on slippery and treacherous banks, while others hazarded the passage from inside jolting hulls. In Spring the Dnieper would be in flood, the snow broth from melting ice and warming days lifting the smaller craft up to clear many of the boulders. Here, at the dawn of Winter, the rock-strewn riverway was an endless course of obstacles.

To Eskil and Runulv, it was far more difficult than they had imagined. There was bitter contrast between how quickly the water rushed by them and the slowness of every toilsome hour. Of all the discrete passages in their journey, this leg of over three hundred furlongs took the longest, and the most from them. This river they had sought, the Dnieper, was now a tangle of rapids, some spanning broad areas, others narrow defiles. Its waters had become a living entity, one desirous of their ruin. It was a wild stallion no man could break or back, allowing none to fetter it. Any attempt to pass was grave insult to the beast, and their boats of no more account to its roiling waters than the brown leaves and dried sticks which tumbled on its surface, only to vanish and be spat up again.

The banks were utterly desolate. No folk lived here. Eskil began to think he might welcome the appearance of even some Pecheneg, as proof they had not been cut off from all human contact and wholly forsaken to the dangers of the rapids. And their provisions were running low. Once they passed the rapids and could turn south, there would be riverside tribes ready to sell them provender. Until then they must eke out what supplies they had. There were no greens for the gathering in this wintry landscape, and the vegetables they had procured from Kyiv were now gone. Their daily sustenance were bowls of boiled barley or wheat, mixed with dried and flaked stock fish, or a dwindling supply of the cured meat from Oleg's rangy cattle. At night they set weirs to catch fresh fish, lowering them between boulders, and came up with enough pike, perch, and chub to freshen the salted herring in their cauldrons.

They passed the second rapid run, one called 'Islet rapid' for the many small atolls arising from the river bed. This lacked the stone towers of the first, but carried its flow even faster, for the channel through which it coursed was narrower. Happily, fewer large boulders lay near the banks, and though it was a mighty effort to control the craft from the banks and from aboard, all made it through.

The third cataract was shorter and bore the name 'Water roarer'. Once through the worst of any run, the men camped as far downstream from its foaming torrents as they could. It did not keep the sound of the rushing waters from ringing in their ears.

They continued on, working in shifts, every day switching those crew who walked alongside, holding the lines to the boats, and those who worked within with paddle or oars, pressing their hulls away from boulders. The river Gods, so often invoked by their hosts, were not entirely callous to their plight, for the weather could have tested them severely. It rarely snowed but they were plagued by rain. Their woollens kept them warm even when wet, but sodden boots made for cold feet, even when encased in stockings looped by nålbinding and fashioned by caring female hands at home. At night they built what fire they could and warmed and dried themselves.

On the tenth day of the rapids Brani, working by the fire's glow, took out several carved flat sticks from his pack, on which he had noted distance in number of days.

"Tomorrow we reach the greatest cataract of all, 'Aeifor'. There is no word for it in our tongue; no man I made this journey with knew its meaning. But it is a fall so high that we must carry our goods and boats up steep paths and down ravines, along the cliff face, to avoid the crushing water of its force."

The guide looked to Runulv. "We must take your drekar apart, and carry her in pieces, as I told you back on Gotland at the hall of the Dane."

The entire journey Runulv had hoped to avoid this. But having gone through the punishing cascades as they had, he no longer clung to the hope Dauðadagr could withstand more abuse.

In the morning Brani and Eskil walked ahead along the bank, scouting for a broad enough area to serve as their staging site. The river here was serpentine, each twist blocking the view of what lay ahead, but when they returned they told of steadily dropping ground, and of seeing the cliff edge from which Aeifur fell. For staging ground they could grow nearer, and did so, fighting against the water which ran more swiftly than over the prior rapids. They stopped late in the day at a smooth rock bank, broad enough to set their camp and begin their work. All their craft must be unloaded, the boats hauled to shore, and then Dauðadagr must be broken down, disassembled into her many component ribs, planking, decking, and bags of rivets. Her mast, spar, and sail must be furled together for portage, her long oars lashed in pairs.

Runulv had never undertaken any ship work with a heavier heart. He broke her apart with the help of Berse and a few of his men, pulling rivets, hammering out pins, peeling off the straked planking of her hull, and knocking out ribs. She was rent as the carcass of a fish would be, picked apart by a large bird. It was almost painful for him in the doing, reducing her to parts.

The carving of Odin would be too large to be carried by a single man. They made a sling out of a piece of extra sail cloth, so two could carry it between them. Runulv would be sure to be one of them. He felt the God to be mightily disgruntled by Dauðadagr's dismantling, and hoped his taking personal charge of the carving might assuage those feelings.

While this was underway, Eskil and the rest of the men were stacking and sorting supplies and cargo as to weight, collecting and lashing into bundles the dugout and karv paddles, and otherwise preparing their goods and boats to be carried overland.

When they had finished, Brani made assessment. "It will take us three, four trips to carry it all," he judged. "Boats first, so we can load them with the goods on the following trip." He looked to Death-Day, now a stacked pile of shaped ribs, curved planks, ironmongery, and the mast, spar and sail. The carved image of Odin stood alone on its wooden base, next to the near-naked keel. "It will take us one trip through just to carry her," he decided.

In the morning they made their start. It was cold, grey-skied, and though a drizzle had fallen overnight, dry enough now so the men could see the smoking of their breath when they spoke. Brani led, unfettered save for his own pack, for he need be nimble enough to go ahead and choose the best footing for those burdened behind him. The dugouts were flipped so that three men could walk within them, the thwarts resting on their shoulders, with the fourth in front, guiding. For the two larger karvs the wheeled axles were brought into play, though the unevenness of the rock meant that their crew must be in constant and steady hand contact with the hull, to keep it from tipping. Runulv and several men were left behind on this trip. Though they had seen no sign of Pechenegs or any other folk, he and Eskil could not leave their goods and supplies unguarded.

There was no path alongside the Aeifur falls; the water fell through a narrow defile carved by the surging waters. They must climb above the falls, shouldering the dugouts and hauling and pushing the karvs. At no place above could they see the falls, only hear its roaring beneath them, though around them the water vapour rose from the pool the flow tumbled into. For a man lightly burdened with a pack, it was possible to descend on a steep trail, which at last terminated beyond the pool, alongside a broad opening of water. Led by Eskil and Brani the men laboured up the hill, struggling under their loads and with the footing, which ranged from bare and slippery rock to scree which shifted under every footfall. When they reached the apex, they all took breath. The track leading down was at such an incline that the men carrying the dugouts could never keep their footing. They had to lower them to the slick track, fasten them to lines, and with two men walking before each dugout, and two in the rear acting as brake, allow them to slide down in as controlled a fashion as they could muster. Men slipped and slid and fell upon the track at this, bruising themselves, tearing leggings, and uttering more oaths than any had ever heard, even those who had known battle. Brani went ahead, so he might check the way down, but Eskil worked alongside the men, helping in first guiding and then braking on each dugout as the course demanded. As the last dugout reached flat ground, half the men climbed back with Eskil to retrieve the karvs, while Brani and the others who had lowered the dugouts took to righting them in the water and securing them, ready to receive the coming cargo once the karvs were safely down.

One boat did not make it. Berse had stayed behind with their crew to move the karvs, and he and the others had done what they could to secure the river boats in their wheeled axles. But the keels of the karvs were narrower than those of the drekars, and the men worked to hammer shims in to tighten the grip. When the first karv was hauled and pushed up the incline, and the men halted so they might rest and survey the track down, they saw Eskil and the others with him climbing back to them. Then, in an unlucky moment, one of the men still steadying the karv in its wheeled cradle slipped on the loose scree. He knocked against the hull, just enough to jar the stern, tipping it. The karv slid out of the cradle and one long moment later was jolting down the track. Eskil was in the lead climbing up and lifted his head at the yells of those above him. He and the men with him dove to the left, scrambling and rolling out of the way of the karv. None of the men at the bottom could have heard the uproar over the noise of the falls, and the karv broke up long before it reached the end of the downward path.

The shock was such that Eskil was as ashen-faced as any of them. He and the others who had narrowly escaped being struck by the barrelling hull picked themselves up and took a long look at the wreckage of the karv. Some of its planking was strewn along the track, some had been flung over the cliff face to the long drop below, and the remainder lay in a heap at the bottom of the track, where it settled against a tall and up-thrusting rock. They turned from it to make the climb to where the crew stood, open-mouthed, at their loss.

By the time Eskil reached them he was able to give orders. "Go down and retrieve any planking you can safely reach," he told the crew. "Carry it to Brani and the others. We will need wood for repairs to the other craft. Gather even splintered wood; it will be our cook-fire."

To none was the loss harder than Berse. He had taken the lead in hauling the karv up, and it weighed heavily on the blade-smith that the boat had been lost on his watch. There was nothing to do save get the second karv down safely, once the track was cleared. They did so, and in every man's head was the knowledge that having lost one of their larger boats, the coming weeks would be cramped indeed when they were once again afloat. There was consolation that no man had been injured and no trade goods lost, and they must cling to that.

Next was the retrieval of their supplies and cargo. Brani and another man stayed ahead with the dugouts and remaining karv, while all the others doubled back to where Runulv and their goods awaited. The news, unwelcome as it was, of the runaway karv must be delivered and accepted. At this point the most pressing need was to get past the Aeifur falls and down to their camp site. But standing amongst the bales, chests, and casks gave little comfort. There was so much to carry that it was readily apparent it would take two trips, even with nearly two score men at work. Runulv and those who had stayed on guard with him joined them; it made no sense to lose the manpower when there was no seeming threat to their waiting supplies. Runulv, turning his back on the skeletal remains of Dauðadagr, felt an almost bodily pain at abandoning her like this, even for the time he must be away.

Each man shouldered a pack, or when possible, lashed the burden upon their backs. They started up, a long line of men snaking their way along the edge of the cliff face. The footing was uncertain, that same mixture of slippery bald rock and crumbled scree the first group of men had need to traverse. Approaching the apex the noise from the unseen water crashing below was such that Runulv gave his head a shake, not easy with the crate he rested against it and on his shoulder. He and Berse were bringing up the rear, and had good view of the men ahead. In places by the cliff edge enough dried vegetation remained that it became an alternate path, and several men took that. The ground it sprang from rapidly muddied into a slime. One of the men, Arni by name, shouldered a small cask. He slipped and turned his ankle in the mud. Arni gave a yell, heard over the rising roar of the water, as the cask dropped from his shoulder and he went down. The man just behind him lurched toward him, arm extended, but weighted as he was by the pack on his back, fell. The folds in the cliff were such that Runulv and Berse were almost directly opposite the men. They watched as the two slipped over the edge of the cliff face and were lost to view.

Those trudging onward had no knowledge of what had just happened. Runulv and Berse dropped their burdens, and Berse ran ahead to stop the descending men before they were lost to view. Runulv meanwhile had dropped on his belly and was trying to crawl toward the cliff edge, that he might see where the men had fallen. Berse returned with several men, who saw the discarded cask Arni had been carrying. The man behind Arni had been another Gotlander, Farulf, who had slipped over with the pack on his back. Arni's younger brother Emund had been next in line, and had flung himself down by Runulv, grasping him by one ankle so their captain could near the edge. The abandoned cask, and position of

Emund and Runulv on the ground, told the returning men much of the story.

Runulv pushed himself up and went to the men. "I can see nothing," he told them. He looked to Berse. "I need a harness; you can lower me over the edge."

A short length of line was handed to Runulv. He wrapped it about his waist, dropped the ends through his legs to pull them up behind him, and draw them through. Two quick half-hitches and a square knot later, Berse stood before Runulv, ready to loop his long line through the harness front, so that Runulv could approach the slippery edge on his belly and be lowered down the cliff face. Runulv took another coil of line and placed it over his shoulder, ready to use to haul another.

Runulv gave Berse a single nod, signifying he was ready. The hazard was such that at the last moment the blade-smith delayed Runulv so he might pass a second line through the harness at the waist.

"Feed out the line as long as you feel the pull of my weight," were the captain's final words as he edged nearer. "Once it grows slack, let it remain. Two quick tugs means pull me up."

Two men held the lines taut, Berse first, and at his side a second Gotlander, nearly as strong. Arni's brother Emund resumed his position near the edge, mittened hands guiding the lines as well as he could to help keep them from needless abrasion. They all watched Runulv as he was lowered. His hands were still visible when he turned his head to the right to see what lay below. They saw him shake his head, but over the sound of the falling water none would have heard him even if he had yelled back at them.

It was not a sheer drop at this point. Instead, a number of knobs of rock projected out from the cliff face, an echo of the boulders blocking their passage by water. Beneath these, and at depth equaling the height of three men, lay a jagged shelf of jutting rock, blocking further view. No waters other than rain or snow had smoothed it. Long ago when the cliff fell away, tumbling into the chasm beneath, this shelf remained. The rock was wet, not only from the recent rain, but from the perpetual mist arising from below.

Runulv could not see beyond its bulk. But the two lay there. The arch of his back told him Arni was dead; Runulv could see it in a glance. He was forced to turn his head back to the cliff face and the knobs of rock he must pass to reach the shelf. The lines he was tethered to kept on with their gradual slackening, allowing his feet to touch. By the tail of his left eye he saw Farulf, lying on his belly, and as Runulv's heels touched the shelf he saw the fingers of Farulf's right hand move.

Runulv could utter no more than the man's name, and did not think Farulf heard even that. His eyes were closed, and other than the slight movement of his fingers nothing gave Runulv hope. Both men had been battered by hitting the projecting rock as they fell, but Farulf still breathed and his captain must try to lift him to his fellows. Fastening the additional coil as harness around the man's body was one thing. But Runulv was aware that Farulf could never be hoisted alone. Runulv must hold on to him, and they both be lifted together. At least Berse's foresight had equipped him with a second line. He untied one of them and tied it to the front of Farulf's harness, then tried to lift the inert man to his feet. The best he could do was hold him round the waist, and count on his feet to keep them both away from the punishing rock face as they were pulled up.

Runulv gave two mighty tugs on the lines. It took a moment, but the slack line grew taut.

The strain on the lines was terrific. The two hauling had been joined by two more, with Berse setting the pace for each heave. The weight of the pull told them they hauled more than one man, and added resolve to their strength.

Arni's brother Emund, tasked with guiding the lines, had been passed a wooden roller when they slackened. Without this to spare them the cutting edge of the rock, they would have frayed and snapped.

As for Runulv, the distance back up, clutching the grievously injured Farulf, and pressing the rock face away with his legs so he might not be further harmed, demanded every particle of his resolve.

At last he was up, his head above the cliff edge. Farulf's own head was on his shoulder, blood dripping from his mouth. Emund was near enough to reach his hand to Runulv, and with the help of others they pulled both men up and over.

Runulv was still on his knees when a wild-eyed Emund spoke. "Arni – where is Arni?"

"There is a ledge beneath us," Runulv panted out. "Both hit it. Arni broke his back." He took a breath, and must look in the young man's eyes as he said the next. "He is dead, Emund."

Emund gave a howl, one which Runulv cut short. "Farulf tried to catch him."

He had crawled away from the edge, and now hands reached out to pull Farulf to safety as well.

It was too late. Farulf heaved a single sighing breath, and died before them without opening his eyes.

"I will go down and get your brother," Runulv told Emund. The younger brother had his hands to his face, but shook his head as he lowered them. "Nai. I will go."

"You will stay here as I order," Runulv told him. He did not want Emund to feel the weight of his brother's body in his arms, nor did he think so slight a man might have the strength to make the short but arduous transit up.

Runulv was lowered again, and again must secure the limp body of one of his men into a hastily formed harness. All about him the mist rose from the waterfall, a cascade he could only feel and hear.

By the time he was hauled up, Eskil and several of the dugout carriers had made their way back up to the top of the cliff. Only Brani and the few with him, far distant below and building their camp, remained ignorant of their loss.

Runulv sunk down on a boulder, his eyes upon his two dead crewmen. Emund knelt at Arni's side, bent over his brother's body. Berse came to Runulv and placed his hand on the captain's shoulder.

Runulv rose and looked about him. To one side the track widened into a small clearing. They could never gather wood enough for a burning, but Arni and Farulf might be laid side by side here on the ridge, and covered with rock, and their spirits thus flow with the river and find release.

He went to Farulf's body first. Two of the men who were friendly to him knelt at the man's side. Runulv reached for Farulf's belt, and slid off his purse. He emptied the contents into his hand. A few pieces of silver sat there, and some amber beads.

"Is this his trading stake?" he asked of the men gathered near him. One nodded sombrely; there was so little to account for, save his life. "He had a few fleeces from his sheep, as well." Runulv nodded. "When we reach Miklagårdr, give them to me, and I will trade on his behalf, for his mother, so that she might know the same reward he would have brought her."

He moved to Emund, at the side of his brother Arni. "Take his purse, Emund. We will mound rock over them, so that any passing this way sees daring men preceded them." Emund lifted his wet face to his captain. Arni was wed and had left his wife and two small children for this adventure.

It was grown late in the day. In haste the bodies of Arni and Farulf were carried to the apex of the ridge. Runulv drew the men's mantles as shrouds over their faces, the last time daylight ever touched them. Then began the piling of rock over the bodies. It was custom that kin lay the first and the final stone, and Emund performed this solemn task for Arni. Runulv did so for Farulf.

Then they must make haste down the track, before night caught them. The falls of Aeifur had claimed one karv and the lives of two men. The carrying of Dauðadagr would have to wait until dawn.

⚜⚜⚜⚜⚜⚜⚜⚜⚜

That night around the cook-fire the men spoke of their dead companions. There was no mead with which to celebrate them, no wine or even ale to lift in cups and speak of their lives and deeds. Water which had tumbled over the falls at which Arni and Farulf died was all that filled their cups. But the men could make boasting promise of the delights of

Miklagårdr to come, and how the two would be remembered there over many a cup.

In the light of morning Runulv could fully see their camp site. Its setting was at the side of the large pool into which the falls of Aeifur dropped, far enough from the cascade itself so that its noise was not ringing in their ears. There were waterfalls on Gotland; sheer cliff faces from which underground springs poured forth their waters unto the Baltic shore below. But Runulv and the other Gotlanders had never seen a cascade as was this behind them. It was split into three main parts, none of them broad, but all of them contributing to the wild spill of water churning in a whirlpool at its feet. This broadened and calmed into the pool by which they had slept. It looked bereft of any life, though fish must swim beneath in its depths.

As they made ready to head back up the track to retrieve Dauðadagr, two large white birds, unseen before, appeared from behind a broad boulder rising above the water's surface. They were so striking in form and size that men stood, the better to see them.

"They are called pelicans," Brani told them. The birds took flight, violently flapping to lift from the surface, water streaming from their bills. With their huge pouched beaks the fowl could bear much within. Ungainly but powerful, they prompted Brani to speak of those dead.

"They head east to Asgard, and bear the spirits of Arni and Farulf."

THE RIVER GODS

THEY reloaded the boats. With one less karv, and Dauðadagr in pieces, they were sorely taxed for space. The remaining karv must serve to carry the drekar's longer parts, and her mast, keel and gunwale planking protruded fore and aft. Even the smallest of the dugouts was forced to carry additional cargo. The loss of two men freed up but slight space, space which none of the crew wished vacant. They walked the craft as they had before, with tow lines, and with some crew aboard to guide and keep the boats from striking the rocky shores.

Runulv was without a command. Eskil had eight of his ten men upon the karv he commanded, and Death-Day was a pile of tarred wood and sailcloth stacked within it. And Runulv had lost two men.

The cold worsened as Winter thickened about them. Snow was mercifully light, but a bitter wind blew down the Dnieper channel, as if through a funnel. Eskil had been wise to gather every stick of the runaway karv, for they had need of it. At dusk they were hard pressed to gather any dry branches to boil their browis. In truth, it was scarcely worthy of that name, with but scant stock fish, lacking any vegetables, and a savour mainly of salt.

At one of the rapid runs the boulders protruding from the rushing waters were so closely spaced as to serve almost as the teeth of a comb. There was nothing for it but to again unpack everything, and haul the boats alongside the waterway.

The crews had now loaded and unloaded each boat numberless times. There was grumbling amongst the men, and both captains heard it. Slaves would have made this all much the easier. Both ignored such talk, until Eskil in a flare of anger snapped at one of his own. "Slaves need to be fed. And we would need many more boats, which would only slow us further."

Runulv was weighted down by the knowledge that Dauðadagr was become their greatest hindrance. Once they reached flowing water unimpeded by rapids she could be put to rights and again resume carrying her full complement of men and cargo. Until then he bore the burden of self-reproach. Almost since the moment Sidroc had told him he would sail the drekar and not his knorr he had pictured his entry into the harbour of Miklagårdr. Eskil's Sharp Tooth might be much the larger, but Dauðadagr was as fine as any small drekar as could be sailed. It had been Runulv's own pride in that vision which had forced him to keep her with him, that and his real affection and concern for her safety. Death-Day had been stolen once and it had taken Sidroc the favour of Odin and all his skill at gaming to win her back. Runulv did not want to be the instrument of losing her again.

Once they had again reached more free-flowing waters, they set the boats in the river and re-loaded them. They resumed their progress, with men guiding and braking the boats from the banks, and others remaining aboard. The afternoon was far gone when the current quickened, a signal of danger ahead.

Brani did not know the name of the coming rapids, and in truth it was hard to keep count. But as the land dropped the river followed, flowing ever swifter. Still, there was more or less free passage alongside the bank, which meant taking advantage of the pull of the current to speed them along. Eskil's karv, so heavily loaded now, did not take the lead. Instead the smallest of the dugouts did, one being walked by two men, with two within, paddles always in the water to guide her away from the bank or any near boulders.

They continued on, each small crew focused on the task of moving their given boat forward safely. Then the lead dugout hit a hidden rock at her bow. She rose high from the water and pitched to port, ripping the bow line from the hands of the man walking on the bank. The two aboard were enough jolted that the man in the bow lost his paddle. The man on the bank holding the stern line leant back, attempting to dig his heels into the unforgiving rock he stood upon. A moment later he was pulled forward, falling hard upon the rock, while the dugout, now free, pitched and turned in the speeding waters. It was caught and sucked into the middle of the current, where it was jostled over and around the rocky bed and its hidden cross-currents. The bow of the dugout shot up in the air, and the two men within it were thrown out. One was near enough to almost reach the hull and grasp onto the netting of line securing the cargo within. He did not. The rest of the crew watched as the dugout tumbled, half flooded, against the rocks, continuing its run down the river. The heads of both men vanished from view.

A heart-stopping period of time passed, until one head popped up. He was close enough to the bank to fight his way to it, and the men in the second dugout were tracking him, extending a paddle out that he might grasp it. He did, and they hauled him closer, until he could cling to the cargo netting at the bow. With the help of those with the guide lines he made it to shore, badly scraped, soaked with icy water, but alive.

The second man was nowhere to be seen. All marked where his head had emerged, his arms flailing as he fought for purchase against the slippery rocks and surging water. He had been trapped underwater, or carried away as the dugout had been.

Eskil had leapt from the karv; these were two of his Svear who had been upended. He joined the men at the lead dugouts as they increased their speed down river, trotting alongside them to try to catch sight of the man, and the dugout he had spilled from.

Past the next slight bend they spotted him, wedged between boulders. It was a macabre discovery. Regardless of how his body had been twisted and turned by the action of the waters, he now lay pinned almost sitting up, shoulders held by the boulders, facing them. There was no question he was dead; his head was thrown back as if his neck had broken.

Further ahead lay the dugout, half full of water but in shallows. The bow netting had held, and those goods lashed within remained, but the stern netting had been ripped away and every pack once secured there had been claimed by the river.

They pulled the dugout closer, using boat hooks until they could grapple with its bulk. Recovering the body was harder. A thrown lasso was tried by one who had experience wrangling horses, but the position of the dead man's head and inability to drop it around his shoulders soon made them abandon the attempt. There was nothing to it but to send a dugout, tethered by no fewer than four lines to shore. Four men crewed it, and with paddles and the braking action of the men ashore they reached the dead man. Stopping to pluck his body proved the most dangerous part of their mission, and they were nearly upset themselves as they worked to do so.

When all had reached shore an end to the day's travel was called. A fire was built, and Thorbjörn, the man who had made it to shore, was placed by it. Though now in his change of clothes, he could not keep his teeth from chattering from the cold which had settled in his very marrow. Only when he was red-faced from the fire's heat did the rattling cease.

Attention was turned to Sigtrygg. It was not clear if he had drowned first or been killed by the pummeling of the boulders he had struck. But another man was dead and a mound must be built over him. Eskil went through much the same acts as Runulv had, emptying Sigtrygg's purse, and making promise he would use what trading goods the dead man had carried to good account. Four of the Svear carried his body a little up the river, and all of them took part in the piling of stone to make his mound. Brani, hardened as he was by travel, was perhaps the most affected, remembering the trip in which his captain, Hedin, had died, and recalling that mishap until Eskil ordered him to silence.

Each night about the fire men told stories of their homes, or of other adventures they had taken part in. Such tales made even their humble bowls of thin browis gain flavour. Yet that night almost no one spoke. The death of the three had shifted the mood of the entire crew. Together they had faced hardship and danger, threats from plainsmen, the extortions of Princes, heat, cold, and soaking wet. Through it they had stood strong as brothers and companions. Now was a rent in that brotherhood. Three of their members were dead, their bodies left far from their families and homes. Emund, the brother of the dead Arni, was most changed. The loss of a brother while adventuring was a common enough bereavement, but a painful cut just the same. Emund kept thinking about the return to Gotland and showing up at his brother's farm to face his widow. Arni's younger brother Emund had lived with them, and her own brother had come to stay with her in their absence. But her brother would be needed at home. What would she do then?

Eskil, tasked with being the instigator of the journey, and Runulv, responsible to the Dane for his treasure and his ship, and to so many Gotlanders for their very lives, were both deep in their own ruminations. They could not admit aloud the track into which their thoughts had begun to run. Even dreams of Miklagårdr's pleasures and riches seemed scant goad to keep them going; they wanted the journey to end, and not to die along the way.

Next day they moved forward, as they must. Every dawn saw the same, or similar challenge, the same or similar hardship. Brani recalled the names of the racing waters as he knew them. 'Little roarer' was one, and 'Boiling water', another. On the rare days when the waters were not overly fast, they all hazarded boarding and used their paddles to keep them driving forward and away from snags and boulders. Most days they divided, with half the men walking alongside the tethered craft, the second steering from within. Moving forward and feeding themselves were their two and only goals.

Where the water flowed out from the deeper pools, they found abundant fish. Their weirs, built of curved wooden staves, and laced with lines, kept them from starvation. Wedged or staked between boulders they could find five or six pike or chub in each one by morning. These were gutted, scaled, and thrown whole into the cooking pot with a few handfuls of grain, extracting every bit of nourishment.

At the end of the rougher cataracts where the stream widened and smoothed, a few burial mounds sat upon the banks, some rock-covered, others there long enough to have sprouted grass and be clothed in wisps of dried and withered greenery. This was where the bodies of those thrown from their boats were washed down, to be claimed by their brothers and given burial. Their appearance was enough to surprise the men each time they saw them: others had been this way before, they seemed to say, and known the losses you have known. Brani looked long at one mound before speaking. "Hedin. Hedin was laid there," he said.

After this they ran out of bank on which to walk or set camp. The Dnieper was wide here, almost forming a lake, with all the smooth bank on the far side; on their own was now a sheer cliff face. The water was calm, and deep enough to paddle across, and they did so. From there they spent a day afloat, keeping along that eastern edge and setting their camp upon it that night. But when the lake narrowed again, they watched the eastern margin narrow, and must return to their western bank. Though the river was shallow here and dotted with boulders, it was not fast flowing. Still, none wanted to risk a sudden current that might catch one of the dugouts and hurtle it onward. Half the men took up the tow lines and waded knee deep into the icy water to keep them secure. Some chose to go barefoot to save their boots the soaking, and emerged with feet red from cold.

The next day, just after the Sun had reached its highest point in day of rare brightness, the river Gods smiled. They were all aboard, paddling, when the noses of the men in the lead dugouts began to twitch. It was smoke, of the most welcome kind, that from a cook-fire. Ahead on a flat and sandy spit bordered with barren birches and flat-topped pines was a small settlement. Its palisade of pine logs was more of a stock fence than protection from marauders. Brani found his brass horn and blew out a few notes announcing their arrival. He did not recall this place, but was as glad as any to see it before them.

Folk came out to meet them, men and women both, blue-eyed and fair-haired like Slavs. These seemed to be almost as happy to see visitors as were the crew to be welcomed through the gates. All boats were beached and the men leapt ashore with new vigour in their limbs. In all the upheaval of packing and repacking the two captains still knew where lay their treasure boxes, and a pair of sharp-cutting shears made by Berse's sons was presented, along with a handful of tiny bells and open-worked beads fashioned of silver. Ale was handed round by their hosts, infused with that soft roundness that wheat imparts to the brew. After the ales, sour or bitter in turn they had been offered on their travels, this was no small boon.

They shared no common tongue, but the word 'Miklagårdr' and their quest for it was understood. It was a settlement of two or three families, with milking cows, flocks of ducks and geese, and a number of short-legged but sturdy chestnut horses, now shaggy in their Winter coats. The crew spent a full day and night there, eating, resting, and buying with silver coinage what food stuffs the folk could spare. They had much grain in the way of wheat and barley, and could fill the near-empty sacks held open to them. Cabbages and apples were carried out of root cellars and added to the store of what the captains bought. The folk had thriving droves of grey-spotted pigs, and could offer plump haunches, smoked and ready to eat. Indeed, their first meal with their hosts featured slabs of this, thick-cut and fried in salted butter from their spring-house. The aroma alone made the men's mouths water with expectation, just as some of their eyes misted in grateful thanks. This was passed with crusted loaves which all tore so they might soak up the savoury butter pooled around the red and sizzling meat.

After so much hardship their sojourn there presaged the good they hoped to encounter there on in. Eskil felt so revived that he found himself watching a yellow-haired maid with the same interest he had shown toward the women at King Oleg's fortress. It took a stern look from Runulv to curb the travelling of the Svear's eyes over her comely form.

Before they departed the two captains made Offering on the beach fronting the settlement. They must give thanks for the distance travelled, and despite their losses, ask for further good fortune on the way to their goal. Eskil obtained a duck from the folk, deeming it, a creature of both water and land, most suitable as a gift to the river Gods. Runulv chose a shorn fleece from Gotland, from whence he and his men had come, and to where they hoped to return.

They dug a shallow pit in the sand to receive their oblations. Eskil dispatched the duck with his knife, duly stamped his thumb in its blood, and placed the smeared drop in his mouth. Runulv rolled the fleece around the body of the bird, and laid it within. Both men filled the void with shovelfuls of sand, mounding it above to mark its place.

When they left on the second day, their provender had been enough replenished to carry them the remaining distance on the Dnieper, and beyond. They would see these folk again, they hoped, when their trading was over and they headed northwest for their homes. With nodding heads and smiles on both sides they took their leave and pushed off. And may we be rich as Ladja, Runulv told himself, on our return.

Past this settlement there was but one run of rapids. It was not a treacherous run, but it occasioned the men again walking the boats from the shore. It felt the river had exhausted itself on its earlier efforts to thwart their progress, and now gave feeble if grudging acceptance of their having survived its trials.

Then it was over, Brani assured them. That was the last challenge. From here on the Dnieper resumed the habits and tendencies of a free-flowing waterway.

They paddled on until they found a landing broad enough to beach and unload the many parts of Dauðadagr from the remaining karv. It took them over three days to put her together, but it was effort which each hour rewarded those who toiled over her.

They were glad for every sound piece of wood salvaged from the broken karv, as it came in handy to replace shorter pieces of decking splintered in their removal. Berse had to set up a forge and fashion many new rivets for her hull. The blade-smith's fire was partly fueled by the shattered remnants of the first karv, fragments too small to be put to service otherwise. "From boat to boat," he muttered to himself, as he fed the fire.

The work to Runulv was joyful, almost exultant. He had been forced to break her down, and now with Berse and Eskil and a few other men he could restore her fully. She might, Runulv thought, as he packed the tar-soaked fleece between the wider slits in her straked hull, be better than ever.

On the fourth day they pushed her onto the rollers and from thence into the river. Runulv kept her there for two full days and nights, tethered by a bow line to shore and by her iron anchor off the stern. Her planking had scarcely shrunk, so wet had been the environs in which she had been moved, and those few places from which water seeped were once more visited with fleece and tar. Only when she was perfectly sound was Odin lifted aboard, and placed again in the stern.

Now deemed sea-worthy, Dauðadagr could be loaded. This relieved the stress of the overcrowded boats; and she could carry so much. Freed from the bulk of her parts, the mast on Eskil's karv could again be raised, and its sail unfurled. From there they sailed swiftly ahead, a flotilla of six. Now Dauðadagr took the lead, with the dugouts behind her, the men aided in their paddling by the current steadily pulling them down river. Eskil, sail hoisted on the karv, brought up the rear. After so much confinement to their small boats, navigating the threatening defiles and deadly chasms of the rapids, to again run free before the wind felt the greatest pleasure.

Four days later the Dnieper again broadened. The sky ahead was lighter behind the trees. A bend in the river later they stood gaping at the vast expanse of the Black Sea before them.

I WANT TO GO HOME

The Fold, Defenas
The year 897, Spring

AELFWYN of Cirenceaster was brought to child-bed under the gaze of the four winds her husband had shaped for her. Raedwulf, Bailiff of Defenas, had carved faces for the seasons at the top of the bedsteads. Winter and Spring were behind her, Summer and Autumn before her. Mute but benevolent, they witnessed the birth of the child she brought forth.

The ever-faithful Burginde took charge, ably assisted by Lioba, wife to Indract, the steward of the hall. Ælfwyn's daughter Ealhswith was busy fetching and carrying for the two older women, and young Blida, Burginde's special help, had charge of Cerd, who now knew four years of age. Blida's task was the simplest, to keep Cerd outside and at play with the hounds of the place, and lead him on his pony. Blida's older brother Bettelin joined in this, so that the boy, active and engaged, was far enough from the hall so that any sound of a travailing woman might not frighten him.

There was perhaps little need of this concern. Burginde had attended her mistress at all three of her prior births, and expected little more than stifled groans and gasps from Ælfwyn. And though Ælfwyn would be newly made a mother once more, and her youngest was in her seventeenth year, this birth would be her fourth. The Lady of Defenas did not disappoint in her delivery of this new life. When she felt the first pangs, she said her prayers most devotedly, commending her soul to God and asking only that her babe should live, even if she herself should die. Her nurse had already seen Raedwulf out of the bed chamber; and even if he had been present Ælfwyn would not utter such a prayer in his hearing, as he had lost his first wife following child-bed.

The travail was mercifully brief, the endurance of but a long afternoon, and without excess of violence. With Lioba at Ælfwyn's shoulders, and Burginde at her knees, the shining babe emerged. Ælfwyn's ending cry was one of almost joyous freeing. Burginde had cause to recall Ashild, whom she had attended at the birth of Cerd. The nurse must smile at the thought. Ashild's mighty war-whoop when her babe finally emerged was heard, Burginde thought, throughout all Four Stones.

When Burginde stood, she placed a perfect boy-child on his mother's breast.

Without the chamber, Raedwulf had stood with Indract, the first pacing, the second gripping an ale cup, now empty. When Burginde opened the door to announce mother and child were hale and hearty, it did not fully assuage the Bailiff's great concern. He wished to enter at once, but Burginde, well used to how much care Ælfwyn took of her appearance, would delay him until she had unbraided the flaxen length of her mistress's hair, combed it smoothly, and had placed a shawl made dainty with thread-work over her shoulders.

It was occasion for joy and thanksgiving, but as Raedwulf bent over his wife he was not alone in blinking water from his eyes. Tears were running down Ælfwyn's face as she held the babe to her, her hand across her son's back, pressing him to her. Raedwulf kissed her, and then the head of his son. Ealhswith was standing back where she had been with Lioba, and that good woman had her arm about the girl. Ealhswith had not been allowed in the birthing chamber for the birth of Cerd, and now knew more of the great mystery of passing from wife to mother.

When the babe had been swaddled and tucked up in his mother's arm, Ælfwyn slept. When she awoke her husband was there, smiling upon her and the babe. She had prayed for a healthy child, and been granted a boy. Raedwulf's sole offspring from his brief marriage had been Wilgyfu, his much-loved daughter, now wed to Worr, the horse-thegn of Kilton. Now he would have a son as well.

The age-old ceremony of claiming the child took place. Before Burginde, Ealhswith, Indract and Lioba, the babe was lifted from his mother's arms and placed in those of Raedwulf, sitting at the side of the bed. As Burginde passed the tiny bundle to his father, her own cheeks were nearly as rosy as the babe, so full of happiness was she.

The Bailiff of Defenas lowered the child to his lap a moment and acknowledged him as his own. "In gratitude to God I welcome this true child of mine, thankful for the life of this boy and my beloved wife, his mother." Raedwulf himself rose to place the boy back in the crook of his mother's arm. Her blue eyes were glistening with joy.

Ealhswith, standing there as one of the witnesses, blinked away her own tears. So much had happened in the last two days. By being invited into the birthing chamber, Ealhswith felt propelled into a level of womanhood heretofore denied to her. She had been frightened by the pain her mother suffered, and distressed by the bloody after-birth, which made her almost faint. The girl had wanted to be of service, and hoped she had been. Now she stood here before her mother's great happiness with a new babe. Ealhswith loved her mother, and desired her to be happy. But there was no denying she had been stunned when told her mother was in love with the Bailiff of Defenas, and preparing to start a new life with him. A further shock was the news of the coming of their babe. Ealhswith felt abashed that she had not considered that a likely, or even possible end, for the newly wedded pair. But she had not. She remembered her mother asking her to be happy for her sake, that day she had shared the secret with her daughter in her nascent garden. Now here was the child, before them all. Ealhswith wished also to feel happy. Instead she felt confused, and overlooked. She was no longer her mother's youngest; her mother had embraced an entirely fresh life with her new husband. Ealhswith felt crowded out for attention, what with her sister's son, Cerd, and now this new boy.

After the other witnesses had left the room, Raedwulf lifted an eyebrow meaningfully to Burginde. He wished a moment alone with his wife. The nurse had not been away from Ælfwyn's side since the first birthing pang had announced the coming of the child. Now she understood, and with a quick bob of her head, hustled from the room.

It gave Raedwulf the time he needed to present a gift to the new mother. It was the sapphire he had carried to Four Stones to present to Hrald as Ælfwyn's bride-price. The Jarl, in a great and generous gesture of approval, had in return handed it to his mother as his wedding gift. After Ælfwyn's arrival in Defenas, the sapphire had sat in an iron strong box here in their bed chamber. Raedwulf had in private taken the stone, and while on one of his trips to Witanceaster, had it set in a bezel of gold. This he had strung from a fine chain of gold, a pendant most rare for his wife. He carried it to her now from the strong box where he had kept it hid. The sapphire was oval, and fully as large as the egg of a quail. Never was gold set to better advantage than to embrace this gem.

The setting transformed it. Raedwulf still had clear memory of the bloody combat against the Danes in which he had won it. The stone was cut, but unset, the prize amongst several of lesser worth in the Dane's small treasure-store at his waist. So great was its value that he had after offered it to Ælfred. The King was still Prince then, and he waved it off, telling Raedwulf it was booty well won. Raedwulf had it in his possession all these long years.

He placed it about Ælfwyn's neck. "A blue not as rich as your eyes," he whispered. "But close." And he kissed her.

The first days of the child's life bode well. He cried lustily to be fed, and fell happily to sleep at the breast when full. Ælfwyn too was well. In asking that she might bear Raedwulf's child, she had compared herself to Sarai, aged wife to Abraham of the Bible. This last gift she asked, to make their love perfect. It had been granted.

There was no near priest; the family would need to travel to Exanceaster, as they did once a month to attend

Mass, so that the babe might be baptised. And the boy needed a name. Ælfwyn wished that Raedwulf choose one. After thought he combined his own, with that of his wife's long-dead father, Ælfsige. The result, Wulfsige, bore a strong meaning: Wolf Victory.

"Wulfsige," Burginde mused. "A right fitting name for a noble boy." She looked down at the babe, latched to his mother's breast. "Small as he is now, I will call him Wulf until he grows." She thought a moment. "And with the Pup" – for this was the way she still referred to Cerd – "we will nearly have a pack."

Burginde also took charge of bringing Cerd so he might meet the new arrival. She lowered the babe in her arms for Cerd to see. "This be your uncle, Cerd," she told him, with a merry laugh. "He is but a mite, now. But when he is grown you must obey him!"

Cerd approached with interest, studying the tiny face, eyes closed in sleep. He reached out a finger to touch the far smaller fingers curled on the top of the blanket the babe was wrapped in. Cerd grinned, then laughed.

Later that day, when the new parents were alone with their babe, Ælfwyn took deep and quiet pleasure in seeing how Raedwulf gazed upon him. She reached out her hand and placed it over Raedwulf's. My blessings are many, she thought. We have been granted a son. And I am at peace with all my children. Ealhswith holds such promise, and is a maid who Ælfred takes interest in. Ashild is honoured, and an asset at Oundle. And Hrald, wed to so good a woman as Pega, and a father himself . . .

This was what Ælfwyn contemplated, holding her new babe, and with the man she loved at her side. Just now she needed an unclouded horizon, with so much in the near foreground of her sight. Ælfwyn had not told Raedwulf about Hrald spending the night with Dagmar while they were at Witanceaster. She determined to shelter this knowledge in her own breast. It was not her story to tell, and she hoped nothing more would come of it.

XXXXXXXXXXX

"I will ask Prince Eadward to be God-father." This was Raedwulf, holding his son at the side of the babe's mother.

Ælfwyn's lips parted in astonishment, then formed a warm smile. A Prince, and one who might soon be King, as God-father to her child.

Ælfwyn posed her own candidate now. "For God-mother, let us ask Ealhswith. She is of age, well-schooled in the Church, and more importantly, herself devout. It might mean much to her, this service. One I hope she sees also as honour."

So it was decided. As they must travel to the cathedral at Exanceaster for a priest, they might select a date two months out. This would give the Bailiff's letter ample time to arrive at Witanceaster, or any other hall the Prince might be resident at, and to receive an answer in return.

The letter was written out and entrusted to one of Raedwulf's men. A week later he returned, with answer. The Prince was more than willing to serve as God-father, and would meet the family at Exanceaster at St Helen's Day, in the third week of May.

The journey from The Fold, even by waggon, was only of two hours. They could set off early in the day, take their places at Mass before the Sun was overhead, and then, when the sanctuary had quieted, have the babe anointed and blest.

Cerd remained at The Fold with Blida and the rest of the household, which meant that Burginde could devote herself entirely to Ælfwyn and the babe. Ealhswith had indeed been surprised to be asked to act as God-mother for her little brother, and more surprised still when Raedwulf told her who would serve as God-father. She had nodded and curtseyed to the King at Witanceaster, and now would stand shoulder to shoulder with the Prince.

The cathedral was as full as it ever was for Sunday Mass, and a noticeable murmur of recognition rippled through the congregation when Prince Eadward, accompanied by a few of his captains, entered. He could not but be noticed, as they walked the length of the nave to stand near the chancel. Eadward was arrayed befitting a Prince on a festival day, in a tunic of russet brown, and with a single heavy chain of linked gold spanning his chest. The Mass was celebrated by three priests in chasubles of green, and the smoking censor swung by the youngest of them wafted incense through the nave. The morning was brilliantly sunny, and the beams cast through the glass casement set the motes of incense dancing about all. Little Wulfsige, gowned in a chrisom of linen snowy white and sewn by Burginde, was blissfully asleep through chanting, singing, and smoke. Held in the arms of both his mother and Burginde he was untroubled by the movement before him at the altar, or the rustle of the congregants behind him.

When Mass had concluded, and paten and chalice replaced in the aumbry, the priests vanished through the door to the vestry. The congregation processed out, save for a few who lingered at the eastern door, curious to see the

Prince and the family he was now conversing with. Raedwulf could make but the briefest of presentations of his wife and her daughter to Eadward before a single priest returned, in a simple white surplice. The two women were of unusual comeliness, the Prince judged, their striking resemblance making it almost as if the same woman, some twenty years apart, stood before him. Both were dressed in rich but sober gowns, Raedwulf's Lady in a dusky blue, the maid in pale lilac embellished with yellow. He allowed his eyes to rest on Ealhswith long enough to make the girl colour. This, then, was the prize Edwin of Kilton had spurned, thought Eadward. His father had told him all; Eadward must know such things, and it might fall to him to find a suitable match for this girl.

The conferring of the sacrament of baptism began. The stone font had been uncovered, and the water within warmed by the dropping of a round stone, heated in a brazier, to remove the chill. A silver tray held by the altar boy was presented. Burginde had charge of Wulf, now awake and looking at all with wide eyes. The nurse was also dressed in her best, a gown of green upon which was pinned a large brooch of silver at the neck, and a silver chain which now Wulf had curled his little fingers around. The priest spoke in the tongue of Rome, except for when he asked who stood as God-parents to the child; then Ealhswith had the thrill of stepping forward with the Prince. They were asked their names, which Ealhswith had not expected.

"Ealhswith of Four Stones. And Defenas," she answered, in a voice scarce above a whisper. She felt discomfited, unsure, and unable to identify herself by one hall or one Kingdom.

The Prince's answer was much the simpler, and firmer.

"Eadward of Wessex."

Burginde turned to Ealhswith, and with a smile of reassurance handed her Wulfsige. Ealhswith felt herself tremble under his slight weight. She must strip off the dainty gown of linen he wore, and pass him, naked, to the priest. She did so. Uttering prayers, the priest lowered the babe to the water, and with quick firmness immersed him three times. Wulfsige's face screwed up in surprise, then scrunched in a wail. After the third dunking the babe was out, and placed in the linen towelling Burginde had sewn for the reception of the new-christened son of her mistress. Ealhswith held the crying child while the priest made the Sign of the Cross over his head, and pressed a drop of rare oil upon his brow. Then it was over, the priest smiling at all. Burginde and Ealhswith dried the now-sniffling Wulf, returned him to his little gown, and restored him to his mother's arms. The party retreated to the vestry where the register was kept, and the baptism recorded, along with the name of Wulfsige's parents and God-parents.

After this the party walked with Eadward and his waiting men to the royal residence kept there for the King's use. A meal awaited them, one which celebrated the bounty of Spring, with succulent lamb, tender new peas and their tendrils, and eggs and cheeses showing off the glories of dairy and fowl house. Raedwulf sat at the right of the Prince, and the two were much in converse. Ælfwyn sat to her husband's right, and then Burginde with Wulf, and finally Ealhswith. The left of the Prince was entirely taken up by his chief men, many of them young and as yet unwed, who denied clear view of the pretty maid amongst the Prince's guests, made excuse to sometimes half rise from the table so they might see her better.

Raedwulf, as assured as he was as warrior and envoy to Ælfred, took little for granted in relations with his son. Thus Eadward's ready acceptance of standing as God-father for Wulfsige held meaning to the Bailiff. This time with the Prince afforded Raedwulf a chance to speak of one who was never far from his mind, Ceric of Kilton. Ceric had served with great distinction under Eadward, and Raedwulf had made certain that monarch and Prince in Witanceaster were kept apprised of his recovery, and of his marriage. It was of this Raedwulf wished to speak to Eadward.

Neither Ælfred nor Eadward had ever dismissed Wales. It shared a long border with Mercia, the Kingdom from which the King's wife, and thus Eadward's mother, had hailed. But relations with the Cymry had often been frayed, with periods of outright hostility. Now one of their Princesses had come to Kilton, and the Bailiff broached the topic of a diplomatic visit to Wales of the young woman and the son of Kilton she had wed. The Bailiff felt certain of Eadward's plan to continue the fortifying of Wessex; the Prince had amply demonstrated that. To bring Mercia under the golden dragon banner was a more delicate topic, and one Raedwulf could only allude to. It was enough for him to touch upon the importance of a secure western border, and strong allies numbered beyond it amongst the Welsh.

"The Princess of Ceredigion is a remarkable young woman, My Lord," he explained. "And I need not remind you of the abilities of Ceric of Kilton; his judgement, forthrightness and intelligence. You have seen them yourself. Together I think they shall make a formidable pair in diplomatic efforts.

"With your approval I will bring this up to the King," Raedwulf went on. "He has already expressed his full pleasure in the union of Ceric and the Lady Dwynwen. Assurance of your support going forward would be a great asset to the workings of the scheme."

Eadward listened with apparent interest. He was young, ambitious, and teeming with aspirations for a flourishing Wessex. "I too will speak of it with the King," he vowed.

The party from The Fold departed not long after this. Eadward and his men would be riding their way in a day or two, and promised to stop at the holding when he left Exanceaster.

That night, once again gathered in Raedwulf's hall, Ealhswith looked about her. The hall, small but solid, lime-washed and fitted out with every comfort, felt more alien to her than the first night she had slept here.

"I would like to go home," Ealhswith said.

She was sitting at table next Burginde as she did every night. Blida was to her other side, attempting to corral Cerd, who as always wished to walk upon the table. The cradle Wulfsige lay in had been brought into the room, and he lay in it, behind his parents. Burginde did not seem to have heard her, or rather knew that Ealhswith had spoken, but had not caught her words.

"I would like to go home," she said again. Her voice was louder this time, but free from any quaver.

Her mother had turned her head to look down at her babe, and now turned back to her daughter.

"Home," Ælfwyn repeated. She would not insult her daughter by suggesting she was in fact there. Ælfwyn understood what Ealhswith meant.

Raedwulf spoke. "To return to Four Stones," he asked. His tone was one of gentle inquiry, one of interest, with neither surprise nor condemnation.

Ealhswith stood up, and nodded her head. "Yes. I would like to go back to Four Stones." She did not need to remind her mother that she had been promised that this option would always be open to her. Now Ealhswith wished to take it.

Raedwulf looked to his wife. It had been a day of great happiness for Ælfwyn, with the formal welcoming into the Church of her newborn. Now her surviving daughter wished to leave her, and return to the hall in which she had been raised. She found herself nodding her head in silent agreement to Ealhswith's demand.

Burginde stifled a splutter. She had no chance to speak, for Cerd had in fact escaped Blida and was standing, both feet upon the table. "Come up here with me!" he invited Burginde. The nurse swallowed her laughter at the thought of climbing up to join him. She rose and swept him off in her strong arms, handed him another bread loaf, and placed his restless feet on the floor.

The Bailiff again took the lead. "Prince Eadward is coming here, tomorrow or upon the overmorrow. Perhaps he can take you as far as Witanceaster, where word can be sent to Four Stones."

"Yes, please," Ealhswith answered. She had asked to go home, and suddenly she might be sent there. If Eadward consented to take her, she would go.

Ealhswith could not speak more; she had already said that which would change her life. It felt there were often conflicting sensations, warring emotions, fighting for precedence in her heart and mind. She could feel fear and desire at the same time, or trepidation and daring. She felt this now, that and things much easier to give voice to. She missed her friends amongst the maids of Four Stones, and the still and calming presence of her Aunt Eanflad, always at her loom. Though it made her cry to go there, she missed standing in front of her sister's ledger stone in the church of Oundle, then kneeling to pray for Ashild's soul. She wanted the reassurance of being near her brother Hrald, and the hope to win his approval. Most of all Ealhswith wished to be noticed, and valued.

※※※※※※※※※

Ealhswith's belongings were made ready for travel, such was the Bailiff's confidence that Prince Eadward would oblige the girl's request. The Prince and his troop of men numbered just over two score, and arrived the following day with a pair of horse-drawn supply waggons, heading east.

After greeting the Prince with the rest of the household, Ealhswith excused herself from his presence, lest he refuse to be burdened with her. Her absence allowed her step-father to be as direct as required.

"We have no small favour to ask of you, my Lord," Raedwulf began. He and the girl's mother were sitting together with the Prince at the high table. Ælfwyn had already poured some of Lioba's good ale from her silver bird ewer into waiting cups. Burginde sat some little distance down, holding Wulf in her arms.

"My step-daughter Ealhswith wishes to return to Four Stones for a visit. Would it be possible for you to take her as far as Witanceaster? With her I will send a letter to one of my men, asking that he rides to Anglia to tell of her arrival."

Eadward cocked his head, but did not seem overly surprised.

"I recall her answer to the priest, when asked to state her name and home. She seemed to be one of divided loyalties," he conceded, with a smile. "But from here I head not to Witanceaster, but back to Lundenwic. My wife Ecgwynn is of there."

Raedwulf and Ælfwyn knew the Prince had now two children, a boy and a girl. He would return to his hall where they, and Ecgwynn, awaited him.

The Prince went on. "That will bring Ealhswith to the Anglia border, where word can speedily be sent to Jarl Hrald, of his sister's arrival."

This was an even better solution, and would bring the girl much closer to her destination. And she could scarcely travel upon the road with more protection than Eadward's own body-guard afforded. Both mother and step-father expressed their gratitude to the Prince, though the tightening of Ælfwyn's throat gave her excuse to find Ealhswith and continue with their preparations.

There was much swirling in Ælfwyn's head. Her girl would be travelling without the aid and companionship of a friend, or even a serving-woman. Eadward had arrived with a troop of his body-guard; there was no woman amongst them. His father Ælfred rarely left Witanceaster without a priest. If it had been the King, the girl could be placed in the care of the cleric. And small as the household of The Fold was, there was no ready serving-woman or maid to send with Ealhswith.

When Ælfwyn found Ealhswith in her garden with Cerd and Blida, she pointed this out to her. Her wish would be granted, but she would be travelling alone with a group of men, one of whom was Prince of the realm. The highest level of decorum must prevail in all Ealhswith said and did.

Ealhswith bit her lip in thought. The notion frightened her, but excited her at the same time. She began at once to plan. If ever there would be chance to be favourably noticed by a member of the royal family, it would be now. She would be discreet, and quiet; this was her nature. She would be uncomplaining, even cheerful, she resolved. Eadward would regard her well, and remind his father of her; perhaps he even knew of some perfect match for her, himself. And soon she would be home at Four Stones.

The Prince could not be delayed, and his quarter-master began at once to shift certain supplies from one of the waggons, which would house her for the coming trip, to the second. Bedding and her two clothes chests were placed on the waggon bed. Ealhswith had a fine gelding given her by Hrald as a parting gift, and he was tied behind, giving the girl the option to either ride or sit within the waggon.

There was little time for fare-wells, and all must be enacted under the gaze of Eadward and his men. Ælfwyn fought tears, as did her daughter. Assurances were given that Ealhswith could send word at any time and be recalled to The Fold. It was Burginde who took the girl aside in the last few moments before she was helped aboard the waggon.

"You be off on an adventure. Both now, with the Prince, and then back at Four Stones. Do nothing to shame your mother, or your brother," was her pithy advice. This was sternly delivered, and followed with a kiss.

※※※※※※※※※※※

That first night with Ealhswith away, Ælfwyn lay abed and awake. The babe had roused her, needing to suck, and now that he had fallen back into his own sleep she could not. Though she knew the reassurance of a peacefully breathing Raedwulf at her side, his wife's thoughts were troubled indeed.

Ealhswith's mother was well aware that her girl was not as happy as could have been hoped. There was some listlessness about her, one that began even before they left for their new life at The Fold. It was as if Ealhswith yearned for something she could not voice. Her asking in so direct a manner to be returned to Four Stones was unlike the girl, and hopefully a sign of her understanding herself better. Ealhswith's choices in life were circumscribed, the lives of all were, but she had asked for something which she and Raedwulf could grant. She was returning to her brother, and life at Four Stones.

Just as Hrald lost his wife Dagmar and then his sister Ashild, Ealhswith lost her much-admired sister-in-law, and then her sister. And Ealhswith felt the sting of rejection by Edwin. She was so tender a girl, Ælfwyn knew. She had known her own profound losses, yet not enough attention had been paid to those wounds. Hrald had looked as though he had moved on from the disaster of Dagmar. He had not. Ælfwyn wondered if her daughter had not healed sufficiently from her own hurts, either.

A Caesar's Road, some of it still in good repair, lay part of the way between Exanceaster and Lundenwic. Eadward used it, and other well-travelled roads of packed earth as well. It took eight days to reach the teeming town of Lundenwic. Ealhswith made use of her experience travelling from Four Stones to Defenas; it had been the first great journey of her life, and now she was making a second, also by waggon. She had every comfort supplied her in the conveyance, just as she had on the first trip, and the solicitude shown by the Prince made her feel a valued and indeed honoured member of his party. The great difference was the lack of her mother and Burginde. In the train of Prince Eadward, she was no mere cossetted child, as she could not help feeling when subject to the loving presence of the two women who had raised her. On this foray to Lundenwic Ealhswith was treated with esteem, and, more significantly for her, as a woman, one of marriageable age and thus a particular asset with as yet unknowable possibilities. She kept to her own promise to remain calm and of good cheer, and though spending much time alone bethought herself of how her mother would respond to being the sole female on such a journey; or imagined Ashild in lively converse with the man driving her waggon, and moved herself to emulate their actions. One fine afternoon after they had stopped to water their beasts, she even made bold to ask help that she might mount her horse, and ride alongside the Prince. It was one of his captains she asked aid of, and he called a second man to hold her gelding's head while the captain steadied her on the waggon board, making it easy for her to gain the saddle. Eadward smiled upon her as she joined him, and though she felt the heat on her cheek, she told herself it was her right to ride with him; an expectation of courtesy, perhaps. Alas, she had never attended much at table to the discourse of her step-father Raedwulf when he, in broad terms, discussed affairs of State with her mother. Ealhswith found herself almost mute after the first few pleasantries with the Prince, and, fearing to broach topics of which she knew little, resigned herself to agreeing to his observations about the landscape they passed through with an innocent and artless simplicity.

Lundenwic, when they gained it, was not as large as the Kingly burh of Wessex Ælfred had made Witanceaster. But the great river bisecting it was itself a thing of wonder to Ealhswith, and the wooden bridge spanning it a structure as she had never imagined. Witanceaster had impressed; now she was awed.

She was received with prompt hospitality into the hall of Prince Eadward. In fact it was the family hall of his wife, Ecgwynn, who, along with her mother, welcomed her. The hall stood in a square, a dry distance away from the river. Its tidal ebb and flow left it a morass of thick brown mud twice a day, and narrowed its channel to a fraction of its width in full flood.

The hall in which she stayed was as large as Four Stones, and many young women filled it, those in attendance to the royal family as either kin, or serving maids. Here the pride she had felt in the Prince's esteem fell away from Ealhswith like a dropped mantle. Many of the women were richly attired, making Ealhswith in her travel dress dowdy by contrast. The first night at table she studied them all. All were of marrying age, and many, like her, would have rich dowers appended to them. She saw with a painful clarity how slight a package she might be. Though she was guest of Prince Eadward and his wife's family, here amongst so many maids Ealhswith sensed herself small and unnoticed. After her trip to Witanceaster where she was called to meet Edwin of Kilton – who rejected her out of hand due to her father – she had slipped from Ælfred's mind. That was last Summer, now it was late Spring. Who would she wed? No one wanted her.

It took Eadward's fast riders a little more than three days to reach Four Stones. Both men would remain, and accompany the party sent to meet Ealhswith in Lundenwic to fetch her home. When they arrived eight days later, Hrald was fronting the group.

He was led to the hall of the Prince, Jari at his side, twenty men behind them, and two waggons. Ealhswith was out in the enclosed gardens behind the hall, almost a cloister, with a number of other maids. When she was summoned within and saw the height and leanness of the man silhouetted there by the doorway she gave a shriek of joy and ran to her brother.

The Prince was away in another part of town and must be sent for. It gave chance for all the dusty troop to lead their horses to the stable block, and for ale to be handed round by Lady Ecgwynn.

Prince Eadward returned, and he and Hrald retired to a small structure in the garden, one fitted out as a private bower. They stood within, and kept their feet, even after a serving man arrived with cakes and ale, and left them. Eadward had never before met the young Jarl of Four Stones, though his father the King had direct dealings with both Hrald and Sidroc.

Now he could take the measure of the man. Eadward was six and twenty; the Jarl before him, three or four years younger. Yet his brow was marked with seriousness, and the Prince could see, a faint scar, barely perceptible, which folded into a furrow when Hrald showed concern. In stature and bearing Hrald could stand with credit with many an older and distinguished warrior. His voice was low, and every word well chosen, yet without any semblance of artifice in intent.

He was a considerable man, in parts and in sum. Looking upon him Eadward understood why his sister Æthelflaed had awarded the choicest prize of Mercian womanhood, the Lady Pega, to Hrald as wife.

Eadward's eyes dropped to the sword Hrald was wearing. The Prince knew it at once; it had long hung on display in the armoury at Witanceaster. Seeing it belted at Hrald's waist prompted his next words.

"You killed Haesten."

Eadward had heard the tale from his father the King, and knew of the reward. It was a kill of such distinction that he must comment on it himself.

"My losses to him were great," Hrald answered. "Including my sister."

"Ashild of Four Stones," Eadward murmured. "Yes."

Eadward and Hrald had been linked for years, if by second degree, through Ceric of Kilton. Ceric had determined to wed the elder daughter of Four Stones, strengthening that link. If Ashild had lived it would have formed a bond of estimable value to Wessex.

"The King told me you let his boys live, though they watched the combat."

Hrald had answer and reason both. He need not add that he would take no child's life. "Ceric told me the King had the boys baptised, in attempt to save them body and soul. The mother stood next them as we fought. I sent them to Frankland."

"Let us hope they remain there," the Prince said. A moment later he made a vow.

"If they do not, the house of Æthelwulf will be at your side."

The Prince's calling on his grand-sire's name was a mark of the highest esteem. Hrald was enough taken by this he could but utter acknowledgment of the promise.

Eadward turned his thoughts to the present. "Your sister, the Lady Ealhswith, is a noble maid."

Wed as he was, he could not add that if the girl had been of age a few years ago and he had seen her, he might have asked for her himself. She was from the lineage of Cirenceaster, anchoring and uniting two lands through her mother Ælfwyn, and her brother, Jarl of Four Stones.

"Rest your horses a day or two," Eadward said instead. "The hall is large, and the road north will wait for you."

SHADOW

A smiling Pega stood at the gates to greet them. Mealla, her companion and chief attendant, was at her side. In Mealla's arms was Pega and Hrald's child, Ælfgiva, rosebud mouth agape as she watched the horses and waggons pass through. Pega's hound Frost sat obediently at his mistress's feet. Kjeld stood off to one side, the key to the treasure room already in his fingers. Once again he had taken the occasion of the possession of the key to hearten him in asking after the hand of Mealla, the black-haired maid of Éireann. Once more the key had failed him.

Any troop of a score of warriors was an impressive sight, and this arrival home with the returned daughter of the hall was no different. Amongst Hrald's men were two youths, Hrald and Ealhswith's half-brother Yrling, and the orphan Bork. It was the first long ride in service for each, and they were given the task and responsibility of bringing up the rear. Light in the saddle, spears in hands, and ready to whistle out approaching danger in a moment, they took pride in this assignment, and were rewarded by being treated as near equals by the other men. Beyond this, they had seen the wonders of Lundenwic, and been in the company of the Prince of Wessex. Bork was no longer a stable-boy. He showed such promise in his training at arms that Hrald moved him out of the stable, and Mul's employ. Bork now lodged with Yrling at the house of Jari and Inga. Bork's gladness at being accepted fully into the ranks of those young in training was sincere. Hrald had realised the boy would always be at a disadvantage while living at the stable, and told him so. Bork's thoughtful answer gave Hrald pause, as the boy quietly pointed out that Christ was born in one.

The horsemen crossed through the gates two by two, crowding the stable yard and being greeted with cries of welcome. Then Hrald, Jari, and all were off their horses, and Pega, who had come to the waggon board where sat Ealhswith, reached her hand out to the girl in welcome.

The first days home were ones of near-delight. Ealhswith had a kind of upwelling of affection for the place which she had kept kindled during her year at The Fold, and had stoked to a burning flame on the road here. Yet there were surprises as well. The first sign of change was the building-works beyond the paddock. The stone preaching cross outside the palisade was fine for the village, but the house of Wilgot the priest made but a poor substitute for a true and sanctified church. Pega was building one now, on the site where the old one burnt when the keep was taken by Yrling. Jari had scant memory of the structure save that it was one that fire had destroyed, but amongst the oldest of the kitchen staff Pega coaxed memories of where it stood. She wished it on the same hallowed ground. It would be made of timber, something Lindisse possessed in abundance, in planks set upright. Pega had such wealth that she could order stone and masons alike to be brought in, but building in wood would make it easy to expand. The foundation had been laid when Ealhswith arrived, so the outline was readily discerned.

Having been greeted and kissed by Pega and Mealla, and surrounded with welcoming cries by the friends she had left behind, Ealhswith could give happy report of the little son, Wulfsige, born to her mother Lady Ælfwyn and the Bailiff of Defenas.

"We will send the child a gift with you, when you return," Pega told her. She had her own child in her arms as she said this. If there was a moment's regret that Pega's first born had not been a boy, she did not allow it to cloud her brow. She gave Ælfgiva an extra squeeze and looked over the child's head to the girl's father. Hrald returned the smile, and Ælfgiva lifted her hand to her father and smiled as well.

After this Ealhswith must again see her Aunt Eanflad. She did not wish to startle the woman, and climbed the wooden stairs to the weaving room fearing she might. She knew a deep affection for her aunt, but in truth was grateful for Pega going with her, assuring her in words and looks that Eanflad was well. Both knew this was not always the case.

Eanflad as a girl had remained largely silent following the attack and fall of Cirenceaster. After her arrival at Four Stones, Eanflad almost never left the upstairs weaving room to which she had been escorted with her mother, and sister Æthelthryth. But she had been devoted to Burginde as a little girl, and her eyes followed her about the room. With Burginde's steady coaxing, Eanflad began to follow her footsteps as well, joining her across the landing to the drying room, where the girl could help hang their wet laundry. After some months Eanflad would venture down the wooden stairs with Burginde, and became a useful aid to the nurse during trips to the kitchen or laundry yards, or at such gentle tasks as gathering eggs from hens in the fowl houses. Eanflad's small hands slipped almost without notice under the roosting birds, and sometimes the flicker of a smile would light the child's face as she filled her small basket. She began moving more about the work yards, at times without Burginde at her side, a sign to all that the girl grew in comfort and mayhap, surety, as she expanded the narrow limits of her horizon. The silent girl was notably fearful of men, and likely to flee to the safety of the weaving room if she took fright, but all Sidroc's warriors knew to give her a wide berth.

One morning when Eanflad had been at the hall for two years, she went out alone to gather eggs at one of the fowl houses. No one knew the exact events that followed, as Eanflad was unable to tell of them. But Sidroc happened to walk by the narrow alley between fowl houses which formed a run, and there found Eanflad pinned against a wall by one of his own men. The girl's gown had been pulled up to her waist, and the man was forcing himself upon her. Eanflad was uttering sounds, akin to the cries of a small animal caught in a trap. At her feet was her woven basket where it had fallen, the eggs tumbled and broken upon the earth.

Sidroc was on the man in an instant, wrenching him by the neck away from the girl. He turned him enough so the rapist might see Sidroc's face as he felt the thrust of his seax in his belly. He killed the man, there in front of Eanflad, still flattened against the wall and whimpering as if her ravisher were still upon her.

From that day Eanflad returned to the weaving room, and rarely left its confines.

Ealhswith had not been told of this episode, and did not know her father had killed a man before the eyes of the panicked girl. Ealhswith knew only that as a child her Aunt Eanflad had suffered assault so severe that she lost her grasp of speech. Eanflad's silent life in the weaving room had been a fact of Ealhswith's life. Eanflad did little but weave after this, and as long as nothing more was expected of her, seemed content. She liked to hear singing, and would nod her head to the tune when Ælfwyn and Burginde, and later, Ashild, sang together. It made the work of their hands at spinning, weaving, or sewing the more pleasurable.

When the Lady Ceridwen had visited and she and Ealhswith's father had been abducted from the cliff lookout at Saltfleet, Eanflad again spoke. She came to her older sister Ælfwyn in her distress, and offered words of comfort, telling her all would be well. Since that distant day she had spoken when moved to do so. At times she had gone with Ælfwyn to Oundle to visit their mother, a consecrated nun there, and walked the convent gardens with Burginde. But her life was largely lived at her loom.

So it was that after a year's absence at The Fold, Ealhswith was not certain how her aunt would receive her. She need not have concern. Eanflad glanced over her shoulder from her work when the weaving room door opened and Ealhswith and Pega walked in. She lifted her hands from the working of her loom, leaving her charged shuttle between the warp strings. A smile flickered over her still face. Though Eanflad had seen more than thirty Summers, her face was as smooth and unlined as a child's, as if she had stopped ageing long ago.

Ealhswith ran to her in gladness, to be greeted by the gently opened arms of her aunt. Pega, always discreet, took this for the encouraging sign it was, and withdrew.

Once released from that embrace, Ealhswith spent a long moment looking about her. Now returned to the room in which she had been largely raised, she felt surprised by her surroundings, or rather, how they made her feel. It was not just the absence of her mother and Burginde, and reaching further back, that unbridged gap left by the death of Ashild. Ealhswith felt she no longer fit here.

Eanflad had turned back to her linen loom, narrower than its woollen counterpart. Her niece followed her, to look upon row after row of linen weft, evenly compacted, its glossy sheen a harbinger of the comfort this fabric would become.

Ealhswith touched the taut warp strings and wondered aloud to her aunt.

"Why is your weaving so much better than mine?"

It did not take Eanflad long to answer. She bowed her head, then returned her eyes to the weft.

"I think of it. I think only of it. I watch my hands and think only of what they do."

Ealhswith took thought at this. Her aunt wove without distraction, intent on the task at hand. Her powers of concentration were ideally suited to reap reward from everything her mother, and Burginde, had taught her about spinning and weaving.

In contrast, Ealhswith felt her own mind nothing but distraction. Eanflad's work was near to perfect, for her attention was there. Ealhswith in her restlessness knew not what to focus on, or even how to do so.

"You – you are best of us," Ealhswith told her. In answer her aunt flashed a smile at her, brief, but a true smile none the less.

That night Ealhswith experienced the second change her sister-in-law had wrought. At table Pega had initiated the use of knee coverings as were used in the court of Mercia. These were squares of hemmed linen placed for each diner, to be laid upon the lap, and used to wipe fingers and mouth. They proved no small saving to the laundresses, as food which dropped from spoon or knife fell onto the cloth, and not tunic or gown. Such cloths were used at Oundle; nuns and monks were known for their thrifty fastidiousness in all things. Not long after Ælfwyn and Ealhswith left, Pega brought the custom to Four Stones. Not all Hrald's men used them, but a few expectant and then reproving looks from the Lady of the hall encouraged those seated at the high table to do so. Kjeld, second in command, was careful that first night in watching how Mealla unfolded hers and spread it over her knees, and tried to do so with the same air of practised ease.

Ealhswith was happy to be back at Four Stones. But she was dismayed at how quickly her initial pleasure and sense of satisfaction passed, and all fell into the rhythm of the old days. It was true her mother was not here, but Pega, with her quiet command, was much the same presence in the working of the hall and its yards. Black-haired Mealla was more than equal to Burginde in both assisting her mistress and in chaffing any of kitchen or yard staff she deemed fell short of her standards. Mealla saved her tartest scolding for Kjeld, who the other men consoled by saying it was a sure sign of favour.

Despite the alterations large and small at Four Stones, Ealhswith decided the most changed was Hrald. He seemed distracted, and more quiet than she had recalled him. He had much on his mind; she knew this. Not only the hall and lands of Four Stones, but that of Turcesig, where their Uncle Asberg and Aunt Æthelthryth presided. The warriors of both halls still young enough to serve as such must be kept in fighting trim, through weapons-training and sparring. Those older, such as Jari and Asberg, had sons and daughters, some now bringing grand-children to the halls.

With his mother Ælfwyn gone, it also fell on Hrald to concern himself with the affairs of Oundle. It was true that no Abbess was more capable than Sigewif. But the devotion the Lady Ælfwyn had showered on the doubled foundation and its good works had been no small part of its growth and success. Her direct gifts, in gems and in silver, had been many, and though her flocks at Four Stones still provided much of the fleece needed for wool production at Oundle, she had also helped with building up a flock there for the creation of parchment. Hrald had taken on his mother's role there in the foundation's many endeavours. It and Abbess Sigewif had been a part of his life since boyhood. He was invested deeply in Oundle, and Ashild now rested there. And Pega could not do all.

About the hall Hrald was lovingly mindful of his daughter Ælfgiva, now scampering with the other toddling young. No one could deny his attachment to this first born. If he sat at the table in the treasure room, absorbed in some work of figuring accounts, or numbering stores, Hrald never asked Pega or Mealla to lift Ælfgiva from where she crawled at his feet, and pulled herself up his leg, demanding to be held. The child was lisping her first words with a sense of command patterned after that of Mealla, but the girl looked at the world through the same deep set grey eyes as sat in Pega's face. Those serious eyes lent the round visage an oddly old look, like a carved poppet of some show-conjurer reciting speech too wise for its tender years. Yet she had a laughing smile for her father whenever he scooped her up and held her in his arms. She delighted to be held up over his head, so that her wide eyes took in all, even above the view of her tall father.

Having returned to the hall there was something more which stood out to Ealhswith. There was nothing to recall her to Dagmar. No trace of Hrald's first wife remained. All had been expunged, from the hall itself and seemingly from memory. Yet when she entered Wilgot's house the first morning to celebrate Mass, her eye fell on the chair against the wall. It sat next to the table he used as writing surface, and when dressed in white linen as it now was, as altar. The tall chair was that in which Dagmar had sat at the high table; Hrald had it carved for her as welcome gift, and after her banishment from the hall, had it banished as well, by sending it to the priest. Even Wilgot kept it shrouded, and it seemed, never sat upon. Some indeterminate fabric was draped over one arm and the back, obscuring the rich carving of leaping deer and running hares; the embroidered cushion on the seat held a wooden tray bearing the priest's writing supplies, ink mixing dishes, knives, wiping rags and all.

How like a throne the chair was, Ealhswith thought. She considered the chair from the tail of her eye as she mouthed her prayers. She would not be surprised if none had ever sat on it, since the day Dagmar had been sent away. It was her place, one that no other could take.

Though they shared a father, Ealhswith did not consider Yrling her brother. Yrling scarcely felt kin to her, just as it was hard to think of the man Sidroc as her father. The man she hardly knew; and Yrling had arrived at the hall a rambunctious youth, and now had some fourteen years. Hrald had brought him from Gotland, and Ealhswith assumed he would one day return there. She heard from the other maids of the hall the upset Yrling had caused when he ran off, an action which did not endear the boy further to his half-sister. But he was well-mannered when he remembered to be, and good with animals.

Yrling had asked for one of Frost and Myrkri's pups. They had been born during his absence from Four Stones, and Hrald gave serious thought if his brother should receive one in light of the concern he had caused. When he realised he might not receive one of the animals through his thoughtless wrong-doing, Yrling displayed such regret that Hrald must relent and grant him one. But Yrling did not know which of the four to choose. There were three males and one female, and this last had run on wobbling legs to Yrling the first time he had seen the litter, in Bork's company. Yrling had always assumed he would ask for a dog and not a bitch; males were taller, had larger jaws and heads, and were more impressive to look at. Yet Myrkri, the pup's mother, was a courser of unusual ability and success. Even when Lady Pega's dog Frost had been trained, and gained the advantage of going to field with Myrkri, it was she and not Frost who the hunters most followed, and praised. As an archer Yrling hoped to one day take his hound into the greenwood and with it stalk, and down, game.

Then Yrling remembered a story his father had told him, one related to his name-sake, and to the drekar Death-Day.

The boy's grand-uncle Yrling prized a mare who brought him much silver through the foals she produced. The mare produced many good colts and fillies, all which added to the growing store needed by the first Yrling. It was true a stud or breeding fee could be charged from stallion, bull, or ram. But with good hunting hounds it was the owner of the female who profited most. A well raised and trained breeding female would bring silver many times over the cost of any stud fee. As his final act on Jutland, Yrling sold his mare to bring him the sum he needed to complete his ship, and leave Dane-mark forever. It was enough to make young Yrling choose the female pup he favoured, and resolve to care for and train her the best he could.

Ealhswith was not alone in sensing the change in Hrald. She did not mention it to either him or his wife, and though Pega would have asked her mother-in-law's counsel, she could not speak of her concern to a maid such as Ealhswith.

Pega had only one clue to give form to her unease. Months ago she had noticed the small wooden box was no longer in his clothes chest; she had seen it there after her discovery of it, and for months thereafter; though she had not again opened it. Now it had vanished. Then one day she spotted it inside the small chest Hrald used to store those few ornaments he sometimes wore, the gold cuff which had been his father's was one. There sat the little box, closed, plain and unadorned as when she had first seen it. Now that it had been moved here she could not resist the urge to again open it.

It held nothing; the red ribband which had been coiled inside was gone. She did not know how to take this; had Hrald then finally discarded it, even destroyed it, and thought to again put the small box to another use? It was nothing she could ask him of, not after his reaction when she had first opened it and he looked over to see the ribband in her hand.

But Pega had seen, had felt, the change in Hrald. Not that he was inattentive to his duties and role as husband and father. It was far more subtle. If she could have articulated it to herself, it would be a sense of disengagement, of inner and unexpressed melancholy, a shadowed and unspoken sorrow. Yet he remained kind and thoughtful to her in all his dealings.

Despite his outward acts, Pega held a thought that pained her, that Hrald's kindness to her was almost too great. At times, when Hrald embraced her in the act of love, it felt there was an added ardency to his touch and actions, which she hoped she was returning in full measure.

Hrald had not in fact destroyed the scrap of fabric which had tied Dagmar's hair as she lay abed. When he returned from Witanceaster he felt drawn to it, and once he had opened it, must finger it. He could not shut it away again, as it had been. His hand moved to his belt. It was of doubled thickness, for inside it were two slits. Into one lay secreted the key to the treasure room. The second slit had never carried anything; he had no other item both small and precious as was the key. Now he slipped off the belt, and pressed the coiled hair ribband into the waiting opening. He could not wear it against his skin, as Dagmar had laid that night with him, but hidden here within the belt it would act as gird to his every day. Having had that night with the woman who once wore it, he must keep his memento always at his waist.

Months had passed since that night. One day he rode, with only Jari at his side, to Turcesig. The Tyr-hand, faithful as he was, had counselled Hrald to forgive himself his transgression, and forget the woman with whom he had made it. But this was a cloak Hrald could not shrug off. He must speak to his Uncle Asberg. Jari could guess the mission, and said nothing.

Asberg saw Hrald's troubled face and lifted his hand to the armoury of the hall; it served as a kind of treasure room. But his nephew shook his head. "Will you walk with me, Asberg," Hrald asked. "What we will talk of must be spoken under the sky."

They set out, alone and together, passing through one of the four gates of the great garrison, and thence into the woodland beyond. Hrald was silent, and Asberg, mindful of the young man's distress, must wait until he could speak. When he did, Asberg was much surprised by his question.

"The runes of forgetfulness," Hrald said. "Do you know them? My father told me of them, runes to be painted on the body to free a man from the desire for a woman."

Hrald had stopped walking, and was looking at his uncle. Before Asberg could answer, Hrald went on. A note of true desperation rose in his voice.

"All shame is on me, to resort to such. I have been shriven but not released, as my confession was false. It profited nothing, and I mocked my faith in penance for an act I did not regret."

Asberg's hand rose to his brow. Jari had told him nothing, but he could guess.

"Guthrum's daughter, Dagmar. Is it her?"

Hrald swallowed in assent. Even hearing her name spoken caused heat to rise within him, a flare of spilled oil upon a smouldering fire.

"I saw her at Witanceaster, when I went at Ælfred's bidding. Dagmar was living there. The Dane I packed her off with was killed, in Dane-mark. The King and his wife had taken her in, as token, she told me, of esteem for her dead father. She was as shocked to find me there as I was to see her."

Having begun the tale he must go on, so his listener could see the depth of his need.

"She wished to beg my forgiveness for the hurt she caused, and swore upon all sacred to her that she was about to send the Dane away when I entered the room.

"We parted that night, but I could not leave her alone. I must see her again before leaving her forever. I could do nothing else. But when I was with her . . . To know she loved me – it was all I need hear."

"Having had that one night with her, I cannot keep her from my thoughts. Or my dreams.

"The runes – are there such things?"

Asberg's answer was as grave as was the question, but delivered in a far more sombre tone. "There are," Asberg told him.

"Men can be bewitched by women. The runes must be painted, nine times each, on hands, chest, and loins. They are Nid ᛉ, Lagu ᚱ, and Is ᛁ. Nid to end the attachment, Lagu for the woman you crave, and Is, the action of ice, to seal the spell. Then a rich sacrifice is made to white-armed Freyja, Goddess of love and lust."

Asberg related this of the freeing runes. He did so with deep reservations. Using such runes called the Gods near, in this case, Freyja. The Goddess could be fickle, and scorn the man who had tried to free his body from such yearning. She could send even greater torment of desire. Men had thrown themselves from cliffs, or slit their own wrist to escape their love-sickness. Asberg had seen this himself. When he was a boy in Laaland, a young man on the next farm had fallen in love with a woman set aside for another. He had painted the runes of forgetfulness on his body. They availed not. He hung himself from a cross-beam in his father's barn on the day the woman he loved made hand-fast.

Hrald listened, and inwardly repeated the names of the three runes. Instead of hope, he felt a growing despair. Asberg, watching Hrald's face, was moved to place his hand on his nephew's shoulder in attempt to give comfort.

Hrald's lips moved, but he spoke not. A new sensation spread within him, that of a deadly and yet calming certainty. Runes of freeing would profit nothing. He would not rid himself of that sensation of bodily longing, however painful it was for it to remain unsatisfied. He wore her hair ribband at his waist even now. There was no freeing for him; this was the curse, and the gift, he had been left with.

THE VISITATION
AT OUNDLE

A FTER Ealhswith had been at Four Stones nearly a month, she asked something of her brother, and Pega. "I should like to go to Oundle," she said, "to see grand-mother. And Ashild."

Pega at once embraced the idea. "The Feast of the Visitation is nearing; it would be a good time." She smiled at Ealhswith. "The church there will be dressed in flowers, lovely to see." Pega turned her eyes to her husband and reminded him, "You need see Abbess Sigewif to review the abbey's affairs soon, anyway."

Thus it was decided. Ealhswith would be sent to Oundle. In a week Hrald would join her there, so he might meet with Sigewif, and he and his sister would return together.

Ealhswith had never been to Oundle except in the company of her mother and Burginde. Though she was escorted by five of Hrald's men, led by Kjeld fronting the waggon, she felt a small thrill of excitement at making this trip by herself. She had brought her gelding with her, and the animal was tied to the back of the waggon. Ealhswith had never been a strong rider, but it might be pleasant to

ride out about the grounds while there; the place had a
needed sense of confinement about it which a ride could
alleviate.

The day was as fine as any could be, and as it was just after
Mid-Summer, long with bright daylight. Ealhswith was seated
on the waggon board, unusual for her; she was always within
the waggon when she came with her mother, and under the
waxed tarpaulin hooped over it. Now she sat in the open air
by the driver. It gave her a new perspective, and she found
herself staring up into the copse of trees which marked the
real beginning of the approach to the foundation. The road ran
through it, making the branches arch over their heads.

She lifted her chin to study them. The leaves, though still
fresh and brightly green, revealed some openings in their
cover, and her eye was drawn to a few clusters of objects
held in the branches above. She could not make them out;
perhaps they were the abandoned nests of great birds who
had nested there. From one or two she thought she glimpsed
white sticks, like those of birch perhaps, protruding.

Then they were out of the shadowed copse and into
the sunshine again. The palisade surrounding Oundle lay
just ahead.

No word had been sent ahead to Abbess Sigewif of the
girl's arrival. As an abbey it was used to receiving visitors,
expected or not, and as the men were depositing Ealhswith
and returning almost at once, the demands upon the
foundation would be slight indeed.

Ealhswith was in secret glad she had arrived during the
service of None, as the Abbess and nearly all the community
was within the church. The lay folk about the place were
many, and she was received with the benignant hospitality

accorded to all, and with that special warmth attached to any of Lady Ælfwyn's kin.

When the service concluded the young visitor stood at the church door. The Abbess was the first to process out, and Ealhswith found herself swept into her firm embrace. They waited together for the girl's grandmother, Ælfleda, to join them. Sister Ælfleda was freed from her vow of silence through a slight inclination of the Abbess's head, and the old woman's happy tears brought water into her grand-daughter's eyes as well. Soon though it was time for Ælfleda to return to her afternoon duties. The bright days brought fine light for sewing, and she was at work hemming linens, something which she promised Ealhswith would join her with.

The evening meal would come after this, but the parting left Ealhswith time to enter the empty church alone. Just as she had never travelled to Oundle without her mother, Ealhswith had not stood before Ashild's tomb by herself. The church, devoid of any others, seemed vastly larger to her this day, or she herself felt small. She walked towards the altar, crossed herself with her genuflection, and then moved beyond, towards the corner to one side of the altar. As soon as she had stepped inside she saw the flowers placed upon the floor. It was Sister Bova, she knew, the brewster, who faithfully picked flowers or greenery Summer and Winter, that Ashild's resting place might always be dressed. Ealhswith drew closer. A cluster of wild field flowers had been gathered, with some pinks and roses from the abbey's garden. And there was a sprig of rosemary; that signal of remembrance must appear every day in Bova's offering, she thought.

Ealhswith bowed her head and crossed herself a second time, and uttered a prayer for the soul of her sister. She did not kneel this visit, but stood upright and with bowed head, looking at the words ASHILD OF FOUR STONES carved in the white stone.

Are you happy here, Ashild, Ealhswith wondered. Is any part of you still here, she asked.

Then her thoughts expanded to include herself. You did not know how I admired you. Your choices were your own. I did not understand them, but I yearned to be brave like you. You made exception to every rule; you were exceptional.

Ealhswith recalled Ashild comparing her to their mother, and telling her that lovely as she was, she would wed a Prince or even a King. But she had wed no one. And she was not, Ealhswith thought, so much like her mother after all, her mother who was loved by a good and handsome man and had a new babe in arms.

Ealhswith turned, looking out through the opened door. So much was here at Oundle. Hrald wed Dagmar there, on that threshold, on a day clouded with rain. But how happy he was.

She should not dwell on Dagmar. Dagmar too was exceptional. She could not live within the rules and was cast out. Yet Ealhswith admired her almost as much as she had Ashild, and Dagmar had disgraced herself. No, she thought, I am more like Pega. I lack daring.

Pega was exceptional only in the treasure she brought. But in her person and manner she was like Ealhswith herself. Pretty, well-schooled, discreet. Folk would nod approvingly when she entered any hall. But they might not set their eyes upon her, wondering more, as they did with Ashild or Dagmar.

To stop her thoughts she walked to the corner of the sanctuary, where Ealhswith was drawn to touch the spear affixed upon the wall. She had not done this before.

〰〰〰〰〰〰〰〰〰

The next morning Ealhswith was leaving the women's hall after having broken her fast. The weather was still fine, and as she had no particular place she must be, she thought she might walk through the garden on the sisters' side, to see if she had recalled it correctly. It was not one, but many gardens, different plots of flowers, herbs, vegetables, bordered round by low clipped hedges, and backed by fruit trees. These grew nearest the tall timber wall which separated the sisters' garden from the garden of the brothers. She was about to step onto a gravelled path leading in when a man's voice stopped her.

"Forgive me, Lady. May I speak to you?"

She turned her head to face a young man, possibly no older than herself, who stood standing and smiling. He was well dressed, held himself upright, and now bowed to her most respectfully.

"My uncle is a priest, otherwise I would not deign to arrest you in your walk," he went on. Again he smiled. His mouth was slightly crooked, off-centre the smallest amount. It gave his smile an impish look. But his eyes were sparkling, and warm.

"I bring this up as we have not been introduced, but Father Edfrid – my uncle – claims that a shared roof alone can serve as introduction. As you and I find ourselves behind the walls of an abbey, I will claim that as our roof, and therefore grant myself leave to address you."

He made a second deep bow to her.

"I am Congar," he said, upon straightening up.

Ealhswith took him in. His hair, almost touching his shoulders, was in perfect trim. It was mid-brown, like good loam, and Sun-streaked in the most pleasing way. He tucked a lock of it behind his right ear, an act that Ealhswith soon saw was habitual. He was clean-shaven; most young men attempted at least a moustache, and if he had, perhaps it had not grown in well. He had a nose long and straight, the nose of a scholar, which made the impishness of the crooked smile beneath it a fine contrast. Above that scholar's nose was a pair of blue eyes, bright, perhaps questioning. At any rate Ealhswith found him compelling, and even handsome. He was, she thought, a youth of ready and quick charm.

She could do nought but smile back.

"And I am Ealhswith." She gave a deep and flourished curtsey, wishing to match him in extravagant presentation.

His smile in return gave her boldness enough to ask a question. It was one more direct than she would have dared if they had not been alone.

"Why are you here, at Oundle?" It was clear he was of good birth, and dressed to show this.

"I am here in discovery," he proclaimed. The words might have been mysterious or profound. But with his dancing eyes and crooked smile, they were mirthful.

He did not let her wonder.

"I have three older brothers. Thus I have discerned that my parents can spare one for the Church. And I have not discouraged them in that inclination; I have ever enjoyed my conversations with my uncle, Father Edfrid, and pondering the larger questions of Eternity with him."

Though she tried to stifle it, Ealhswith must laugh at this, so merry was his tone.

"I have had weapons training, yes," he assured her. "No sword at the moment; it is under my box bed in my alcove." Congar lifted his hand toward the monk's hall. "I am just as happy with that rule. It is awkward to move in close quarters wearing one, and impossible to dance."

"Dance!" Now she did laugh, and openly. When there was dancing at festivals, men who owned them never wore swords; many even freed themselves of their knives.

Congar was not quite done. "My good parents would like me to enter the Church, for the benefit of their souls, and because they have means to elevate me." He paused a moment, and grew more serious. "Perhaps if I profess here and do well under the Abbess, she could recommend that I be sent to Rome. Where many possibilities would open, or so says my uncle. But it is for my own sake as well I would like to see Rome."

He made a gesture with his hands, opening them as if all had just been revealed, and there was nothing more to tell. Now he inclined his head, in invitation that they walk amongst the garden Ealhswith had been in the act of entering when he had stopped her. She was happy to oblige.

Ealhswith had learnt a few things about this young man already. But Congar had left certain points unsaid.

"Are you a postulant," she asked. This was the first stage before becoming a novitiate. Postulancy was a period of initial exploration in monastic life, to observe at close hand a life given over to the worship of God and service to man.

Congar nodded. "I think I am expected to be."

His voice took a more serious turn. "My father wants this for me; my mother as well."

He took a breath, and with it claimed a pause.

"Just now it is hard to know. I feel no strong calling, either way."

He said no more. Ealhswith was much struck by this; so close it was to her own uncertainty. She yearned for a calling, to be summoned to some worthy end. A few years ago she did not care if it were cloister or keep. After the death of Ashild she saw she must somehow gird herself and try to take her place, and serve her brother as the daughter of Four Stones. But nothing presented itself save the union with Edwin, which she could not have. The cloister was always available; and her mother had sometimes questioned her, to see if she thought she might find a sense of purpose, and even joy, here in Oundle. But Ealhswith did not know. Her imaginings only carried her so far; someone or something else must take her the rest of the way.

Ealhswith's long silence prompted Congar to speak. He gave a small laugh, and lifted his hand to the blossoms about them. "I am like those flower heads, being blown in the wind. My family is of Cantwaraburh. My uncle Edfrid serves at the Cathedral there. He knows the good Abbess and wrote to her about me. My parents thought it best I leave, that coming here would help me decide what is the right path."

"They wished you to leave Cantwaraburh," she repeated. Was there temptation there, she asked herself. Or distraction. The monastery there was perhaps equalled only by Glastunburh; why should his parents send him here instead, she wondered.

She asked a different question instead. "Your uncle is a priest there. Who is your father?" This was the common question asked by all. He had said much, but had not volunteered his direct lineage.

"A King's thegn. One I think who would be Reeve one day, but is not yet. But Cantwaraburh suits him, as between cathedral and mint there is much to protect."

"Congar of Cantwaraburh," she said, and smiled. "That is pleasing to the ear."

He laughed. "Do not tease me about it. One day I might be Brother Congar, or if I excel, Father Congar." He gave thought and said the rest. "Or even, Bishop Congar." At this they both laughed. He finished by again mentioning that great capitol of pilgrimage and devotion.

"Going to Rome would be good."

Ealhswith gave a nod of agreement. She could not conceive of going to such a place, though she knew of many whose fondest desire was to visit. Her mother had told her that even King Ælfred of Wessex had been, as a boy, taken by his father, King Æthelwulf, on holy pilgrimage.

"And you, Ealhswith, are you considering a vocation?"

She blinked.

"My grandmother is here as nun. But I am the sister of Jarl Hrald of Four Stones."

Ealhswith never thought of herself as half-Dane, but she must admit to being Hrald's sister, so Congar understood her own responsibilities.

"Ah. I have been here long enough to understand. Your father, then, was Jarl Sidroc."

"Yes," she answered. It felt almost an admission of guilt to say it. "But he left when I was quite small."

So much lay attached to this admission. Ealhswith was half-Dane; her father one of the raiders who had taken Four Stones from its rightful folk in bloody conflict. Did Congar now think less of her, she wondered. A sudden urge ran through Ealhswith, to tell this young man that she had last year been intended, by his own King, for no less than Edwin, Lord of Kilton. But any mention of Edwin's name must lead to the fact that she had been rejected, based on her father and his past actions. Ealhswith could not lie and suggest she had spurned so worthy a hall as Kilton.

Congar thought again. "Ashild. You are then her sister."

"Yes."

"The Archbishop gave me a gift to bring, in her honour. She is known there, in Cantwaraburh."

"She would be," Ealhswith murmured, then feared it sounded peevish. "I meant, her act here in the defence of Oundle was something to be remembered."

"And so it is," Congar agreed.

"I saw you brought a horse," he said next. "Would you like to ride out this afternoon?"

As sudden as the request was, it seemed a decision of some moment, and it was one she could make herself.

"There is a wood, just before you see the palisade," she told him by way of answer. "The road winds through it. When I came through yestermorn I saw something, nests of birds or some such, in the trees. Could we go there? I will ask the Abbess if we may do so," she offered, for she must have permission to ride out.

Congar's reply was more decided. "I will ask Brother Balin. Of all the monks here he knows me best. We will have a stable-man with us. If we do not exceed the limits of the parkland, there can be no objection.

"I could bring a spear," he added, as if in jest.

"Please do not."

It was said so quickly that he must look at her. She was thinking of Ashild, having killed a man with her own spear, before the gates.

"It was a jest," he said. "We will need no protection. And we will have our horses." Danger could often be outrun, it was true.

Congar's eyes shifted back and forth in playful action, as if he scanned for danger. There was such ease about him, she thought. For Ealhswith, always so aware of herself, his untroubled light-heartedness was something to envy.

⁂

Congar received permission to accompany Ealhswith on a brief ride. He must attend service at the hour of Sext, but after that they were free to go, accompanied by one of the stable workers. This was a grown man, no stable boy, and mounted on one of the dray horses, but the animal could move smartly enough if needed.

As Ealhswith approached the barn she saw her horse awaiting her at the mounting block by the stable wall. A good animal which must belong to Congar was tied at the post there, and Congar stood, smile on his face, ready to help her mount. Now that he was so close, Ealhswith realised he was scarcely taller than herself. Well, he is yet young, he will grow, she thought. And she was rather tall, it was true. The hand he offered her was strong, really that of a man. But she feared asking how old he was, lest he be younger than she.

They set out, the stableman behind them. Ealhswith would learn more of Congar, and took advantage of riding side by side to do so.

"You said your father was a thegn of Cantwaraburh. Are you then also a thegn," she wished to know.

He gave his head a shake. "That would be yet another vow, one in service as a pledged man. I am again," – he laughed – "betwixt and between."

He gave a sigh. "I have ten and eight years now, and must make decision between a sacred or a secular life. Soon I will be too old to make a good start at either."

She would have laughed along with him, save that she was struck at his age.

"I too have ten and eight years," she confided.

"We could be twinned," he declared, "in our age, and in our uncertainty."

She gave her head a laughing shake, but wished to be serious again. "How long shall you be here," she asked.

The period of postulancy usually lasted half a year. After this, one was expected to know if they wished to progress to becoming a novitiate. She was not sure if he had yet reached this point.

"Until I decide," he said. "It could be some time. And I have only just arrived, last month." His look was more thoughtful as he told her this.

"And you, Ealhswith. How long will you remain at Oundle."

"Only this week. Then I will be fetched back."

Congar gave a grave nod of his head. "In that case, we must lose no time," he told her.

His tone was also grave, but his face now held that hint of mirth which it so often wore. Still, his words surprised, and perhaps thrilled her. He valued her company and wished to make the most of the scant time afforded with her to enjoy it.

She felt flustered and so said the next, to distract her own thoughts.

"What must you do, as postulant?"

"Observe Divine Service, every hour of it. Also all tasks that might be asked of me. Working in the garden, or kitchen, or at the baking ovens. Caring for the animals. Even laundry."

These menial labours were things he had never done at home, Ealhswith knew. She was here as a guest; nothing was asked of her. She was free to join the sisters in any or all of the services of the day, but had no firm hand upon her shoulder awakening her in the middle of the night so she might rise and join them at Matins. For Congar, considering the life of a monk, it was different; he was expected to join more fully in the life of the brothers. Just as Christ had washed the feet of his disciples, one must learn humility and obedience, and to treat every task as inherent service to God.

"Of more interest is the brothers' scriptorium," he went on. "I am now helping Brother Balin in the preparation of parchment; we have the sheep skin stretched, and I did some of the lacing upon the frame. And the grinding of roots and mineral pigments for inks is I think, always a pleasure. One never knows what the final colour will be. At least I do not," he quipped, with a smile.

Congar lifted his right hand from the reins. The pad of thumb and forefinger were stained from such work. He showed them off with a laugh. "When I am truly good, I will be as blue-fingered as Brother Balin," he intoned.

She laughed as well. But his next words proved his attraction to the work. "I think if I applied myself with the quill I might develop a fair hand." There was a note of hopeful pride in this, and no mockery, and Ealhswith felt herself taken into his confidence.

How different was Ealhswith's own experience with quill and ink. She dreaded being called into the Abbess's writing room. Hrald could write with assurance, and formed his letters in a strong and open hand. Ashild had hated her own scribblings, as she termed them, and used to make Ealhswith laugh making fun of them. Ealhswith fell somewhere between her two siblings in ability, she thought. She could write well if she spent reasonable care on it, but took little enjoyment in doing so.

They rode on, sometimes speaking, sometimes in that companionable silence which is a pleasure to those in tune with each other. Ealhswith was reflecting on all which was demanded of Congar while he was here. It provoked a sudden thought. If she did attend more prayer, she might see him there, in the church, standing on the men's side. She could almost imagine this, standing a bit behind him with the sisters, tapers flickering about the walls, and Congar feeling her gaze and turning to see her there. Then she dismissed this thought for the wickedness it was.

As they neared the wood, Ealhswith spoke again of the reason for their destination.

"I saw something in the trees above," she told him. "I wanted to return and puzzle it out. Some kind of nests,

I think, made of sticks. Birch, perhaps. And there was something else, tangled in the sticks."

"The nests of some large bird," Congar suggested. "Crows build nests of ever-increasing size, and will carry objects to their nests as well." He gave a smile. "We shall find out."

When they had almost reached the copse Congar turned in the saddle and spoke to the stableman. "Will you stop here," he asked. "We will be within sight." The man nodded, and pulled up. Congar turned to his riding companion and grinned. "It will be more of an adventure if we discover it alone. And together."

The two rode on, halting under the arching branches above them. Congar looked up, and then about them. He too saw the clusters above. The largest of the trees was an ash, and its reaching boughs made it the easiest to climb. He jumped off his horse and made for a lower bough, while Ealhswith remained on her mount. Congar hooked his hands around the ash bough and pulled himself up and onto it. Ealhswith followed him with her eyes as he moved; so limber and agile was he that she knew it was not many years ago he climbed trees for boyish sport. He partly disappeared underneath clusters of leaves as he shimmied his way along, and then further up, the bough.

Ealhswith, her face lifted below, heard Congar's quick release of breath. The leaves rustled and shook as he moved amongst them. Something fell from the tree, a long white stick of some kind. Then he reappeared, shimmying down in haste, and jumping to the ground.

He stood before her, wiping his hands on his leggings. "Let us come away now," he told her. His face and voice were troubled enough that she turned her horse's head at once in obedience. But she could not help asking, "Why? What is it? Is it the nest of a great bird?"

"No. They are human bones. Men were hung here once. The white sticks are their bones, and the rags, remains of their clothes."

Ealhswith's hand rose to her mouth, but could not stifle her gasp. She moved her horse away from the trees, and awaited him.

When he had mounted she spoke. "It was my father did this. There was an attack on Oundle, and Danes laid siege to it, threatening fire. My Uncle Asberg and my sister Ashild led the defence, charging from within. They killed them all. My father Sidroc was there; he had come from Gotland to defend Four Stones. Though the Danes were ready with fire and oil to burn the convent down, Sigewif wished to give the dead burial. Sidroc claimed the bodies instead. I was told later he and his men hauled them into the trees, where they rotted."

Ealhswith gave thought and went on. "He did it as warning to other Danes."

"Yes," Congar agreed. "And I daresay as Offering. The un-Churched Danes do such things."

Ealhswith must nod. That was what her father was, un-Churched.

Ealhswith would never ask Abbess Sigewif about Congar. Nor could she pluck up the nerve to enquire of one of the brothers about him, either. Oundle was a holy place, one where men and women left their past lives behind, and any hint of curiosity as to their standing in secular life, or their prior doings, would be both inappropriate and indecorous. And Congar had told her far more about himself than she had about her own life.

He was so well spoken, she thought. So light and free in his manner, and in his speech. To converse with him had made her happy, and must bring happiness to all who heard him. She was content with that.

Ealhswith did not see Congar the next day, and realised she began to find cause to look for him. The working areas common to both nuns and brothers included the fowl-houses, cow-shed, stable, and paddocks. She took a sudden interest in the welfare of her horse. Going to the paddock to visit the animal took her past the monk's garden; she might hazard a glance to see if he stood there, hoe in hand. But their paths did not cross.

She busied herself with her grandmother, hemming linens, and stitching with coloured thread a border on a scrap of linen, a design she might wish to replicate on the hem of one of her gowns. But after two more days of this, she must excuse herself from the old woman's company. She wished to spend more time with the sisters at their gardening work, she told her.

Yet how could Ealhswith hope to come across Congar there. The sisters and brothers had their separate large gardens. Each hall was served by its own laundry, and kitchen-yard and staff. Congar had made remark to her about this on their ride together. "I hear the sisters eat better than we brothers; more skilful cooks," he jested. "But we all drink the same good ale." This was brewed by Sister Bova. Remembering his crooked smile, and how she had smiled back, gave her a pang. She felt bored and restless; why did she not see Congar?

Then when she was in the nuns' garden, she saw Congar pass, along the far end of it. He was in fact heading to the brewing-shed, and pulling a small hand wain. Ealhswith watched as the slight figure of Sister Bova came from one of her herb sorting tables to greet him, and then saw Congar lift two thick-walled crocks of her brew into the wain, to haul back to the brother's hall. She hoped he might turn his head and see her at the distance, standing there. Yet if he did so, he would see she waited for him to do just that. She forced herself to move on, lowering her eyes as if absorbed in the costmary and sage growing at her feet. When she heard the creak of the wheels of the wain he pulled, she looked back at his retreating figure. He had not seen her, she thought. She turned and faced the bed of spent cones of knapweed flowers. Their bloom is over, just as mine shall soon be, she told herself.

The next afternoon, when Ealhswith least expected him, she saw Congar again, in the church. She pulled open the heavy oaken door and entered the sanctuary, cool and white in the Summer's warmth. The altar was dressed in flowers, as the Mass for the Feast of the Visitation would be celebrated on the morrow.

Ealhswith hardly saw the blossoms. Congar was there, his back to her, facing the upright spear bolted to the wall. Ashild's spear. He placed his hand upon it, as she knew many others had done; as she herself had done.

She grew closer. He turned. He was not startled; there was that ease about him, in nearly all things. Ealhswith did not move, so he came to her, and with a nod, began to pass her. She had meant to kneel at Ashild's ledger stone and say a prayer. Now she realised that in respect to her entering the church, he would leave it himself. She turned and went with him. She could pray for the soul of Ashild anywhere.

They stepped outside.

"I would have liked to have met her," he said.

"Ashild?" Though Ealhswith had come to pray for her, she did not want to think of her just now, with Congar at her side.

"Yes, of course; Ashild, your sister." He was smiling, but not unkindly, at her questioning him. "Women of daring are admirable. Exciting," he added.

"Some thought her reckless," she answered. The moment it fell from her lips she regretted it. "I admired her, in almost every way," she ended.

"I am glad to hear that. One would not wish to feel shame at someone one loved, and lost."

They stood, shoulder to shoulder, blinking at the bright sunlight flooding the garden before them.

"I have wished to see you, Ealhswith, and could not," he said next. "But I have thought much of you."

Her heart gave a leap in her breast. No man had said these words to her, or any words of endearment.

"Soon I must leave," she answered. She did not mean to whisper, but that was how it sounded, a fact too hard to be spoken aloud.

She felt a touch of her hand. His own slipped into hers. Her hand was down at her side, almost hidden in the skirts of her gown, but his found her own and took it.

Ealhswith waited for him to say more. He did not, but gave her hand a squeeze before drawing his own away. Then, with a nod of his head, he left her.

Hrald arrived. The trip to Oundle and back could be made in one long day, even given the business he must conduct with Abbess Sigewif. The church and grounds had been backdrop for key moments in Hrald's life, and he did not feel he could spend the night surrounded by Oundle's shades. It was here he had wed Dagmar, and it was to the Winter-blasted garden outside the church he had fled following his casting her out of his hall. He had brought Pega here after their marriage, and it was here, in that same garden, she had told him of their coming child. And Ashild was here, the sister he loved and admired and let get killed.

He and Jari and a few other men made good time without a waggon to slow them. The return would be slower, but Hrald knew Sigewif would have all ready for their meeting. After that he would visit the church, then start back with Ealhswith and her waggon.

His little sister was there to greet him, as was Prioress Mildryth and Sigewif herself. Ealhswith joined them in the Abbess's writing room for the welcome ale. Then the Prioress and Ealhswith excused themselves, as Jarl and Abbess rose to move to the table where the account book awaited. A young nun joined them, to assist Sigewif as needed; one new to the task. The Abbess had instructed her in her duties, a signal honour for one who had recently professed her perpetual vows.

The account book was opened and gone over first. Oundle received support from the Church, as all foundations of its kind did, but its relationship with the former Lady of Four Stones had been deep. Ælfwyn's endowments of treasure and land had accelerated its growth five-fold, and the flocks of sheep that Lady had so carefully built up at Four Stones were the major source to Oundle of shorn wool, meat, and sheep skin for parchment. Sigewif was scrupulous in keeping Hrald appraised of this yield, and also showing him any gifts of note which had been received in his sister's name.

Oundle's treasure was held in two places. The gold paten and chalice, the silver ewer for wine poured at Mass, and other sacramental objects used in divine service were kept in the aumbry in the chancel of the church. Its silver coinage and other treasure were held by the Abbess here in her writing chamber. A great store was kept, numbering any silver or gold which novitiates of both sexes had brought, which were kept in trust for them; silver, gems, and other goods donated for the founding or continuance of the abbey and its acts, of which Lady Ælfwyn had continuously given over the years; and the newest source of treasure, that given in honour of Ashild. This combined store was kept within three strong boxes, one placed within the next, and all kept locked, requiring separate keys of diminishing size. Sigewif handed the three keys to the nun, who under the gaze of the Abbess and Hrald, opened the first strong box, lifted its lid, unlocked the second, and then the final. Two wooden trays sat side by side within, and the nun carried the first to the table and set it down before them, a glittering array of gems and precious metals. She returned for the second. To one side of this, against the wall of the strong box and not within the tray, sat a cup of silver, richly made. Though it was set apart it was surely treasure, and she made space for it on the second tray and carried it to the table. The cup was Dagmar's.

Hrald saw it for what it was, as did the Abbess. With a quiet word she dismissed the nun. When the door had closed behind her, Sigewif spoke.

"Forgive me, Hrald. You were not meant to see this. You gave the cup to Oundle, and asked that I melt it down. I did not.

"My excuse is simply this: it is a thing of beauty. It was also dear to you. I wished to keep it, to see if it could go to some higher end than the crucible."

Hrald remained mute. Confronted by Dagmar's cup, he resisted the urge to again reach for it. When he had picked it up in the treasure room to bring it here, he had wished to crush it in his hand, as he himself felt crushed. He wished to touch it now, not to destroy it, but to hold it again, as she had once held it.

The eyes of the Abbess had not left Hrald's face, though his own were trained on the silver cup before them.

"I will keep the cup," Sigewif went on, "in trust for that higher end."

⚶⚶⚶⚶⚶⚶⚶⚶⚶⚶

When Ealhswith left that afternoon with Hrald, she did not see Congar. He knew her brother was coming to collect her, and she had hope the two would meet. It would at least give her another chance to see Congar before she left. Her packs and a small handbasket in which she kept her sewing goods were packed into the waggon. She walked with her brother to the church, but let him go in alone so he might have time at Ashild's tomb. Then with a hug and kiss from each her grandmother and the Abbess, she took her place on the waggon board. Hrald was riding ahead with Jari, and no one kept pace with her. She did not wish to talk. When the waggon passed under the ash tree she did not look up. The bone which had dropped to the earth was gone; some animal must have carried it off.

When she got back to Four Stones she found a note in her handbasket. It was from Congar. It was a scrap of parchment, jagged at one edge following the shape of the hide, and cut straight on three others. She had not seen his writing before and it felt almost as if he stood before her.

MY DEAR LADY EALHSWITH
I have made no vow to forsake here at Oundle. I cannot envision a life in Cantwaraburh as the fourth son to my parents. I would be but a burden to them, for I know as the youngest there is no great provision for me. I have, though, a sum to see me to Rome. Will you go with me? . . .

She read on, hardly believing her eyes, though her lips formed the words as she read them. He named her, My dear Lady. He signed himself, Your Congar.

My Congar. Mine.

But go to Rome – what did that mean? She was intrigued and frightened and knew she must see him again.

She must return to Oundle. She let two days pass, days spent in an inner delirium of expectation. She read the letter again and again. On the third day she went to Pega in the treasure room, careful to see her alone. Mealla was out in the pleasure garden with Ælfgiva, and Hrald as well out of the hall.

"Oundle," Ealhswith said. "Is there a waggon heading near? Could I be left there?"

A kind of mild wonder was in her sister-in-law's voice. "Oundle again? Of course." Perhaps the girl was drawn to a vocation. Pega asked as much.

"Are you perhaps . . . in search of a vocation?"

Ealhswith lowered her eyes. "I think I am," she answered.

"Certainly we will send you," Pega replied. "I will ask Hrald if Kjeld can take you, as soon as may be."

Pega paused and looked at the girl. She was uncertain of King Ælfred's plans for the girl, or even if at this point he had any. Her trip to Witanceaster was almost a year ago. Should Ealhswith go as a nun, she would be removed from all such speculation, and potential utility. Pega had but one stipulation.

"But if you feel called, you will not profess your postulancy without telling Hrald. He must know, of course."

Ealhswith nodded. She must say something, so added, "I think the stay might not be long."

Pega nodded. Ealhswith might be on the cusp of a decision, and need to speak with Abbess Sigewif to aid her.

Kjeld could in fact take Ealhswith back, two days hence. When the waggon pulled up to the door to take on her belongings, Pega must comment on the number of packs and baskets Ealhswith had lined up and waiting.

"You are taking much, for a short stay," Pega teased.

Ealhswith must think, and do so quickly. "I have clothing which I thought to donate. There are poor women of the area, who Abbess Sigewif told me would welcome what I can spare."

This was an outright lie; Sigewif had mentioned no such thing. Ealhswith felt an inner shudder as she told it.

To Pega such charity from a young woman was a sign of renouncing the world and its vanities. "That is a kind act," she said, and kissed her on her forehead.

The girl gave a heartfelt, even tearful Fare-well to her brother and sister-in-law. "Surely," Pega said, as they had waved her off, "she must be considering dedicating herself at Oundle."

※※※※※※※※※※

Two days later a stable boy at that foundation, moving hay in the barn, struck something solid with the tines of his rake. Four leathern travelling packs. Two he recognised, marked as they were with the crest of Cantwaraburh, burnt into the hide. These belonged to young Congar of that place. The other two packs he did not know. But why were they here? He knew the young man in question was working much with Brother Balin in the scriptorium. The boy felt troubled enough upon discovering them to go to Brother Balin, and report his find.

When Balin arrived at the barn, he stood a moment staring at the packs.

"Please to bring Congar," he asked the stable boy. When he returned, Congar in tow, Balin dismissed the boy. Congar swallowed at the sight of Brother Balin's discovery. His eyes rose to the monk's face. He was not used to seeing such displeasure written there; a look far more irate than when Congar had dropped a tin tray of powdered walnut gall upon a clean leaf of parchment.

"These are your packs," Balin said.

Congar must admit to this.

"And these?" Balin demanded, indicating the other two.

"Ah . . . they are those of Ealhswith of Four Stones."

Brother Balin did not attempt to corral his anger. "With whom you were riding off? Are you mad? This is abduction. Or close to it. And she is the sister of the Jarl!"

Balin strode to the open doors and gestured to a passing serving woman, bidding her to at once find Lady Ealhswith and bring her thither.

Ealhswith was in the garden, and thus easy to spot. The serving woman's demeanour when she relayed this command so distressed Ealhswith that tears were springing to her eyes as she crossed the courtyard and approached the doors to the barn. There stood Congar, with a monk.

"Lady Ealhswith. Congar has suggested to me that these packs are your own."

Tears were running down her cheeks, and she but nodded her assent.

"Very well. Please to go into the sisters' hall, and wait there."

Ealhswith could do nothing but curtsey to the monk.

As she was led away, she turned her head over her shoulder to look back. Congar was staring at her, the lips of his crooked mouth gently parted, as if no words could pass forth. She forced her throat to open enough for speech.

"Fare you well, Congar," were her final words to him.

***

It did not take Balin long to report the thwarted plan to the Abbess. Despite her shock, Sigewif's first response was to cross herself and give thanks the two had been apprehended at this point.

"I will see Ealhswith first. Then Congar."

He left her, and she awaited the tap on her door which would signal Ealhswith's arrival.

When it came, Sigewif rose. This was not an interview to be conducted seated.

Ealhswith's face was already wet with tears. Were they of contrition, or frustration that she had been caught, Sigewif wondered.

The Abbess folded her hands. They covered the silver crucifix at her breast, a pose that to Ealhswith looked as if she did not wish to offend the Son of God by being confronted by the miscreant girl before her. The voice was low, steady, and firm.

"Either Brother Balin is mistaken, or you and Congar were soon planning to elope."

It was poignant, even in its absurdity. But to wed Congar would be to wed far below Ealhswith's station.

Ealhswith nodded. "He wanted to take me to Rome."

"To Rome," the Abbess repeated. "And how were you to live? I am holding most of Congar's silver."

"Congar said that Hrald would perhaps send us silver, once we were wed."

Sigewif's eyes rose Heavenward. Her exasperation could barely be kept in check. "Once you were wed." Those eyes, grey as the sea and just as angry, now nearly bored through the girl. "Or rather, once he had laid you on your back in a hayfield, he would attempt to extort funds from your brother. Once there was no redeeming you."

Ealhswith trembled under these words. She wished to be defiant, sure of herself and of Congar, but was close to dissolving in fearful tears.

"You do not know – you do not know!" the girl sobbed.

"I do not know," the Abbess repeated. Her words were slow and each was wrought with meaning. "You see this" – and here the Abbess swept her large hand in front of her, in indication of her imposing self – "and cannot conceive of me at your age. Cannot imagine me young. Nor comely. Nor in love, and burning with passion."

This was so unexpected, so direct, and the vision it conjured so ardent as to be almost indecent to the frightened reverence in which the girl held the woman before her.

Sigewif stopped herself at this. The words the Abbess had spoken had exceeded the wants of the task at hand, but not those of her own history. But the girl could be brought to her senses, that was clear.

Ealhswith's chin dropped. Sigewif went on.

"Do you understand what this would do to your prospects? Do you understand? Did you stop and think for one moment?"

"I have no prospects," Ealhswith cried.

"Did he touch you?"

"He held my hand. He helped me at the mounting block."

"Nothing more?"

"Nothing more."

Two wanton children, Sigewif thought. One could give thanks for their foolish innocence. At least the boy was not a rake, she must credit him that.

The Abbess looked back to Ealhswith. "I believe you. But I am shocked at this behaviour. What put you in mind of this?"

The girl's cheeks were wet with tears, but she would defend herself.

"I – I like Congar. And I wanted to be – like Ashild."

Even as she said this, Ealhswith saw her behaviour placed her far closer to the actions of Dagmar. But she could not risk naming Dagmar here.

"And exactly how does the act of running off with a young man you hardly know recall you to your sister?"

"It was – bold."

"Bold," Sigewif repeated. "Bold. Would it be bold to bring shame to your mother, to discredit the hall of Four Stones, and destroy your value to your brother, who wishes a good marriage for you? Is that the kind of boldness Ashild possessed? I think not."

Ealhswith was now sobbing, openly and without reserve.

"No, you are right, Reverend Mother," she choked out.

She recalled Burginde telling her upon leaving The Fold to do nothing to discredit either her mother or brother. This meant considering the result of her own actions on those she loved. Heedless to this advice, she had nearly flung away her reputation, recklessly choosing to follow her own confused desires rather than her conscience.

The Abbess began to walk up and down before her, her hands now tucked into the wide sleeves of her habit. She made several passes before she stopped and spoke again.

"I have a decision to make, Ealhswith. One I cannot make without you. It is this. Do I tell the Jarl about this transgression?"

Ealhswith could scarce believe that end was in doubt. But the Abbess suggested otherwise; not perhaps for her sake, but out of consideration for Hrald and Pega.

She could not answer, but looked all her hope to the Abbess.

It was answer enough.

"Congar leaves today," Sigewif went on. "You will remain here another week, in penance and charitable works. Then I shall send you back to Four Stones with good report of how helpful you were.

"Go off to confession now. A crime of gross thoughtlessness needs to be told to your confessor. After that, go to your grandmother Sister Ælfleda. She is in her cell, sewing. Spend the rest of the day being of help to her."

Ealhswith must delay a moment, long enough to touch her knee to floor before the Abbess in thanks.

When Congar entered the writing chamber he saw the Abbess, standing and awaiting him. The four packs were now sitting on the long deal writing table in the centre of the room. With a sweep of her hand, one commanding in its size and apparent strength, the Abbess gestured to them.

"What hurtful prank is this," she demanded.

She did not expect an answer. The boy's blanched colour was enough. She moved to the smaller table where she wrote, and read.

"Congar. Do you see what I have before me?" She opened her hand to her writing materials, laid in order on the ink-stained surface. "With a few strokes of my quill I could tell Father Edfrid of your misadventure. Your near misadventure, thanks to Brother Balin. It would form a blot upon your name, and prospects. Your parents and brothers would suffer the embarrassment of your act, and you the shame of a diminished future.

"You are neither the first nor the last to question your calling. But this decision must be yours alone, reached through self-examination and reflection, and not dependent on a sudden fancy for a lark with an innocent maid.

"She is the daughter of the greatest patron of this foundation," Sigewif went on. "Ealhswith's brother is Jarl of East Lindisse. King Ælfred himself has taken interest in her. You came close to robbing her of all this. Great should be your shame, and great, your repentance.

"And – you arrived here in the spirit of discovery. To see if you might be called to serve God and His creation as a monk, or even priest."

She stopped. The force of her words struck the young man for the truth they were. The scales dropped from his eyes, as he saw his heedless actions as the Abbess did.

Congar must speak, and could at least address this last remark.

"Abbess Sigewif, having disgraced myself as I have, that door is now closed to me. I beg your pardon for the hurt I have caused. And the greater hurt we were spared."

Sigewif responded, and not unkindly. "I am sending you home to Cantwaraburh. My letter will not mention this, only my suggestion that you require more reflection to move forward with a vocation. You may never reach Rome, unless you go there as pilgrim.

"But I will say this: those who have a calling will always find themselves in God's service." She went on, more pointedly, "As a candidate I would say it was good you were yet a postulant when you wavered."

LAND OF
THE RED DRAGON

To Cymru

Late Spring 898

D WYNWEN delighted to be at sea. The ship that carried her was the greatest of living beasts, freed from earthly confines, skimming the white-plumed waves. No horses' manes curled and spilled as these did. The thrilling drive of the prow cleaving the cresting swells was an exultation to her. She rode above and through them, laughing at the power of the hull ploughing the furrow of the salt water beneath the keel. The ship was wild beast and man-made tool in one. Ceric must stack two sea chests, one upon the other, so she could see above the high-rising curve of the bow. There she clung on to the gunwale, just as she had when he and Worr had taken her out in the small boats at Kilton.

They drove west and then north, in two of Ælfred's war ships, laden with supplies and treasure. In the lead vessel was the small Princess of Ceredigion, heading to her Welsh home. At her side was Ceric of Kilton, and at his side, Worr, the horse-thegn of that place. Together Ceric and Worr had selected a score of the pledged men of Ceric to accompany them. The priest Dunnere, a man of Cymru, but having lived many years at Kilton, rounded out their numbers.

Along with the ships, Ælfred had provided a score of warriors, skilled seaman all, to crew both vessels. The twenty men of Kilton were divided between the war ships. Together, and counting the King's two captains, they totalled a little over two score men. There was always a balance to be struck between adequate protection, and the over-burdening of one's hosts with a large troop to feed and house. Two score men meant the ships were manned but lightly; the craft were large enough to have carried half again the number. Yet they sailed in tandem, and any raiders at sea would think twice before challenging them.

The young Princess was the lone female. She had asked her serving maid Tegwedd if she would like to again see Ceredigion, but the girl shrank back, nearly running off in fear. Elidon's hall was where Tegwedd had been a slave, and nothing could convince her that her days of scrubbing pots in his cooking yards was over. She begged to be left at Kilton, and Dwynwen, whose personal needs were slight, was happy to comply. She and Ceric had a tented canopy in the stern, fitted out with every comfort Lady Edgyth could provide.

The Kingdom of Ceredigion would be their first landfall. From there they would progress by sea to the Kingdom of Gwynedd, where they would ask its King Anarawd to summon the other Welsh Kings. Much preparation had preceded their sailing; more than Ceric had ever imagined.

They must wait for Spring and smoother sailing before setting out, but this gave time for the fashioning of gifts, and the writing of letters to be presented with them. These missives were written out in the tongue of Rome as well as that of Cymru, so that each King's priest might be able to read the letter aloud to the monarch for whom he acted as scribe and spiritual guide.

If Dwynwen had her way, they would have set out at once, in the tightening grip of approaching Winter, as soon as Ælfred's letter had arrived.

"The King inquires of Dwynwen, Princess of Ceredigion, what gift would bear most meaning to the sons of Rhodri Mawr," Ceric read. "Such gift will be a token of my esteem, and symbol of increasing alliance between our lands, and our respective folk."

Dwynwen needed no thought. "He should send dragons," she proclaimed. "King Ælfred flies a golden dragon on his pennon. And we of Cymru, one of red.

"The King has men whose skill in metals is such as the dwarves; his gift to us proves this." Here she lifted her hand to the disc of highly polished silver they had just unwrapped. In it one's reflection smiled back, true and undistorted, and with the cool gleam of that precious metal enhancing face and hair. The looking disc had a handle, also wrought of silver, and shaped like a slender fish, pleasant in the hand. It was large enough that Dwynwen could see the full length of her hair, if Ceric held the new disc behind her, and she, their old.

"A small dragon of gold for every King," she directed. Her face was alight with pleasure as she thought of such a creation. "Reddish gold, made ruddy by some copper, to make it glow the more.

"One to Elidon," she counted. "One to Anarawd of Gwynedd to the north. One to Merfyn of Powys to the east. One to Llywarch of Dyfed to the southwest. And in the southeast, one to Meurig of Morgannwg. Five dragons of gold."

Her smooth brow furrowed a moment in thought. "But the eyes must be red, for the red dragon of Cymru."

"Garnets," Ceric suggested.

Dwynwen's own eyes fairly danced at this. "Yes, garnets."

"Should they be alike?"

Her smile was bright and broad. "No Kingdoms are alike. All are different, just like dragons. Some should be standing, others rearing, others flying."

Ceric nodded his head. "Five dragons of gold, with eyes of garnet," he repeated. "These will be rich gifts, indeed."

Dwynwen gave a little shrug of her shoulders, and laughed. "Rhodri had many sons. Some from different mothers. He divided what he had conquered amongst those sons he most favoured. These became Kings. Others, who were younger, were named Princes. Dunwyd, my father, was one. But five dragons, yes."

The last news Ceric read was the best.

"And King Ælfred asks that we deliver the gifts ourselves."

"Ourselves!"

He turned his eyes back to the parchment. "It is my respectful request that Lady Dwynwen and her husband Ceric of Kilton serve as envoys in this task."

"We – we are going to Ceredigion. I will see Luned." She flung her small self into his arms.

Now, after three days of sailing, they were nearly at her shore. King Elidon must be their first stop, not only for Dwynwen's sake, but as show of respect from Ælfred to the monarch of a far smaller and yet vital Kingdom. Raedwulf, the Bailiff of Defenas, had written early to Lady Edgyth, asking her advice in this matter. It was clear from Raedwulf's short visit to Kilton that Dwynwen had early placed her confidence in the Lady of that burh. On her nuptial day, Dwynwen had told her that Elidon wanted silver from Kilton, but more than this, to be connected to the King of Wessex. Edgyth thus assured the Bailiff that honour and recognition were more important to King Elidon than treasure. Ceric and Dwynwen coming to Ceredigion brought him both.

The long crescent of the bay where lay the Kingdom was bounded by sand beaches, and backed by forests of white-barked birches. Amongst these were stands of hazel, willow, reaching pines, and distinguished by their girth, ancient and spreading oaks. These all slipped before the eyes of Dwynwen and Ceric as they stood side by side on the deck of the lead ship. It was late in a fine and fair day, and both ships and those who gazed out from them were bathed in the glow of the Sun. Dwynwen looked with growing recognition at landmarks she knew: an uprooted trunk of an old tree, sprawled upon the beach where it had been knocked by a wind storm; a cluster of boulders from which women went out to seine shrimp in their huge baskets.

The arrivals were dressed in their best clothing, demanded by a visit of state and by the importance of those whom they had journeyed to meet. Dwynwen wore the red silk gown she had wed Ceric in, and he too had chosen that outfit he had donned that day, a tunic richly blue. At his side was the seax he had ever worn, that of Merewala. But this day he wore also his sword, for he was here as envoy of his King.

Ælfred's ships each carried a flag topping its mast, upon which had been laid an image of a sharp-clawed golden dragon. As they neared the river outlet beyond which stood the fortress of Elidon, a second banner appeared on the lead ship, run up above the prow. This was the flag that Dwynwen had stitched, there in the pleasure garden of Kilton, the red dragon of Wales, and the golden dragon of Wessex, sporting in the air. It snapped in the fresh breeze, drawing all eyes to it. The palisade of the hall and its parapets were within sight. Driving as they were for shore, any approaching ship would be spotted at a distance, and those within alerted to the near arrival.

"They have had no word of our coming; your stepmother can have no idea it is you returning," Ceric cautioned.

"She will see me from afar," Dwynwen assured him.

And in fact she was right. As they drove into shore, a woman in a dark cloak stood there upon the sand, alone and apart from the line of armed warriors behind her. The wind blew her cloak about, revealing the creamy white of the gown it covered.

The war ships beached side by side. With no pier to tie to, a small tender was dropped into the shallow water to spare their feet from wet. Ceric jumped down into it. Worr took Dwynwen by her waist and lowered her into his waiting arms. From there it was the work of a moment for the Princess to scramble over the side, dry-shod, and run to the woman standing and awaiting her.

Ceric watched as Dwynwen was embraced by the woman, all but enveloped in the dark cloak she wore. He heard her cries of joy, and the muffled response from she who held her. He came up, slowly, and respectfully, Worr just at his right shoulder.

Ceric saw an older woman; at least her hair was white. In form she was as slender as a girl, yet moved with a gravity which made fitting backdrop to the darting grace and quick laughter of his child-wife. This then was Luned, the woman who had largely raised Dwynwen, and who had schooled her in many arts.

Both females were now facing Ceric. The Lady's arm was about Dwynwen, whose smile for her husband was all the greater for the water glistening in her eyes. Luned looked at the man before her. The lids of her eyes were shadowed, adding to the somberness of her gaze.

Ceric made a deep bow. "Lady. I am Ceric of Kilton."

The Lady Luned studied him. Her face, though still, underwent a subtle change as she looked upon him.

"And more than that," she answered. Her voice was low, resonant, and despite the whistling wind and the waves striking the hard shore behind them, readily heard. "You are the son of Ceridwen. The daughter of Luned."

Ceric was struck dumb. Ceridwen. The daughter of Luned.

His mother was half-Welsh; all knew that. He stood before his grandmother. She who had raised Dwynwen, his cherished wife.

He must repeat what he thought he heard. "You are the mother of Ceridwen, daughter of Cerd, of the River Dee."

Luned smiled. Her response was correction and amplification, both. "Ceridwen, daughter of Luned. Luned of Ceredigion, and for some years, the River Dee." She let these words settle, and then went on. "And yes, Ceridwen, daughter of Cerd."

Her expression was benign, and perhaps expectant. Or was it gentle triumph which bowed her lips, that sense of inexorable closure of a long running circle? Ceric did not know.

He had embarked upon this journey fully aware this meeting with Lady Luned was important. He could not know how deeply that importance ran. Her words had struck a vein akin to an underground river flowing within him. What design had Fate drawn, spiraling him back like this, to enfold them all? It was as complex as any of the designs Dwynwen painted upon her slips of birch bark.

Ceric looked to Dwynwen, her eyes rounded with startle, a gasp upon her lips. She had not guessed.

Luned lifted her arms to Ceric. She must be the first to make this gesture; she was a woman, and older, and respect and courtesy demanded the choice to touch him must be hers. Now she did so, welcoming this man to Ceredigion, and into her life.

Grandmother and grandson held each other. It was a long and needed moment for Ceric, one of stillness. He must have time to recover from this shock, and time to absorb its vast significance.

Then they parted, while still keeping hold of the other's forearms. Ceric looked for trace of his mother in the face gazing upon his own. So many years had passed, more than a decade; he recalled his mother's hair more than her features. But for Luned, beholding Ceric was seeing Ceridwen, so strongly did he favour her.

Then Dwynwen clung to both, drawing them to her, and again to each other. She looked to her step-mother.

"This is why you knew I would save the life of a man. You knew, for he would be part of you."

Luned's answer was in her kiss to Dwynwen's brow. "I drew half the circle," she murmured. "It was you who closed it."

Worr stood silently and almost unmoving, taking this in. The horse-thegn had been privy to moments of unexpected revelation concerning Ceric, and his Lady Mother. This was another. Worr risked his life in his regular duty for Kilton, and his belief in the workings of Fate were of uncommon depth. It was a web where no string could be touched without another vibrating in response. Every loss was balanced with a gain, Worr believed. Ceric had lost much, and now much, in different form, was being returned to him.

The horse-thegn thought of dead Lady Modwynn, and what this revelation would have meant to her. That good Lady of Kilton had uncommon attachment to Ceridwen. His thoughts passed to his wife's father, Raedwulf of Defenas, Modwynn's good friend. Raedwulf had taken special interest in Ceric; more, Worr thought, than in Edwin, Lord of Kilton. There was something Fated about Ceric, and this, now witnessed by Worr, was part of it.

When Dwynwen moved aside she could see the silver pin her step-mother wore, that of the young Moon in the arms of the full Moon.

"That is the pin Lady Edgyth sent," Dwynwen whispered.

"It is," Luned replied. "I wear it at my heart, each day."

Dunnere the priest had joined them. It prompted Dwynwen to look about her and speak.

"Where is uncle?"

"He and Gwydden are at their Mass," Luned answered. In fact, the day was the Sabbath-day, and such was to be expected.

The King was not long delayed, for as the party turned to the gates he appeared, his priest at his side, hastening towards the arrivals. His captain had met the ships, and more importantly, his sister-in-law, as Dwynwen stood with her. The King halted, and let his guests come to him. Elidon made no attempt to hide his pleasure at seeing the man his niece had wed. His eyes swept from Ceric's face to the rich seax across his belly, to the gold-trimmed sword he wore.

The presentation to the King was made by both priests, who had but a moment to greet each other with a kiss of Peace. Neither man had witnessed the Lady Luned revealing herself to Ceric, and so presented him merely as Ceric of Kilton.

"The God-son of your King Ælfred," Elidon added, with satisfaction.

The bow Ceric made was one of deep homage, fitting both for a monarch and for the nearest male kin of his bride. Ceric saw an old warrior of more than fifty years, who wore the sign of battle on his brow, for a broad gash, long healed, ran there above his eyes.

The King spoke again, words carefully formed. "I have enjoyed the contents of the wine jug you sent," he said, with a trace of glee. That huge jug, brim-full with silver coinage, had been the price of his young niece's hand.

Then Dwynwen herself came forward and curtseyed to her uncle, earning a benevolent smile from the monarch. The King offered her his arm. She took it, with a ready smile, and then gestured Luned to take her own.

All were welcomed in, through the palisade gates and into the forecourt. The thegns of Ceric, and the ships' crews, were led to the kitchen yard to take ale. Ceric, Worr, the two priests, and the captains of both ships followed Elidon, Dwynwen, and Luned.

Gaining the hall yard, Ceric looked about him. The size of the timber structures within the palisade was perhaps not impressive, but the range was. Elidon's hall was easy to mark, foursquare, broad, and bedecked with a red dragon pennon from its roof ridge. They headed towards its opened door. A stable of considerable size flanked it, and on the other side, a store-house of some kind, granary perhaps, Ceric thought. It was the highest of all the buildings, three tall floors, he gauged from the window openings, with a gabled roof and a window near the peak. Beyond the great hall were other structures, many outbuildings of small but sturdy make, roofed with timber planking or with thatch. Set off to one side, and fenced, sat an orchard and seeming garden space.

The day was fine enough to take a welcome ale out of doors. When Ceric stepped within the hall he saw why Elidon would wish to greet visitors here. The side door had been left open, and the lowering Sun sent a shaft of piercing brilliance into the place, striking what was there displayed. The high table at the end was backed by a wall from which all manner of armaments was hung. Clusters of bristling spears were hooped in iron holders. Shields of many colours, some nearly new and untried, others battered almost to fragments held only by their bosses, studded the wall. Swords and knives were fastened against the timber planking.

Even a passing glance told Ceric and Worr these were trophies. Captured weapons were given to one's men as reward. But certain might be kept and displayed as these were, by Elidon. Weapons of many fallen men hung from that wall, warriors of other Welsh Kingdoms, those of Mercia which had long battled the Welsh, of Wessex, and very many, Ceric and Worr saw, of the Danes.

A plump but pale young woman, well dressed and gemmed, stood at the table. It was Elidon's wife, who with no time to prepare, yet was ready with her serving folk to pour out ale. Dwynwen went to her and was given a kiss upon her brow.

All stood for the lifting of ale cups, as was meet for a greeting cup and the presentation of gifts. The first was gift from the King of Wessex to Lady Luned. It was couched in a wooden box, long as a hand, but narrow as three fingers. Worr had charge of it, and handed it to Ceric, who accepted it in both hands.

Ceric turned to Lady Luned. "King Ælfred of Wessex sends this sign of his esteem to Luned, Lady of Ceredigion, in honour of the granting of the hand of the Princess Dwynwen to the hall of Kilton."

Ceric had not told his wife of this gift; she knew of that Ælfred had created for her uncle, but not this, for her step-mother. She thus stood most expectantly at Lady Luned's side as Ceric presented it. Both looked down on a box which was in itself an object of beauty, for the dark wood had been inlaid with strips and squares of many other woods, in every hue trees grew, yellow to red to black.

The Lady lifted the lid. Within lay a necklace, of white pearls.

The gasp of joy Dwynwen gave was reflected in Luned's far quieter smile. But the Lady deigned to hold the necklace up for all to see. There were perhaps thirty pearls, lustrous as the Moon, strung together, and set with a looped fastener of silver. Each pearl was the size of a pea, matched in shape and hue, and nearly flawless.

Luned spoke, her words gratifying to hear. "The King's gift is well chosen. As is he who offers it." Uttering this, she looked to a beaming Dwynwen.

All Ceric could do was bow again under this praise. Being kin would alone not confer this endorsement, not from such as Lady Luned. But she had spoken it, and before those gathered here. It was a most public acknowledgment of her approval.

Ælfred had sent two signs of favour to Elidon, King of Ceredigion. The first was in recognition of the union between Elidon's niece and Ælfred's God-son. It was Dunnere, the priest of Kilton, who had advised on this gift, a manuscript of the Four Gospels, written and illuminated on vellum, and bound in boards, leather-covered and set with gems. Dunnere had pegged Elidon as both devout, and vain. Such a gift would flatter his self-regard, and make him feel the closer to the learned King to whom he was now connected by the hand of his niece.

Dunnere presented the Gospels in a box of carved wood, laid it before the King, and Elidon himself opened the lid.

The eyes of the priest of Kilton met those of Elidon's own priest, Gwydden, standing at the King's shoulder. Dunnere, much the elder, saw the satisfaction and gratitude in his brother priest's face. The gift had been perfectly devised, uniting Heaven and Earth, the realms of eternal God and those of two Kings whose reign upon the land would be over in the blink of an eye. This volume was testament to those monarchs and their linkage. And the book was an object of sacred devotion, and of beauty.

Dunnere's words were perhaps even more impressive than the lavishness of the gift.

"In honour of the union of Dwynwen of Ceredigion, and Ceric of Kilton, Ælfred King of Wessex sends to Elidon King of Ceredigion this sign of his kinship."

He spoke them twice, in the tongue of Wessex and in that of Cymru.

Elidon's eyes lifted to the cleric, then dropped to the volume before him. Sign of his kinship. Dwynwen had known which brother to wed. Elidon found himself looking at Luned, and further found himself presenting her with a single nod of approval in the girl she had raised.

The second gift was that Dwynwen had ordered made. Ceric turned to his right and took from Worr the small box he offered him. He bowed to Elidon again, and placed the box on the table before him as he spoke. The first two gifts had been signifiers of wealth and esteem. This next was a matter of statecraft, and the voice of Ceric conveyed this in full measure.

"King Ælfred further sends you this, made by request of Dwynwen, Princess of Ceredigion. She asked that each Kingly son of Rhodri Mawr be presented with a rich gift, as a bond of unity and friendship to the Kingdom of Wessex. This, my Lord, is yours."

Dunnere repeated the message. King Elidon lifted the lid of the box and set it aside. Within, on a cloth of dark blue, sat a gleaming object, of a size to cover a man's palm when laid in the hand. The King picked it up, the garnet eye glinting as the Sun struck it. Elidon's wife gasped, and even those who had seen what lay within were silent.

Elidon spoke so all could understand. "A fire-drake."

He need not add it was cast of gold; all could see that. It was the figure of a dragon in full flight, wings uplifted, jaws open, coiled tail streaming behind. It was encrusted with tiny beads of gold, forming scales and sinews along its gleaming body.

It was Dwynwen spoke now. "With your help, uncle, Ceric and I will take them as Ælfred's gifts. We will go to Anarawd, in Gwynedd, eldest of Rhodri Mawr's sons. He will gather the other Kings at his hall, that we might present them all together. One to Anarawd there in Gwynedd. One to Merfyn, in Powys to the east. One to Llywarch of Dyfed in the south-west. Another to Meurig of Morgannwg in the southeast.

"After this we will return to you, uncle. Each dragon is beautiful, but each is different."

She smiled at Elidon. "This one I chose for you is most beautiful."

Little could have pleased Elidon more. He was now to become the conduit of alliance between Wessex and his brother-Kings in Cymru. It would add immeasurably to his standing amongst them. All knew it had been his niece who had wed Ælfred's God-son. He had spared no resource in bruiting this about. Now Dwynwen would deliver gifts from Ælfred to the other Kings under the aegis of Ceredigion.

The King looked from Dwynwen to Ceric.

"I will help you," he vowed.

Ceric had begun to offer his thanks, but Dwynwen was not done. There was more she must tell. Elidon had just received two gifts of signal importance. He was made to feel valued by no less than Ælfred, King of Wessex. Strapped to the body of Ceric was a trophy proving her own husband's history and worth, and she would have Elidon know of it.

"Uncle. The sword Ceric wears."

Elidon's eyes narrowed as he again considered the young man's weapon. He said something to his priest, who repeated it for the sake of Ceric.

"It is not new-forged, the King says," Gwydden reported. "It is of an age to have tasted the blood of many men."

Dwynwen picked up her telling again. "It is the sword of Offa, of Mercia," she said.

Mercia had been the great enemy of Wales, running the length of the eastern border as it did. Dwynwen naming its fabled King at the height of his influence imbued the weapon with immediate power and interest. She went on.

"It came into the possession of Ceric from his grand-sire, Godwulf, Lord of Kilton, who was given it by King Æthelwulf, Ælfred's father. It is thus the sword of two Kings."

Dwynwen said this, and then repeated it for her uncle in the tongue of the Cymry. But it was clear the King had understood at least part of the history of the weapon on the first telling.

"Offa," Elidon repeated. The impression the name made on the man was there upon his face.

His niece smiled. "I told Ceric that we Cymry were grateful for his great dyke, which kept them out, and we in," she said.

Ceric had been listening with some little startle to Dwynwen's words. She was celebrating he who wore the sword now, as being fitting bearer of a distinguished weapon. But there was boldness in his child-wife's tale; a kind of caution to her uncle that Ceric was apart from, and perhaps equal to, Elidon and his brother-Kings.

Raedwulf had confidence in Dwynwen, and her abilities as Peace-weaver. The Bailiff had made this clear to Ceric, and to Dwynwen herself. Ceric reminded himself of this now. Her manner might be disarming, but the effect was direct, even penetrating.

Ceric looked to Lady Luned. She was watching her step-daughter with lowered eyes, and with an untroubled brow. Her face, so placid, revealed her feelings only in the slight upward curve of her mouth. Pride was there, Ceric, thought, and quiet pleasure.

He let his eyes move to Worr. Dwynwen had reframed the story of his sword in her pert way, and not without charm in the telling. Worr could do nothing but convey his admiration for the Princess in his returning look to Ceric.

There was time before the evening meal for the travellers to settle themselves in their new lodgings. Dunnere would stay with Gwydden in that priest's own house. Ælfred's men would sleep upon the ships, and Ceric's be divided between Elidon's hall and a secondary hall for guests. The King had a small timber building, a kind of bower, for Ceric and Dwynwen to stay in, and had a serving woman ready to take them there. But Dwynwen insisted they sleep in the gable of the granary building. It gladdened Ceric; he had almost feared that Dwynwen might stay with her step-mother, and he did not wish to be parted from her for even one night.

"It was always for me an eyrie," Dwynwen told him. "If our bedding and packs can be brought from the ship, we will have all we could desire," she promised. "The palisade shuts out much, but from the granary peak the whole sea is before you, and the beach, and the way leading into the palisade." Her smile grew across her face as she recounted this. "Certain fire-drakes perhaps choose to live on cliff-tops, where all is open to their eyes." She thought a moment and added, "It is from there I first saw the golden dragon of Wessex."

Ceric realised this was true; Edwin had come to see if Ceredigion had a bride to suit him, and rode with the dragon banner Edgyth had made.

She led him to the granary, pushing open the door. Several cats, tabbies and mackerel spotted, lounged about, on the tops of casks and piles of full and empty woven sacks. "Our sentries," Dwynwen smiled. "We lose little grain with their service."

There on a shelf stood an oil lamp with base of bronze, and with it flint, striking steel, and dried moss as tinder. Dwynwen struck out fire and lit the lamp, one screened with panels of parchment set in a wooden frame to shelter the flame from any breeze.

They climbed the broad stair to the upper floor, and a second narrower stair to the next. All was covered with the dust of ground meal. But at the top, beneath the gable, stood a closed door. Dwynwen pushed it open to reveal a room, spare but spotless. There was a table, upon which sat a shallow basket filled with strips of white birch bark. Another basket held the kind of feathers Ceric had seen Dwynwen turn into brushes. Two oil cressets, fashioned of glazed pottery, rested next the baskets. A bench was there, and a few cushions. The room was as tidy as if she had used it a day ago.

Dwynwen gave a happy sigh. "It must be Luned," she judged. "She did not know when I would return to her, but she has kept this ready for me." They moved within. A single casement in the gable peak bathed the room in a golden glow.

"You were up here, when Edwin arrived?" Ceric asked.

"I was."

Ceric moved to the window opening. It was just as she had said. Up here they were free of the confines of the palisade. The whole sea was before them. He saw their ships beached upon the sand, and the rippling tide stretching out to the dropping Sun.

They stood looking out together. Sea birds dipped and soared, those who would sleep upon the water, and those who must seek land for their night's rest.

Still looking out, Ceric spoke of what he had this day learnt.

"Elidon. He does not know."

Dwynwen wrapped her arm about his waist.

"I did not, either. Luned will tell, or not. It is all of Luned; as you are. And me, through both of you."

He understood. He and the Lady Luned shared a deep bond, one he had never expected. But more than his own tale, it was the Lady's to tell.

Ceric looked about the small room. It was a space Dwynwen had spent happy hours in, alone, he thought. Tonight they would sleep here as man and wife.

His arm encircled her, pulling her to face him. He bent to kiss her lips. "I will have our packs brought," he agreed.

Gwydden poured out a second cup of ale for Dunnere. They sat in Gwydden's trim house, alone and content. Always circumspect, they could in each other's company relax the prudence with which they conducted themselves each and every day. Facing each other across Gwydden's single table they could not help but smile. For Dunnere it was great pleasure to speak his native tongue, and that alone. And Gwydden, younger by more than a score of years, looked up to the older priest. The two had corresponded as they could for years. Their first meeting had been in the company of Edwin, Lord of Kilton, come as suitor. This second saw the happiness Dwynwen took in the man she had actually wed, and King Elidon honoured with rich gifts, and high esteem, from Ælfred.

Gwydden and Dunnere had reason to take satisfaction, for their own acts, and those of their ilk. Monks and priests of Cymru had served notably and well throughout their native land, and the Kingdom of Wessex. Ælfred's personal confessor, and the scribe recording the life and acts of the King, was a Welshman, Asser, who left the monastery and cathedral of St David's in Dyfed at the King's request to live at his side. Wales had extended its influence throughout the great island in innumerable ways.

The two who sat at Gwydden's table had no such lofty calling. Yet each had played a vital role of service, the one at Kilton, the other, here at Ceredigion.

It had been Gwydden who had answered Dunnere's original query about the young Dwynwen, and it had been Gwydden and Dunnere together who had hoped that the Lady Luned would find Edwin, Lord of Kilton, a suitable match for the girl. It had been Gwydden who had the task of reading the letter penned by Dunnere to Elidon, informing the King and Lady Luned that the Princess had instead wed the elder, and not the younger son of Kilton. The two clerics were steeped in this marriage, but the union they had attempted to forge came from the anvil in different shape than either man had intended. Yet it was more beautiful, and more valuable than they had thought possible.

They spoke of the couple, of Elidon's pleasure in the man Dwynwen had wed, and of the King's enhanced role as ally to Wessex.

After a while they fell into silent satisfaction. Dunnere recalled something else, and he shared it with his brother priest.

"There is still Edwin. And he is still unwed."

⛬⛬⛬⛬⛬⛬⛬⛬⛬⛬

The welcome feast that night was marked by mead being poured first, and for all. Dwynwen, gowned in red, had brought her fillet of gold, and wore it upon her brow. Luned had donned a gown of dark red, making stepmother and daughter resemble embers, the young vivid red, the elder a deep and smoky carmine. Ceric too wore his golden fillet, casting him very much a Prince of this place or any other. As he and Dwynwen approached the high table he saw that before the salver shared by Elidon and his Lady something glittering had been placed. It was the small golden dragon with garnet eyes Dwynwen had given. Elidon's eyes kept returning to it throughout the feast.

As a sign of high esteem Ceric was placed at Elidon's right. Dwynwen sat next him, and Lady Luned next her. Then came a captain of the King's guard Ceric recalled from the meeting on the beach. Worr sat next him. To the left of Elidon's wife sat the priests Gwydden and Dunnere, and the two ship captains of Ælfred who had brought them safely to the shores of Ceredigion. The rest of the table was rounded out with the picked men of Elidon, and at one end sat his bard, modest in presence but mindful of all before him.

This night, after the salvers were carried off, Elidon's bard sang of Winter-white Arawn, one of two Kings of the Otherworld of Annwn. Arawn had great power, but could not defeat his rival King, and asked Pwyll, an unintended interloper in the Otherworld, to take his place and do so for him. Arawn gave Pwyll his own bodily form to fulfill the task, but Pwyll was so honourable a man he did not press his advantage and sleep with Arawn's wife in his guise. When the true Arawn returned to her, she rejoiced to be no longer spurned by a husband she knew loved her. The resulting friendship between the realms of the everyday and the Otherworld continued long after.

As he sang Dwynwen recounted to Ceric the key points of the bard's lay, but even if she had not, he would be struck by the beauty of the telling. When the teller of tales at last silenced the harp strings with his hand, and all were calling out acclaim for his skill, Dwynwen again whispered in her husband's ear. "Sometimes one man must fulfill what another has started," Dwynwen told him.

She said no more than this, but Ceric felt she spoke of his brother and himself. It was Edwin who had journeyed here, and sat at this very table, but Ceric who had wed the Princess thereof.

Later that night Ceric and Dwynwen lay abed in the gable room of the granary. They had climbed the steep stairs by the light of Dwynwen's lantern, which still lay burning upon the table. Its diffuse brilliance radiated like a tiny Sun across the small space. Such light bathed all in an auric glow, giving charm to even commonplace items. The same warm radiance heightened the gloss of objects of value, instilling them with added mystery and thus, a kind of enchantment which could be felt but not easily described. The eyes of Ceric rested upon two such things hanging from pegs upon the wall. The first was Dwynwen's gown, falling in rich folds, which in the little light shaded to nearly black. The second was his gold-trimmed sword in its scabbard.

He was moved to speak of the blade.

"What you told Elidon about my sword . . . it surprised me."

He had learnt today something of great magnitude, that Lady Luned was his grandmother. This finding had robbed him of his breath for a moment. Far smaller but significant to Ceric was the surprise of his young wife's words about the sword of Offa. All she had said was true of the weapon. But she had made a point of who bore it now. He gave his head a shake, and with it, a small laugh. She was so young; how did she speak thus, with such insight, even wisdom? He thought too, of when he had come across her wearing the weapon, or attempting to, and how she had touched it and said a sword with such a history bore power, left within it from each man who had wielded it. One can work magic with such a blade, she had told him.

In her way his child-wife had done just that, and before him today. Ceric turned on his side to face her. There was tenderness, and wonder, in his words.

"You surprise me. You have, from the first time I saw you."

She smiled, that quick and almost secret smile that was hers alone. Then her face grew serious.

"I have sat at the table of Princes and Kings all my life," she said, as if in answer.

"You could have wed a Prince, or a King, of any land," he returned. "I am neither. I am not even Lord of Kilton."

"You are everything," she answered. "You have given me everything. Even fire-drakes guarding our bed at Kilton. And now you bring fire-drakes of gold to my kin.

"And," she added, "we are both stories. Arawn and his Lady are one. But like the tale of Trystan and Esyllt, the ending can be changed. I came to change your ending."

His arm reached about her, pulling her to his chest. "You gave me a new beginning," he whispered to her.

⚇⚇⚇⚇⚇⚇⚇⚇⚇

The next morning was drizzling and grey, wearing the chill of uncertain Spring. All, save Lady Luned, met to break their fast in the hall, and then many of those from the high table remained, clustered about Elidon, to speak of the journey north to Gwynedd. Anarawd's hall was remote, on a craggy hilltop, and a full day's travelling on horseback from the river nearest it. Upon landing they would need to buy or hire horses and waggons. An escort of Elidon's own men would thus join them in their journeying. They would rest another day, and then set out north, to King Anarawd in Gwynedd.

By late morning the clouds had thinned to a pale wash overlaying a brightening sky. Worr had noticed something when the ships had landed, and wished to see if his conjecture was correct. He and Ceric and Dwynwen walked out together through the opened gates of the palisade, and turned to the left.

"I thought I spied an old earth-work," the horse-thegn explained. "If so, it could be flooded at high tide, and then closed off to hold the water."

They came upon its remains soon enough, a gully which might have once extended around the entire fortress. Here and there a few worn and rotted posts protruded from the sand as if they had once served as reinforcement to a deep trench which had been dug.

"It does look like a moat," Ceric mused. He questioned Worr, who stood, studying the ruin. "Could it be the remains of an earlier fort?"

He knew from Dunnere of the vast amount of metal extracted from Wales to serve the needs of the Legions, and of the Emperors of Rome. The men of the Caesars took copper, lead, tin, silver, and even gold from Cymru. They must have built their own burghal system of fortresses to patrol and keep all in order, for those who worked the mines for them were the enslaved Welsh.

Ceric looked to Dwynwen, and gestured to the palisade and those buildings enclosed by it. "Did King Elidon build this?"

Dwynwen shook her head. "My grand-sire, Rhodri Mawr. But he never saw my face." She looked about her, as if his shade could be listening and watching. "But perhaps he does, now. I was not born yet when he died in battle."

She went on, in less serious vein. "Rhodri built the fortress, but the sea has changed since then." She smiled. "The sea is always changing," she noted.

As they were turning towards the gates, an aged serving woman walked through them, and stopped to scan the beach. She saw Dwynwen and raised her arm to her.

"It is Luned's woman," Dwynwen said. The three walked to her. She bowed, and spoke to Dwynwen in the tongue of the Cymry.

Dwynwen turned to Ceric, her surprise upon her face. "Lady Luned invites you to her bower," she said. "No man, I think, has crossed her threshold, since the day its building was complete."

Worr was forced to let a low whistle escape his lips, but with a smile of his own, left them as they entered the forecourt of the hall.

Dwynwen led Ceric past hall and stables, and the house which had been pointed out to him as Gwydden's, the priest. They reached the garden he had seen upon arrival, its wattle fencing no deterrent to a few speckled hens which had flown or strutted over from the fowl houses. Seeing them made Dwynwen laugh. "They are my favourites," she told him, and made a shrill little cry which made the hens look up at her.

They passed the timber church, small but of handsome make. Beyond this was the Lady's bower. It was round, and of greater size than was the bower Ceric and Dwynwen shared at Kilton. It had been built with care, and structured to last, the timber posts and ends of the roof rafters sized for a much larger dwelling.

There was no window giving out to their approach, but Luned discerned their arrival, and opened the stout door before Dwynwen could tap at it, or even call out.

The Lady stood in the opening, just behind the broad threshold, one marked with painted designs in red and yellow over which one stepped. The waving patterns extended up the height of the door frame to meet overhead. Luned was again garbed in a gown of ivory hue, making the pureness of her white hair the more striking. That hair was looped up in several winding ribbands of white, confining it while somehow amplifying its abundance. On her breast she wore the silver pin she had worn yesterday, a circle of silver with iridescent shell representing full and new Moon.

Dwynwen crossed over first, and into the arms of her step-mother. Ceric took a breath and stepped in after.

He stopped short, and marvelled at the contents of the place. The first thing that struck him were the flowers. Masses of dried flowers, flower head down, floated above, suspended from the rafters of the roof, in numbers beyond counting. They formed their own sky, of pale pink, deep red, light yellow and rich blue, with many paled to white. To look up was as close to beguilement as anything as humble as single flower stalks could offer. Many maids and women hung bunches of herbs or a posy of flowers to dry in their rooms; this was far beyond and apart from that homely act. The flower heads roofed the entirety of the house. It was strange, and beautiful. And as unique as the two women who stood before him, Ceric thought.

The Lady was looking at him, watching his wonderment. A benevolent pleasure showed on her face, and Dwynwen, at her side and with her arm about the Lady's waist, also showed that pleasure in her own face. Luned nodded at Ceric, inviting him to look further. He dropped his eyes to the walls. A large glass casement lit the room, one which could be shuttered both inside and out by hinged wooden panels. Near it was a table laid with fine pierced-work linen, and upon that another piece of costly glass, a clear bowl with three legs of the same stuff. The bowl was as large as a basin, larger than he would have believed if he were not beholding it himself. Yet it was clearly not for bathing face and hands; it was placed as a sacramental object, and Ceric thought this must be the bowl the Lady looked into to descry the future.

He let his gaze travel further. The place was built of timber, but almost nowhere could it be seen. The rafters were concealed by the rain of flowers, the planked walls hung with draperies of patterns unknown to him, the chairs and benches laid with fleece and furs. A curtain of some filmy stuff was drawn across one portion of the room; concealing and revealing the bed that lay beyond it, piled with cushions and rolls of blankets. Upon one wall were shelves where sat cups, stemmed and straight, wrought of bronze, and of silver. Small bowls of silver companioned these. Other shelves held pottery jars, stoppered all, and beneath them a tray of some white metal which held implements with which to write and paint with the tips of feathers, much like the carefully gathered kit at Kilton Dwynwen set her hand to.

Ceric had seen the work sheds of dyers, and the private chambers of learned Ladies such as his grandmother Modwynn, with her many abilities. Never had he seen such a space as this created and inhabited by his second grandmother, Luned. It was hard even to think of her this way; the knowledge of their kinship was so new. If he had entered this space without that knowledge, he might have thought it the bower of a sorceress, a diviner, a witch. From what Dwynwen had told him, Luned must be a healer on a level beyond any herb-women he had seen, excelling perhaps even such as the Lady Modwynn, or Edgyth, schooled by nuns and monks in the use of plants and roots. The trappings of this woman's interests should make him wary in her presence, but no disquiet did he feel.

She was not a witch, but as Dwynwen had named her, a wise-woman. Her power was palpable, yet he sensed no evil about her. Some churchmen railed against the secrecy of old women, their mutterings and sly knowledge. Be mindful of what you are taught, he told himself. What you feel may be truly what you know of someone.

"Will you take wine, Ceric," Luned asked. "It is of my own making, of last Summer's elderflowers, and has mellowed now enough to drink."

Dwynwen clapped her hands at the prospect, and moved with her step-mother to a lidded chest sitting upon another. This was opened, while Luned glided to the wall which held the cups Ceric had noted. A stoppered jug appeared from the chest, and three cups were filled. Dwynwen's was a straight cup, of silver, small, but embossed round with running forest animals which led each other on an endless race. The one Luned brought to Ceric was stemmed, also of worked silver. The Lady held it as a special vessel, and passed it to Ceric with some little gravity.

"This is the cup from which your mother drank, by the River Dee, when she came to visit me," she told him.

Dwynwen gave a small gasp of delight, and Ceric took the proffered cup with a silent but significant bow of his head.

Luned turned back to her step-daughter. "Ceridwen was no older than you," she told her. The smile that played upon the Lady's lips was perhaps for both girls.

Luned took up her own cup. It was also stemmed, also of silver, but set about with pure rock crystals; a gemmed cup such as a Queen would lift to her lips.

"And this cup is that which your mother watched me drink from," she told Ceric.

The three raised the cups in salute, then tasted the nearly colourless liquid in their cups. Though it be cool Spring, the flowery fragrance transported them to Summer's promise.

"The flower white, the berry red, and the wine it gives from each, distinct as night from day," Luned told them. She smiled at Dwynwen, and at Ceric holding his mother's cup, and he wondered if in this way she compared her two daughters.

She gestured they sit, and Ceric and Dwynwen placed themselves next each other on a fur-covered bench, while Luned sank into the lone chair.

"Your wine is of rare savour," Ceric praised. He lowered his eyes to the depths of the cup, imagining his mother, no older than Dwynwen, drinking from it.

There was much Ceric wished to ask, but no way to frame his questions that did not seem gross intrusion. Still, he must make a start, and couched his query in as low and gentle a tone as he could.

"Our connection," he began. "Will you tell me when you knew of it?"

Luned smiled, and gave a nod of her head. "When I inquired of Edwin of his mother." The pause that ensued went on long enough that Ceric feared no more might follow.

Then she picked up the thread of her thought, inclining her head to the table which held the rare bowl of glass.

"It was nothing I foresaw. Sometimes the curtain is drawn, and we must pull it back forcefully.

"I admit I dismissed your brother, until he spoke your mother's name."

"You dismissed him."

"I did." She turned her eyes with sudden penetration on Ceric. "You two are not alike," was all she said.

"And it was always to be Dwynwen's choice," the Lady went on. "She took a path of high judgment for one so young, offering to travel to your home, and there to make her decision."

Luned's eyes now rested on her step-daughter. "And you knew, my girl, whom you had truly come for."

Dwynwen smiled back at her step-mother.

Ceric was not eager to revisit the turmoil of that day. He found himself speaking of his son.

"Lady Luned," he began, unable to name her grandmother, out of respect. "I have a small son. Your great-grandson. His mother named him Cerd. She was a woman half-Dane, half-Saxon. She died, on a field of battle."

It was the bare minimum of the child's story, and at the same time, all he could now bring himself to speak of it. Dwynwen knew the tale, without stint; she could tell of it to the Lady as she saw fit.

The dark lids of Luned's eyes closed over her gaze. "Cerd," she repeated.

He was not sure how this mention of the name would be received; his mother might have been the product of rape.

She seemed to take this in, the fact of the boy, and also the circumstances of his mother's death.

"The child has unusual blood . . . "

"He will come to live with us, when the time is right," Dwynwen offered.

Luned nodded her head. "He will," she agreed. "You must know him, Dwynwen," she ended.

"You will round the island of Ynys Môn on your sailing to Anarawd, King of Gwynedd," Luned next said. She went on, in form of a directive. "You must stop there. Saint Dwynwen, for whom you are named, dwelt there, on a tiny island of her own."

Dwynwen leapt up. "How I would like that!" she sang out.

"But the Saint requires no dragon of gold," Luned advised, with the trace of a smile. There was lightness in her tone. "She cares nothing for such things. Your speaking your name there, and showing her Ceric, will be veneration enough."

OF KINGS,
AND SAINTS

I T was Worr who held the remaining four golden dragon ornaments in his keeping. The morning they were to set out to King Anarawd, Ceric brought them up to the granary room, where Dwynwen might again see them. She had been originator of the gifts, and he wished her to choose amongst them, selecting which ornament was best fitted for each King. Some of the Kings were uncles she had seen but once, but she knew of their Kingdoms, their rank amongst the kin of Rhodri Mawr, and Ceric trusted her to make selection.

Ceric opened each small wooden box and set them before her, one by one. Dwynwen carefully considered the four beasts, unique in aspect and character. Each was exquisite in form and workmanship, their warm gleam amply expressing the precious metal from which they had been wrought. Massed together the effect made her catch her breath.

Her eyes, quiet and intent, lingered on one. It had a tail which rose and extended back over its head, there to terminate in a small circle above it.

"This one," she decided. "It wears a crown. If there were to be an over-King in Cymru, it would be Anarawd."

They had gained the help of Elidon, and having done so, must set out for his powerful brother-King, Anarawd of Gwynedd, and win his help as well. He was eldest of all Rhodri's sons, and Rhodri had left him his own birth-Kingdom, Gwynedd. Anarawd had built a large and potently skilled band of warriors to help him keep it.

To reach Anarawd's fortress they must sail round the northern tip of Cymru. Before they did so, they would make land at the promontory of Ynys Môn, to stop at the island where Saint Dwynwen had retreated. They took both ships and the full complement of crew and warriors, abetted by eight picked men of Elidon, to act both as escort and guides.

They left at dawn with good wind, assuring they would reach Dwynwen's island later that day. Sea and sky shared a milky quality, a blue haze of light fog which made the two merge into a mist which concealed at one moment and revealed the next. As the morning wore on, the Sun burst forth in fitful rays between shifting clouds. Puffins bobbed in the wavelets, their bright orange beaks and white faces in sharp contrast to their dusky backs. The ships sailed steadily northwards, rounding a long headland, hugging the coast. Sand beaches stretched alongside their starboard side, oftentimes swelling with peaked dunes, or crested with rocky outcroppings. Plovers in great numbers ran along the sand, gleaning for tiny mollusks. A lowering range of grey-brown mountain peaks, one of them still white-capped, formed a vast spine in the distance, reminder that the Kingdoms of Cymru were better sailed than crossed by waggon or horse.

It was late afternoon when they reached the island. Fingers of rock crept from the isle into the watery flow, a mooring of its own. They saw the church first, small, built of stone, set amidst freshly-green beach grasses which waved in the strong breeze in echo of the sea. No folk were in sight, though sea birds soared overhead, sharp cries spilling from their beaks as if in welcome.

Wave washed as it was, Saint Dwynwen must have loved the water. As a tidal island, her home was sea-girt for much of every day. Upon their approach, one of Elidon's men directed they could not touch the prow of the ship to the saint's island; those who come to honour Dwynwen must cross the sand to do so. They dropped anchor and lowered the tender, and Ceric and Worr again took Dwynwen into it, and rowed to shore on the mainland side. Once beached, Worr and Ceric pulled the small craft up well beyond the tide line. Worr nodded that he would stay with the boat; until Ceric and Dwynwen entered the church they would be well within sight and sound.

The tide was ebbing, but still calf-deep, and the distance to the saint's island that of five or six horse lengths. With a smile Ceric pulled off his boots and handed them to Dwynwen. He picked her up into his arms and stepped into the cold and foaming water to make the crossing. She laughed in protest, but must accept his refusal that she walk across herself. Even shallow water could deepen quickly, and tidal currents in such places might sweep one off in an undertow.

When he set her down he sat upon a low ledge of rock and replaced stockings and boots. The church of grey stone was before them, smaller than that of Kilton, and edged at its foundation with blown sand of light brown. There seemed little growing save the narrow-bladed beach grass, but the air was fragranced with a green and herbal scent, beyond the salty smack of the sea.

Ceric stood and looked to the church. "Tell me of Dwynwen," he invited.

His own Dwynwen gave a delighted laugh.

"Lovers honour her, those who are happy in love and those whose hearts have been broken. She was the daughter of a King, Brychan, who lived long ago. He was father to St Ninnoc, as well, she who you honour at Kilton."

Ceric gave a small shake of his head in surprise. He had scant memory of his sister of that name, who had died as a babe. Of the Saint for whom she had been named, his knowledge was also slight, save that she had sailed across to Frankland and there founded a nunnery. With a nod of his head, he bid the story go on.

"Dwynwen wished to become a nun, but met a young man named Maelon. She was torn in her desires. Her heart turned finally to God, and she knew not what to do. She prayed to fall out of love, and that her burning passion be transformed to ice. An angel appeared and gave her a potion, which turned Maelon truly into ice. The Princess was struck with pity, and with sorrow, for him.

"She knew not her own power," Dwynwen recounted, "or that the angels listened to her. Dwynwen then prayed to be granted three things: That Maelon be restored to his natural form; that God in his mercy would nurture all true lovers; and that she herself might dedicate herself to His service. She left her home."

Dwynwen now looked about her, and breathed a sigh of satisfaction at their surroundings. "She found her way here.

"She became a healer. The sick and ailing came to her for help, not only for ailments of the body, but of the heart and mind. She loved all animals, wild things like birds and foxes as well as cattle and sheep. She could heal them, as well."

"And what of Maelon," Ceric was moved to ask.

"Ah! Of him we do not hear," Dwynwen admitted. She smiled, and summed, "It is her story; we must imagine the right end for him.

"He became a monk, likely, as he was moved by her holiness," she suggested. "Or wed one of her three-and-twenty sisters."

"Three-and-twenty?" Ceric gaped at the number.

"Her father was a King," she answered, with a small shrug. "But Dwynwen was said to be prettiest."

"As you are," he answered.

She laughed again.

There was no path or worn track to the church; or the blowing sand refreshed all it touched, so it seemed they were the first to set foot on the Saint's isle.

The nearer they came to the building, the smaller it looked to Ceric, a kind of diminutive chapel, a chantry really, or a place of true hermitage. It was sized correctly for she he approached it with.

The door was sturdy enough, and set with iron work fashioned with great craft. The strap hinges spreading from one edge had been hammered into dragons, clawed paws extended, holding and supporting the planks of the door in their grasp. Ceric pulled it open.

There were but three windows within, a large one above the altar, and two set in the side walls. He would have left the door ajar for the light it lent, but the blowing sand eddying at the base of the building made him pull it closed behind them. At once the soughing wind and rippling of the tide was shut out, and they stood in perfect silence.

The altar was of the simplest, like that of a chantry, and laid with a plain cloth of linen. Set upon this were two candlesticks of silver, and between this, a slender upright cross of silver. Off to one side stood a half-size statue of a young woman, a maid really, with open arms of welcome and a broad smile upon her face. It was not of painted wood as were many statues of saints Ceric had seen. It had been gilded in its entirety, so that it gleamed in the sunlight thrown through the window near it.

They were not alone. A woman was there, kneeling in prayer before the statue. Under her knees was a tiny cushion set upon the stone floor. She crossed herself, rose, and came to them.

She was not a nun; at least she wore no known habit, but her gown of simple make suggested a life of like simplicity. Ceric could not readily gauge her years; the place was dim, but more than this, there was a timeless aspect to her person. If nun she were, he thought her of unusual youth to be placed in charge of such a shrine, but then, she may have distinguished herself in the eyes of her superiors. She was dressed in a gown of dove grey, and a white linen veil laid over her heavy plaits of fawn-coloured hair lent light to her face.

She looked upon the two visitors and nodded.

Dwynwen curtseyed deeply, and spoke.

"Sister," she told her, as she thought her a nun. "I am also Dwynwen."

The woman smiled at her. "And so you are."

The smile that spread across Dwynwen's lips was wide and sincere. Did she then know of her coming? Or were perhaps all women who made pilgrimage here an aspect of Dwynwen, who had sought succour in love, and found refuge on this windswept shore?

The woman made a small gesture of her hand.

"A cheerful heart is all, and this you possess. You may present yourselves to the Saint," she invited. "I will be at Dwynwen's well."

Saying no more than this, the woman turned from them and left. The opening of the door threw a shaft of sunlight onto the floor, striking their backs and ending at the gilded statue they faced. It fairly blazed under those rays. A low gasp escaped from Dwynwen's lips. Then the door was closed, shutting off the beam of light.

Dwynwen fixed her eyes upon the statue and spoke.

"Saint Dwynwen, you who were torn asunder by love, who prayed for ice to help you make the choice of courage, we have come to ask your blessing. I too am Dwynwen, and this man Ceric is my love. Under your gaze we proclaim ourselves as one. Our Offering is our hearts, bound one to the other.

"You were healed of your longing, Saint Dwynwen, then went on to heal others, and the beasts of field and forest. May you help me do the same.

"May our love cause harm to no one, only blessing. And if we must suffer, let us do it for love, and with love."

Dwynwen spoke again, but this time in the tongue of the Cymry. Ceric did not know what she said, save that he heard his own name. Then she crossed herself, and turned to him with smiling lips.

They made genuflection at the altar, and then Ceric pulled open the door to the sea and sky.

"There is a holy well," Dwynwen said. "I did not know this. We must drink of it."

They scanned the landscape. Across the sand flats, now merely wet with sea water caught in its low ridges of sand, was the boat they had rowed over in. Worr was walking upon the beach. Beyond him were the two ships, riding at anchor. About them were dunes of tawny sand in which reaching grasses had emerged, with a higher cliff of dark and craggy rock above. And behind the church, a small copse of trees. They made for it. Trees could not grow without fresh water; a spring or underground source must be there.

They found the well, a spring which had been circled round with stone, and a deep pool formed. A font of holy water it looked, one offering a cooling tonic to all who had made the trek to the isle of the Saint. A wooden bench of rustic make had been set before it, and on its time-worn seat, a dipper of copper with which to ladle up water. This burbled, ever renewing, from the rock, spilling to the dark pool. Mosses grew about the well, and saplings of wych elm and white willow nodded over it. A flash of silver in the water told them a fish lived there; such were sacred messengers to those who made query before them.

"The nun – she is not here," Ceric said. There was no trace of her. The ladle was dry; if she had come here, she had not drunk from its waters.

"She spoke of this well to tell us it was here," Dwynwen offered. "We must drink of it."

Dwynwen had offered him water from a silver hand-fast cup. Now Ceric took up the ladle, dipped it into the pool, and held it to her, so she might drink from its copper lip.

She did so, holding the bowl of the ladle in both hands, and then passed it to him. As he lowered it from his lips, the fish surfaced, breaking the water for a glistening instant before vanishing into its depths. They both smiled. It seemed benediction indeed.

They sat down upon the bench, the ladle still in the hands of Ceric. Their eyes rested on the pool, and the water tumbling gently from the rocks just above it.

"All you told me about Dwynwen – did your birth-mother, who named you, tell you this?"

Dwynwen thought. "I think she must have; I do not recall Luned speaking of the Saint, not before telling us we must stop here."

"Tell me of your birth-mother," Ceric went on. "She died when you were a small child," he guessed.

"The Faeries bore her off. That is what my father told me, Prince Dunwyd. He said he could never quite grasp her in his hand, though he be very gentle with her. But yes, she dwells in another realm. In the land of Faery. And with the Saints."

This telling, uncertain and at the same time decisive, was so like her innocent knowing that Ceric could only accept it, as he did all things of his child-wife.

Ceric nodded, then noticed the growing shadows of the trees about them. He rose, and set down the ladle. They stood a moment side by side looking at the dark surface of the well. Its water, cool and sweet, was now within them. It was shrine of its own, and to have shared its refreshment an added benison.

They walked back to the church. There were no other structures in sight, and no sign of the woman who had greeted them. Was it the Saint herself, Ceric had to wonder.

Worr, waiting on the beach, raised his arm to them. Ceric waved back, then spoke to Dwynwen.

"Lady Luned said we need leave nothing. That instruction was for you, namesake as you are. I would like to leave an Offering. Stay here and I will do so."

She smiled and nodded her agreement. He went in, stood before the statue of the Saint, and crossed himself.

"Dwynwen, Saint, you who gave your name to my bride, I know you are truly patron of those who love, to have helped her find me. I give you this as token of my thanks. But do not, I beg you, let her know any suffering."

Ceric must add this last, for he thought it was what Dwynwen had asked, for his own sake.

He opened his purse. Dwynwen knew fourteen years. He counted out the same number of whole coins of silver, and laid them down at the feet of the statue.

⁂

They sailed on, stopping to drop anchor at dusk. Next morning brought them to the broad mouth of the River Conwy. A coast-guard was set there, hailing them with brazen horns, for Anarawd's fortress lay down river. The captain of Elidon's men called out to them, and was invited ashore. There he delivered a letter from Elidon to Anarawd, asking that it be carried to the King forthwith. Within was news that the party was envoy of Ælfred, King of Wessex, urging Anarawd to send word to Merfyn in Powys, Llywarch in Dyfed, and Meurig in Morannwg. These three monarchs must ride at speed to join Anarawd at his fortress here in Gwynedd, so that Ælfred's God-son, Ceric of Kilton, and Dwynwen, Princess of Ceredigion might present each with a rich sign of favour, King to King.

Those aboard ship watched the courier ride away, with the assurance from the coast-guard that Anarawd would have the missive by nightfall. They were waved onward, and hoisted sail. They could travel the Conwy only so far, and then must themselves go overland by horse, and with a supply waggon.

Though the Conwy flowed northward, it was so broad at its mouth the wind could be put to good use in driving them south. Late in the day, after passing several narrow islands in the river, they reached a small but stoutly fortified river port, set on the western bank. Rising hills backed it. A road, well laid and maintained, led through them. The fortress of the King of Gwynedd lay at the end of it.

With Elidon's escort they were now nearly fifty men. Gathering enough horses for such a large troop would be daunting, as the port kept but few. It was determined Ælfred's men should stay with the ships, and the men of Kilton and Elidon be horsed. Then there was the needed waggon, both for supplies and for Dwynwen, who would be companioned by the two priests. This luckily the captain of the port could supply. Two-and-twenty horses, and two for the waggon team could be gathered, and the captain of the headland port set his men to doing so. The travellers spent the night upon their ships, but with the freedom of going ashore as they liked. It took a full day for all the horses to be procured, with Anarawd's men heading inland in pairs and returning with the needed beasts. Thus two nights had passed before the waggon could be loaded, horses saddled, and the party set off.

Along with the escort of Elidon's eight men, the port captain gave them two, so they were as heavily protected as any could wish. They journeyed with a fortune of gold, a secret unknown to all save those who had stood before Elidon and told of their plan. Anarawd's two men led, followed by four of Elidon. The lead two of these bore the King of Ceredigion's flag of a dancing red dragon. After these came Ceric and Worr, riding side by side, followed by eight of the thegns of Kilton. Then came the waggon in which was seated Dwynwen, Dunnere, and Gwydden. It was hooped over and covered with tarpaulins, protection from damp, and from just behind the waggon board, on the right, rose another flag, the two sporting dragons, red and golden, which Dwynwen herself had sewn. The waggon was driven by a thegn, and one more rode at the team's near side in front, and another trailed the waggon. Following it came the remaining thegns, riding two by two, and then as rearguard, four more of Elidon's warriors.

Though the day began in a mizzle of rain, it could not dampen the spirits of the troop, embarking on a venture they hoped would prove advantageous not only to Wessex but the folk of every Kingdom of Cymru. The road they travelled rose swiftly from rolling hills to flank narrow defiles edged with steep cliffs. Unseen birds chirped in treetops, their leafy canopies so high one must crane the neck to glimpse. Massive boulders, dark with wet, were roofed with mosses of resplendent green, and in several places rivulets of water came splashing from an undergrowth of veridian brilliance. The path to Anarawd's hall provided its own natural defence, one not to be taken lightly. Yet other tracks were in evidence, paths which crossed their own, coming from both east and west.

They arrived late in the day, to find a fortress crowning a hill top. Palisade and buildings were largely screened by the trees lining the final twist of the road, until of a sudden Anarawd's forest stronghold loomed.

The palisade followed the contour of the hilltop, making it hard to gauge its full expanse. The doubled gates stood open in welcome. Just within, in startling contrast to the wildness of the country just travelled, and the numberless trees surrounding them, rose an upright of stone. It was a preaching cross, and loomed above even those on horseback. The upright and cross piece were chiseled out of one slab of stone, its arms circled by a wheel of stone. It was carved over with figures, tempting to the eye.

Beyond this lay a timber hall larger than that of Kilton, and with a range of stables, barns, and workshops to serve a garrison of some two hundredfold.

Ceric and Worr, riding side by side, could only look at each other in awe. "This indeed is the hall of a King," muttered Ceric.

Most powerful of Rhodri's sons, Anarawd had won the trust of his famed sire. Rhodri rose from King of Gwynedd to dominate all of Cymru. Anarawd was a considerable warrior in his own right, and Rhodri had given him Gwynedd. In the score of years since his father's death the new King's gaze shifted far beyond his own borders, though, and Anarawd had forged alliances with the Danish Kings of Jorvik, engaging both in trading and raiding with their men. Nor had he been beyond familial dispute. Over the years he had attacked the smaller Kingdoms of his own brothers, and provoked both Mercia and Wessex. And he had long ago defeated Ælfred's son in law, Æthelred, Lord of Mercia, in a telling battle that ended Mercia's attempts to conquer Wales. He was also canny enough to recognize Ælfred's capabilities, and to present himself a few years past at Witanceaster with pledges of peace. Anarawd was in short an estimable ruler, one better kept a friend than made a foe, and Ælfred, in the twilight of his reign, was attempting to keep him as such.

King Anarawd was ready for them. He stood within the opened gates at the head of a long file of spear-bearing warriors. At the King's side was a woman, with a range of children behind her. True to what Ceric had been told of the Welsh monarchs, a priest was at his other side. It was, Ceric thought, as much a demonstration of true piety as claim to Christian lineage in Cymru, an unbroken belief which ran back to the faith of the early Christians of the Caesars. Ceric well knew the quiet pride Dunnere took in this; that the True Faith had been kept alive in Wales when the Kingdoms to the east were awash in heathen idolatry.

As they neared Ceric got a closer view of the welcoming party. Anarawd was grey of hair and beard, and powerful of build, the shoulders of a breadth that made the man a fortress of his own. Like most Cymry, he was not overly tall, but there was a solid strength to his person, even in his sixth decade. The woman at his side was of noble mien, perhaps a score of years younger than her husband, and having survived the bearing of the six or eight children behind her had a dignity well earned, and well worn. The priest was, like Elidon's own, young and vigorous, his eyes skimming the arrivals to rest on Gwydden and Dunnere in the waggon. Unless Anarawd himself possessed the gift of letters, this must be he who had read Elidon's missive aloud to announce their mission.

The escort halted, giving Ceric and Worr a chance to nod their respects to the King, and allow Ceric to ride back to the waggon. He quitted his horse and reached his hand to a beaming Dwynwen. Gwydden gave a hand to the elder priest, aiding his descent from the waggon board, and both clerics went ahead, to present the envoys.

Dwynwen walked with measured step at the side of Ceric. When they stopped before Anarawd and his Lady, Gwydden began addressing the King in the tongue of Wales, first presenting Dunnere, who inclined his head at Anarawd's greeting, and returned it. Then Ceric and Dwynwen came forward. It was the priest of Kilton who made this presentation, a long stream of words from which Ceric could discern only his own name and that of Kilton.

His child-wife did not await the end, for she stepped forward and ran to the King. She gave a deep curtsey to each her uncle and to his Lady, and then fairly sprang into their arms. She spoke, words mingled with laughter, until Anarawd's lined eyes crinkled with his smile.

Anarawd began to speak, first to Dwynwen, and then to Ceric.

It seemed as though the King was making some comment of her size, or growth, for he gestured with his hands a remembrance of her person the last time they had met, one to indicate a very young child. Anarawd then looked from Dwynwen to Ceric, as if confirming that small as she was, she was now wed.

The party was welcomed within the great hall, and their tired horses taken off to water and a needed rubdown. The refreshment awaiting those who had travelled from Ceredigion began with basins for hand-washing, followed by the passing of bronze cups filled by the Lady of Gwynedd. Within foamed a nut-brown ale flavoured with the seeds of fennel, which Ceric was to learn was a favourite of the King.

Anarawd had no command of a tongue other than his own, and Ceric and Worr stood by as Gwydden spoke to the man, gesturing often to Ceric. Then the priest turned to Ceric and addressed him directly.

"The King will receive the gift from Ælfred, esteemed King of Wessex."

Worr was ready with the small wooden box sheltering the precious thing. He placed it with ceremony upon the flat palms of Ceric, who presented it to Anarawd. The King set it upon the table and with lifted eyebrow relieved it of its lid. There lay the gleaming dragon, crowned by its circling tail, as Dwynwen had chosen.

Anarawd freed it from its box and held it up. A murmur of admiration rose from those assembled. It was then Dwynwen stepped forward. She addressed her uncle, the King, but by a turn of her body included all who stood before her; his Lady, priest, the many children hovering just behind, and Anarawd's chief men who backed him. She spoke with simple grace, but with firmness, though a smile lit her face.

Ceric could not know what his young wife was saying. Dunnere had moved closer to him, and Ceric looked to the priest.

"She is telling of Kilton," the priest whispered. "Extolling its glories. The church of stone. The bound and gemmed books. The fact that I am myself Cymry. Now she is speaking of the piety of Ælfred and his munificence to the Holy Church. The closeness of the King to the Cymry, the fact that the King, who could draw holy counsel from Frankland or even from Rome, sought the wisdom of a priest of Cymru in calling Asser, monk of St David, to abide with him. Now she speaks of the rich gifts Anarawd received of Ælfred when he and his brother Kings visited Witanceaster in the past."

There was some little admiration in the priest's voice as he breathed these words in the ear of Ceric. The Princess remembered all he and Gwydden had told her, and told it well. Indeed, Dwynwen's shining face, and small hands which moved in expressions of abundance, joy, and reverence, fixed all eyes upon her.

Then she turned and looked to Ceric. She took up her speech, but this time he knew of what she spoke, for he heard the name Offa and knew she was again relating the story of his weapon. He took the smallest step forward.

Anarawd's reaction to being confronted by the sword of Offa was nearly identical to that of Elidon. Striking as it was with its gold trim, his eyes opened the wider at the weapon as he learnt of its history.

"Offa," the King said. His eyes lifted to meet those of Ceric, and gave a nod.

It was time for Ceric to speak. The King of Gwynedd had been reminded of Ælfred's power and devoutness, and Anarawd had direct knowledge of the monarch. Now in addition to prior bestowals, he had received a magnificent dragon figure to further cement the friendship between the Kings. What Ælfred required in return was a covenant, signed by all the Kings of Cymru, pledging alliance to Wessex.

There was a balance which must be maintained with the man, and Ceric took the tack of celebrating the attributes of the Cymry as a distinct and heroic folk, vassals to none. He furthermore must introduce the notion that soon the crown of Wessex would pass to Ælfred's son. The alliance with the Kings of Cymru would continue, under the new King, Eadward. This condition was of sensitive nature. The death of a King was a fraught time in any land, and succession often times occasioned a bloodbath. Challenges could be sudden, fierce, and successful. To pledge to honour a compact made with one King, and carry it on to his son, was nearly unheard of.

Ceric spoke at length of the King's son, Eadward, of whom he had intimate knowledge, having served under him on many a campaign, most notably that in which the infamous Dane Haesten, scourge of both Wessex and Cymru, had been pursued. Anarawd and his brother Kings must see that Eadward would continue the same policies established by his father, and extend the same liberalities, or even greater, which the Kings had come to expect. With expanded peace, this included an increased fostering of trade between Kingdoms, an act of bringing them closer together.

Ceric outlined this, sentence by sentence, with Dunnere, and Gwydden too, speaking his intent to Anarawd and his court. When he was done, Anarawd responded, and Ceric learnt that he had, as requested, summoned his remaining brother Kings to join them here in Gwynedd; the furthest might be here within the week.

At the table that night Ceric and Worr were surrounded by those who did not speak their tongue, dependent on Dwynwen and Dunnere to explain the words of the King, and later, songs of the bard. Yet their reception was marked by an open-handed welcome, and Dwynwen's own enjoyment in the night gave him pleasure. The meal was unstinting. The kitchen yard had three days to prepare for this welcome feast, days well spent. Several yearling pigs had been split and roasted, rendering the flesh both succulent and crackling. The running fat from the roasting swine had been carefully preserved in drip pans beneath the turning spit, and used to enrich the browis to follow, providing added savour. More of the excellent ale was poured out, followed by mead washed from upland honeycombs.

Anarawd's fortress was large enough to house several smaller halls, one of which was designated for the party from Kilton. Ceric and Dwynwen were led by a serving woman to an alcove within, large and deep enough to proclaim it reserved for guests of importance. Worr was given the alcove next them, and as was usual for the clerics, they clustered with their fellow priest in his own house. It would take several days for the remaining Kings to arrive, but the waiting would be carried out in comfort.

The isolation and difficulty of access of the King's stronghold limited the ability to explore much beyond its confines. Yet there were views from the ramparts as broad and far as from a mountaintop. The next morning Anarawd invited Ceric and Worr, with the King's two eldest sons, to walk them with him, that they might exult in the views. The fortress was well concealed from below in several aspects, but there were openings in the forest growth which allowed unrivalled views over vast distances, stretching as far as the sea to the north.

Hawks were brought, that they might hunt with them from these heights. Ceric and Worr were each given one of the King's trained harriers to fly, and spaced themselves out along the length of the ramparts, taking turns releasing them against likely prey. Rock doves and wood pigeons, large and clumsy flyers, fluttered in the cross currents sweeping up the ravines, and the hawks once unmasked took off like flown arrows after them.

Ceric, standing alone with his hawk on his gauntleted wrist, was aware he had not partaken of this sport for years. Kilton kept no hawks, but Hrald did, and at Four Stones he and Hrald and Ashild had ridden out, goshawks on their wrists. It was a lifetime ago; Ashild's own life was over. He looked at the bird on his wrist, silent and still, awaiting the removal of its hood and then release so it might have a chance to snatch prey from the sky. It was part of the strangeness and beauty of life, Ceric thought, that he should be here now, guest of a King of Cymru, and wed to a Princess thereof. His young wife had been invited up, but had demurred; wishing Ceric and her uncle to share this together, and knowing that hawking needed no common speech. And, Dwynwen wished to spend time with some of her same-aged cousins, who, like her uncle and aunt, she had not seen since the death of her own father, Prince Dunwyd.

When Ceric and Worr descended from the ramparts he went looking for Dwynwen. The doors to the great hall were opened to admit light, and he heard the strains of music within. Dwynwen stood at one end of the high table, singing to her cousins. They sat about the table, elbows upon the scarred surface, some with chins resting in their hands, eyes fixed upon her small figure. Women who were spinning, and those weaving at the wall looms in the light of the open doors also turned their faces and listened. Ceric knew of what she sang. Dwynwen recounted the tale of Trystan and Esyllt to her cousins, her voice taking on a sonorousness her spoken words never did. Ceric, intent in his watching, realised he heard the tone of Lady Luned in her singing, a pitch low, resonant, and full of import.

She held no harp nor cymbal to enhance the telling, but her small hands moved with the rise and fall of her voice, adding shape and meaning to her words.

The song ended with the peace and content the lovers knew, its final notes lulling enough to sing a restless child to sleep. When she was finished her cousins cheered her effort. Dwynwen's quick smile was followed by a laugh of happiness at this praise.

She came to join Ceric.

"It was that you taught Garrulf, at Kilton," he said.

Dwynwen nodded. "It was."

She thought a moment before going on. "I do not think love should be punished, not when it is true."

Ceric gave a nod of his head. He had been thinking of Hrald when he stood upon the ramparts, and thought of him again now. When love is shared, it was hard to condemn it.

He spoke the words rising to his lips. "Life is over in the blinking of an eye."

"It is," Dwynwen agreed. "Our lives are short, and we must love as we can. It is the only way to give ourselves and others the strength to face it."

She stood on tiptoe, so she might kiss his cheek as he lowered his head to her.

Within the week all the Kings had gathered. For Dwynwen, it was a reunion of uncles she had not seen since her father's death. The Kings of Powys, Dyfed, and Morgannwg were men in their fourth decade, now assembled in the presence of their diminutive niece. Elidon was away in his own fortress, but in Dwynwen before them was Ceredigion embodied.

Again, the two priests Dunnere and Gwydden made introduction of Ceric to the monarchs. Again Dwynwen spoke of Kilton, and then of Ceric and the fabled sword he wore. And Ceric then spoke of Ælfred, and of Eadward. The golden dragon figurines were presented by him, as Dwynwen had instructed, and to each King according to age. Unfeigned pleasure was in their faces as each held up the gleaming dragons for all to admire.

Now the covenant pledging friendship with Wessex could be read out by the priest Gwydden, and signed. Two names stood upon the parchment when it had been carried to Kilton, that of Ælfred, King, and Eadward, Prince of Wessex. A third had been since added, and first of the Welsh Kings to sign, as was meet, that of Elidon; for Dwynwen, conduit of this compact, was of Ceredigion. Anarawd was now the fourth signatory, then Merfyn of Powys, Llywarch of Dyfed, and Meurig of Morgannwg. Ceric was not surprised that Anarawd took the quill in his own hand and dipped it in the tiny ink pot before them. His signature was bold and clear, the letters showing sign of diligence in the scribal art. Merfyn signed with equal confidence, if not equal skill, but Llywarch and Meurig each had Gwydden sign their names, after which they placed their mark, the sign of the cross.

Cups were filled and raised again, this time with wine. Rare were the times the Kings had gathered for peaceful ends. Ceric, looking on this, knowing his own small part in it, and the far larger one of his young wife, was suffused with pride. Dwynwen stood just at his shoulder, her face alight with happiness. At his second sip he again raised his cup, and to her alone.

As their ships rounded the island of Ynys Môn and headed south, Dwynwen gazed in the direction of that far smaller isle where dwelt the Saint whose name she bore. Stopping there had been both gift and benediction. She thought too of the Lady of the place, or holy sister; Dwynwen was not sure. I will return, her heart sang out; I will return to you.

Though they must beat against the wind, the return to Elidon's coastal fortress was marked by the high spirits of all aboard. A day of sodden rain could not dampen it. The rain abated somewhat as they neared, and as they landed not only Luned but Elidon himself awaited them, hooded, but expectant.

Once within the hall the King was shown the signed covenant. He looked upon it with true satisfaction, asking Gwydden to again read it aloud, and with his finger tracing the outlines of the signatures of his brother Kings. Ceric found Luned's response as veiled as were many of her reactions, but the slightest upturning of her lips, and a glint in her eye as she looked upon Dwynwen, and then turned her gaze to him, seemed rich approval.

Next morning they readied to sail. They arose early, for Dwynwen wished to share a walk with Ceric. They followed the old moated channel they had traced with Worr, but went on. Almost directly behind the fortress lay an open expanse, which had been cleared of timber. Beyond it was a wood of mixed broad-leafed trees, extending its reaching grasp year by year, for a flourishing growth of low shrubs and saplings sprang up in the cleared space. The woodland beyond was fresh and inviting in its spring dress.

"There is something pretty here," Dwynwen said, and led him in.

Arching trees met over their heads, and mosses gave way to lichens creeping along rocky outcroppings. Branches thinned, telling of a small clearing ahead. They heard birds chirping, and then the flutter of wings as they took flight. Their gathering point was a water source, a flat rock from which an underground spring burbled. The rock was slightly hollowed, unto a basin, with an opening near the centre from which water plashed up. It overspilled into other rocks, leaving shallow bowls from which the birds had been drinking. As they stood, a few of them returned, including whinchats with their white striped heads and copper-hued breasts. It was a true rock fountain, the charm of which was not lost on Ceric.

"Have you drunk here?" he wished to know.

"Many times," Dwynwen answered. Her smile grew. "But my gown gets wet, kneeling down to reach it." Her merry laugh suggested this had been little deterrent in the past.

They moved forward. The yellow blossoms of gorse led them on, and hawthorns nodded in greeting, hung with the white buds of coming bracts of flowers. Further on a stand of round-leafed aspens clustered together, like so many slender sisters. Running up the pale bark of several were twining vines, evergreen, but bright now with new growth. Dwynwen snapped a few free, and with nimble fingers fashioned two wreaths for their heads, one for Ceric, and a smaller for herself. She placed hers on her head and then stood before him with the second.

"You may bow your head," she instructed, with mock gravity. He did so.

She placed the green circlet on his head, bright contrast to the dark gold of his hair.

"I make you Prince," she told him.

She smiled, and he laughed as well. But as they walked on, he gave thought to her words. They were deep enough in the wood that the palisade encircling Elidon's hall felt far away.

"Would Elidon truly make of me a Prince?" he wondered aloud.

Dwynwen made a small sound, one of remembrance, of the morning she had claimed that before a raging Edwin.

"He would," she answered calmly. "He would make you a Prince of Ceredigion.

"And if he did so," she went on, "we must live here. But he would give us our own hall. And folk to serve us, and men as warriors to back you."

Ceric lifted his eyes to the aspens. And Elidon did not yet know he was grandson to Lady Luned. Ceric was forced to pause, thinking on this.

He was pledged to the Lord of Kilton, Edwin; and pledged further both to Eadward, and to Ælfred. Nothing he could now countenance could make him break these bonds. Yet the knowing of this, that there might await another home for him, Dwynwen's home, and the home of his surviving grandmother, held true meaning.

They must turn back. Dwynwen, grateful to have shared this place with the man she loved, clung to his arm. She was as full of glad cheer as ever, and spoke of her happiness that they would return to Kilton having accomplished all they had set out to do. If Ceric felt a twinge of reluctance to quit this new found path, his bride's good humour soon dispelled it.

Worr, attending to the lading of the ships, saw them and grinned. Ceric's hand almost went to his brow to remove his leafy crown, then stopped at Dwynwen's words.

"You must wear it within the palisade, to mark you as a true Prince," she advised.

He did so. They walked in, together.

"I must see Luned again. But I will not be long," she told him. "Come to us in the orchard garden." They had packed at dawn, and Ceric need only bring a man to help him carry down their bedding and packs.

When he entered the garden he became aware of its transformation during the time they had been away. He did not at first see Dwynwen or Luned, screened as they were by new growth. Dwynwen was garbed in light green, the same gown she had donned upon arising, but here she looked to Ceric's eyes a living part of this orchard. Lady Luned, wearing her customary ivory, might have fallen from the pear trees. They had begun to blossom, a haze of white above their heads. Soon the apples, their buds already showing tinges of pink, would follow. As he neared he greeted them with a truth.

"This orchard suits you," he told them with a smile. Luned smiled back, and Dwynwen laughed merrily. But then thought Ceric, all places were made the lovelier, hallowed even, by her presence.

Lady Luned wore about her throat the necklace of white pearls King Ælfred had sent her. Ceric must smile with further pleasure at this, to see that she favoured it enough to wear it now, and before him. As he looked at both the elder and the younger females, the Lady's hand went to the clasp of the softy gleaming strand. She unhooked it, and draped it about the slender throat of Dwynwen. Kissing her step-daughter's forehead, she told her, "I give you this, gift of your new King." Dwynwen's mouth opened in surprise, but the Lady went on.

"Pearls are of the sea, after all. Like a wave, you will always return to me."

As Dwynwen's very name meant "wave", she laughed in delight at this rich bestowal.

They walked on. The grasses they trod were hung with dew droplets, but cheerful with flowers of blue and yellow. On the dog roses, already leafing out, clusters of rose buds trembled under their own weight.

Dwynwen led him to an apple of many years' growth, gnarled, twisted, with boughs hanging nearly to the ground balancing those which rose heavenward. It made fine contrast to her youth and freshness. Dressed as she was, pearl-bedecked, and with the delicate crown of living green, she could have stepped from the land of Faery. "We will hang our crowns on this old apple," she proposed. "It will be more fruitful than ever, this year." They did so, his larger wreath encircling that of hers.

The three were largely quiet, sharing but few words, as so often presaged those soon to be parted. Yet they were not alone in the orchard garden. Four or five of the black and white speckled hens were there, flown over from their fowl house, pecking through the grass with their bright beaks and uttering tuck-tuck as they found beetle or worm. Dwynwen had told Ceric that hens of many colours dwelt in the flock, but these had ever been her favourite. The spotted hens had companion of their own. Standing upon the wooden garden table was a handsome speckled cock, with red comb and dark and glossy crested tail. He heard Dwynwen's chirrup to him, or seemed to notice them admiring him, and began to strut upon the wooden boards, almost a small dragon in his pride.

A slack tide lay upon the beach; Ceric had seen it, and soon it would turn. They must be off. But there, before they reached the wattle fence enclosing the orchard, he was moved to speak of the future.

He turned to Lady Luned. "My mother has not met Dwynwen, nor my son. If one day I should travel with both to Gotland, would you come with us? I want my mother to know Dwynwen, and see her grandson. And if you were there, to see her own mother again.

"Would you sail with us?"

It was plaintive in its simple directness. Ceric did not know what more to say. He stood unmoving, looking at his grandmother, over whose face a shadow seemed to cross. Ceric could guess why, and said the next.

"Not to Mercia. Nor Wessex. Your feet will not touch ground there unless you wish it. But with Dwynwen and me, and my boy, to Gotland. If you would like to see my mother."

The slightest movement of her throat told that Luned had swallowed. She followed this with a long but gentle breath. "I would like to see your mother," she answered.

"Then we shall sail, the four of us!" This was Dwynwen, joyance in her voice.

It forced her step-mother to smile. "Yes. We shall, one day, sail to Gotland."

The three embraced, as they had upon the beach after arriving. Luned kissed them upon the brow, first Dwynwen, then Ceric, in blessing to both.

Worr and Elidon awaited them in the hall. The King, well pleased with the outcome of their efforts, surprised his niece with an offer.

"I would like to grant you a gift, my child. Tell me what you desire."

Dwynwen paused but a moment. "May I have three speckled hens, and a speckled cock to take back with me?"

King Elidon threw back his head, and laughed. "You may," he told her. As the final part of the lading, two withy baskets were handed up, the hens and cock snug on heaped beds of straw within.

When all were aboard, Dwynwen stood with Ceric, looking at the figure of a woman, wrapped in a dark cloak, who stood motionless watching from the beach. The sail was hoisted, and the wind, catching it, pressed the ship westward. Luned extended her arm towards the girl on the deck, palm upright, as if they might press their hands together at this distance. Dwynwen responded in kind with her own arm and hand, reaching toward her step-mother, as if they touched.

⚜⚜⚜⚜⚜⚜⚜⚜⚜

At Kilton the Lord thereof found sleep long in coming. After a few fitful hours Edwin rose from his bed after a day of no special note, and in which no added care had been placed upon him. Yet a series of formless phantoms shadowed his rest. Ceric had been gone the better part of a month; and if all had gone well, he and Dwynwen should soon return. A thought, unbidden, came to Edwin: of their not returning. Mishaps at sea could be many, and misadventures on land posed their own hazards. And it was not solely these which had occasioned Edwin's unhappy thought. Rather it was the danger he felt inherent in his brother journeying to Ceredigion. The surety with which Dwynwen had announced that King Elidon would make Ceric a Prince of the realm still sounded in his ear. Losing his brother like this – Edwin could not allow such a concern, and he shook the thought from his head.

He had lit a cresset in the darkness, but his sole shadow in the room underscored the fact he was alone. A surge of resentment flooded him; followed, and paired with, shame. His resentment was rooted in the fact that he could not have the kind of love which his older brother so readily attracted. The Princess of Ceredigion, whom Edwin had wooed and brought here, had returned to visit her home – but with Ceric.

Edwin had seen the kind of love and devotion Ceric had for Dwynwen, but could scarce imagine it for himself; it seemed a kind of obsession to him. Edwin had no name for that kind of absorption and attention. He is under a spell of some kind, he had told himself more than once. Yet part of Edwin desired this, yearned for this.

This discomfiture, this lack in him, reached back before the Welsh girl, to a woman of Kilton. Recalling his thoughtless usage of Begu brought a flush of shame to Edwin's cheek. He was not unkind to her; he knew this; but his was a thoughtless use, just the same; a lack-wit when it came to appreciating her. She had not even left a message of Fare-well for him. He knew now it was always Ceric foremost in her mind. It was his brother she cared for, even loved. Edwin saw now she must have felt pain at this hopeless attachment – and he knew that hopelessness now, if not bearing an attachment worthy of despair. He had no one to want, or to love.

Edwin could stay in the treasure room no longer. He pulled on more clothing, unbolted the door, and stepped out into the dark hall. His captains Alwin and Wystan slept nearest to his door, and as he drew it shut and locked it Alwin's face appeared from behind his alcove curtain. Edwin hissed that he needed air, and would not be long, signalling the man back to his pillow.

He must disturb another man by the hall door, a man who had in years past noted Edwin's nocturnal comings and goings to the hamlet in which lived Begu. Once free of the hall he walked with purpose toward the sound of the sea. A half Moon was dropping in the heavens, and as he cleared the beech hedge of the pleasure garden the light of its descent was echoed in pale ripples in the oncoming tide. He passed the pavilion, not wanting to sit, not liking the place, as it was where he had discovered his brother and Dwynwen together, and already pledged as man and wife.

He neared the cliff edge and let his eye travel over the ladder of moonlight cast in the water.

Sidroc had told him to pray and sacrifice. He did not know how to do that; he did not even understand the kind of love Ceric and Dwynwen had, nor the kind of bewitchment his brother was under.

He thought of the night of Modwynn's funeral, when Ceric had vanished, and he had come here fearing to look over the edge lest he find his body below. It made Edwin now move a little away from that sheer drop, though his thoughts remained fixed on his brother.

Ceric had pledged to Ashild, who had given him a child; cared for him enough for that. Begu had loved Ceric, and now this elfin sprite from Ceredigion. Why was Ceric worthy of such devotion? He answered himself with this truth: He is like his father. I am like mine. It was a despairing summation of his failures.

Edwin would not think more of this; that lineage was utterly out of his hands. He thought again of what the Dane had told him on Gotland.

Pray. Dunnere had preached there was no bargaining with God. Yet what else could he do. Not even the King of Wessex could help him to a proper wife. And sacrifice? Even if Edwin removed any hopeful expectation from the giving of the sum, he would perhaps receive benefit from the act of giving. Many acts of good had flowed from urgent pledges to God.

If Dunnere were here at Kilton and not away with Ceric, Edwin would go to the priest for direction in this. But he could go alone into the church and attempt to speak, so God would hear him. He found himself turning, back to the church he had passed on his way here. The oak door was never locked, but tonight felt a hundredweight to open.

Only the single sanctuary lamp was aglow, hanging there by the altar, and never allowed to flicker out. But moonlight struck the casements, casting the stone floor in a spectral hue. Edwin approached the altar, shrouded in white linen, and made his genuflection. He looked down at the grave of his grandmother Modwynn, and that of the old Lord of

Kilton, Godwulf, whom he had never known. Modwynn, he felt, had paid scant attention to him; he had felt Ceric to be the favourite. Yet he still believed his grandmother had loved him. Now perhaps after praying for her soul, she might intercede. He uttered a prayer for her, that if she did not yet enjoy the blessings of Paradise, that she might soon be purged of all sin and found worthy of doing so.

Having made this start, he might now ask a boon for himself. Edwin's first duty was to wed a woman who could serve capably and with honour as Lady of Kilton. But those were not the words which found their way to his lips.

"I ask that God send me a woman to care for, and who in return, will care for me. Please send her to me."

It was all he could do. But he felt a freeing upwelling, in having asked.

Now for the required sacrifice. Edwin must make, or promise, an offering. He had nothing of value on his person, but much he could spare in his possession. He named the sum, and the act, with firmness, as if his prayer had been already granted.

"In thanks I give fifty pieces of silver, entrusted to my mother Edgyth, for the care of the poor women of Kilton."

The Dane had said something more to him – the counsel that most troubled Edwin. He had told him that he must be ready to abandon all he knew. Edwin did not know what that meant. There was so little he could abandon; honour and duty forbade it. But in the vault of his breast, he surrendered to this. If it would not dishonour Kilton, he would be willing to abandon all he knew, all he expected, to win a fitting wife.

As Edwin stood alone in the church of Kilton, his brother Ceric lay on his back aboard one of the King's ships, his arm about Dwynwen. She was sleeping, untroubled by the creak of wood and the soughing of wind in the sail. There was good light from the half Moon setting outside their tented shelter, and by its sheen they drove steadily for Kilton.

Their venture north had been crowned with success. It did not surprise Ceric that Dwynwen, a Princess of Ceredigion, should be made welcome by her kin as she had been. It was his own reception that caused him wonderment. All the Kings had responded to Dwynwen's telling of his sword in the same manner; it was as if Ceric had won the blade from the great Offa himself, though that monarch had lived and died long ago. Ceric and his gold-trimmed sword had been woven into an endlessly-running story, one to which all had been eager to add his own name. The tension between the folk of Cymru and the Saxons had ever existed, and was still recalled. As a boy Ceric had heard from Dunnere of St David, the patron of all Cymru, and how, a generation after the Saint's death, he appeared to King Cadwallon on the field of battle against the invading men of Northumbria, and helped the Welsh to victory. It was as if Ceric, bearing the sword of their sworn enemy Offa, was cast in the light of a victor against a former oppressor.

He had not understood how different he would find Cymru. It was not just the language, nor the fact that the rollicking tunes and plaintive songs played in the King's halls were all unknown to him. It ran deeper than that. He thought of the worship of David, and Dwynwen, and of Ninnoc too. The Saints of Cymru seemed vital and real, as if they still walked amongst them. From the mouths of their bards he had heard more of the realm of Faery, that other-world which Dwynwen cherished, one he felt she glimpsed while walking in deep forest, or gazing into still waters. As devout in her Christian faith as she was, as revered as were her famed Saints, hers was a lineage entrenched in its own ancient Gods and heroes, men and women and beasts as well; their own red dragons, which had been honoured, celebrated and sung of far longer than the Old Gods of the Saxons had been by his own folk on this great island. His attachments to his kin, and home of Kilton, and even the Kingdom of Wessex, strong as they were, might pale next the glow of the fierce bonds Dwynwen, blood-linked to many Kings, had been born into.

Whether it was the result of the nature of the Cymry, the blithesomeness of Dwynwen, Ceric's close connection to Ælfred, or the history of his weapon, none could fault the return from their efforts. Both Ceric and Dunnere would write letters to Ælfred, describing what they witnessed. And beyond their testimonies the signed covenant would accompany their missives. Ceric thought of the Bailiff of Defenas, and the pleasure the man would take in what had been achieved. He trusted he had repaid Raedwulf's faith in him; he knew that Dwynwen had.

Beyond this, the return to her home had brought his young wife immense joy, and both had learnt the true connection between himself and she who had raised Dwynwen.

Luned had agreed to join them if they journeyed to Gotland. It gave his going added purpose, and was now become almost a pilgrimage. He must see his mother again, just as Luned must see her daughter. And his own mother must meet Cerd. The Bailiff was now serving as father to the boy, just as Hrald had, and for two long years, in his own absence. He did not know when they might undertake this journey; perhaps next year; but its certainty grew. Ceric wished Hrald were near, that he might share news of his found kin, and of his planned voyage to Gotland. He wondered if perhaps Hrald could come to Saltfleet, and meet them there, however briefly, on their way to the Baltic. Ceric needed to assure himself that all was well with his friend; most of all he wished for Hrald the happiness he himself now knew.

Dwynwen stirred against his chest, a momentary shift of her lissome body in the crook of his arm. Her eyelids did not flutter, but a soft sigh escaped her lips as he bent his head to kiss hers.

ST PETER'S PENCE

Anglia and Wessex
The Year 898

P EGA had no expectations of a letter. One had just
arrived for her at Four Stones, carried by a horseman.
The content of the missive was no less than a royal summons.

It was ten days before Mid-Summer. The first hay crop
had been scythed and gathered, and early rye and barley
fields showed signs of ripening to gold under an ever-
lingering Sun. Spring lambs were well-grown, and the ewes
now milked for the making of cheese. The Lady of Four
Stones had been with two of the dairy maids in the spring
house; it was there the women pressed the soft milky curds
into the wooden forms lining the shelves in which the rounds
would rest. Mealla was just outside with Ælfgiva, and it was
to her a serving woman brought the rider. The man had
already been divested of his horse, and stood holding a thin
but stiff leathern wallet which the maid of Éireann knew
must hold a square of parchment. Mealla stuck her head

into the open doorway and called down to her mistress; the spring house was dug into the ground several steps for added coolness.

Lady Pega emerged, having wiped her hands on a piece of the abundant linen the cheesemakers made use of for straining and wrapping, and was greeted by the courier. The man was little more than a youth, and the respectful pride with which he handed the wallet to its recipient told Pega he felt proud of having accomplished the task.

"From Lady Æthelflaed of Mercia, to Lady Pega of Four Stones," he told her. "I will await your response, by word or letter."

There was nothing suggestive of ill tidings in the youth's bearing or tone, allowing Pega to dismiss the first, and natural response of mild alarm at any arriving message. She thanked the letter-bearer and entrusted him to the woman who had escorted him thus far into the hall yards. He was very close now to ale, bread, and cheese to tide him over until the evening meal in the hall.

"Come Mealla, let us take it to the garden, and read it there," she told her companion.

Mealla picked Ælfgiva up to speed them along; she was as curious as Pega to learn the contents, and the child was of an age when much caught her attention, and would not be hurried along. The girl's shrill little yawp of complaint was readily silenced by Mealla placing the string of coral beads she wore into the child's hand. This was a special gift from Pega, and Mealla cherished it as such.

Once in the bower garden the two women sat at the table there, whilst Ælfgiva was set free to scamper about the gravelled paths and flower beds. She dropped down into one and began pulling cornflowers, their bright blue buttons gathered into a tiny posy.

First Pega must fetch her fine sewing shears, for the leathern halves of the wallet had been laced together with loops tight enough to try the patience of any. She snipped away at the seam with care, freeing two sides so she might tap the contents out.

It was indeed a letter, and in Lady Æthelflaed's own hand. It gave Pega a small but joyous burst of recognition to see it, and a smile rose to her lips knowing that no scribe other than the Lady had penned it.

It was but a few lines, each forcing the smile on Pega's lips to deepen. She read it to herself, then lowered the letter and spoke to Mealla.

"We are going to Witanceaster, Mealla, and soon. The King is this year sending his offering of St Peter's Pence to Rome, and Lady Æthelflaed is coming to her father, that she might herself deliver the alms of Mercia to be added to the gift. There will be a special Mass, a feast, and the ritual send-off of the horsemen bearing the silver."

"And we shall see it?" Mealla's black eyes had grown large, not only with the prospect of seeing the royal burh, but attending the festivities surrounding this gift to the Holy Church.

"We shall see it!"

Ælfgiva had now approached her mother, a handful of crushed cornflowers clenched in her fist. "You shall see it too, little one," her mother promised with a laugh, "and Æthelflaed, who has been as an older sister to me, shall at last meet you."

The traditional date for the gathering of this gift was at the Feast of Saints Peter and Paul, just after Mid-Summer. This was a full fortnight away. It would give Hrald time to arrange for his absence as he accompanied his family to the royal burh.

It was of her husband Pega spoke next. "I cannot wait to tell Hrald; he will be pleased indeed that we have been included in so important a feast day as this."

Hrald was away at the valley of horses, but should return shortly. His absence did not keep Pega and Mealla from their planning. When Hrald and Jari had ridden with a troop of men to Witanceaster nearly two years past, the journey had taken six days. On that occasion the Jarl had been called by King Ælfred to join him at the royal burh, where he had in mind a match for Ealhswith. Alas, the King's hope was dashed, as Edwin Lord of Kilton refused the girl. Hrald was further delayed in returning to Four Stones, as he rode with Edwin to see his friend Ceric. But Pega had good memory that the ride south to Witanceaster had taken six days, supply waggon and all.

Pega's first thought of preparation was for their little daughter. "Ælfgiva will need a new gown, one fitting in which to meet Lady Æthelflaed and the King," she posed. In fact, the dyer in the village had but recently delivered a length of rose-pink linen to Pega, enough for gowns gracing both mother and child.

"If we start now, we will have time for new gowns for each of you," Mealla promised. She was an expert seamstress, and such a commission, to be worn before a royal audience, felt a satisfying challenge to her skill.

Pega laughed in pleasure. Dairying was forgotten; the milk maids knew far more than she how to press good cheese. Now she and Mealla must begin cutting and sewing.

The maid of Éireann arose in her customary brisk manner. "'Tis time to take up shears; I'll away to the weaving room and lay out the linen."

Pega, still holding the letter of summons, promised to soon follow.

Mealla left the confines of the bower garden and headed across the forecourt. As she passed one of the armourer's forges, Kjeld turned round and spotted her. Instead of lifting her chin in the air and assuming an air of disinterest, the raven-haired maid actually slowed her step so Kjeld might join her. She was smiling, which was enough to make him wish to enjoy her gaze. But her words revealed what had put that smile on her lips.

"I am going to Witanceaster," she announced, with a note of triumph in her voice.

"Witanceaster?" Kjeld rarely ventured anywhere; as second in command he must remain at Four Stones when Hrald was gone.

Mealla seemed unwilling to explain why, so Kjeld was forced to go on, with no hint as to what was calling her there.

"Well – make sure you come back to me," he offered.

Mealla bristled, as he knew she would. It was become a game between them, seeing how quickly she might feign offence. At least Kjeld hoped she was feigning offence.

"Huh! Back I shall come, but for my own sake, and that of Lady Pega and Ælfgiva," was her tart rejoinder. "And I am going at the side of Lady Pega, for she has been called by

Lady Æthelflaed herself to join at the collection and sending of alms to Rome."

Kjeld thought a moment. Mealla had not mentioned Hrald going; if he was excused from doing so, Kjeld felt certain he could convince Hrald to send him as head of the body-guard. He would be in a position of high responsibility protecting the Lady of Four Stones and her little daughter, and be in the almost constant company of Mealla.

As Kjeld considered this happy possibility, two horse-men entered through the gates. One was Hrald himself, accompanied by Jari, back from the valley of horses. Hrald was still astride when Mealla called up to him, that Lady Pega awaited him in the bower garden, and with cheering news. Having delivered this, she bestowed but a quick bob of her head to Kjeld, and went on her way.

As Hrald walked to the garden he saw Pega, washing the hands of Ælfgiva in a basin kept there for just this purpose. Ælfgiva called out to her father and raised her dripping hands to him. Hrald laughed and picked her up, wet hands and all, as her mother tried to dry them on a linen towel. Pega was laughing too, and as soon as her own hands were dry, lifted the small square of parchment in the air between them.

"A rider has just come, from Lady Æthelflaed in Mercia. She is travelling to Witanceaster that she might bring alms to her father's St Peter's Pence offering. Æthelflaed bids us join her there at the royal burh. Mealla and I were just planning it out, Hrald; we have time to reach Witanceaster by the Feast of Saints Peter and Paul."

Shining expectation stood on her brow, and Pega had rarely looked prettier as she delivered this news, and its hope.

Ælfgiva, in her father's arms, was now fussing to be set down upon the table top, and Pega took the child. She did not at once register the change in Hrald's countenance.

"Witanceaster," he repeated.

"Yes – Witanceaster! At last I shall see it; Æthelflaed goes so rarely that she never had chance to take me, but now I may again see her, and King Ælfred, and the great burh itself. And there shall be a rare feast. Mealla is starting on new gowns for Ælfgiva and me."

"Have you sent message back," was all Hrald could ask.

"The courier has only arrived, and is in the kitchen yard. But of course we shall go; it is a most happy occasion for us all."

She saw he did not share her own eagerness, and wondered if there was some impediment to his leaving; he had mentioned nothing pressing in recent days.

"And this is but another honour the King, and his daughter Lady Æthelflaed, grant you, Hrald, inviting us as they have," she went on.

He only nodded.

"We will go, of course," she added. A growing note of concern now rippled through this wish.

Hrald looked at her. Ælfgiva had circled her arms around her mother's neck and was again smiling at him.

Hrald nodded his head, this time with decision. He had no choice but to say the next. "Yes. We will go," he ended.

After Pega and Ælfgiva left, Hrald stood a moment in the confines of the garden. His eyelids had dropped over his eyes, shrouding them against the bright blue of the sky. He lifted his chin and let his gaze fasten on the leafy beech hedge surrounding the space. From there he tipped back his head to look directly at the sunlit sky, dazzling above him. He closed his eyes against it. Witanceaster was the last place he wished to venture. The royal burh meant only one thing to him: Dagmar.

Ealhswith was up in the weaving room with Eanflad when Mealla entered. Ealhswith was spinning wool at one of the windows, and her aunt stood at her loom, weaving more of the creamy stuff. Mealla smiled, and wordlessly carried the bolt of pink linen from a storage chest to the long cutting table. Ealhswith asked about it, but not a word Mealla would share; it was Pega's news, and hers would be the pleasure of telling it.

Ealhswith had not long to wait. Pega and Ælfgiva came up the stairs, the child chattering away as she did so, refusing to be picked up and carried, wishing to make the climb herself. When they finally arrived Pega's good spirits were undampened. She greeted Eanflad with her customary kiss, and turned to Hrald's young sister.

"Ealhswith – the happiest of news. Lady Æthelflaed has invited us to Witanceaster, for the collection and sending of alms to Rome. We must be there by the Feast Day of Saints Peter and Paul. I shall be so happy to be in the Lady's presence again; what joy. And I have always wished to see Witanceaster. Ælfgiva is old enough to travel safely; there will be a splendid Mass in honour of the Saints, and a feast.

"Please to come with us; we are all bidden, and thus all welcome."

Pega's excitement rang in every word. Ealhswith remained unmoving, yarn in hand, having allowed the spindle to strike the floor. She found herself looking down at the worn planks she stood upon. Witanceaster was the place of her humiliation, where she had seen the man Ælfred had intended for her, a man to whom she was at once attracted. And that man had rejected her. No, she did not wish to return to Witanceaster.

She bent down to retrieve the spindle, and straightened up with a returning smile. She kept her voice as even as she could.

"I am glad for you, Pega. I am certain it will be splendid. But I shall remain here, with Aunt Eanflad."

Pega's hope for Ealhswith's company was dashed, and her face clouded a moment. Witanceaster, she then realised. Ealhswith must not have fond recall of it. She knew almost nothing about the refusal of the young Lord of Kilton to accept her; Hrald had so little to say of it. But it must have stung, and deeply. Ealhswith had been living with her mother in Defenas then. But she seemed not quite herself since her return here to Four Stones.

Days of happy anticipation followed for Pega and Mealla. The new rose-pink gowns were cut and sewn; one for the mother, a diminutive copy for the daughter. Pega selected with care which of her jewels to take, including the gem-set fillet of gold she had worn at her wedding, which she imagined adorning her brow at the feast. There was a leather-worker of skill in the village, and Pega asked the woman to cut and sew a new pair of shoes for her, of soft pale leather. They were shaped with a few eyelets up one side at the ankle, and Pega planned to use narrow lengths of pink ribband to lace them. And she spent careful time sorting through the best of Hrald's tunics and leggings, that he might be as richly dressed as she.

At the feast Mealla would be sitting with Ælfgiva at a children's table. While being modest in show and appearance, the maid of Éireann was possessed of a prideful nature when it came to her attachment to Lady Pega, who had not only been born into an ancient lineage, but was the favourite of the Lady of the Mercians. Mealla determined a new head wrap of fine gauge linen, etched with embroidery along the length of the trailing hem, would set her apart. She also looked at, and then decided to bring, the splendid silver bird brooch Kjeld had given her; she could wear it to fasten a shawl, or pin it to the bodice of her gown.

In short, preparations were many. Pega would not be gone long; she felt Æthelthryth need not be called away from Turcesig. The serving folk of the hall, well trained by Lady Ælfwyn and dedicated to their roles, would be more than adequate to keep it running. Kjeld would preside over a near-empty high table, but would invite those men he felt had promise to join him there for the duration, a foretaste of what could be earned through future service to the Jarl. And Ealhswith had blushed becomingly when Pega had pointed out she would act as Lady of the hall in her absence. This meant sitting not at the table for unwed maids, but at the high table, and the task of pouring out the first round of ale for all seated there. And Ealhswith would also bear the keys of the treasure room, and more, at her waist.

There was also the matter of the silver Pega wished to contribute to the alms heading to Rome. "I will bring silver of my own," she told Hrald one night. "I know Æthelflaed will do the same; carry not only offerings from the treasury of Mercia, but from her own store."

This roused Hrald enough to prompt his next words.

"I will open a silver chest for you; count out what you feel is fitting, from Four Stones."

Pega smiled, and bestowed on him a kiss.

Within a day or two word had travelled through hall and village that the Lady of Four Stones, near and dear to the ruling house of Wessex, had been called to the royal burh for the honour of attending the giving of St Peter's Pence. A few women of the village even approached her, clutching a fragment of a silver coin, asking that it might be added to that treasure of alms their good Lady carried with her.

Hrald had his own preparations to attend to. Given his wife and daughter were travelling with him, and the amount of silver they would be carrying, the Jarl could take no fewer than thirty men, all mounted. To these must be added two wag-gons, one for provisioning, the other in which Pega, Ælfgiva, and Mealla would sleep. He and Jari decided to bring five extra horses, should lameness strike any of their mounts. In all it would be a considerable party which set off from Four Stones.

Two who had special interest in the planning were Yrling and Bork. They were away at Turcesig with a number of youngsters, where Asberg, that master of shield and spear work, held regular drills to perfect the skill of fledging warriors. They learnt of the coming expedition on their return, and both sought Hrald, and together. They found him with Jari in the treasure room, where they had been told by a serving woman to look.

Yrling rapped on the door, and called out his name. "And Bork," he added, with a nod at the youth at his side. Bork had always been taller than Yrling, but now had filled out as well. From gangling boy he was becoming a well-knit young warrior. Yrling too had grown, but retained the compact build of his boyhood. Both Asberg and Jari had commented on how he favoured the Yrling who had conquered the place. They had learnt to be careful not to say so within earshot of his great nephew, lest they spur the lad to more adventures than he, or they, could handle.

Hrald rose from the table and let them in. The eyes of both youths widened. There on the scarred table top sat five swords, which Hrald and Jari must have been examining. They were all worthy blades, the grips or guards trimmed with beaten copper or silver wire. They were no common weapons, but had been forged for warriors of wealth.

Yrling let an oath of admiration escape his lips. Bork, ever more moderate in speech and action, merely looked upon them with awe.

"Já?" was what Hrald asked, of their gaping.

Yrling remembered their mission.

"Witanceaster. We heard you are going. Let us go with you, Hrald."

Hrald took a breath. "Most of the high table rides with us; Jari has chosen the rest."

"But a rear guard," Yrling pressed. He and Bork had already served thus, when Hrald had travelled to Lundenwic to fetch Ealhswith.

Jari had answer. "This ride is far longer than to Lundenwic. We have men who have served as rear guard since before you were born."

Yrling would not be deterred by this; in fact it provided fuel for his next argument.

"All the more reason to have young eyes and supple backs amongst them!"

Jari had to laugh, and even Hrald smiled at Yrling's jibe. It was true that serving as rear guard required tiresome turning in the saddle. And sharp eyesight, able to detect movement at a distance, was a necessary gift. Here were two with both supple backs and young eyes.

"Hrald – Witanceaster," pleaded Yrling. "Jari and Asberg have told us so much about the thegns of Wessex. It is our chance to finally see them." And perhaps spar, thought Yrling, though this he did not say.

Bork had remained silent, but now had cause of his own to speak.

"Jarl Hrald," he began. "Abbess Sigewif and Father Wilgot have both spoken of the cathedral there. I – I would like to see it. To offer a prayer for my father."

The simple sincerity of this request gave Hrald pause. He had not planned to invite either Yrling or Bork, but found it hard to deny a fatherless boy this request.

Hrald was forced to study the two. Much was on his mind, but he and Jari had in fact been speaking of them when they knocked. Yrling seemed to sense when he was the subject of any discourse, and appear.

"Do you see these swords?" he asked of them.

Both moved forward to get a better look.

"You may join us and serve as part of our rear guard." Neither Yrling nor Bork had time to do more than turn to each other when Hrald went on.

"If you serve well, Jari and I will select two of these blades as your own. Your sword-bearing will be upon our return here."

As kin to the Jarl, Yrling was almost assured of receiving a sword from him. But these weapons were beyond any first sword most warriors carried; they were those a seasoned warrior would be proud to bear.

Bork, an orphan who lived under the disgrace of his own father having been involved in an attack against Hrald, had no expectation of ever owning a sword unless he was fortunate enough to win one on a field of battle. He could not speak, and was blinking away sudden water in his eyes.

Jari addressed them now, and gruffly enough to make impress. "I did not have weapons this good until I was almost twice your age. Prove you are worthy of them. Obey every order, keep from fighting, and most of all, when we are at Witanceaster, we are guests of a King. Do nothing to bring shame to Hrald or yourself."

The youths could do little more than mumble their thanks. Each took a step closer to gaze upon the shining steel laid out before them. Warning notwithstanding, Jari took notice of which lad's eye lingered the longest on any one weapon.

Bork still was in charge of Hrald's own horses, and asked a needful question. "Jarl Hrald – your bay?"

The stallion had made the journey to Witanceaster before, and remained Hrald's favoured mount. Hrald nodded.

Yrling and Bork left. Hrald was left alone with Jari.

"It is good you took them on," the Tyr-hand noted. "The long ride will help toughen them up, though to Yrling, riding with us will be no more than camping. Bork – he knows better."

Jari had been with Hrald at that long-ago attack, and seen the starving men and boy behind it. Kjeld was there as well, and had been entrusted with bringing Bork and his father's body to Four Stones.

Jari rose, and placed his large palms at the small of his back to stretch, as if it already ached from hours in the saddle.

Hrald had said nothing, and was looking at the steel upon the table, though without his eye fastening on any one blade.

"You do not want to travel to Witanceaster," Jari hazarded. As acknowledgment of a truth, it was not much above a murmur.

"You are right, my friend. And I must."

Hrald did not think he could allow even so trusted a man as Jari to speak more of it. All he could do was rise, signal to the Tyr-hand that they were done.

⚔⚔⚔⚔⚔⚔⚔⚔⚔

Before their departure the family of Four Stones and those closest to them attended a private service in the new church. Despite its modest size it was a well-proportioned structure, stoutly erected of hewn timber, and sporting a wooden tower from whence a bronze bell, ordered from Lundenwic, would one day hang. Depictions of vines and sheep had been carved around the door frame set in its western end, two motifs Pega judged to be appropriate to Four Stones as it grew in faith.

Indeed, it was planned that one day the entirety of it should serve as its chancel, and a new nave be built to house the gathered congregation. Months had passed since the priest Wilgot had offered his first and consecrating Mass within, yet the wood still bore that forest scent, and in the warmth of the morning the aroma enveloped those within.

Wilgot read psalms, and spoke of the honour due to the Heavenly Father, and the privilege of contributing to the collection of silver destined for Rome. It served as blessing to those travelling, and a plea for judicious conduct for those staying behind. The first group was comprised of Hrald, Pega, Mealla, and little Ælfgiva. Yrling and Bork were invited, and in fact Bork, early to the church, went and found Yrling to remind him his presence was expected. Young Ealhswith would act as Lady of the hall in Pega's absence, and was thus representative of those who must stay behind. Kjeld knew Mealla would be in attendance, and entered the church as well. He lost few opportunities to demonstrate his devoutness before the demanding young woman he sought.

Hrald stood, listening to the worshipful supplications of the priest, asking that if it be the will of God, all would be speedily reunited in a service of thanksgiving. All he could do was bow his head under these words. Hrald had no excuse to remain behind. He had almost wished for some brewing trouble at his border, some report of marauding bands of brigands to be hunted down, so he would have excuse to send Pega with Kjeld and a body of two score men.

He added his own silent prayer to those mouthed by the priest. Hrald's prayer was of the simplest, that whatever challenge lay ahead, he might rise to meet it.

Every denizen of hall and village gathered to see them off. In the past Hrald had ridden to fight, to meet King Ælfred, to travel to Mercia and once before to Witanceaster, amongst many other forays. No prior leave-taking matched this in interest. But then, the folk loved Pega. They were glad in her, glad that she was honoured in this royal summons. Hrald was aware of all this, and worked to hide his own discomfiture. Yet as he swung himself up into the saddle, he thought of his dead sister. The ghost horse that was Ashild's stallion stood there in the paddock, motionless, but looking at him. How much he needed Ashild now.

All he could hope was Dagmar would be gone from Witanceaster; that she would have taken his advice, acted on his plea, quitted the place, and made a life for herself elsewhere. He tried even to imagine her in the strange city of stone called Paris; wed to a prosperous trader. It availed not. In his mind's eye he could summon the broad river, the island set therein, the stone buildings crowding it; but he could not place Dagmar there, wed to some wealthy merchant, or even a nobleman of the court. He could picture her no place but in the small house she had built against the north wall of Ælfred's fortress. Yet almost two years had passed; she must have quitted Witanceaster and moved on.

Perhaps Dagmar had moved on. Hrald had not. Rare had been the days, and none the nights he had not taken thought of her. That scrap of ribband from her hair was even now in his belt, concealed, just as his desire must be hidden.

He shook his head and touched his heels to the flanks of his horse. They set out, amidst the waves and calls of his folk.

Given the fair Summer weather, the troop made better time than any might have expected. They kept the two waggons centred in the double rank of horsemen, as further security for their occupants and the silver they bore, a precaution happily untested. Little Ælfgiva was restless in the waggon, and at times Pega and Mealla, grateful themselves to escape the ceaseless jolting, took turns walking alongside it with her. Hrald rode there as well, but more often switched between riding behind the first two horsemen, and turning his horse's head to the rear to check up on Yrling and Bork. Serving as rearguard was tedious work, and the Jarl's frequent presence kept all the men so assigned alert. The two were also part of the night watch over the horses, so they had full taste of the roles warriors on the road must play.

The trip recalled to Pega the long journey from Mercia to Four Stones. She had just been wed to Hrald, and had Mealla at her side as they faced their new life in Anglia together. Now she headed south, with a healthy little girl, one beloved by both her parents. Lady Æthelflaed had a sole child, a daughter; and though Pega hoped to soon have a son, she knew the Lady would take pleasure in Ælfgiva. Hrald's distraction – she was not certain of it, and wished that Lady Ælfwyn was near, so she might ask her counsel. But her own happiness was enough to carry her on, that and her and Mealla's pleasure in what awaited them.

They faced but one bout of rain, a sudden cloud burst just after dusk which left the men scrambling into their tents, but the females snug in their waggon. As they travelled at this point along the Caesar's road it had little effect on their progress next day; the track they followed was still lapped with cut stone, sparing them from being mired in mud. Towards the afternoon of the fourth day they approached a sentry point from which a winding horn called out. Hrald and Jari rode ahead, backed by two men, and were waved on with the knowledge that they would reach Witanceaster before noon next day.

Indeed, as they grew nearer they began to see folk upon the road, not only coming from the royal burh, but heading to it, upon smaller paths which now met theirs. Every type of conveyance that might be expected appeared before them, or fell in behind them. Waggons drawn by oxen and loaded with bushels of green beans and plump white onions, or plugged crockery jugs and jars of unknown contents; carts upon which were stacked withy baskets holding clucking hens; men pushing and pulling hand-wains in which masses of carded wool roving peeped from linen sacks; and bypassed by all, two aged shepherdesses, crooks in hand, guiding their small flock of black-faced sheep well out of the danger of the King's horsemen who also hastened by.

The troop from Four Stones set their final camp by a small watercourse. The night was dry and clear, and as they spooned their browis around the cook-fire, many spoke of their eagerness to see Witanceaster next day. Hrald and Jari may have been alone in their silence on this point, but Yrling and Bork, sitting with Pega and Mealla, asked so many questions of the young women about life in a great burh that none would have noticed the reticence of the Jarl and his chief body-guard. Yrling had at least seen Jorvik, but it seemed a rough and ready place compared to his imaginings of King Ælfred's fortress city.

None needed to be roused next day. All took advantage of the good water supply to wash face and hands, wipe down their horses and tack, and for those who would come into contact with any of importance at the royal burh, don clean clothes. As Hrald strapped on his sword he was most aware that the costly blade had been presented him by Ælfred, one taken from a Danish war-lord, and given him in grateful recompense for the killing of Haesten.

After they broke their fast around the cook-fire Hrald and Jari waved Yrling and Bork to them. They had been at work with the rest of the men, striking camp, and the two approached Hrald with expectant faces. His orders laid yet another responsibility on them, one they took as the honour it was.

"Yrling and Bork. While we are in Witanceaster, you are on quartermaster duty with Jari. He will depend on you."

Both lads were living at the house of the Tyr-hand and his wife Inga, and since they had come to peace with each other, pairing them in every task was become more and more natural.

"We carry grain in our waggons to be turned over to the kitchen yard, to aid in the provisioning of all. You will help Jari with that."

The two looked at both Hrald and Jari, and nodded. Hrald went on.

"Lady Pega was a royal ward of Lady Æthelflaed. I think we may be given our own house in which to lodge. Jari will likely sleep in the main hall, and you two be billeted with the younger warriors of the burh in a second hall. All must be on their best conduct. We are guests of the King. You are expected to remind our men of this as needed. Drink will be plentiful, as will gaming. Keep your heads and watch for trouble. If any of our men give cause for concern come to Jari or me at once."

The gravity of this charge was not lost on either youth. Their Jarl was trusting them to protect his own name, and the reputation of Four Stones, while its warriors enjoyed the hospitality of a King with whom he had forged alliance. Yrling was suddenly brought to mind of all he had learnt about his father's actions when he was Jarl, and how as one of King Guthrum's chief men he had signed the treaty ending a bloody conflict of many years. This was nothing his father had told him on Gotland, or rather Yrling had not known what questions to ask of his father's life here. But once at Four Stones Hrald, Asberg, and Jari had told him much. He saw with sudden insight that he was being tasked to serve his own father, and the treaty he had helped make. It made him stand up the straighter as he listened.

After Yrling and Bork left to saddle their horses, Hrald walked to the waggon where Pega and Mealla stood. They were speaking of Witanceaster, with both eagerness and a hint of wistfulness in their tone, for they spoke also of Weogornaceastre and Gleaweceaster, the great towns in which they had lived with Æthelflaed and Æthelred. Hrald had seen Weogornaceastre himself, while courting Pega, and had himself marvelled at the impressive stone structures left behind by the men of Caesar, the vast height of the walls; and how grand was the cathedral before which he and Pega exchanged their vows. The young women recalled many pleasures and sights they had missed; the religious pageants, friends, lively markets held not only on Feast Days but every week, the chance to see and buy goods from distant Frankland, and even further away. How isolated Four Stones must be to them after having lived amongst such towns. They keenly awaited seeing Witanceaster, imagining its grid of many streets, its order and prosperity, the sense of earned importance of its folk as they went about their business in the royal settlement. It would be different from the noble burhs of Mercia they had known, but would restore them to that kind of setting.

Ælfgiva had already been lifted to the waggon bed, and Hrald helped both Pega and Mealla up. Pega's happiness was full upon her face; her deep-set eyes, which could look thoughtful even when she smiled, danced with light.

Soon the traffic around them grew thicker, and the doubled walls of Witanceaster loomed. They were greeted at the opened gates by an under-steward who directed them. "Lady Pega, Lady Æthelflaed arrived yestermorn. I will tell her of your own arrival."

Pega clasped her hands in pleasure, and Ælfgiva laughed at her mother's happiness.

Once within the vast forecourt the troop divided. Jari took charge of men and horses and the supply waggon. The steward sent a man with Hrald, and still mounted, he escorted the second waggon to their assigned bower house. It was one of several in a line; Hrald recalled that in which his mother and the Bailiff of Defenas had stayed. Under Mealla's brisk supervision the serving man unloaded the waggon for them, carrying in clothes chests and baskets. The serving man then drove it off, taking the dray horses to a paddock.

Hrald had quit his horse, but stood just without holding the reins. Both Pega and Mealla were moving about, looking into the alcoves, and admiring the oil lamps of brass upon the table.

Hrald spoke. "I will stable my horse, and go find Jari at the great hall."

Pega looked up with a smile. "Yes. There is so much to see, and we are eager for it. And I yearn to greet Æthelflaed. As soon as we have unpacked, we will find you."

Ælfgiva had been stamping her feet in excitement, and ran to the open door to follow her departing father. As he mounted his horse she called to him. He lifted his hand to her, and rode on. Mealla closed the door, not only to confine the eager child, but against the dust being churned up by waggons and horses.

The two women considered the chests and hampers which had been carried in. For all the effort taken in packing, unpacking was but a simple task, and one which could wait. Pega opened a single chest. Everything was laid with order. She looked at Mealla and smiled again. "Let us walk about a bit," she offered. "Ælfgiva is restless – as am I."

THE APPLE

HRALD had not forgotten the way to the King's own stable. He guided his bay to it, past the larger stable and its paddocks, and a smaller one which served for mares nearing their foaling time. He was expected to stable his horse here; the steward who had greeted them at the palisade gates had even mentioned it.

Hrald stopped near the open doors of the stable and got off his bay, pulling his reins with him. A youth came toward him from the dimness within. Hrald did not recognise him, but the lad, Ultan by name, recalled him at one look. This tall Dane had once presented him with an entire coin of silver. The youth stopped short, bobbed his head, and looked in Hrald's grave face as he spoke. Ultan dropped his voice, but pitched so that Hrald could clearly make out the words.

"Guthrum's daughter." The stableboy seemed uncertain as to what to say next, and ended with, "Do you want her?"

Hrald's eyes closed against this question. He had convinced himself that Dagmar would not be here; that she would have gone to Paris; or that she would have met a man from all the many who passed through this great burh, wed him and travelled away.

But no. Her words came back to him: I will remain here, under the King's protection – here, until you call for me, or come yourself.

"Her house is the same," the youth went on, "that by the northern tower."

Hrald could do no more than nod. He turned back to the stark brightness of the day, but could move neither right nor left. Dagmar was here.

She might have no way of knowing of his arrival, and with his family. If they should chance upon each other in the hall, or while crossing a work-yard or forecourt . . . Hrald could not complete this thought. He only felt that coming upon her unawares would occasion some betraying sign that they had before met each other in the royal burh. Hrald was alone now, freed for a brief spell even from Jari's companionship. He must take the chance to warn Dagmar they were here.

Hrald turned. His footsteps took him swiftly to the northern wall. He passed the watch tower thereof, and the narrow side road which emptied near it. He glimpsed two or three folk upon his way, intent on their own errands, but no one more. There, against the palisade wall, stood Dagmar's small house, with its stout brown door. No neighbouring abode had sprung up next it; it was as solitary as when he had last stood before its timber planks. But one thing had changed; or he had not noticed it before. A small apple tree, too young to bear fruit, grew to the left of the house, tucked just round the corner where it would not be trampled by passing waggon wheels. The planting of any tree was ever a sign of hope in a future to come, even if they who had done so never lived to see it to fruition.

Hrald drew breath and stepped before her door. He was not aware of his breathing, only the beating of his heart, which pounded also in his ears. He rapped, to no response. He rapped again, leaning to the door frame, and spoke.

"Dagmar. It is Hrald."

Still silence. There was no sound of movement within.

Hrald stood there, looking at the door, attempting to collect himself; recalling in acute, indeed painful, detail the last time he had entered and then left that door; thinking he would never see its broad planks again.

Dagmar might be anywhere within the expanse of the walls. He could not remain, but must take his chances that their paths would not cross.

He turned, and his eye again fell on the sapling apple. Dagmar must have planted it, in future hope, or mere acceptance that this would be her dwelling place. Whether it signified expectation or resignation, he let his eyes rest upon it. A movement made him lift his gaze.

There beyond the tree he saw someone coming his way; a female figure, bent at the waist, arms extended in front of her as she clasped the uplifted hands of a small child. The child was running on tiptoes and laughing, the little feet barely skimming the ground, upheld by the hands of the mother. The woman who held the child thus was also laughing.

The child, still chortling, dropped abruptly down on the ground, releasing her. The woman looked up, and saw the man studying her.

It was Dagmar. The child at her feet, a brown-haired boy, had twisted on his short legs and turned, pulling himself up to his feet to cling to her skirts. The boy grasped at the dark blue linen with one hand, extending the other out, as if in greeting to the tall man who stood staring at them both.

"Dagmar." Hrald's voice sounded no more than a dry husk in his mouth.

One of her hands had risen in the air, towards him. Her lips formed a smile. The boy was chirping a little sing-song melody, as he clawed at her gown to be picked up. Dagmar's hand went to the child's head, then she bent to lift him in her arms. She moved closer.

Her first words to Hrald were of their parting.

"Do you recall our night together," she asked. Her voice was low, but not without a tremor of remembrance. "I told you at its end I knew much sweetness would come to us." She looked to the boy in her arms. "Here is the sweetness."

Hrald looked mutely upon the boy, nearly too staggered to speak.

"It was a single night . . . "

Dagmar's generous mouth curved into a smile. "It is always a single night."

It was true of course, a babe did not come by degrees, but by a single coupling. Hrald gave his head a clearing shake; he felt thunder-struck. She was not barren; here was their child – a boy.

Once again, all had changed in his world. Once again this woman before him had re-ordered all he knew. Here was his son, one born of Dagmar.

He glanced about, as if trying to reel in time, or to better grasp its unspooling. "How – how was this accomplished . . . ?"

"Accomplished?" she asked, with a slight smile, though her answer was one of gentleness. "The way it ever has been for women. I went away, to a convent. Ælfred arranged it, after I spoke to him. His kindness was such he did not even ask of the father. I returned months later, with my child."

The boy was nuzzling in her hair, grasping a handful which was free of the yellow headwrap over it. She went on.

"No question was asked of me, by the King, or by any other. Do not forget, I am a Dane – Guthrum's daughter, of a Danish wife – one of his many Danish wives. Little is expected of my conduct.

"I was shriven, yes. The priest asked of me both prayers, and penance. One thing I could not grant – contrition for my act. That I hid from him."

A long moment went by for Hrald, reflecting that he too could feel no remorse for their night together. As to what it had led to – he considered what she had been through.

"You did this. Alone."

"Not alone," she answered. "Your child was with me."

He had no answer to offer to this quiet courage.

The high esteem he accorded this response, and her entire action, was shown in the respectful note of his next words.

"What did you name him?'

Her smile shown again, slight, but warm. "He has just learnt to say it. You may ask him yourself . . . "

Hrald looked at the boy, and inquired. The boy puffed out his round cheeks, as if pleased to answer. "Hro . . . ft," he breathed.

Hroft. The name of Hrald's great-grand-sire, back in Dane-mark. Hrald repeated it, in a voice betraying his wonder. It was a name wholly of Dane-mark, and his son was almost wholly a Dane.

"Hroft," Hrald repeated. The child gave a little crow of acknowledgement and reached his tiny hand out to his father. Dagmar stepped closer, shifting the boy nearer Hrald in invitation. As he took hold of Hroft, he saw the glistening of Dagmar's eyes as she relinquished the child. Those wet eyes crowned a smile, warm, one for both Hrald and their boy.

Hrald's free arm came up and clasped Dagmar about the waist, pulling her to him. Little Hroft was encircled by both parents. Hrald's face was lifted skyward for a moment, then with a stronger grasp about the woman in his arm he pressed his lips against hers. Dagmar's arms came around them both, father and son. The few moments of this embrace served as the passing of an eclipse in Hrald's shadowed life, a sudden transformation from dark to light.

When they parted they saw two women emerge from the narrow side road, and turn towards them.

The first was Pega. She was in the act of speaking to Mealla at her side, who held Ælfgiva by her hand. The lightness of their tone suggested they were on a treasure hunt of sorts, looking for the man they had so suddenly found.

Both groups stood motionless. The only sound arose from the two children. Mealla hastily stooped to pick up Ælfgiva in a protective hold. The little girl merely looked over at her father and chortled out a greeting. The boy in her father's arm was chanting his own name over and over, and with each soft singing repetition patting his father's cheek.

Pega's eyes fastened on the family group before her. She took in the tall, dark, and striking woman at her husband's side. They next rested on the little boy, dark haired, looking, she knew, as Hrald must have looked at this age. Everything she saw only strengthened the connection, this likeness of father and son. Hrald kept hold of the child. He could not make this simplest and slightest correction, Pega saw; it would be some manner of repudiation to place the child down upon the ground, or have handed it to its mother. Hrald held firm to the boy.

Pega's lips parted, but the whisper of air that escaped could scarcely be called a gasp. Yet she trembled at the side of Mealla, so that the black-haired girl's arm came up around her waist in support. Pega sensed that every drop of blood in her body had rushed into her head; she felt she would topple from the weight of it. In contrast to the near crushing pressure at her temples, all colour had drained from the faces of the man and woman she stared at. No one spoke.

No one need speak to tell Pega what she had just learnt. The boy was a toddling child of little more than a year. Pega thought back. Hrald had ridden here to meet with Ælfred about Ealhswith. On his return he was distracted. Now Pega knew why. Now she knew almost everything.

Something snapped within her breast. Not the breaking of a branch, ready for fire; but rather the turning of the workings of a lock. Something had snapped, not in two, but snapped shut. She saw it all, saw it for what it was, saw it for what it had always been.

Pega then turned away, turned her back on Hrald, and those with whom he stood.

The pain in her chest was such that her heart must rent; cracking into shards and fragments. I will die, she thought. Pega realised the sin it was, to wish this as she just had. She stood singled out and alone, eyes staring ahead and at nothing. She was aware only of the near-palpable fracture of that vital organ in her breast, and the utter destruction of what had been her ordered and happy life.

Pega lowered her head in a bow, and with Mealla at her side, left.

Hrald stood at the side of Dagmar, their son still in his arms. His face had grown ashen. It was Dagmar who found voice, a tremulous plea rooted in her own shock, and reflective of the shock of all.

"Hrald. You – you must go to her."

She said this, with the damning realisation that though he had at last met his son, she herself might never see Hrald again. Despite the fear clutching at her narrowed throat, the words arose again, a pressing and painful rasp, and possibly fatal to her own future hope.

"You must go to her."

Hroft, alarmed at the sudden tension about him, now reached out his arms and whimpered to his mother. She took him. Dagmar kept herself from saying anything more. She blinked her welling eyes, and gave the slightest nod of her head in dismissal to her child's father.

"I will see you soon," Hrald answered, a hoarse but urgent vow.

Pega and Mealla had returned to the bower house. Pega's shock was too great for tears, but a river of them was flowing behind her eyes, gathering like a dammed flood.

"Stay here with Ælfgiva," she told Mealla. "Unpack nothing. I must see Æthelflaed.

"No tears, Mealla," she said, brushing away one of her own with her hand. "Not yet. Now I must go to Æthelflaed and tell her."

When Hrald arrived at the bower house the door was shut against him. Approaching it, he heard his blood pounding in his ears, a thrumming as insistent as the beating of a drum. He tapped on the blankness of the door, a light tap, the tap of one not staying there, yet who sought one who did. A long moment later Mealla opened to him, her milky skin gone even paler.

He saw Ælfgiva lying in the box bed of one of the alcoves. But Pega was not there. Mealla's eyes and nose were red from crying, but she drew herself up. Hrald remained silent, almost willing her to speak, but she held to her silence. His eyes moved about the room once more. It made Mealla speak.

"My Lady is not here," she told him.

Hrald nodded his head. Mealla stood before him as stiffly as she would before an un-looked-for visitor. Hrald, having broken trust, saw he was now a stranger to the maid of Éireann. She herself had witnessed, along with Pega, the fruit of his infidelity.

Mealla went on. "She is with the Lady Æthelflaed of Mercia." This declaration, though quiet, showed in its formality the distance Mealla now saw between Hrald and the sphere of Pega.

Mealla did not move aside, so he could enter, and indeed, there was no reason for him to do so. "I will await her outside," he told her.

Mealla gave the smallest of curtseys, that given an unwelcome guest.

At the hall reserved for Lady Æthelflaed Pega was given speedy entrance. One of Æthelflaed's companions brought the tear-stained young woman to the sleeping chamber of her mistress. Æthelflaed was within, sitting at a table over which parchments were spread. She rose at the sight of her former ward, but the smile on her lips faded as Pega approached. The young Lady of Four Stones was trembling, and seemed barely able to keep her feet. Æthelflaed had no time to speak; Pega was ready with her awe-ful discovery. It spilled out, in a fury of heartbreak, the telling broken by Pega's choking sobs.

"Hrald . . . I just found him with a woman, his arm about her waist, a toddling child in his arms; a boy. The image of him at that age, I am sure.

"He came here almost two years ago as the King asked him to, on behalf of his sister Ealhswith. The boy he held was a year or so in age.

"I think she is Dagmar. His first wife."

Æthelflaed's erect form stiffened the more, as if she had received a jolt to her person. The Lady must fight her own disbelief and anger over this outrage, an offence to both Pega and herself. She believed all Pega had told her, and without question, the girl was ever truthful and levelheaded. Still, Æthelflaed felt shock at her own misapprehension of the Jarl of Four Stones.

Many men fathered bastards. This, though, was uncommon, in that the child had been born to Hrald's first wife. It was no casual encounter prompted by mere lust or boredom, but proof of a deeper connection. The Lady of Mercia recalled how Hrald had spoken of his first wife; that he had no cause for complaint. He had been more than happy with her, she remembered him saying. She had also noted the change in his countenance as he spoke of their failed union, and had thought then that it had cost him a great deal to sunder it. And sundered it had not been; not fully, or it had been re-kindled by chance, and here in her father's royal burh.

Pega gave Æthelflaed no chance to advise, or even console her. Her former ward next spoke her resolve.

"It is over, my Lady. My marriage is a sham. This boy proves it. I will not return to that bower house, or to Four Stones. Please to take me in, that I might go back with you to Mercia."

Pega spoke with breath-taking decision. She did not dwell on the hurt to her, which was vast, but on the action she must take to remove herself from its source.

Even as she admired Pega, Æthelflaed must warn her from such sudden determination.

"My dear girl, do not act in haste. Many men father children on other women, as well as the wife they truly love."

Pega's next words rang with bitter grief. "I am no wife to him! He is already wed. And to her."

The ugliness of this realization was stamped on Pega's contorted face. It was as close to a claim of gross duplicity, or at the least, marriage under false pretense, as one could get.

Lady Æthelflaed was admired for the coolness of her judgement, and she did not want Pega in her pain and sorrow to bring down unneeded grief on her own head. Most of all Æthelflaed must exert herself to salvage the union between Four Stones and Wessex. She had worked hard to create it, and now must work harder to maintain it, for Pega herself seemed determined to shatter what she had so carefully built. It was Pega in fact who addressed this.

"I know the effort spent in pairing me. You have been as kind as a mother to me, and as caring to my future. But I will not return to him. It is over."

Tears sprung in Æthelflaed's own eyes. There would be nothing she could say. The girl had come to her, a hurt irrevocable, her mind made up. All of Pega's movements had been directed and ordered by others. She had twice been told who to wed. It had all come to nought.

The Lady of Mercia regarded the young woman before her. As seemingly tender as she was, Pega had a core of steel. It had been formed and tempered through her former losses, but now had been brought to unbendable strength through this crisis. And Pega was so deserving of being first in the heart of her husband. This was what was galling, the injustice of her Fate; the way the girl had accepted Æthelflaed's pick for her, and then with only a few hours of acquaintanceship, went gladly to her marriage bed, to bind herself to a man incapable of fully loving her.

This severance from the man she had wed was the first real decision, unaided and unguided, that Pega had made in her entire short life. Æthelflaed could not abrogate it now; it would be insult too great to the girl's spirit and character.

Æthelflaed must consent. "Yes," she answered. Her next words were both truth, and pledge.

"You are of Mercia, and I, its Lady. You are under my full protection." She placed her arms around Pega's shoulders, and kissed her. "I will have your goods brought here."

Æthelflaed released Pega, and looked about her. The girl had come here for refuge; her hall must remain such.

"I will speak alone with Jarl Hrald, and in the great hall."

Hrald was in fact standing outside the bower house door, awaiting Pega's return. She did not appear, but a messenger did, bidding him follow to the King's own hall. Hrald's sharp intake of breath was audible to the man, just as the messenger must note the sallowness of his cheek, and slackness of his person.

Hrald was led within the hall. A few pit-men worked in its centre, scraping a quantity of cold ashes from the long fire pit. By doors and casements women stood at looms, weaving in the good light thrown from their openings. Hrald took scant notice of any of this; his thoughts were churning. If he was to face Ælfred, he did not know how to proceed. He had sought out Dagmar to warn her, but it was she who bore great tidings. The surprise and joy of seeing their son had been still upon his brow when Pega, guiltless and without guile, witnessed all, and in a single glance.

The messenger knocked upon the door. A low voice within answered, and he opened it for Hrald. Hrald found himself alone, facing Lady Æthelflaed. She moved to the door and drew it closer to its frame, but did not close it.

That Lady had been alone in a room with only three men in her life: her father, brother, and husband. When conferring with other men, she was always attended by at least two of her Ladies. But this was a matter of State, and she could not risk being overheard. The messenger who had brought her guest stood outside. Now she walked deeper into the small chamber, and Hrald followed.

"Pega has come to me," she said in greeting.

Hrald's mouth moved, but he was unable to speak, for the Lady went on.

"She has told me of your – return, to your first wife. A return in act, and now, in substance." This was as close as Æthelflaed could come to naming the child.

"It is Pega's stated desire that she travel to Mercia with me, where my Lord Æthelred awaits. It was there she was wed, and there the union will be sundered.

"As you wed under false pretenses, the marriage shall be speedily annulled. It will be as if it never occurred."

The baldness of this statement forced Hrald to object. "A child resulted," he protested, thinking on Ælfgiva.

"Two children, if I am not mistaken," returned the Lady. A trace of scorn had crept into her voice, and she gave her head a small but angry shake as she fought to control her words. She turned from Hrald, and took a few measured steps before the table.

Æthelflaed must master her own ire; too much was at stake. There were paired currents moving in her thoughts, just as a river might flow slowly on its surface, and a far quicker current be active along the river bottom. So it was with this union she had forged. Pega's haste in breaking her tie with Hrald could sweep away all. She must try to salvage the Peace.

The Lady's voice was now as steady as if she recited stores needed for her own kitchen-yard.

"You will return her dowry. They are articles of antiquity long in her family.

"Your bride-price," she went on, turning to face him. "The waggon of weaponry you presented. It has been dispersed, and the weapons are irrecoverable. The King made estimate of its value upon receipt. We will send you that, in silver, some two hundred pounds."

Hrald listened, and with a shake of his head, gave answer. "The bride-price. I forfeit it."

As reparation it was a staggering sum to offer; a considerable impact to his treasury.

Æthelflaed might have laughed. She could scarce contain the bitter harshness rising within her. Handsomely done, she thought. Those who wreak the greatest damage are too rarely those who offer the deepest recompense. Yet even two hundred weight of pure silver would not assuage the insult this Dane had visited upon her hall. Still, she must acknowledge the gesture.

"You have a sense of fitness about the injury you have caused. One appropriate to the offence."

With a nod of her head she went on with her demands.

"Ælfgiva stays with her mother; there is no question of that."

Hrald had lowered his head under the force of these pronouncements. This last was the law of Ælfred; mothers took custody of offspring. All had been decided, by Pega, by Lady Æthelflaed, and by her father's law. He had not spoken a word to object.

He had no defence; did not know where to begin before this imperious woman, a Queen in her own right.

Another thought had come to Æthelflaed. As unpleasant a task as it would be, it was hers to inform her father and brother of this breech. She could delay the telling a day or two, until she had more time to think. But it put her in mind of both male kin.

Her next words were an observation, one which would be chilling if Hrald were not already numbed by all he had felt and heard. "My brother will not be pleased to learn of this," she went on. "In the collapse of your marriage you place yourself rather outside his circle of concern."

Hrald must lift his head at this. The Lady met his gaze, and fully.

"It was one of the reasons why alliance with me, and my Lord-husband, was beneficial to you, Jarl Hrald. As buttress to your position. Eadward will be King. Wed to Pega, you became almost as kin to him. Now –"

She did not complete the sentence. She did not need to; Hrald understood. Displeasure through the royal family would be great. Yet it felt close to a threat, and he would answer.

"I offer no defence to my actions. Yet I tell you now that I will always hold firm to the Peace created by King Ælfred and Guthrum. I am myself a part of it. My father Sidroc, when he was Jarl, was witness to that pact, and signed it."

Hrald need not remind the Lady that Dagmar was the daughter of the Danish King who went so far as to accept baptism as proof of his pledge to adhere to the terms he had hammered out with Ælfred.

Hrald could have said much more; that he had fought to the death to protect and uphold that Peace, downing Thorfast in single combat. The cost of his fidelity to the treaty had been enormous. He and his warriors had consistently repelled Haesten's attempts to destroy the Peace, attempts which had caused Hrald to fight bloody skirmishes and an all-out battle, in which Ashild was killed. He could not recount this now; but the spectre of all which had been expected of him, all he had expected of himself, rose before him.

The Lady had inclined her head in acknowledgment of Hrald's statement, but now returned to the pressing subject at hand.

"I will not dissemble, Jarl Hrald. I am aggrieved at this parting. Yet Pega is insistent. Her union with you is at an end."

Æthelflaed had one more demand to make.

"Your sister – send her to me," she said.

Mention of Ealhswith was the last thing Hrald expected. Yet Æthelflaed had voiced this as firmly as any command on a field of battle.

Hrald fixed his eyes upon her face, one stamped with the firmness of her character. Here again the Lady of the Mercians had proven in possession of a mind as decisive as her father's.

"Ealhswith," he said, feeling he must voice her name.

He considered her demand, but must speak the next. "As a pledge?"

Was his little sister then forfeit, he asked himself.

Æthelflaed nodded.

"Yes. As a pledge. My earlier efforts having failed, through Ealhswith I will forge alliance between Four Stones and Mercia. And Wessex," she added, in a quiet tone. "I can place the girl in a marriage advantageous to both my interests and your own. Send her to me."

Hrald could not answer this. He had lifted a hand in seeming protest, for the stipulation that he surrender his younger sister caught him utterly unawares. For an instant he pictured Ealhswith away in a royal hall in Mercia, lodging with Pega, and happy to be there in her company. In that setting she might by degrees turn against her brother for the way he had used her former sister-in-law. Hrald's eyes shifted upward to the roof rafters. He could not now entertain either sending Ealhswith away, nor the loss of her affection and respect.

He swallowed back this concern. His throat was dry; the Lady had made no offer of drink, nor would he be able to take more than a mouthful, so tight was his belly.

Hrald made his sole request.

"Lady Æthelflaed. Pega – I must speak with her."

"She does not wish to see you. Respect that."

Hrald could not respond to this final command. Though he kept staring at Æthelflaed, she did nothing but dismiss him.

"You may go."

He made his bow, passed through the door, and went to look for Pega.

Pega did not remain at Æthelflaed's hall. There were certain things of Hrald's packed in with her own, and she wished to herself remove them, and in the bower to which they had been brought. This small act of separation had taken on sudden importance in her mind. Hrald returned to the bower to find the door open, and Pega within.

"Pega," he said.

She turned and looked at him. Her solemn eyes, deep set and almost smoky by nature, were rimmed in red. Hrald had not seen such evidence of sorrow on her young face, and keenly knew himself to be the sole cause of it.

He looked about; she was alone.

"Where is Ælfgiva?"

"At the hall of Æthelflaed. Where I am now going."

Pega finished at her work, lifting the last of his tunics from the chest. She laid them on the table, and spoke again.

"That woman is Dagmar."

"Yes."

"And that child is yours."

"Yes."

"That boy is not your bastard. Ælfgiva is."

Hrald's mouth opened.

"Yes," Pega went on. "She is the bastard child, for you were still truly wed to Dagmar. Your first and only wife. My daughter has been baptised, and she will be raised as if her father is dead. For that man is dead."

Hrald closed his eyes against this truth. He had dissembled for long months, ever since he had seen Dagmar in Ælfred's hall, and spent a night with her. It was a lie he attempted to tell himself, and could never believe, that he would, after that night, go forward in his life without her. Pega had come upon him with Dagmar and their son, and in a single glance seen the truth.

But Hrald had another, and beloved, child; one with Pega. He must ask of her, and what rights he had relinquished in Pega's mind.

"Are you saying I will never see Ælfgiva again?"

"I could keep you from that, yes. But I will not. Only that if you wish to see her, you must travel to Mercia to do so."

He could not respond, and she went on.

"Our union will be sundered, Hrald."

He began to speak, but she lifted her hand. "It has been sundered."

Her next words, so quietly uttered, were yet a heavy door closing on their past, and shared life together.

"You had made a decision. Now I make mine own. I will leave this bower, now. I will not return to Four Stones.

Ælfgiva and I will travel with Æthelflaed, back to Mercia. Mealla will return with you and pack up that which is mine at Four Stones. She has my blessing to wed Kjeld; I will tell her that.

"The forest land you granted me as my morgen-gyfu. I will make it over to the foundation of Oundle, for their use and profit."

Once again Hrald made a sound of protest, to be cut short by her next words.

"Say nothing – hear me out.

"I thought you were mine, as I was yours. But I was mistaken. You could not give yourself as I could; you had already done so. To her.

"You were forced to wed me; I know this. Æthelflaed and Ælfred fixed you in their aim as surely as any archer."

She saw how he bridled at this, saw the beginning of new words of protest form on his lips.

Pega looked down, and shook her head gently as she reconsidered her words. "Forced – that is too harsh a word. Led is better – you were led to me by their hands, as I was led to you."

Hrald must overcome the growing lump in his throat to make answer.

"Pega – to have hurt you like this, you who are so undeserving of pain – I . . . "

Pega lifted her hand to stay his words. There was justice only after death; she knew this. And perhaps only true happiness could be found there, as well.

She did not weep before him, though she saw the water standing in his own eyes. Now in his presence she felt little more than an awe-ful sense of finality, of ending.

"Fare-well, Hrald. I am sorry I could not make you love me."

Pega dropped her eyes and saw the ring of twisted metal upon her finger. She pulled it off, wrenched it with something near to desperate violence from her finger, and placed the golden ring on the table by his tunics. She uttered her final words to him.

"I keep nothing you gave me, save Ælfgiva."

Once back in the hall of Lady Æthelflaed, Pega began instructing Mealla on the tasks awaiting the maid of Éireann when she returned to Four Stones. The hall keys were safe with Ealhswith; having given back the ring of twisted gold, there was nothing to pass over to Hrald.

"Nothing do I want from him," Pega ordered. "I have Ælfgiva, and all I came with. Nothing more will you pack for me. Anything of value you find which he gave me – give it to Wilgot, for the poor."

The idea of returning to Hrald's hall without her mistress and friend was abhorrent to Mealla, and she said so. Pega had ready answer.

"No, Mealla, only you can pack for me. And then I want you to remain there. Kjeld must stay at Four Stones; he is second in command. And you must stay with Kjeld. I only need you to pack my goods, and place Frost in the trust of one who will care for him as they travel to me. Then you must stay, Mealla. Kjeld will be a good husband to you, and I believe you bear affection for him. He has spoken to me of you, twice. He knows I approve of him. And this way your life will be much the easier. There will be no split loyalty; you will be Kjeld's wife, and care for him, and your coming babes. It is the best path for you, far better than if you returned with me to Mercia."

This sent the raven-haired maid into a fit of weeping.

"Nay," she wailed. "My life has always been with you, and the house of Mercia. Do not take that from me . . . "

"You need not think of it now," Pega replied. "When you are there, you can make decision. But I urge you to remain at Four Stones, with the man who loves you. It will be a richer life for you."

Little Ælfgiva, napping in an alcove, awoke at their voices and began to whimper, drawing both women to the child's side.

❧

DAUGHTER
OF A KING

ONCE Æthelflaed had dismissed Hrald from her presence, she had another brought to her in the great hall: Dagmar. The Lady of Mercia had no occasion to venture to Witanceaster in the past two or three years, and had no knowledge of her father sheltering Guthrum's daughter. Now there was a knock on the chamber door, and they were brought face to face.

Æthelflaed looked upon a tall and dark-haired woman, whose person and presence could only be summed as stately. Dagmar might be a few years younger than she, but there was no mistaking the distinction of her manner and appearance. The deeply arched eyebrows, again dark, lay over large and lustrous eyes, eyes which were becomingly still. The mouth though, rather wide and with well-formed lips, spoke of a real, if latent, sensuality. The woman before her was gowned not as a Dane, but in the same kind of long-sleeved dress Æthelflaed herself wore; it was of dark, almost midnight, blue, and with the dark hair and deep blue eyes set the woman's handsomeness off well. It was significant,

Æthelflaed thought, that Guthrum's daughter had cast off dressing as a Danish woman. Was it in attempt to stand out less in a Saxon court? Or in effort of a true adoption of the ways of Angle-land; religion, mores, gown, and all?

The two women spent a long moment considering each other. Then Dagmar bent one knee behind her and dipped her head into a curtsey.

"My Lady," she murmured.

Æthelflaed waited until her guest stood upright before giving her the courtesy of a nod.

"Lady Dagmar," returned Æthelflaed.

Dagmar had been granted that title for the mere half year she had been Hrald's wife, and Lady of Four Stones. To hear it now, and from the lips of the most powerful woman in all Angle-land, struck her.

The Lady of Mercia saw this, and went on.

"I am the daughter of a King," she told Dagmar. "As you are."

Having placed them on equal footing, the Lady of the Mercians paused here. She had made no motion that they should sit. As with all unpleasant exchanges, it would be a discourse as brief as that Lady could make it. Æthelflaed went on.

"We were tasked from girlhood to fulfil a role to further the aims of our Kingly fathers, our brothers, and, if they could be attained without conflict to the aforementioned, the aims of our husbands."

This preamble over, Æthelflaed's voice rose slightly in reflection of her stifled anger.

"I knew of Jarl Hrald's first marriage when I presented Lady Pega of Mercia to him. Pega has been my direct ward, and this contract was made by her – and by me – in belief of Jarl Hrald's full faith in entering into marriage with her.

"You have sundered that union. And you have deranged my plan."

Dagmar's lips had parted at this news, but no response was expected, for Æthelflaed went on.

"You have borne him a child?"

"I have."

The Lady of Mercia's penetrating glare demanded more, and this she asked.

"A boy, I understand."

"Yes. A boy. He is named Hroft, for Hrald's great-grand-sire."

A son, Æthelflaed inwardly repeated.

When her own child was born, she silently rejoiced. She had prayed for a girl and this prayer had been answered. A girl could fully inherit her goods, that was enough. A son would have changed everything for her, and likely, for Mercia.

Æthelflaed had been no stranger to hard decisions. She determined to have no other child. She ceased sharing the marital bed with Æthelred after the birth of their firstborn. Bringing forth a boy, one who could be held up as a future King of Mercia, was to be avoided at all costs. She loved her mother's homeland, Mercia, had dedicated her life to it, but was forever loyal to the Kingdom of Wessex, and her father's cause of uniting these former rival lands as one. Her younger brother Eadward would be King of Wessex, and the great entity of Mercia, if all went well, would one day be absorbed into that Kingdom. Ælfred's daughter wanted no son of hers to lay claim to Mercia as a future King. She must be able to hand it to Wessex intact.

Æthelflaed went on, in measured tone, one which like a sheathed knife, still held its edge.

"You will understand how great is my disappointment at the failure of Jarl Hrald's alliance with Mercia. It is a union in which I placed considerable effort."

Dagmar again fought against her startle. Æthelflaed spoke as if Hrald's marriage was fully at an end. Despite the shock of discovery upon them all, it was rare indeed that any union at this level was ruptured so abruptly. She herself had been cast off summarily when found with another man; but the bond with Hrald had been purely personal; Dagmar had brought nothing to the marriage in the way of treasure, land, or living powerful kin. And she could not fail to notice that the Lady spoke only of the broken alliance with Mercia, with seeming disregard for the pain caused in the betrayal to Pega. Æthelflaed showed herself as calculating as any war-lord in weighing the cost of the acts of others.

This next must be voiced with care, and Æthelflaed slowed her words as she sought the proper tone. Friendship between she and the Jarl was no longer possible, but the trust of a Jarl with so great a holding as Hrald, and in the key territory of Lindisse, would ever be an asset to both Wessex and Mercia. Æthelflaed had taken true satisfaction in the fact that Hrald had dismissed a Danish wife, daughter of her own father's most canny enemy, and could be brought to make a marriage with her own Mercian ward. Now that union would be dissolved, and Hrald was back with a woman who, despite her outward appearance, could likely summon many Danes from their ancestral homeland. Æthelflaed's father could not live long; his death would bring a period of instability and possible vulnerability, a perfect time for attack. Æthelflaed would address this, and directly.

"You may exert some influence over the Jarl's decisions in future. If that be so, I will stress to you the vital importance that the intent of the Peace of Wedmore, forged by both our fathers, and signed by that of Jarl Hrald, be adhered to.

"Jarl Hrald has made no chartered pledge, signed no treaty with Wessex," Æthelflaed went on. "Yet he has ever adhered to that signed by our fathers, and witnessed and signed by his own. And he has stood here within the hour and insisted this shall remain so."

Several moments went by as the women eyed each other.

"I will count on you to help him remain loyal to that pledge."

Dagmar's answer, though low, was as firm as Æthelflaed's own words.

"I will count on you to help Eadward, when he is King, do the same."

After leaving Pega, Hrald could not return at once to Dagmar, though he knew her own distress must be great. Right now he needed as clear a head as he could keep. He found himself near the main stable, and stopped before its door. Several benches of planed wood flanked the broad opening; he sank down on one of them, alone. He sat upright for a moment, before clasping his hands and letting both them and his head drop towards his knees. His eyes remained open, seeing the brown of his boots, the lighter brown of the hard and pounded soil beneath those boots, and little else.

He felt, as well as heard, Jari's approach. He looked up at the faithful Tyr-hand, seeing the paling ruddy hair framing the man's lined face.

Jari raised his marred hand in greeting. Though he ate, held a spear and a sword, and used other tools with his left hand, that had come by necessity, and as a young man. To greet others, he still found himself raising his right, maimed as it was.

Jari began with his report. "The grain was delivered to the kitchen yard. All our men are quartered, Yrling and Bork with the young men in the second hall. Our horses are in those paddocks" – here he raised his hand to two near enclosures – "and have been watered and fed."

Hrald nodded and rose. Jari began moving toward one of the paddocks, where their horses stood over piles of hay. The two men stopped at the rail. It took a moment for Hrald to speak. Despite the strain shadowing it, his voice was as even as he could keep it.

"Dagmar is here. And I have a son."

Jari could not repress the whistle that came from between his lips.

Hrald went on. "Pega – she has sundered our union. She came across Dagmar and I, and the boy."

"Sundered?'

"Já. It shall be annulled. In Mercia, where it was made. She will return there with Lady Æthelflaed."

Jari stood looking at Hrald in stunned silence. Hrald went on.

"I must go to Four Stones, and soon, so that I might pack up all her treasure."

The big man had lowered his head, absorbing this.

"Whatever you must do," Jari answered. There were no other words he could think to say. "I am ready for it."

"I am going to Dagmar," Hrald said in parting. Jari gave a silent nod in response.

The Tyr-hand stood alone at the rail. Here, under the brightness of a noon Sun, the smell of dust and horses, a daily part of Jari's life, enveloped him. His grey stallion had lifted his head when Jari whistled, and now ambled over, greeting him with a nicker. Jari reached out a hand to scratch between the horse's ears. The beast bobbed his head in pleasure, nickered again, and moved back to the nearest clump of hay. Jari's eyes watched him, until some kind of response to this news arose.

"Sidroc," Jari muttered.

He was all Jari could refer to, the fact that Hrald took after his father in more ways than met the eye. But then, certain women did that. Jari had stood at the base of the stair to the weaving room at Four Stones and watched Sidroc nearly kill his own cousin Toki, because Toki had grabbed the maid Ceridwen. The right woman – or the wrong woman, Jari mused – could make a man lose his reason. Yet Ceridwen had proved to be the right woman for Sidroc, no doubt of that. But Guthrum's daughter – she had caused the entire hall deep upset, and Hrald the kind of grief that was hard to witness. But he had forgiven her. Now the surprise of the child. A son. Jari gave his head a shake at the speed with which so many lives had been upended.

Jari's gaze rose to the roofline of one of the stables. I am here to safe-guard your body, he had told Hrald on their first visit to Witanceaster. More than this I cannot do . . .

No harm had come to Hrald's body, but much to his life. The young Jarl's actions and beliefs differed in striking ways from those of Sidroc. But their natures were alike, Jari thought. Hrald would need every bit of his father's strength to deal with the outcome stemming from that single night spent with Dagmar.

On his way to Dagmar's house Hrald heard two voices in his head. The first was that of his mother, Lady Ælfwyn. She had been at Witanceaster when he had found Dagmar here. He had told her of his struggle to resist his desire for his first wife, and she had warned him that no good end could await him if he succumbed.

The second voice he heard was Dagmar's own, words she had told him following their night together, and repeated to him this very day. There is much sweetness ahead for us, she believed, and holding their son she answered that belief by adding, Here is that sweetness.

Hrald passed the small apple tree, that symbol of hope she had planted. He tapped upon her door. Dagmar opened almost at once, as if she had been on her feet, awaiting him. She did not touch him, though her face betrayed her yearning to do so. She took a step back that he might enter, and then closed the door.

Hroft was sitting on the floor by his cradle, and looked up at him. "Hroft," the child said again, and went back to playing with the small wooden horse grasped in his hand.

The boy's parents faced each other, unspeaking. Dagmar could not guess the outcome. She knew but one certainty, that over the nearly two years since he had last stood before her in this house her response to Hrald had not changed. But Hrald had changed; she saw that by the look on his face, and the light in his eyes as he gazed upon their son. As she had vowed, she had remained here at Witanceaster under the protection of the King. Now Hrald was back, and would take up the broken thread or let it lie. All hung in the balance. If this day was to decide her life, her very Fate, so be it.

Dagmar was the first to speak.

"I was called to Lady Æthelflaed. Is it true, what she told me, that Pega made swift decision?"

Hrald nodded. "I spoke to her, and to Pega. All was decided before I did so. The marriage with Pega will be annulled."

Dagmar could scarce say the next. The sudden finality of it was much to compass. The consequences were vast, and her heart racing from fear. Hrald could be vilified, and she most certainly cast as evil incarnate.

"No one will understand," was all she could utter.

Hrald countered her claim, in words low, but steady. "My father – he would understand. I know it. And Ceric."

Both men were far away, and neither had met her. They could be of no aid to Hrald. Dagmar drew a breath; tried to steel herself from the tumult in her breast. She could scarcely voice her question to him.

"Could it mean war?"

Hrald shook his head. "Eadward, and the King himself – they have been well disposed to me. My stance in upholding the Peace has not altered – will not alter. Pega will receive all her goods back. And – I have forfeited any claim to the bride-price. I want none of it."

As recompense for the distress caused it was indeed a large gesture.

"I will lose Ælfgiva," he said next. "Also Ealhswith."

The first, though cruel, was to be expected.

"Ælfgiva must remain with her mother," Dagmar murmured.

It was the second stipulation, about Hrald's sister, that surprised. Dagmar must place the best face on it. "And Lady Æthelflaed can help Ealhswith to a good marriage."

His throat had tightened so the next came out as a whisper.

"I might never see either again," he answered.

His own pain led Dagmar to hide her face in her hands. Harm after harm she had caused him.

"It is too great a price to pay," she cried.

She felt his own hands cover hers, and gently pull them towards him, drawing her near.

He shook his head and answered. "But to have gained you – and Hroft . . . You must know this, Dagmar. Not one day has passed without my wanting you."

Dagmar had closed her eyes, in attempt to keep the water gathering there from spilling forth.

Hrald's next words would have filled her with joy, were she not mourning his good name.

"We will wed again, soon, and at Oundle."

She must stifle her tears, at what he had lost, and how much more he might lose.

Hrald drew her hands to his lips and kissed them. He lifted his eyes to the rafters for a moment, then brought them to rest upon her face.

"Even if it burns me, I must turn to the Sun. You are that Sun."

The afternoon grew late. Pega, Mealla, and Ælfgiva had been installed in Lady Æthelflaed's hall. It was as royal residence comprised of three rooms, a square common room where meals could be taken, and two narrower chambers to be used for either writing or sleeping. The three guests were resting in the second of these. Pega was excused from appearing in the great hall that evening; if needed Æthelflaed would make quiet excuse for her absence. The Lady of Mercia had food and drink brought to the young women, urging them to partake, and restore themselves as they might after the tumult of the day.

So much having been decided and in such rapidity, Pega and Mealla were largely quiet, playing with Ælfgiva and then soothing her to sleep. Lady Æthelflaed had her own duties and responsibilities to return to, but found the consideration of amendments to the tax requirements she had been studying when Pega had first arrived could scarce capture her attention.

The hour grew near; Æthelflaed must prepare herself for her father's hall. Those invited were still arriving to partake of the coming festivities two days hence; she must be there with her mother to welcome them. She bid an early good night to her guests, and went back to her own chamber. She took from a chest an armful of sewn fabric, its hue the deep purple-brown of a ripe plum. Tonight the Lady neither needed nor wanted aid from her own women to gown herself, and wished to be alone with her own ponderous thoughts.

Æthelflaed reflected upon her upbringing and life, the limitations she was subject to, and the sacrifices she had made. Born at a time of crisis, the predation of attacking Danes a constant backdrop from her birth, she had known little peace. Everything she had undertaken since girlhood – education, effort, marriage, and all else – had been in the service of one goal, the survival and continuance of Wessex, and her father reigning over it. She had been rewarded with power, and with responsibility in rare measure for a woman.

Her thoughts circled round to Pega. The girl had been raised to wed at the highest level. It was no less than a trust held between Pega's parents and herself as their Lady. And Pega had proved sensible, tractable, and as an unlooked-for boon, loveable. Æthelflaed felt true affection for the girl.

Now Pega had surprised her, in the swiftness and absolute quality of her resolve to sunder her marriage. She admired her – Æthelflaed had not expected this in a nature she had adjudged little more than dutiful and sweet. This sudden action had been summoned from her by a tragedy, but Pega had answered it with the decisiveness of a Queen. The Lady could not help but see herself in the girl.

Æthelflaed dropped a necklace of linked and multi-coloured gems set in gold about her neck. She paused a moment, still thinking on Pega, and the abrupt turn her life had taken. She had risen to this challenge, and those concerned with her and her welfare must grant her that. Chief of these was she herself, Æthelflaed of Mercia. She would not allow Pega to closet herself in a convent, or otherwise make short shrift of what were surely natural abilities of a high bent.

Æthelflaed's head lowered a moment, her lids dropping slightly over her eyes. Then with something like a start, she stood. She moved with swift decision to the door connecting to the second chamber, tapped upon it, and let herself in.

Pega was standing at the window, looking into the gloaming, as a prisoned bird might. She turned at the sound of the door, and looked at the Lady.

Æthelflaed had but a single word for her.

"Kilton."

———

HERE ENDS BOOK ELEVEN OF
THE CIRCLE OF CERIDWEN SAGA.
THIS IS A NEVER-ENDING STORY.
MORE BOOKS WILL FOLLOW.

———

You've read the books – now enjoy the food. Your free Circle of Ceridwen Cookery Book(let) is waiting for you at www.octavia.net.

Ten easy, delicious, and authentic recipes from the Saga, including Barley Browis, Roast Fowl, Baked Apples, Oat Griddle Cakes, Lavender-scented Pudding, and of course – Honey Cakes. Charmingly illustrated with medieval woodcuts and packed with fascinating facts about Anglo-Saxon and Viking cookery. Free when you join the Circle, my mailing list. Be the first to know of new novels, have the opportunity to become a First Reader, and more. Get your Cookery Book(let) now and get cooking!

THE WHEEL
OF THE YEAR

St Dwynwen's Day – 25 January

Candlemas – 2 February

St Gregory's Day – 12 March

St Cuthbert's Day – The Spring Equinox, about 21 March

St Walpurga's (Walpurgisnacht) – 30 April

St Elgiva's Day – 18 May

St Helen's Day – 21 May

High Summer or Mid-Summer Day – 24 June

Saints Peter and Paul – 29 June

Feast of the Visitation – 2 July

Hlafmesse (Lammas) – 1 August

St Mary's Day – 15 August

St Matthew's Day – The Fall Equinox, about 21 September

All Saints – 1 November

The month of Blót – November; the time of Offering for
followers of the Old Religions; also time of slaughter of
animals which could not be kept over the coming Winter

Martinmas (St Martin's) – 11 November

Yuletide – 25 December to Twelfthnight – 6 January

Winter's Nights – the Norse end of year rituals, ruled by women, marked by feasting and ceremony

LITURGICAL
HOURS OF THE DAY

The Canonical Hours – special daily prayers, as practised by Oundle and other religious foundations, are as follows:

Matins, or night-watch, about 2 A.M.

Lauds, at dawn

Prime (the "first hour") about 6 A.M.

Terce (the "third hour") about 9 A.M.

Sext (the "sixth hour") about noon

None (the "ninth hour") about 3 P.M.

Vespers, the lighting of the lamps, at sunset

Compline, on retiring to sleep

ANGLO-SAXON
PLACE NAMES,
WITH MODERN EQUIVALENTS

Æscesdun = Ashdown

Æthelinga = Athelney

Apulder = Appledore

Basingas = Basing

Beamfleot = Benfleet

Beardan = Bardney

Bearruescir = Berkshire

Bryeg = Bridgenorth

Buttingtun = Buttington

Caeginesham = Keynsham

Cantwaraburh = Canterbury

Cippenham = Chippenham

Cirenceaster = Cirencester

Colneceastre = Colchester

Cruland = Croyland

Defenas = Devon

Englafeld = Englefield

Ethandun = Edington

Exanceaster = Exeter

Fearnhamme = Farnham

Fullanham = Fulham

Geornaham = Irnham

Glastunburh = Glastonbury

Gleaweceaster = Gloucester

Hamtunscir = Hampshire

Headleage = Hadleigh

Hreopedun = Repton

Iglea = Leigh upon Mendip

Jorvik (Danish name for Eoforwic) = York

Legaceaster = Chester

Limenemutha = Lymington in Hampshire

Lindisse = Lindsey

Lundenwic = London

Meredune = Marton

Meresig = Mersea

Middeltun = Milton

Readingas = Reading

River Lyge = River Lea

Sceaftesburh = Shaftesbury

Scireburne = Sherborne

Snotingaham = Nottingham

Streaneshalch = Whitby

Sumorsaet = Somerset

Swanawic = Swanage

Turcesig = Torksey

Wedmor = Wedmore

Welingaford = Wallingford

Weogornaceastre = Worcester

Isle of Wiht = Isle of Wight

Witanceaster (where the Witan, the King's
advisors, met) = Winchester

ADDITIONAL PLACE NAMES

Frankland = Much of modern-day France and Germany

Haithabu = Hedeby (formerly Denmark, now in modern-day Germany)

Aros = Aarhus, Denmark

Laaland = the island of Lolland, Denmark

Land of the Svear = Sweden

Miklagårdr = Constantinople (Istanbul)

Cymru = Wales

Éireann = Ireland

Dubh Linn = Dublin

Frisia = modern Netherlands

Dorestad = former trading town on the Rhône in modern Netherlands

Hunefleth = Honfleur, France

GLOSSARY
OF TERMS

Althing, and Thing: a regular gathering of citizens to settle disputes, engage in trade, and socialize. Gotland was divided into three administrative districts, each with their own "thing" or meeting, but the great thing, the Althing, was held at Roma, in the geographical centre of the island.

alvar: nearly barren stretches of limestone rock, typically supporting only tiny lichens and moss.

Asgard: Heavenly realm of the Gods.

aumbry: a recess built into the wall of a church, to receive and store sacred objects.

brewster: the female form of brewer (and, interestingly enough, the female form of baker is baxter . . . so many common names are rooted in professions and trades . . .).

browis: a cereal-based stew, often made with fowl or pork.

chaff: the husks of grain after being separated from the usable kernel.

ceorl: ("churl") a free man ranking directly below a thegn, able to bear arms, own property, and improve his rank.

cottar: free agricultural worker; in later eras, a peasant.

cresset: stone, bronze, or iron lamp fitted with a wick that burnt oil.

drekar: "dragon-ship," a war-ship of the Danes.

ealdorman: a nobleman with jurisdiction over given lands; the rank was generally appointed by the King and not necessarily inherited from generation to generation. The modern derivative *alderman* in no way conveys the esteem and power of the Anglo-Saxon term.

ell: a measure of length corresponding to a man's forearm and outstretched fingers.

fey: possessing magical or supernatural powers; one belonging to the Land of Faery.

fulltrúi: the Norse deity patron that one felt called to dedicate oneself to.

fylgja: a Norse guardian spirit, always female, unique to each family.

fyrd: the massed forces of Wessex, comprising thegns – professional soldiers – and ceorls, trained freeman.

hack silver: broken silver jewellery, coils of unworked silver bars, fragments of cast ingots and other silver parcelled out by weight alone during trade.

hamingja: the Norse "luck-spirit" which each person is born with.

lamm: Gotlandic name for a sheep.

leech-book: compilation of healing recipes and practices for the treatment of human and animal illness and injury. Such books were a compendium of healing herbs and spiritual and magical practices. The *Leech Book of Bald,* recorded during Ælfred's reign, is a famed, and extant, example.

lur: a vertical (or curved) sounding horn fashioned of wood or brass, dating from the Bronze Age, and used in Nordic countries to rally folk from afar.

morgen-gyfu: literally, "morning-gift"; a gift given by a husband to his new wife the first morning they awake together.

nard: (also, spikenard) a rare and precious oil, highly aromatic, derived from the crushed rhizomes of a honeysuckle-like plant grown in the Himalayas, India, and China. Mary Magdalen was said to have anointed the feet of Christ with nard.

philtre: a potion to excite love or lust in another.

quern: a small hand-driven mill consisting of two grind stones, the top stone usually being domed and having a hole to insert a wooden handle for turning. The oats, wheat, or other grain is placed between the stones, and the handle turned until the desired fineness is attained.

rauk: the striking sea- and wind-formed limestone towers on the coast of Gotland.

seax: the angle-bladed dagger which gave its name to the Saxons; all freemen carried one.

scop: ("shope") a poet, saga-teller, or bard, responsible not only for entertainment but seen as a collective cultural historian. A talented scop would be greatly valued by his lord and receive land, gold and silver jewellery, costly clothing and other riches as his reward.

scrying: to divine the future by gazing into a looking glass, a crystal, or water.

shingle beach: a pebbly, rather than sandy, beach.

skeggox: steel battle-axe favoured by the Danes.

skirrets: a sweet root vegetable similar to carrots, but cream-coloured, and having several fingers on each plant.

skogkatt: "forest cat"; the ancestor of the modern Norwegian Forest Cat, known for its large size, climbing ability, and thick and water-shedding coat.

Skuld: the eldest of the three Norse Norns, determiners of men's destinies. Skuld cuts with shears the thread of life. See also Urd and Verdandi.

strakes: overlapping wooden planks, running horizontally, making up a ship's hull.

symbel: a ceremonial high occasion for the Angle-Saxons, marked by the giving of gifts, making of oaths, swearing of fidelity, and (of course) drinking ale.

tæfl or Cyningtæfl ("King's table"): a "capture the King" strategy board game.

thegn: ("thane") a freeborn warrior-retainer of a lord; thegns were housed, fed and armed in exchange for complete fidelity to their sworn lord. Booty won in battle by a thegn was generally offered to their lord, and in return the lord was expected to bestow handsome gifts of arms, horses, arm-rings, and so on to his best champions.

treen: domestic objects fashioned of wood, especially tableware.

Tyr: the God of war, law, and justice. He voluntarily forfeited his sword-hand to allow the Gods to deceive, and bind, the gigantic wolf Fenrir.

Tyr-hand: in this Saga, any left-handed person, named so in honour of Tyr's sacrifice.

Urd: the youngest of the three Norse Norns, determiners of men's destinies. Urd makes decision as to one's calling and station in life. See also Skuld and Verdandi.

Verdandi: the middle of the three Norse Norns, determiners of men's destinies. Verdandi draws out the thread of life to appropriate length. See also Skuld and Urd.

wadmal: the Norse name for the coarse and durable woven woollen fabric that was a chief export in the Viking age.

wergild: Literally, man-gold; the amount of money each man's life was valued at. The Laws of Æthelbert, a 7th century King of Kent, for example, valued the life of a nobleman at 300 shillings (equivalent to 300 oxen), and a ceorl was valued at 100 shillings. By Ælfred's time (reigned 871-899) a nobleman was held at 1200 shillings and a ceorl at 200.

yealing: one the same age.

NOTES

Chapter the Seventh

Trystan and Esyllt. Welsh names for the legendary, and doomed, lovers Tristan and Iseult.

Chapter the Eighth

The route to Miklagårdr. Several river routes existed from the Baltic to the great Byzantine capital of Constantinople. That taken by Eskil and Runulv heads first north, to Staraya Ladoga, before continuing on southward to Novgorod, Gnezdovo, and Kyiv, amongst other known settlements, trading posts, and way-stations along the route. I have peopled them with a cast of largely fictional characters, including Ladja, who we first met in *Tindr*. We now return to her in her old age, and in the exalted state of Mistress of Staraya Ladoga.

We cannot know how many died attempting to reach Miklagårdr and its peerless trading opportunities, but we do know men of Gotland were amongst them. A picture stone still here on the island, raised in honour of Ravn (or Hrafn) by his four brothers, commemorates his death en route. The runic inscription reads: "Brightly painted, this stone was raised by Hegbjarn and his brothers Rodvisl, Austain and Emund. They have raised stones in memory of Ravn, south of Rufstain. They penetrated far into the Aifur. Vivil was in command." (*The Spillings Hoard: Gotland's Role in Viking Age World Trade*, p 128.) Rufstain (or Rofstein) must have been a now-lost placename along the route. Ravn's surviving brothers were obviously proud that they raised multiple memorial stones to their lost sibling, both at the site of his death and at home on Gotland.

As bioarcheologist Cat Jarman tell us in *River Kings: The Vikings from Scandinavia to the Silk Roads*, (p 259-260) a grave found in 1905 in Ukraine contained the upper portion of a skeleton resting on a flat stone. When the stone was lifted it revealed a runic inscription on its underside, "Grani made this vault in memory of Karl, his partner." Dr Jarman states this is the only runic stone found in Ukraine or Russia, and that "the style the runes are carved in strongly suggests that the carver, and maybe Grani and Karl too, came from Gotland."

The fearsome and deadly cataracts and waterfalls our Saga adventurers encountered on the Dnieper river near the end of their river journeying were obliterated by a Soviet hydroelectric dam project in 1932.

CHAPTER THE NINTH

Oleg, "Grand Prince" or King of Kyiv. An attested ruler of Kyiv, and one of the Varangians – Swedish warriors and traders – who knew such success in the east. The *Russian Primary Chronicle* states that in 904 Oleg led an attack on Constantinople, numbering some 2,000 ships from various tribes. Mention of wheeled ships is made as Oleg's fearsome fleet drove towards the city walls. A vast tribute was paid to him to leave without sacking the city, though it is said he hammered his shield to its wooden gates as reminder of his might.

Chapter the Sixteenth

The runes of forgetfulness. The carving and painting of runes were employed for many magical practices. Much of Norse magic and spell-work deals with love and lust, and runes and bind runes used in this way perhaps had significance known only to the creator. I have chosen the runes Nid, Lagu, and Is as those suitable to free a man from the forbidden desiring of a woman.

Chapter the Seventeenth

The relationship between Congar and his uncle Elfrid, a priest. Strong relationships between uncles and nephews were common in Anglo-Saxon and Norse culture, and we have seen this referred to many times in the Saga. The bond could be particularly meaningful between the mother's brother and her son. The uncle therefore acted as a representative of her family of origin, advocating its interests as well as the interest of the boy's father and his family. Many such pairs undertook adventures together, in war or trade; Yrling and his nephews Toki and Sidroc are one example. In this instance the priest Elfrid is influencing his nephew Congar in considering a life of religious vocation.

Chapter the Eighteenth

Rhodri Mawr (in Welsh, "Rhodri the Great"). A renowned war-chief against both the Saxons and Danes, Rhodri Mawr was born Rhodri ap Merfyn about 820, and died either 873 or 877/878. Rhodri became King of much of Wales during his lifetime, and was famed for his defense of Cymru against Viking invaders, killing the Danish leader Gorm in 856.

After striking military success, Rhodri was killed in battle against the invading Mercian army, likely at the Battle of Anglesey in 873. At his death several of his many sons each helmed a different portion of what their father had briefly unified. I have simplified the complex familial relations and shifting border lands by appointing four of his known sons, Anarawd, Merfyn, Llywarch, and Meurig, as Kings of their respective territories. The mountainous setting of King Anarawd's fortress is one imagined for the King of Gwynedd.

Chapter the Nineteenth

St Dwynwen. Our own Dwynwen tells us much of this Saint, said to be one of the twenty-four daughters of King Brychan Brycheiniog (c 390–450), the first King of Brecon (or Brecknock) after the withdrawal of the Romans. Dwynwen is thought to have died in 465. The small stone church and holy well on her sandy isle became a popular place of pilgrimage after her death, but following the Reformation her worship was repressed, and the church fell into ruin. During the reign of Queen Victoria interest in the early Saints revived, leading to the erection of a simple cross on Dwynwen's isle, followed by another, of Celtic design, in 1903. Dwynwen's isle is no longer a true tidal island, but is happily a nature preserve of great beauty, where a few atmospheric stone walls and an arch of her church survive. Her Feast Day is 25 January, and in recent decades, with the focus on pride in Welsh heritage, there has been a resurgence of interest in St Dwynwen as Patron of Lovers, providing a native-born alternative to the

Roman St Valentine. Note that Dwynwen is not officially recognized by the Roman Catholic or Anglican Churches, but is by that of the Eastern Orthodox.

CHAPTER THE TWENTIETH

St Peter's Pence. King Offa of Mercia (died 796) seems to have originated the gift of English alms to Rome in honour of the founder of the Church there. Ælfred's father, King Æthelwulf, had twice taken Ælfred as a boy on pilgrimage to Rome, presenting lavish gifts, including on the first occasion a gold crown, a gold-trimmed sword, precious vestments of silk ornamented with gold, quantities of gold for clergy and nobles, silver to be distributed to the common folk, and silver and silver-gilt candleholders and hanging candelabras for various churches, according to the *Book of the Popes*. An annual, sometimes occasional, giving of St Peter's Pence is recorded in the *Anglo-Saxon Chronicle*, and was an offering that the devout Ælfred tried to continue, at least in years when demands on his own treasury for domestic and military needs were not too great. I have used such a donation as a setting for members of the royal family and their close friends to gather and celebrate the alms about to be taken via courier to Rome.

ACKNOWLEDGEMENTS

An author owes her career to her readers, and I have been blessed with some of the best readers on Earth. Your devotion in reading or listening to the books, requesting them at the library, and most of all telling friends about the Saga adventure have carried me forward from book to book. The Saga is a never-ending story, and I hope never to disappoint.

My First Readers are a stalwart band of trusted enthusiasts who read and comment on every new title when it is in manuscript. My great gratitude for doing so for *To the Sun* is due to Wendy Adams, Tony Allen, Lorraine Angelopoulos, Judy Boxer, Liz Faulkner, Mary Kelly, Elaine MacDonald, Kristen McEnaney, Jennifer Morris, Debbie Newsholme, Melinda Osman, Amanda Porath, Ellen Rudd, Linda Schultz, and Lorie Witt. Sharing the excitement of an additional Saga novel with you is a joy.

Two very special readers have companioned me in recent years, Beth Altchek and Libby Williams. Though our bodies may be separated by thousands of miles, both are very much at my side. Their discernment and unflagging support has served me in more ways than they can know.

If you'd like closer engagement with the "world of the Saga," The Octavia Randolph Official Circle of Ceridwen Saga Forum on Facebook awaits you, where you shall find fellowship in discussing the Saga novels and the Anglo-Saxon and Viking Era settings in which they take place. The Saga Forum provides us all with a welcoming and engaging environment in which to explore the books and the richness of their settings. It is a veritable "treasure room" of information and celebration, from medieval foodways to smithing, fashion to fortress building, parchment making to rune carving, early Christianity to the Gods of the Norse, and much more. Such a welcoming home for my books and their readers would not be possible without the tireless activity, creativity, and oversight of Misi, Wolf CrescentWalker and Jessica Charboneau. My debt to you is boundless, as is my gratitude.

ABOUT
THE AUTHOR

Octavia Randolph has long been fascinated with the development, dominance, and decline of the Anglo-Saxon peoples. The path of her research has included disciplines as varied as the study of Anglo-Saxon and Norse runes, and learning to spin with a drop spindle. Her interests have led to extensive on-site research in England, Denmark, Sweden, and Gotland. In addition to the Circle Saga, she is the author of the novella *The Tale of Melkorka*, taken from the Icelandic Sagas; the novella *Ride*, a retelling of the story of Lady Godiva, first published in Narrative Magazine; and *Light, Descending*, a biographical novel about the great John Ruskin. She has been awarded Artistic Fellowships at the Ingmar Bergman Estate on Fårö, Sweden; MacDowell; Ledig House International; and Byrdcliffe.

She answers all fan mail and loves to stay in touch with her readers. Join her mailing list and read more on Anglo-Saxon and Viking life at www.octavia.net. Follow her on Facebook at Octavia Randolph Author, on Instagram and for exclusive access and content join the spirited members of The Official Circle of Ceridwen Saga Forum on Facebook.

Printed in the USA
CPSIA information can be obtained
at www.ICGtesting.com
LVHW041918240824
789143LV00006B/586

9 781942 044420